That Time Daisy Got Tipsy and Rescued a Duke

Heir Hunters

Jennifer Seasons

Heartwrite Publishing

To all the determined ladies making their way in the world. You deserve your own HEA.

Playlist

Girls Just Want to Have Fun - Miley Cyrus ♥
Greedy - Tate McRae ♥
Rumors - Lizzo ft. Cardi B ♥
Dura - Daddy Yankee ♥
The Sweet Escape - Gwen Stefani, Akon ♥
Good Love - Dazeychain ♥
Wildest Dreams - Taylor Swift ♥
Too Sweet - Hozier ♥
Renegades - X Ambassadors ♥
Hopeless Valentine - Dazeychain ♥
Ride with Me - Pink Sweat$ ♥
Earned It - The Weeknd ♥
Take My Breath Away - Berlin ♥
Therapy - Budjerah ♥
Ex's and Oh's - Elle King ♥
Nothing Breaks Like a Heart- Mark Ronson ♥
ft. Miley Cyrus ♥
One Too Many - Keith Urban, P!nk ♥
I Love You, I'm Sorry - Gracie Abrams ♥
Right Here - Taylor Taylor ♥

Prologue

B ramble Estate Investigations
Salisbury Court, London
June 1838

"I found him!"

She'd done it. Once again, Daisy Bramble had found her man. Or well, in this case, duke. And the estate reward that she'd claim on him was huge.

How she loved her job.

Slapping a hand down on the map on her desk with a triumphant thwack, she looked around the headquarters of Bramble Estate Investigations and grinned. "That's right, sisters, I've located the lost Duke of Ashby Hollow. You may bow to my greatness."

She received a crumpled bit of parchment upside the head instead.

"Fat chance in Hades," snorted Violet, thrower of said parchment, and youngest of the Bramble Hill orphan sisters, though at four-and-twenty she was hardly considered by societal standards young.

A blessing it was that they didn't have to give two bollocks about that sort of thing.

Laughing, Daisy retrieved the ball from where it had landed on her desk and deftly slid it into the trash bin next to her. "Say what you will about me as your sibling, there's no denying that I am outrageously competent at tracking down descendants of the aristocracy and securing that beautiful bounty."

From the back rooms echoed the voice of Blossom, another Bramble Hill sister and heir hunter. "I'll concede that you are highly proficient at this task. However, I err on the side of cynicism over the belief that you've truly located this Duke of Ashby Hollow. Genealogists and every estate investigator in greater London have searched years for him. Ever since the intestate proclamation was announced after the old duke died of . . . what was it? Ergotism? How does that even still happen? I thought everyone knew better than to consume moldy grain."

Daisy shuddered. Ugh. Such an undignified end for a person. Hallucination with a side of gangrene.

Though to be fair, in that duke's case, she'd heard that no one had missed him. Which said everything. Character flawed? Quite, apparently.

"It does explain, however, why he was known by the village residents as the Rabid Duke."

Daisy snorted, humor flashing in her rich brown eyes. Violet made an excellent point.

"I wonder if he bit anyone?" she mused aloud. Really, wouldn't that be something?

"He did! I read all about it. A woman's arm. Took a chunk right out."

Rabid Duke, indeed.

"Perhaps the curse caused it."

Violet and Daisy turned in unison to gape at Blossom emerging from the back room.

"Pardon me?" Blossom couldn't possibly believe such nonsense. Not the woman who once spent a night in a Devonshire castle dungeon renowned throughout England for its late-night rattling chains, frigid drafts, and pitiful disembodied moans, simply to catch the wayward descendent of a lowly baron, even though the finder's fee was a pittance compared to the cost expended in locating him.

Blossom's conclusion on spectral anomalies after that night? Nonsense.

It had distracted her a tad that night, perhaps, that the heir had been a weasel of a man that she had a personal grudge against—her former unfaithful betrothed. Awful sod. He'd used poor Blossom to no end. Yet, instead of breaking her, that experience had only made her stronger and more resilient. Blossom might have a delicate name, but she was no fragile flower. Not that one.

Not any of them.

On that note. . . "I'm off to York in the morning to catch a big, fat-pursed duke."

"What makes you believe that you have the correct man?" Blossom pressed, a frown marring the skin between her blonde brows. Pressing a hand to her abdomen in the way she did when her gut intuition began brewing a concoction hot with warning, the tallest Bramble sister tipped her head to the side and leveled her gaze on Daisy. "I don't like the feel of this."

"Oh, you and your feelings." She waved her sister off. "I've got this completely under control. *And for your information,*" she stressed, meeting Blossom's steely gaze with one of her own, "I've never once been impulsive or irrational in my professional pursuits. My success record speaks for itself." Why was she defending her abilities to her sister? She already knew them.

"It's . . . York," Blossom trailed off and gestured vaguely in front of her with her free hand. "Such a distance to go on a hunch."

Daisy sat up in her chair and snapped her vest straight down her collared blouse, offended. "Never simply a *hunch*, Blossom. You know that. I don't operate that way." Standing, she scanned the room, taking in the many filing cabinets filled with their many cases—several of which she had personally solved. For that's what heir hunting really was: a mystery to solve. A puzzle to arrange in order to reveal the hidden image. "You're behaving quite strangely today." She glanced across the space to Violet and demanded, "Don't you think?"

"Mm, perhaps a bit more than usual." Violet pursed her lips and assessed their blondest and most elegant of siblings. Somehow, she'd acquired a polish the other Bramble orphan girls hadn't managed to attain. More's the pity. Undoubtedly, they'd access far more restricted areas of Society were more of them able to so seamlessly infiltrate the *ton*.

Alas, Blossom was their lone Society weapon.

Violet was astonishingly deft with locks and obscure monastic records.

And Daisy was good at *the chase*.

Smiling broadly, she trailed a finger along the glossy wooden top of her desk and collected nary a single spot of dust. That was also Blossom. Tidy as a mouse. Bless her heart. Left up to Daisy, they'd be swimming in dust and sneezing cat hair from the stray Violet thought no one knew she was feeding. "My informant, the York innkeeper Mrs. Buddersham, unflappably proved herself years ago as reliable when she helped us track down our lost Bramble Hill sister, Rue."

Blossom stilled, her statuesque figure outlined in the early afternoon sunlight flittering through the large front windows. "I did not realize she was your source of information," she admitted quietly. "That changes things." Her hand continued to rub her abdomen in small, worried circles. "Though my stomach tells me something is not what it seems with this case. I warn you that much."

"It must be the legend of Ashby Hollow that has you worrying." Violet nodded like a wise old owl, her bright blue eyes earnest. "Every duke for the last seven generations has met with some horrid demise . . . all alone . . . because their wives also met untimely demises before them. It's tragic, really." Those unnaturally bright eyes of hers shimmered with sympathy tears. "Could you imagine such a terrible thing?"

"No," Daisy snapped, unnerved by the sudden concern over one single missing heir. So what if the dukedom came with a rather grim legend attached? "I cannot imagine that. What I can foresee is the rebuilding and reopening of Bramble Hill Orphanage like we've been planning for years. It becomes possible with the ten percent finder's fee of *twenty-five thousand* bloody pounds that I'm going to collect."

Violet released a low, impressed whistle.

"Right." Blossom nodded, her golden strands shimmering about her beautiful face as she squared her shoulders. "Well, what are you waiting for?" she shooed Daisy one-handed toward the front door. "Go get that heir."

Withholding a sigh of frustration, for she planned to do exactly that, she glanced at Blossom and instead asked, "What is your intuition truly telling you?" Because deep down she believed her sister's gut feelings. They'd proven accurate more than not. Blossom, however, would be impossible to deal with if she ever admitted it. So, she affected a placating expression and pretended to only entertain her sibling's superstitions out of familial devotion.

"Oh, don't look at me like that. It's plain you truly wish to know." Blossom took a steadying breath and blurted, "Whatever you think you'll find, Daisy, you won't. You're not prepared."

A shiver ran down her spine, right between her corset stays. "I'm prepared for everything," she retorted, her own stomach suddenly greasy with uncertainty. "This is a case like any other."

He was only a man. And it was a straightforward job.

She stiffened her spine. "Mark me, I'll get my heir."

Daisy always did.

Chapter One

Y ork, England
    One month later . . .

Perhaps she'd miscalculated.

Daisy sighed deeply, hands on her hips as she eyed the guests of The Stag and Lantern currently eating heartily and enjoying the beef stew Mrs. Buddersham had added to the inn's dining menu. "It's been over three weeks without a single glimpse. Not a whiff of the duke anywhere." She turned her gaze to the sturdy-bodied innkeeper standing next to her. "I know I'm becoming obnoxiously redundant, but I must ask yet again if you are *quite* certain that you've seen this Dawson Woodbridge fellow that I wrote to you about?"

"I swear it, Daisy. I do. Three times he's dined here, always choosing the table closest to the door." She pointed to a small round table set for two near the entrance. "Never meets anyone, and watches everything."

"Hmm. Sounds like a person on the run to me."

"I didn't say your missing heir was a quality human, dear. I only said I saw him."

Daisy snorted.

"I do hope spending these weeks in the Yorkshire air has not been without its own merits for you at least, even as you've yet to uncover your . . . shall we say . . . missing item?"

Fighting a rumbling pang of hunger in her belly as she watched two travel-worn men rip shamelessly into hanks of beef, Daisy swallowed back the sudden craving for food, and patted the older woman on her shawl-covered shoulder. "The Dales are glorious this time of year, so no, not wasted. A chance to see you never is."

But this one might have been, she confessed silently to herself, her spirits flagging. Which was aggravating when she usually ran on unwavering determination. Obstacles entertained her, tickled her sense of competition. What was so different this time?

Twenty-five thousand pounds.

By far the largest finder's fee on an estate she had ever attempted to collect. The amount boggled her mind. The poor orphan girl in her marveled at the vastness of the sum, the wealth it would provide them.

All those other lost orphans they could provide for with the fee and home. Give hope to. *Futures* to. It brought her to tears just thinking about it.

She would never give up.

"Hey, wench! Fill 'er back up!" A ham-fisted man across the room bellowed at Daisy and signaled to his empty pint glass. "I don' got all bloomin' day."

Narrowing her eyes, she noted the bellower was the same lout who'd tried to grab her bum last Tuesday and had earned himself a plate of mutton in his lap for the offense. Being a tavern barmaid was tough work. She respected every woman who earned her keep this way. She'd been doing it for only a few weeks as part of her investigation and was ready to thump some inn regulars all the way into Scotland.

"Ignore him." Mrs. Buddersham gently elbowed Daisy's side. "I mean it. John's a lush and a cuckold with nothing to live for since his wife took off with the butcher from Blackfriar Lane two winters past." She nudged her side again. "See here, look. I've got quite the thing for you. It'll dull the disappointment." A bottle appeared before Daisy's nose. "Try this."

Daisy sniffed at the blue bottle, and instantly blinked back tears of a different sort. "What in the devil is that?" She could *smell* the potency coming off it.

"Oh, it's a wee family recipe passed down through the generations on me mum's side. It's made with a dab of barley, a spot of honey, and a few other things I can't recall off the tip of me head."

"I see," Daisy said, considering the drink in her hand. "It's rather like honeyed whiskey."

Mrs. Buddersham chuckled, her expansive bosom jiggling under the soft-looking gray shawl. "I suppose it is. Or a whiskey mead."

"Sounds just the thing." *Exactly* the thing to help her forget what was at stake should she fail to locate and bring in the lost Duke of Ashby Hollow.

"*Wench!*" The regular called again, his expression turning thunderous. "I want me ale!"

"Shut yer cake hole, ye reet berk!" Mrs. Buddersham yelled in native Yorkshire, and whipped out her arm, staying Daisy before she could make a single move. "I'll take care of him." She glanced pointedly down at the bottle Daisy held, her voice once again polite and professional. "You drink. Relax. Take a stroll. Whatever you wish to do. I feel responsible for your current circumstances, so go. I'll pull Lyselle from upstairs and send her to the kitchen to serve in your stead."

"I *could* use some time to ruminate," Daisy murmured, acknowledging the innkeeper's suggestion.

"That sounds unpleasant, bless you."

Releasing a bark of surprised laughter, Daisy flung an arm around the wonderful Mrs. Buddersham and squeezed her close. "Oh, you do make life lighter, my friend."

Twin patches of pink appeared on the woman's apple cheeks before she shooed her away. "Off with you now. I've an inn to run."

"If that churl gives you any trouble, you find me." If John laid a single hand on Mary Buddersham, she'd shove a spoon up his nose. Mark her.

"Don't you worry, dear. I've got me Mason for such necessities," she assured, referring to her giant son. He ran the kitchen with impressive deftness, creating scrumptiously delicate dishes —and he cooked with his massive shoulders rounded while his head scraped the ceiling.

His crumpets were to *die* for.

Speaking of . . . there were still some in the kitchen. "I'll take this bottle of spirits and go ruminate now."

"Ugh. Sounds atrocious. Bless you."

"It's—" Daisy cut off with a shake of her head. "Never mind."

She took three steps.

"If that becomes a problem, dear, let me know. I'll send for Doc Grimbly."

"Thank you!" Daisy choked out, not wanting to laugh out loud and offend her friend. Hustling through the inn, she reached the kitchen door and rushed through, making it just in time. Laughter tumbled loose, the sound cascading from her lips. Oh, Mrs. Buddersham. Bless *her*.

"What's so amusing?"

Her shoulders still shaking with humor beneath her tunic dress, Daisy glanced at Mason. "Your mother is a very sweet person."

The large cook smirked. "What'd she go on about this time?"

How to explain this one?

Daisy simply continued to laugh softly and raised the bottle of homemade whiskey mead in the air. "She said for me to drink this."

Mason's ruddy eyebrows rose in surprise. "Mum don't usually share the family spirits. Either she's trying to impress you, or she cocked up and wants you to forget. Can't be nuffin else." His gaze lowered to the bottle in her hands. "Mindful with it, luv. It'll smack you between the eyes 'fore you can blink. An' have you seeing ghosts in the Shambles to boot."

"Is that so?" How very interesting. She raised the bottle to eye level and squinted at the liquid sloshing behind the cobalt glass, wondering aloud, "Can it make a lost duke appear?"

Shrugging his enormous shoulders, Mason chuckled and began chopping carrots, the slicing sound of his knife rhythmic and comforting and sure. "It can certainly make you *think* he's appeared."

"Ahh," Daisy drawled, unfairly annoyed at Mrs. Buddersham's drink for not possessing magical properties that delivered her duke at her feet. Frowning at it, she added, "I suppose that in dire times that is all a person can ask for, that the illusion dull the pain of the reality." How melodramatic she sounded!

"In me experience," said Lyselle, pushing through the kitchen door to collect a waiting order, "life does nuffin but hurt. Anything that can make it sting a wee less is welcome." The slender brunette hefted the tray and settled it in place against her shoulder, steadying it with both hands. "Three dead and buried, lousy husbands taught me that."

Instantly feeling guilty for having complained when what she was going through was nothing compared to what the barmaid insinuated, Daisy rushed to assure them, "It's not that terrible. Nothing like that, at any rate. I shouldn't be complaining at all, really. It's just a hiccup with a job."

It wasn't *that* bad, true. But she was still allowed to indulge in self-pity for a moment, wasn't she?

Bringing the bottle of honeyed whiskey to her lips, she tipped her head back and gulped. Sweet heat instantly flooded her chest and filled her belly. She held the bottle at arm's length, impressed. "Mm, that's tasty." She could already feel her limbs unclenching and loosening. "Your family's recipe is brilliant!" she declared to Mason, her attention wholly on the whiskey mead concoction in her hands. If she couldn't find her heir, at least she had found this liquid gem. "I've never experienced a drink so cozy and comforting," she took another long pull on the bottle, "and delicious." Like honey cake, but booze. "If you ever sold this, you'd make a fortune."

"I keep telling me mum that!" Mason's hazel eyes lit up with excitement, clearly glad to have someone else thinking the same, and he began chopping more quickly, the pace a staccato rap on the countertop. "Expand the inn to include a brewery that would be capable of producing barrels of our very own York-shire-grown *uisge beatha*." He wiped his huge hands on a towel and flung it over his shoulder. "Mum works too hard. This would provide and let her rest."

"Well, I am all in favor." Daisy raised the bottle in salute. "It's delicious *and* effective." Glancing around the comfortable kitchen with its worn stone floor and sturdy wood furniture, she found a chair perfect for sinking into by a nearby table. Plopping on the age-smoothed seat, she narrowed her eyes at Mason. "Let me ask you a something."

"Fire away."

"If you were hunting for someone and they were being exceedingly disrespectful of your efforts and continued to stay hidden, what would you do?" Daisy took another swig of her new favorite drink and wiped the back of her hand across her mouth, adding, "Right rude, if you ask me."

"Appalling behavior," Mason agreed with complete seriousness, his broad, raw-boned Yorkshire features a mask of sincerity as he added the chopped carrots to a large pot.

"Mm," Daisy agreed with an emphatic nod. "You're a good man, Mason Buddersham, readily agreeing with me. You do your mum proud." All men should be this amiable and compliant. Life would be so much easier.

But what fun would that be? A voice in her head whispered in taunt. The same one that adored chasing after an heir and collecting that wonderful bounty.

Daisy smirked. It had her there.

Brushing a palm across her plain brown skirts and patting her thigh, Daisy pushed to her feet. "Well, I'm off to find my duke." Not *her* duke, her duke. Just the duke she was currently after. "If one missing Dawson Woodbridge happens to come in here while I'm on his trail, please detain him for me. I'll be forever grateful."

"Will do." Mason nodded and tipped his auburn head at the bottle she still held. "Want to leave that here?"

"Nope." Not even a little. "Your mum gave it to me and currently it's my prized possession. You want it? You'll have to fight me for it." She tossed him a smile to let him know she was joking. Mostly. It really *was* good.

Was she feeling a bit protective of her liquor?

Yes, yes she was. No judgement. Well, not much anyway, okay?

"It's been a stressful month!" she blurted, defending herself to the kitchen at large, glaring at the butcher block like it had sniggered at her.

"Positively dreadful month you've had."

Daisy nodded once again, her head bobbing more than she'd meant for it to. "It has been!" she half-wailed, glad for the sympathy. One part of her heard the pitiful tone and cringed. The other part . . . the quickly-becoming-inebriated part of her didn't care at all. In fact, what was she so upset about again? "Aha!" She remembered the duke and snapped her fingers. Impressed at the sharp crack of sound they made, it thoroughly distracted her from her worries. "Hey, that's swell." She snapped her digits again, grinning over the sound. "Did you hear that cracking sound? My fingers made that."

"Go easy there on the *beatha*, luv." Mason set the stew ladle across the top of the pot, and pushed his rolled linen sleeves further up his forearms like he was prepping for physical resistance. "It's not made for the likes of you. You're too soft."

"Beg pardon?" Daisy's chest puffed in indignation. Well, if that wasn't offensive as Hades! "I'm not soft!" she argued, pushing past him toward the door, and shoving his hand away. "I'm hardy as Hamstone!"

"Daisy."

"I will have you know that I am excellent at the consumption of libation."

"I'm sure that's the usual of it—"

"I'm tough," she cut him off. "I'm strong and capable and clever." With a swing of her hips, she thrust her body at the back door, opening it to the cool, fragrant evening air beyond. "Anything I want, I get. 'Cept my family back. That didn't happen.

14

But you can't bring back the dead, can you?" she finished with a woeful shake of her head. "No, you surely cannot." Brightening, she stepped over the kitchen threshold and shot Mason a jaunty salute. "I'm off to scour York for the heir to a cursed dukedom! Good times, good times. Don't wait up!"

Chapter Two

"Now, if I were a missing heir to an offensively rich dukedom, where would I be?" Looking left and right, Daisy debated which direction to wander first. "If I go this way . . ." She pointed with the bottle down the infamous Shambles, the medieval lane stretching before her into the encroaching dusk, and where The Stag and Lantern resided. Well, mostly resided. The inn's entrance faced Little Shambles, leaving only the servant doors and side entrances directly situated toward Shambles itself.

"Here, dukey dukey!" she called into the growing dark as she began wandering the cobblestone lane and broke into a fit of giggles when she realized what she'd said. "Ha! *Dukey*," she repeated and giggled more, passing a small group of pub-goers.

"That one's pissed in 'er cups," a woman whispered loudly to her companions, her gaze meeting Daisy's as they moved by. "I want whatever she had."

"Say . . ." Daisy drawled while she watched them pass, a thought sparking in her sloshy brain. "Have any of you seen a man about this tall," she asked, her hand raising to what she assumed six feet looked like, hovering well above her own head.

"He's quite fit from what I'm told, and he possesses green eyes. His hair is brown and unkempt and perhaps a tad long. I'm also told he might be bearded. Oh! And he's scarred through his right eyebrow." Daisy beamed at them expectantly, "Anyone?"

"Sorry, miss," another woman replied with a shake of her dark head. "No one like that's been by us."

"I'da noticed 'im." The first woman added with a smirk. "Sounds like my kind of ride."

"Any man with a job is your kind of ride, Mildred."

"Don't blame me for having standards."

Daisy laughed and continued strolling down Shambles, taking her time to enjoy the ancient winding street and its quirks. Such atmosphere and history it possessed! All the overhanging upper stories and tiny door frames and odd, wobbly angles. Mason was right that ghosts lived there. She could almost feel them looking over her shoulder and following her every step. Creepy? Why yes, a little.

"Good luck finding your man!" One of the women called behind her as she retreated into the distance.

"Good luck finding yours!" she hollered back, unthinking.

Laughter trailed off into the fully bloomed night.

"Well, my friend, let's have another sip of you." Daisy said to the honeyed whiskey bottle tucked safely away in the pocket of her skirt. "And then you can show me where one Mr. Dawson Woodbridge is hiding, m'kay?" She took a drink and popped the cap back on. "Excellent! That'll do me. Now, where's this missing duke, oh mighty mead? Show me the way!" Placing the bottle back in her pocket, she took a step and stumbled when she dropped down into the carriage track that ran the length of the narrow old lane. "Step there! There's a step there!" she called out to the people few strolling from one tavern to the next. In case someone needed to know it was there, of course.

"Who you lookin' for, luv?" a women with big, frizzy orange

hair and bigger breasts inquired, easing from the relative safety of the shadows clinging to the buildings. "I mighta seen 'im." The corner of her full mouth tipped up in a delf-deprecating half-grin. "Truth is, I seen lots o' things from this spot through the years."

A doxy! Perfect.

Daisy brightened at the sight of her, swaying slightly before righting herself. A proper streetwise informant! She loved those. Reaching into her pocket, she retrieved the bottle again, waggling it enticingly. "Mighta seen 'im, you say? Well now, wouldn't that be fortuitous?" She took a swig for herself and then offered it over. "Care to share what those keen eyes of yours have witnessed?"

The woman grinned wider and accepted the bottle, taking a healthy pull before wiping her mouth with the sleeve of her dress. "Depends. Who's askin', and what's he to you?"

The truth? A version of it? She went with, "Let's just say I'm in the business of finding things. And at present, the thing I am very much trying to find is an heir who has rather inconveniently gone and misplaced himself."

The doxy barked a laugh. "Sounds like he don't want to be found."

"Yes, well, people often have the most peculiar ideas about what they want and what they need. I intend to convince him he needs finding. Preferably before he's arrested for vagrancy, eaten by a street urchin, or—heaven forbid—hired on as an honest laborer. I'd never forgive myself."

"Ain't no street urchin eatin' a grown man, not unless 'e's made of biscuits." The doxy snorted.

"You haven't met some of the hungrier ones," Daisy muttered. Then, louder, "But back to our elusive heir. Have you seen him or not?"

The doxy tapped a finger to her lips, considering. "There

was a feller what fits yer description, mighta been in The Stag and Lantern couple nights back."

Daisy gasped. "Really? And what was he doing? Was he drinking? Brooding? Staring dramatically into the middle distance?"

"He was arguin' with a bloke. Nearly came to blows 'fore the barkeep stepped in. Didn't seem the brawlin' type, though. More like 'e was cornered."

"Cornered?" Daisy frowned. That was interesting. "By whom?"

The doxy shrugged. "Some brute, built like an ox and twice as mean-lookin'. Didn't catch the whole of it, but the bloke ye want slipped out the back soon after."

"And where, pray tell, does one go after slipping out the back of The Stag and Lantern?"

"Could be anywhere," the doxy said. "Could be 'e legged it through the alley to Coppergate. Could be 'e ducked into one o' the lodgin' houses round the corner. Could be 'e's sleepin' rough down by the Ouse."

Daisy groaned and massaged her temple. "So, in summary, he's either in a warm bed, lost in a maze of alleyways, or communing with the local rats by the river. Marvelous. That narrows it down."

"You want him, you'll 'ave to start sniffin' about like a blood-hound," the doxy said, handing back the bottle.

"And my nose isn't nearly sensitive enough for that. I suppose I'll just have to go knocking on doors, shall I?" She took another sip, contemplating her next move. Sighed gustily into the evening air.

The doxy leaned in slightly, eyes gleaming. "Or... ye could ask the right sort."

"The right sort?" She arched a brow, questioning.

"Ones what know things before most. The beggars, the street sellers, the urchins."

"The same ones you said wouldn't eat him?"

The doxy smirked. "They might talk fer a price. A coin, a meal... or a sip o' that."

Daisy glanced at the bottle, then back at the woman. "So, what you're telling me is that I must bribe the underbelly of York with honeyed whiskey in order to locate my missing duke?"

"Aye," the woman said, grinning. "That's 'bout the size of it."

Sighing, she tucked the bottle away. "Right then. Off to grab some bread and bribe someone, I suppose." She turned, then paused. "What's your name?"

"Rosie," the doxy said.

"Well, Rosie, if I don't find my duke, I shall at least die of an interesting evening. Cheers." Daisy grinned and tossed a jaunty farewell. Then she turned on her heel and strode off toward the river, her course now set. With any luck, she wouldn't end the night floating in it.

After a sneaky, quick stop back at The Stag and Lantern (one loaf of slightly stale bread and a wedge of cheese secured with only minor difficulty involving a spinning countertop while Mason was occupied in the loo), Daisy found herself meandering along the river in search of her next informants. She spotted them soon enough, a trio of men huddled near a crumbling wall, speaking in low tones. Excellent.

"Evening, fine gentlemen," she greeted, planting her hands on her hips for added dramatic effect. "I wonder if you might help a lady in distress?"

One of them, a wiry man with a missing tooth, gave her a look of deep suspicion. "Depends. What's it worth?"

"What, not even a moment of chivalrous kindness? Not even for a poor, lost soul?" She pressed a hand to her chest, faking affront.

"Not unless that soul's got coin," the man replied dryly.

Daisy tsked. "Very well. How about a different sort of currency?" She withdrew the loaf of bread from her skirt pocket, waggling it enticingly. "A meal and a sip of something strong, for the right information." She pulled out her favorite blue bottle and waggled it too. But she didn't give it over, not yet. Not unless they became difficult.

The three men exchanged glances before nodding, and she handed over the bread, watching with great satisfaction as they tore into the loaf like starved wolves.

"Now," she said, crouching beside them, swaying slightly. "Tell me about the man who left The Stag and Lantern two nights back. And don't leave out any good bits."

The toothless man bit off a hunk of bread and chewed, eyeing her thoughtfully. "Aye. I saw 'im. Looked a mite troubled, he did. Took the alleyway east, towards the bridge."

"Troubled how?" She waggled a finger in front of him when he didn't immediately answer.

"Kept lookin' over his shoulder," he finally replied. "Like someone was on his tail."

Not another heir hunter.

Damn it, she hoped like hell it wasn't so. That finder's fee was *hers*.

"And was there?" Her stomach tightened.

The man wiped his mouth with his sleeve. "Dunno. But if I was bettin', I'd say aye. He weren't runnin', but he weren't dawdlin' neither."

Daisy nodded sagely, though the effect was somewhat undermined by the way she wobbled slightly on her haunches. Points, whiskey mead. "That's suspicious, all right. And this was... when?"

"Two nights ago."

She exhaled. Two nights. That was a long time for a man to

be missing in York's underbelly. Too long. Either Dawson was very good at hiding... or someone had found him first.

Which would be deeply inconvenient.

She tapped her lip in thought, then leaned forward, lowering her voice conspiratorially. "And tell me, gentlemen... has anyone besides me been sniffing around?"

The men exchanged glances. Then, slowly, the toothless one nodded. "Aye. Big fellers. Built like prizefighters. Didn't seem like they was offerin' bread and cheese, though."

"Interesting. Most interesting. Right then!" she declared, pointing determinedly toward the darkened streets of York. "Time to locate a missing duke before someone else does! Or before I get entirely too sloshed from Mrs. Buddersham's miracle whiskey to care."

"Yer already there," one of the men observed.

"Nonsense," she puffed. "This is my optimal level of deductive prowess." Spinning on her heel, she nearly lost her footing. "Gentlemen," she said as she turned back, her voice as grand as a duchess at court, "you have my sincerest thanks for being right proper sorts and not taking advantage of a defenseless woman wandering the perilous streets at night."

The men, grizzled, sharp-eyed, and street-worn, blinked at her in bemusement.

"To be clear," she continued, straightening with an exaggerated sway, "I know that *I* am not, in fact, defenseless. But you don't know that, which makes this whole encounter rather sweet on your part." She tapped her chin. "Unless, of course, you did know, in which case . . . *very* wise of you."

The wiry man with the missing tooth let out a short bark of laughter. "And what makes ye think ye ain't defenseless, then?"

Daisy grinned, stretching her arms overhead with a languid roll of her shoulders. "Oh, you know. Grew up an orphan in an all-girl orphanage. We didn't have time for niceties like *playing fair*. If you wanted to keep your boots, your supper, and your front teeth, you learned how to fight mean."

"That so?" The biggest of the trio gave her a slow, assessing look.

"Mm-hmm," nodded solemnly. "I bite, scratch, and—if pressed—can throw a punch so wicked it'll make a man rethink his entire life's choices." She wiggled her fingers at them. "But you lot? You're good men. Didn't even try to steal my booze. That's rare and commendable."

The toothless man snorted. "Maybe we just figured we'd let ye stagger off first, then nick it later."

Daisy gasped, pressing a hand to her chest in mock offense. "Oh, you villains! And here I was about to declare you York's most chivalrous ruffians." She raised a brow. "But fair warning, if I catch you at it, you'll find yourself wearing that loaf of bread as a hat before you can say Oi!"

The men chuckled, shaking their heads, and the wiry one tipped an imaginary hat. "Well, if ye get in trouble, little miss orphan-boxer, ye know where to find us."

"Don't tempt me. I will drag you all into my schemes." She winked, waggling her fingers at them.

"Ain't never stopped a lass from trouble before." The biggest one grunted.

"Excellent." She beamed. With that, she spun again—only mildly miscalculating the momentum and having to sidestep a rather inconveniently placed cobblestone—before striding into the night, the river mist curling around her.

Now. Time to find her wayward heir before she ran out of whiskey.

Chapter Three

As Daisy meandered back toward the Shambles, she decided that the street was just a little bit too much, after all. Too twisty. Too tilty. Too *wiggly,* if streets could, in fact, wiggle.

"Honestly," she muttered, pausing in the middle of the narrow lane, and squinting at the way the buildings leaned over her like nosy old aunties. "Did no one, in all the centuries of its existence, think to build one, just one, wall straight?" She tilted her head, then tilted her body to match. "Oh, there, now it looks right."

A passing man gave her a wide berth.

She hugged herself against the cool night air. Good heavens, but she missed her sisters. If they were here, they'd probably be trying to steer her home, tucking her into bed with stern words about how a lady shouldn't drink on an empty stomach.

Well. Joke's on them. She *had* eaten—if honeyed whiskey counted as a meal, which, under the current circumstances, she was quite sure it did.

Continuing down the cobbled street, she reached out now and then to trail her fingers along the rough timber of the overhanging buildings. "It's as if a dozen drunk men got together, built their homes at random, and then stood back and said, 'Perfect! Let's call it a street!'" Yet the air smelled of old wood, stone, and the lingering warmth of baking bread. In the distance, a violinist played a merry tune outside one of the taverns, and somewhere nearby, a cat yowled in protest at something. "Magical," she declared. "Perfectly, wonderfully, weirdly magical."

But time to get back to sleuthing. If her missing heir was hiding somewhere in this topsy-turvy maze, she would find him.

Daisy adjusted her skirts as she wandered, the well-worn brown fabric swishing about her ankles. A proper tavern wench's dress, if ever there was one. Practical, a bit saucy, and best of all, sturdy. It had seen better days, but that was part of its charm. The off-shoulder linen blouse was loose enough to keep her comfortable and just snug enough to keep her from looking entirely like a ruffian. The bodice was laced tight, accentuating just enough to make a man rethink his priorities, and the sleeves —well, they had been on her shoulders earlier in the evening, but Daisy had always preferred a bit of freedom in her movements.

And of course, the best part: the pockets.

Enormous pockets, deep enough to carry an entire collection of ill-advised treasures. Currently, they housed precisely one treasure that mattered most: her half-drained bottle of Mrs. Buddersham's homemade honeyed whiskey, which was easily the finest whiskey ever to be produced in the entire country. Possibly the entire world.

"You're the real hero of the night." She patted the pocket fondly.

"Talkin' to your own pockets now, are ye?"

Turning, she found a stout woman wrapped in a heavy shawl, leaning against the doorway of a crooked little shop. The woman's face was lined with years of wisdom and an expression that suggested she was thoroughly unimpressed with everything.

"Not just any pocket," Daisy corrected, swaying slightly as she turned fully to face the woman. "A *whiskey* pocket. A most important distinction."

The woman sniffed. "Aye, well, ye might need it, wanderin' about this late. The Shambles don't take kindly to the tipsy and unguarded."

Daisy pressed a hand to her chest. "Are you suggesting I'm unguarded? I'll have you know I have exceptional reflexes. Possibly. Unless stairs are involved."

"Then maybe ye'd best be careful. They say a spirit walks these streets at night." The woman gave a knowing little hum.

"A spirit, you say?" She perked up immediately. "I love a good haunt. Who is he? A tragic lover? A vengeful gambler? A butcher, perhaps, come to reclaim his lost sausage empire?"

"Depends who ye ask. Some say it's the ghost of a merchant who was trampled in a street fight. Some say it's a woman who met a tragic end at the hands of a scorned lover. Others say it's the Widow of Greymoor. An' others say it's older than that. A whisperin' thing, always at yer back, just outta sight."

"*Oooh.* That's deliciously unsettling." She shivered with delight.

"Aye. And ye mark me, girlie, if ye hear footsteps where there shouldn't be any, don't turn around."

"That's terrible advice. What if I want to see a ghost?" Daisy pursed her lips.

"Then ye deserve whatever comes of it."

"Brilliant. Thank you for this valuable information. I shall be extra on the lookout."

The woman muttered something about "foolhardy girls" before disappearing back inside, shutting the door with a resolute thunk.

Daisy turned back toward the twisting street, wiggling her fingers at the dark. "All right, moody ghost, you heard the lady. If you're going to haunt me, do try to make it worth my while."

She continued walking, her boots clicking against the uneven stones, her skirt swishing around her ankles as the night deepened. The street had emptied further, save for the occasional flicker of candlelight behind grimy windows. Shadows stretched long in the glow of the few lanterns still burning.

A whisper of wind curled through the narrow lane. She slowed. The air was just a little too still. She glanced behind her. Nothing.

Humming under her breath, she picked up her pace again. "Ghosty ghosty, I promise I'm very fun company."

Step.

She heard it. Not her own footstep. Not an echo. Something else.

She whirled around too fast, wobbling slightly. The street was empty. The shadows stretched, unmoving. The windows were still. Not a single door creaked open.

Daisy put her hands on her hips. "Rude."

But as she turned back, something moved in the periphery of her vision. A shape, a flicker of something shifting just at the edge of the lanternlight. Her breath hitched. A trick of the light? Or something else entirely?

The wind stirred again, carrying with it a whisper—soft, distant, but unmistakable.

She froze. "Well, then," she murmured, adjusting her bodice, standing just a little taller. "Looks like it's going to be that kind of night."

And oh, she *grinned.*

It hadn't just been the wind whispering. Or a ghosts. It had been a voice. A man's voice, rough-edged and cut from the kind of streets that bred knife-fighters and fast hands. The kind of voice that carried the weight of London's rookery, full of dark alleys, whispered deals, and promises that were more threat than comfort.

"Dawson Woodbridge," it had called.

"Oh." That was interesting. Either her heir was nearby, or the ghosts were messing with her.

"Dawson Woodbridge."

Now she'd heard it twice. She swayed slightly on the uneven cobblestones, head tilting as she turned in the direction the voice had come from. The end of the Shambles loomed ahead, spilling into the broader streets where the shadows weren't quite so thick, where the city stretched out toward the river in curling alleyways and twisting lanes.

She took a step. Then another. The street felt heavier now. Like something unseen was pressing against it, urging her forward.

Daisy loved that sort of thing. The ghosts, the mysteries, the ominous whispers in the night. All delightfully atmospheric. And, if she were being entirely honest, she had been hoping for something dramatic to happen tonight. She just hadn't expected the drama to whisper at her first.

She turned the last corner at the end of the Shambles—and ran smack into someone.

A very solid someone. Someone with broad shoulders, a chest like a brick wall, and an *oomph* that suggested he hadn't been expecting to run into anyone either.

Arms flailing for balance, she staggered back. A pair of strong hands caught her elbows before she could topple over completely.

She blinked up. Then blinked again. "*Oh.*" Green eyes. Messy brown hair. A scar cutting through one eyebrow. A shadow of stubble across a jaw that had absolutely no business being so chiseled. "Well," Daisy breathed, wobbling only slightly. "*Hullo there.*"

The man exhaled through his nose, looking at her as though he weren't quite sure if she was real. "What?" He hesitated, then frowned. "What in blazes?"

"I *found* you!" Daisy's grin stretched wide, practically beaming up at him.

Her missing heir, Dawson Woodbridge, cursed. Then scowled. Then muttered, "Oh, bloody hell."

She barely had time to register his scowl before a shadow shifted behind him, fast, brutal, and utterly rude, and—THWACK.

The sound was solid, the kind of impact that made Daisy wince even before she saw the result. Dawson's body jerked with the force of it, his hands slipping from her arms as he staggered sideways, dropping her in the process.

"Oi!" She yelped as she hit the cobblestones, her skirts tangling around her legs. "Absolutely not! You do *not* just drop a lady mid-reunion!"

Dawson, meanwhile, was too busy swaying on his feet, one hand pressed to the side of his head where a fresh welt was forming. His gaze flickered, hazy and confused, but his instincts were still intact. He turned, a hand half-lifting to fight.

And that was when the second thug moved.

She had precisely one and a half seconds to take in the fact that there were two of them—large, burly sorts who looked like they regularly bench-pressed sacks of bricks for fun—before the second one lunged.

"Oh no, you don't!" she declared. Because while Daisy was a little bit tipsy, and while she was very much sprawled on the ground like an unfortunate potato, she was not the kind of woman to sit back and let things happen. Her hand dove into her pocket. Not for the whiskey. (Though she would argue that whiskey could have been a solution, if thrown properly.) No, this time, her fingers curled around the smooth, cool handle of the knife she kept tucked there for emergencies exactly like this.

Because she had grown up in an all-girls orphanage. And when you grow up surrounded by other girls who would absolutely shank you for taking the last bowl of stew, you learn two things very quickly:

1. Fighting fair is for idiots.
2. Pockets are for knives.

She flicked the blade open and, with a truly impressive lack of grace, threw herself forward, aiming straight for the nearest set of ankles.

The second thug (who had clearly not been expecting a fallen woman to suddenly become a rolling badger from hell) bellowed in alarm as she sliced. Not deep. She wasn't trying to kill the poor fool. Just a reminder that he should rethink his choice of occupation.

He stumbled back with a curse, and that was all the distraction Dawson needed. Still reeling from the first blow, the man moved, lurching sideways, using his momentum to ram into the first thug with enough force to send them both crashing into a nearby wall.

"Oh, excellent!" she exclaimed, grinning as she rolled back onto her feet. "You *do* know how to fight. I was a little worried for a moment there."

He shot her a look—half-exasperation, half-incredulity, and entirely put upon. "I wasn't expecting to be bludgeoned upside the head, was I?"

"Well, you are clearly being hunted by nefarious sorts." She yanked her skirt free of its own knot. "You really ought to be expecting *something*."

"You say that like it's easy," he muttered, dodging as the first thug came back swinging.

She hummed. "It is easy. You just assume everyone's trying to kill you until proven otherwise."

"That sounds exhausting." He grunted as he blocked a punch, throwing his own in return.

"Yes, well, I haven't been knocked senseless tonight, so who's really winning?"

Dawson shot her another glare, but she could tell—he liked it. And she was beginning to really like the look of him. Rugged. Capable.

Oh yeah, he looked like a mistake she'd make twice.

But first they had a fight to win.

Ever the connoisseur of both fine whiskey and strategic violence, Daisy reached into her cavernous pocket and wrapped her fingers around the blessedly sturdy neck of her blue bottle. Mrs. Buddersham's homemade honeyed whiskey. She yanked it free, lifted it high, and took a glorious, throat-burning swig. And then . . . she swung.

THWACK.

The first thug's eyes rolled back immediately as the bottle connected with his skull, and he crumpled like a sack of regret, hitting the cobblestones with a heavy thud.

The second thug—a little slower on the uptake, poor fool—blinked in horror, as if his own skull was suddenly feeling very, very vulnerable.

Daisy grinned, wiped her mouth with the back of her sleeve, and swung again.

THWACK.

Another satisfying thud as the second man hit the ground.

Silence settled over the street.

The bottle, miraculously, was still intact. A testament to Mrs. Buddersham's truly exceptional brewing skills. Daisy blew out a breath and gave the nearest thug a little nudge with the tip of her boot.

Out cold.

Perfect.

She dusted off her skirts, casually tucked the bottle back into her pocket, and turned to find Dawson Woodbridge gaping at her.

Just staring, jaw slightly slack, like he had never seen a woman before in his life. "What," he finally managed, voice a little hoarse, "the *bloody hell* was that?"

"That, sir, was an excellent bottle of whiskey being put to exceptional use." She beamed, and then cocked her head, considering. "I could have used my knife again, but that felt a bit redundant, don't you think? Variety is important in these matters."

His green eyes flickered between her, the sprawled-out thugs, and the whiskey pocket that had somehow produced both a weapon and a drink in under ten seconds. Finally, he let out a slow, deeply bewildered breath and scrubbed a hand down his face. "You're..." He shook his head, like that would help. "You're... one hell of a woman."

"I am, aren't I?" Daisy agreed.

He took a step closer, still looking at her like she might vanish if he blinked too hard. "Who—" His brow furrowed. "Who in the name of all things unholy are you?"

Should she tell him? Should she not? Oh, but where was the fun in that? Taking a moment, she considered—but not really.

All mischief and warmth and utter, whiskey-fueled delight, she leaned in a little. "Wouldn't you like to know?" she whispered, winking.

Then, before he could demand answers, she grabbed his wrist, yanked him down the street, and called over her shoulder,

"We should probably run before they wake up, don't you think?"

Chapter Four

Dawson was having a very strange night.

One moment, he was on the run, trying to avoid getting himself either found or killed. Preferably both. The next, he'd quite literally collided with a woman who smelled of honeyed whiskey and bad decisions, only to watch her single-handedly knock out two of Mad Duggie Black's best bruisers with nothing but a liquor bottle and sheer gall. And now he was being dragged through the streets of York like some hapless, overgrown doll, with no idea who the hell she was or what she wanted from him.

"What—" he huffed as he tried to keep his footing, his boots scuffing against uneven cobblestones. "Where—? What the bloody hell are we doing?"

The woman—who, thus far, had offered him no name and only a deeply concerning amount of enthusiasm for violence—whipped her head around, grinning as she yanked him forward. "Securing a carriage, of course!"

Dawson's stomach dropped. "What?" And then he saw it. A fine-looking black carriage, sitting at the edge of the street, its driver conveniently nowhere to be seen. His already pounding head pounded harder. "Oh, hell no."

She didn't slow down. Didn't ask his opinion. Didn't even pretend she was considering another option. She simply hauled him straight to the carriage, threw open the door, shoved him inside with alarming ease, and—

SLAM.

The door shut. Dawson had precisely one second to process the dim interior, to lurch forward, to make a plan before the world tilted. The carriage jerked forward with violent force, and Dawson—large, grown man that he was—was whipped backward like a ragdoll, slamming against the far wall with a graceless oof. "*Oh, for fu—*"

The wheels rumbled fast, tearing over cobblestones, hooves thundering. From outside, he heard his mysterious savior/captor whoop loudly, her voice full of utter, reckless delight. "This is brilliant!" she called. "I love driving!"

Rubbing the back of his head as he pushed himself upright, he groaned. This was not how he'd planned to spend his evening. In fact, when he'd slipped out of The Stag and Lantern two nights ago, he'd had one simple goal: Disappear.

But instead, he'd been discovered by a madwoman who apparently stole carriages for fun.

He braced himself as another sharp turn whipped him sideways. Through the front carriage window, he caught a blur of brown skirts and a mass of long, dark hair, whipping about as his savior/captor urged the horses faster.

"Who in God's name are you?" he roared, half-slammed against the seat.

"That's not important right now!" she called back.

"The hell it isn't!"

She leaned to peer inside the window, grinning entirely too much for someone who had just commandeered a man and a carriage. "Let's just say I'm a finder of lost things," she said with a wink. "And you, my dear Dawson Woodbridge, have been very, very lost."

His stomach tightened. She knew him. She knew his name. *Oh, bloody hell.*

He managed to upright himself, barely, gripping the edge of the seat as the carriage barreled through the streets, wheels rattling against the uneven stones. Outside, his unknown captor whooped again, the sound absolutely delighted, as though this were a joyride and not a high-speed escape.

"This is excellent fun!" she called as she handled the reins with far too much confidence for someone who had just snatched his entire sense of control.

"Would you mind explaining why I'm currently being whisked through the streets of York by a completely mad woman?"

She peered into the carriage window again, grinning as though he were the best thing to happen to her all evening. "Oh, I'd love to explain," she said sweetly. "Truly, I would. But I think we should put some distance between us and the men who just tried to cave in your skull first, don't you?"

Rolling his head back against the seat, Dawson sighed. Fair point. Mad Duggie's men would eventually wake up, and when they did, they were going to be very, very cross.

He should be concerned. He should be trying to wrestle control of this situation back into his own hands. But instead, he just found himself watching her. The way she handled the horses like she was born for it. The way she grinned at danger like it was a favorite old friend. The way her bronzed skin glowed under the dim lantern light, her dark hair tumbling loose, wild and utterly untamed.

She looked like a woman who thrived in chaos.

He sat forward, bracing as the carriage hit a particularly

deep rut in the road. "Alright, love, I'll bite." Dawson arched a brow. "What exactly makes you think I'm lost?"

She snorted. "Oh, come now." She gestured vaguely in his direction. "You were skulking in alleys, getting your head bashed in by criminals, and doing an abysmal job at keeping a low profile. That screams lost to me."

"I'll have you know, I was doing an excellent job at not being found." He gave a quiet laugh, rubbing his jaw.

She smiled wider. "And yet... here we are."

Damn it.

Dawson liked her. He shouldn't, but he did. There was something utterly unshakable about her. She had the energy of a storm, the kind that blew through town and left nothing the same after it passed.

He sighed, leaning against the seat, watching her through the window. "So. You're a finder of lost things."

"That's right."

"And me being 'lost'," he said, slowly, "wouldn't have anything to do with the fact that I'm supposed to inherit a large amount of money and a tedious amount of responsibility, would it?"

She clicked her tongue. "Oh, look at that! He's *clever*. Don't worry, chum, you're going to love it."

"I'd love it a bit more if I wasn't being tossed around like a bloody ragdoll!" he hollered when she hit another rut and sent him flying.

How could he possibly want to take over Mad Duggie's East End Gang? No matter what he owed Duggie for taking him in as a lad, it wasn't that. Like he'd told the gangster when this whole mess had started: find another crime boss to take over. Dawson wasn't having it. Of course, now he was a wanted man, with East End members sent after him as a parting gift from Mad Duggie Black.

She peeked back into the window, her hair swirling around her face. "Oh, don't be dramatic."

"*Dramatic?*" He gestured wildly to the entire situation. "I was minding my business, got cracked over the head, and now I'm stuck in a runaway carriage!"

She snorted again. "You weren't minding your business, you were getting your arse kicked by those two clods when I ran into you."

"Minor details," Dawson grumbled.

The carriage took a sharp turn, and he barely managed to keep himself upright this time. He sighed, running a hand through his messy, disastrous hair, and decided. Fine. If he was being abducted, he might as well get some answers.

"Who, exactly, told you I was lost?" He propped an elbow on his knee, watching her through the window.

"A birdie?" She flashed him another maddening grin.

He'd spent most of his life learning to read people, their tells, their ticks, the way their lies formed in the space between their words. And something about this woman—this whiskey-wielding hellion—was not adding up.

He breathed, rolling his shoulders, trying to work the lingering ache out of his skull. His coat had taken a bit of a beating in the scuffle, but it was still serviceable, dark and plain enough to blend in anywhere he pleased. His shirt, loose at the collar, sleeves shoved up to his elbows, was wrinkled from too many nights spent sleeping in places a man of means should not be sleeping.

If she had truly been watching him, tracking him like some determined little bloodhound, then she should have known he was no gentleman.

"You know," he said, idly adjusting the buttons on his coat, "I was under the impression that Mad Duggie was keeping his little succession plans quiet."

The carriage jolted. Just a fraction. Nothing obvious. But Dawson felt it. Felt the moment her hands tightened around the reins.

He leaned forward, watching through the small carriage window, and caught the flicker of too-casual curiosity in her expression.

"Mad Duggie?" she echoed, not quite turning to face him. "What an intriguing name. Sounds positively ominous."

He hummed. "He is. More so when he's deciding a man's future without asking him first."

Her fingers twitched. Dawson grinned slow and sharp. Oh, she hadn't known. Not about that. Which meant she wasn't working for Duggie. Hadn't tossed his arse in a carriage on Duggie's orders.

She wasn't working for one of his many, many enemies, either, because she looked too damn surprised to be fishing for answers.

So who was she, then? And why had she been so determined to get him in this carriage?

"Must be quite the future," she said smoothly, still watching the road. "What with all that wealth and responsibility weighing on you."

And there it was.

Dawson's brows lifted. She wasn't talking about Duggie's empire. She was talking about something else. Something he didn't know about.

Interesting.

He leaned back, stretching his legs, casually amused as he watched her squirm. "Hell of a thing," he mused, letting his voice trail just enough, watching—waiting—for her next move.

She didn't miss a beat. "Oh, I imagine so," she said, her tone light, conversational, as if they were not, in fact, engaged in a game of very high-stakes deception. "A man like you, someone who's spent his life in the underbelly of things . . . why, you must be positively revolted at the thought of settling down and taking the reins."

Dawson huffed a laugh. "Oh, revolted doesn't begin to cover it, sweetheart."

She tilted her head, as if intrigued. "And yet, here you are. Clearly running from it."

Dawson smiled. And, for the first time in a long time, it wasn't forced or guarded. Because she didn't realize she'd just told him something he wasn't supposed to know.

If she was talking about Duggie's empire, then sure, he'd been running from it since the day the bastard first laid his claim on him. But the way she said it—so vague, so knowing. She thought she was talking about something else. And that meant she was guessing. She didn't actually know what she was chasing. More precisely, who.

Rubbing his jaw, he felt the light scrape of stubble, and decided this could be fun. "Well," he said, settling in, "you clearly know so much about me, why don't you tell me?"

"I'd hate to spoil the surprise." Her lips curled.

He smirked. She was lying through her teeth. But the real question was . . . what the hell did she actually think she was dragging him into?

Chapter Five

The lovely, infuriating, reckless woman currently stealing Dawson across Yorkshire thought she was leading this dance.

She wasn't.

She thought she had all the control, all the knowledge, all the upper hand.

She did not.

He watched her through the front window, thoroughly enjoying himself as she attempted to sidestep his questions with all the finesse of a woman who had absolutely no clue what she had just stumbled into.

"You know," he drawled, "I've met all sorts of people in my time—cutthroats, cardsharps, thieves, the occasional corrupt vicar—"

"Oh, I do *love* a corrupt vicar!" she interrupted, flicking the reins with enthusiasm. "They're so creative in their sins."

That surprised a laugh from him. "Right? All fire and brimstone in the daylight, stumbling into brothels by moonlight—"

"—and pretending they don't have a taste for whiskey and wickedness?"

"Exactly!"

They grinned at each other through the window, the carriage bouncing along the winding road, night stretching out around them as the lights of York disappeared behind them.

"See, I knew I liked you." He let out a deep, easy sigh, stretching his legs out in the cramped cabin.

"Astonishing. I haven't even properly rescued you yet, and I've already won you over." Her enormous brown eyes flicked back to him, mirth dancing in them, lips twitching at the corners.

"Sweetheart, you've concussed me and stolen my peace, but you do have great conversation skills, so I suppose I can forgive you."

"Very gracious of you."

"I try."

"And might I clarify that I did not concuss you?" She shook her head, smiling, and Dawson caught the way her shoulders relaxed, just a fraction, as though she had finally stopped expecting him to protest his fate.

Little did she know he had no intention of protesting anything. In fact, the more he watched her, the more he was enjoying himself. There was something wildly entertaining about a woman who could bash two men's skulls in with a whiskey bottle, steal a carriage, and still make him laugh while doing it.

And if she thought she could outmaneuver him in a battle of wits—

Well. She was in for a very long night.

"So, tell me something, love." He tilted his head, voice dropping into something lower, smoother.

Her fingers twitched on the reins. Not much. Just a fraction. But he caught it.

42

"Something about you?" she asked, all lightness and ease, but he heard the careful edge beneath it.

"No," he said, grinning slowly. "Something about *you*."

Her lips parted briefly, before she caught herself, shaking her head. "Absolutely not."

"Why not?"

"Because I am a mystery, Dawson Woodbridge. A puzzle, a delightfully unsolved enigma."

"You're a woman who drinks straight out of a bottle and drives a carriage like a lunatic."

"A very sophisticated enigma."

He laughed outright, shaking his head. "You are something, that's for certain."

"And you're enjoying yourself immensely."

"I have never been more entertained in my life." Dawson pressed a hand to his chest, chuckling.

"Well, good. Because we've got miles to go before I let you free."

"Darling," he murmured, voice all lazy amusement, "who said I wanted to be freed?"

And just like that, she stiffened. Just a fraction. Just the slightest shift in her seat. But he saw it.

Oh-ho.

So she hadn't expected that, had she?

She had expected him to fight her, to push against this, to rage and struggle and make her life difficult. But Dawson had no intention of doing anything of the sort. This? This was fun.

And if he was going to be dragged into something, he might as well enjoy the journey.

He smirked as he leaned closer to the window. "So then," he murmured, watching her very carefully, "what happens when we get wherever we're going?"

She didn't answer right away. For the first time, she hesitated. And he saw it, felt it, the first crack in her confidence, the first moment where she realized she might have miscalculated.

Oh, he liked that.

He liked that *a lot.*

Finally, she spoke, her voice still bright, still cheerful, but just a little too practiced. "Well," she said, "I suppose we'll just have to see, won't we?"

"Oh, sweetheart," he murmured. "I cannot wait." Dawson leaned back, a slow grin curling across his face.

He had long since given up on trying to reclaim control of this situation. Not because he wasn't capable of it. No, he could wrestle a man twice his size into submission, slip a lock with a hairpin, and disappear into the London streets with a change of coat and the right slouch.

Frankly, he was having too much fun.

"You know," he drawled, watching her, "I have to say, for a woman committing multiple crimes, you seem remarkably unconcerned about my thoughts on the matter."

"Oh, are you concerned? My apologies. Shall I take you back?" She snorted, flicking the reins.

"I'm just saying, most people who abduct a man—"

"—*Rescued!*"

"—in the dead of night have the decency to at least explain why before carting him across Yorkshire." The carriage rattled and bounced over a rough patch of road, and Dawson braced himself, his shoulder knocking against the side panel. "Are you trying to break my spine?"

"Not intentionally," she said lightly.

"Not intentionally," he repeated under his breath, shaking his head. "Just going to be one massive bruise by the time we get wherever we're going."

"Oh, stop whining. You're perfectly intact."

"For now," he muttered.

The town had long since disappeared behind them, the narrow, twisting roads giving way to open fields and shadowed hills. The countryside stretched wide and quiet, the only sounds the creak of the carriage wheels, the rhythmic clop of hooves, and the occasional rustling of wind through the grass.

Dawson breathed out, settling back, watching her as she guided them forward. He didn't know what he had expected her to do. Drive them until dawn? Pull straight into some great hall to lock him in a dungeon? Something about her had suggested as much.

The carriage slowed. Just a little at first, then more noticeably, the speed easing into something steady, rolling, then finally stopping. Dawson arched a brow, shifting in his seat as the horses huffed, faint steam curling in the air.

The carriage rocked slightly as she moved, shifting to climb down from the driver's seat.

He debated for all of half a second whether he should stay put. Then decided against it. Because, really, he had far too many questions to just sit there patiently like a man resigned to his fate. With a quiet groan, he pushed open the door, stepping out into the evening light, boots hitting the packed dirt road.

It was quiet here.

Wide, open country, a narrow lane flanked by fields and the dark shapes of trees stretching toward the sky. A small wooden gate stood just ahead, leading into some rolling pasture beyond, the grass silvered in the pale glow of the moon.

"Well, well. A woman who knows when to give her horses a rest." He rubbed the back of his head.

She was standing by the wheel, arms folded over her chest, watching him with that same bright-eyed mischief. "Even I," she said grandly, "know when to show mercy."

"Oh, do you?" Dawson smirked.

"Indeed. I may be a woman of strong will and questionable

methods, but I'd never run my horses into the ground. Besides," she gestured vaguely toward the vast, moonlit countryside, "it's quite pretty, don't you think?"

Dawson glanced around. It was, admittedly, nice. Quiet. Still. The kind of place where a man could breathe for a moment before deciding what in the hell to do next.

Not that he'd tell her that.

Instead, he leaned against the carriage, lazy and amused, crossing his arms. "Ah, so it wasn't for the horses at all. You just wanted to get me alone in the dark countryside."

"Sir, you wound me! What sort of woman do you take me for?" She let out a mock gasp, placing a dramatic hand over her chest.

He grinned, slow and sharp, tilting his head. "I'm still figuring that out." And damn, but he liked watching her squirm. Because she did squirm, just a little—not much, just enough.

Then she recovered, flipping her hair over one shoulder, tilting her head right back at him. "I suppose you'll have to keep sticking around to solve that mystery, won't you?"

He laughed, shaking his head. He had made many questionable decisions in his life. Apparently this was about to be another one.

The carriage stood quiet, the world stretched wide and open around them. The stars blinked lazily overhead, the night thick with the scent of earth and wild grasses, of crisp air and the faintest lingering trace of city smoke still clinging to their clothes.

And *her*.

She smelled warm.

Like whiskey and honey and something darker underneath, something rich and maddening, something entirely at odds with the sharp, biting wit she wielded like a weapon.

He should have kept his distance. But then—when had he

ever done what he should? Instead, he shifted just slightly, tilting toward her, barely a movement at all. Just enough to let the night breeze carry the subtle trace of her scent to him.

A sniff, barely there. Not enough to be noticed, unless you were looking for it. And she wasn't. She was still grinning, smug as ever, all wild eyes and untamed laughter, as if she thought she had him cornered.

Poor thing.

She didn't realize she had just wandered into the den of a very patient, very entertained wolf.

Not touching, not quite invading her space, but close enough that she would feel the shift of his presence, he leaned in closer, the quiet weight of his attention settling firmly upon her. Then, he bent his head, just slightly, lowering his voice into something low, deep, warm. The kind of voice that curled around a person, slow and steady, full of things meant to be dangerous. "Since you won't tell me your name," he murmured, "I'm afraid I'll have to call you poppet."

He felt it, the small, barely-there shiver that rippled down her spine. The way her breath hitched, so quick, so subtle, that if he hadn't been paying attention, he would have missed it. But he was paying attention.

Oh, he was paying very, *very* close attention.

Dawson smirked, just the barest curl of his lips, and stayed right where he was, close enough that his breath stirred against her cheek, warm in the night air. "Unless," he continued, just as softly, just as leisurely, "you'd prefer I call you darling instead?"

She turned to look at him then, slowly, her huge, dark eyes gleaming with something sharp and unreadable. For the first time all night, she didn't have an immediate response. And damn, but he liked that.

He pulled back just enough to meet her gaze properly, grinning lazily, utterly delighted at the new, fascinating turn of events. "Ah," he said, pretending to sigh. "No argument? No clever retort? I must have startled you, *poppet.*"

She blinked. Snapping back into herself, she huffed, rolling her shoulders as if to shake off whatever that was.

"You're ridiculous," she muttered, folding her arms across her chest.

Shoving his hands casually into his pockets, he chuckled. "And yet," he murmured, "you're still standing here, aren't you?"

That earned him a narrowed glance, but she didn't move. Didn't step away. Didn't correct him.

God help him, he was having the time of his life.

"You seem awfully pleased with yourself, *darling,*" she tossed back at him, all mock innocence, as if she hadn't just felt him test the air between them—as if she hadn't just felt the shift, the change in whatever game they were playing.

"Well," he said easily, slow and silky, enjoying the way she refused to look at him. "Poppet suits you."

"Does not," she muttered, her head snapping toward him, eyes narrowed.

He hummed, watching her, watching the way her throat moved when she swallowed, the way her shoulders stiffened slightly, as if bracing for whatever he was about to say next.

"Oh, it absolutely does," he mused, shifting just slightly, just enough to keep her attention locked on him.

And there it was. The way she turned abruptly—a little too fast, a little too determined—and stalked toward the carriage, like she could just walk away from whatever had settled between them.

Dawson almost let her. Almost. But where was the fun in that?

He followed. Easily. Quietly. And just as she reached for the carriage door, just as her fingers curled around the handle—he moved. Not touching, not quite. Just close enough that his hand came down on the door beside hers, blocking her in with nothing but presence.

Oh, hell.

He felt it immediately, the way she froze, the way her breath hitched, the way her fingers tightened on the handle as though bracing herself for something she couldn't quite name.

Interesting.

"So," he murmured, his voice low, smooth, just barely brushing against the shell of her ear. "Are you planning to tell me where we're going?"

She didn't move. Didn't step back. Didn't even breathe for a moment.

Ah.

That was *very* interesting.

Shifting, just slightly, just enough to let his breath graze against her skin, to see if she would—Oh. She shivered. Barely. Still, he felt it. He hadn't been entirely sure before. Hadn't been entirely certain if that last one had been real or if it had been his own wishful thinking.

But *this?*

This was real. And Dawson knew when he had won a game. He grinned.

"Unless," he continued, letting the words trail, letting his voice drop into something just a touch too warm, "you'd rather keep me in blissful ignorance a little longer?"

She didn't move.

She didn't answer.

For the first time all night, she wasn't snapping back, wasn't filling the silence with quick words and witty little jabs.

Finally, finally, she turned her head, just slightly, just enough to meet his eyes. And damn if she wasn't even more stunning up close. Gold-bronzed skin, kissed by the sun, full lips that were currently pursed in frustration, dark lashes too thick and too long, and those huge, deep brown eyes, still bright with that infuriating, intoxicating intelligence.

He stared at her, suddenly not entirely sure what his next move was supposed to be. There was something dangerous about standing this close to her. Something undeniable about the way the space between them felt too tight, too warm, too charged. Something downright foolish about the way he could still smell the lingering honeyed whiskey on her skin.

It made him want to taste it.

Damn it. This was a mistake. A delightful, stupid, exhilarating mistake. And he had never walked away from a mistake that made his blood sing. He watched her, grinning, knowing exactly what he was about to say before he said it.

"You know," he murmured, just before stepping back, just before letting her breathe again, "if you don't give me a name soon, I might start thinking you like hearing me call you poppet."

She let out a breath, sharp and short, as if she had been holding it for too long. Then, with remarkable speed, she whipped around, chin tilted, shoulders squared, eyes flashing fire. "You," she declared, "are the most infuriating man I have ever met."

"I'll take that as a compliment, *poppet.*" Dawson beamed.

And damn if she didn't shiver again. Excellent. Still, he shouldn't underestimate her. In three moves, this pissed-to-the-wind poppet had laid Mad Duggie's henchmen out cold.

Dawson exhaled, dragging a hand through his hair, wondering what in God's name he was supposed to do with a woman like this. She wasn't just quick-witted, maddening, and absurdly competent with a liquor bottle. She was dangerous. And if that wicked little shiver had meant anything, she was dangerous in ways he hadn't even begun to unravel yet.

"Who are you? You've got to tell me." he asked, his lazy grin deepening. His voice lower now, rougher. An angel? A goddess with a mean right hook? The love of his life?

Good hell, she was gorgeous.

The woman in question inhaled sharply, as if only just now remembering that she had, in fact, neglected to tell him her name.

With absolutely no ceremony, she straightened herself, lifted her chin, and declared, "Daisy Bramble, at your service," she hiccuped and sort of, kind of... bowed. More of a toppling over and righting herself, really.

Dawson blinked.

Daisy Bramble.

That . . .that was not what he'd been expecting.

"You're joking."

"Rude."

"No, truly." He studied her, amused and utterly delighted. "I was expecting something a little... sharper. Something with an edge."

"Daisy Bramble has plenty of edge, thank you very much." She placed a hand over her chest, mock-wounded.

"Right. I'm sure it strikes fear into all your enemies." Dawson bit back a laugh.

"It should!" she declared indignantly. Then, with far too much enthusiasm, she threw out her arms and proclaimed, "I am Daisy Bramble, hunter!"

He lifted a brow, rubbing his aching jaw, still feeling the weight of the blow he'd taken earlier. "Hunter?" he echoed, bracing his head between his palms. "As in hunter of men?"

He thought of Mad Duggie's men, prone and unconscious on the cobblestones. Looking at her now, beaming, delighted, still swaying slightly from drink, well, he believed it.

"That's right!" she said, grinning so damn brightly that he

almost forgot what kind of trouble he was in. "I am Daisy Bramble, Hunter of Men."

He grunted, shaking his head slowly. "Hell," he murmured. What exactly had he just gotten himself into? He blinked slowly, trying to process the absolute absurdity of this moment.

Daisy Bramble.

Hunter of Men.

Bloody hell.

His head throbbed, the ache from earlier pulsing behind his eyes, and he rubbed at it half-heartedly, unsure if it was from the actual blow to the skull or from the sheer force of this woman's personality. Probably both. Because Daisy Bramble—this tipsy, wickedly dangerous, moonlit temptation—was standing in front of him, grinning at him like she had just laid claim to his entire existence.

And the worst part?

He wasn't entirely sure she hadn't.

Chapter Six

Daisy had spent her life getting into trouble—and, more importantly, getting out of it.

She was a runner, a scrapper, a born survivor, a woman who could charm a barkeep, out-drink a swindler, and slip a pocket watch from a man's coat in the time it took him to blink. But nothing, nothing, in her experience had prepared her for the problem that was Dawson Woodbridge.

Because *good hell*.

He was . . .

Entirely too much.

She had been prepared for someone soft. Some pampered, well-kept, easily led heir who would thank her kindly for returning him to his grand fortune, tip his hat, and be done with it. But this man? This man had London's backstreets in his bones, the rough cut of survival in his broadened shoulders and battle-worn knuckles, the kind of rugged sharpness that did not, in any way, belong to a duke's heir.

And then there were his eyes. Green, wicked, sharp with intelligence.

She didn't like them. Didn't like the way they tracked her

movements, the way they lingered, the way they amused themselves at her expense. Or worse, the way they made her feel like he saw something in her that even she hadn't figured out yet.

Putting space between them, she took a step back, because space was safe, and distance was wise, and his smirk was getting far too knowing. She needed to think. Needed to remember who she was and why she was here and not get distracted by the ridiculous, entirely inappropriate thought of climbing him like a tree.

A very sturdy, very tempting, very broad-shouldered tree.

She hadn't climbed a tree before, but she knew the branches, and she was fairly certain that if she ever did, Dawson Woodbridge would be exactly the type she'd start with.

Daisy needed him pliable, agreeable, cooperative—and instead, she was getting the strong, laughing, completely unbothered version of him, and she did not like what that meant for her chances to bringing him back to London.

Exhaling sharply, she focused on anything else. Like the fact that night had fully fallen. Like the fact that she'd driven them into the countryside, where there was nowhere to go, nowhere to take him, and nowhere to sleep but . . . Oh. *Oh, hell.*

Her stomach dropped. She turned slowly, reluctantly, and glared at the carriage. The very small, very enclosed, very *only-has-one-bloody-seat* carriage.

Dawson huffed a quiet laugh, clearly watching the exact realization hit her square in the face.

"Well," she announced, lifting her chin defiantly, "this is a development."

"Indeed." He rocked back on his heels, hands in his pockets, looking infuriatingly at ease. "Seems we're in for a bit of a... cozy night, wouldn't you say?"

Oh, she did not like the way he said that.

Low. Smooth. Amused as all hell. As if he were daring her

to acknowledge it. As if he knew, *knew*, that her thoughts had been far from pure just moments ago.

Daisy cleared her throat, ignoring the wicked little curl of his smirk, the way his shirt was still open at the collar, the way the night breeze played through his hair like it was trying to test her resolve.

Focus.

He is your job. You are collecting him for a payday. You are going to return him to London and get your fee and that is the only reason you are here.

"I assume you'll be taking the floor, then?"

Daisy blinked. "Excuse me?"

He gestured loosely at the carriage interior, where there was precisely one seat and not a single inch of extra space. "Well," he mused, "it would be improper for us to share, would it not?"

"You— I— It's my carriage!" she sputtered.

"And?" Dawson lifted a lazy brow.

"And you are my—" She stopped.

He grinned.

Oh, hell no. She was not about to say you are my captive while standing in the middle of a moonlit road with a man who was taller, stronger, and clearly far too at ease with this entire predicament.

"I'm your what, exactly?" he prodded, tilting his head, watching her squirm with deep and profound delight, looking far too entertained.

She gritted her teeth. This. Right here. This is why she should have tied him up before shoving him in the carriage.

"Fine," she huffed, crossing her arms. "We share."

"Scandalous.' Dawson pressed a hand to his chest, mocking horror in his voice.

"Shut up."

"I should warn you," he said, so, so damn casually, "I am known to be quite restless in my sleep."

Daisy inhaled through her nose. *Do not kill the client. Do not kill the client. Do not kill the—* "We're sleeping in shifts," she declared, pointing at him.

He shrugged easily. "As long as you don't get lonely."

She prayed for patience as she climbed inside and settled. She was going to die in this carriage. Not because Dawson Woodbridge was an unwilling captive. But because he was too willing a temptation.

She had survived many things in her life. Street fights. Drunken brawls. The occasional unfortunate attempt to cheat at dice. But she wasn't entirely sure she was going to survive this. Because this . . . this too-small, too-tight, too-warm carriage situation with a smirking, frustrating, absurdly attractive rogue of a man, was quickly becoming a disaster.

And the worst part?

It was her own bloody fault.

She had picked him.

She had hunted him down, shoved him into this carriage, and now she was trapped with him for the night, his long legs stretched out entirely too comfortably, his damned lazy confidence oozing from every inch of him.

God help her.

Shifting pointedly, she bumped her hip against his because there wasn't enough bloody room in this cursed carriage.

He let out a low, amused sound, lifting a brow at her. "Apologies," he murmured, not apologetic in the least, adjusting his position so that his knee brushed against hers deliberately.

She clenched her jaw. This man. She had hauled him across Yorkshire, rescued him from a couple of goons, and he was repaying her by being entirely insufferable.

The carriage lantern cast flickering light across his face,

highlighting the rough edge of his jawline, the messy fall of his hair, the faint scar cutting through his eyebrow. And she hated that she was noticing. She hated that she was aware of him. Of his broad shoulders, the heat of him, the solid weight of him shifting beside her every time the carriage creaked.

Damn it all.

Daisy straightened violently, pulling her arms tighter around herself, glaring at the ceiling like it had personally offended her. "I cannot believe," she announced, "that I am spending my night like this."

"You're the one who kidnapped me, poppet," he reminded her unhelpfully. The absolute scoundrel leaned his head back against the seat, crossing his arms behind it, looking so damned at ease it was offensive.

"*Rescued*," she corrected, through gritted teeth. "It sounds far more romantic that way."

He snorted. "Oh yes, very romantic. Nothing woos a man quite like being bashed over the head and dragged into the night."

"I did not bash you!" She turned to glare at him, only to find him already watching her. And damn it, he was grinning. A lazy, wicked thing, all mischief and challenge, like he was just waiting for her to snap first.

And she just—*ugh*. She hated how sharp he was. Hated how he was reading her, watching her reactions, taking note of every bloody move she made.

Daisy forced herself to smirk instead. "Well, you're still here, aren't you?" she pointed out. "I don't see you jumping out and making a run for it."

"Maybe," he murmured, "I just like the company." He let out a slow, deliberate hum, eyes flicking lazily over her.

She absolutely did not shiver. Nope. Didn't happen. She

glared at him harder, but he only grinned wider, like he had seen her reaction and was tucking it away for later use.

Oh, he was wicked.

And the worst part? She was starting to suspect he wasn't going to be nearly as easy to deliver as she'd hoped. The more he watched her, the more he studied her, the more he prodded and played and tested her, the more he was figuring things out. And Daisy did not like that.

Not one bit.

She needed him unsuspecting, oblivious, easy to manage. And instead, she had this. A man with quick hands, quicker wits, and a mouth that was going to get him killed one day. Preferably not by her. Hopefully.

"You are the most exhausting person I have ever met." Daisy groaned, tipping her head back against the seat, staring at the ceiling again.

He let out a low, rumbling chuckle beside her. "Flattered," he murmured.

"Do you ever stop talking?" She turned her head, slowly, narrowing her eyes.

"Do you want me to?" He grinned.

No.

Absolutely not. Because if he stopped talking, then she'd be left with the silence. The very, very charged silence. The silence where she could hear his breathing, feel the weight of his presence, be too aware of the way their legs kept touching, the way the heat of him sank into her skin.

Daisy swallowed. "God help me," she muttered.

Dawson laughed.

And damn it all to hell, she liked the sound of it.

The night was too quiet. If it had been louder, if there had been a storm, a howling wind, a raging downpour, maybe Daisy could have ignored him. *But no.*

The June countryside was perfectly still, warm and lazy, wrapped in the kind of soft, golden darkness that made everything feel closer. The faint, sweet scent of wildflowers drifted on the breeze, mixing with the rich, damp earth, the smell of hay and stone and summer air curling in around them like a cloak.

The horses had settled, their soft, rhythmic huffs the only steady sound in the night. And beyond that? Nothing but crickets singing, the occasional low hoot of an owl, and the distant, lazy rustling of trees shifting under the stars. It was the kind of night meant for peace.

Which was very unfortunate because Daisy was experiencing the exact opposite of peace. And it was all Dawson Woodbridge's fault. He was too close. Too solid, too warm, too impossibly large in such a confined space.

She had already tried to shift away, to press herself against the very edge of the seat, but it didn't matter. He was everywhere. Big, broad shoulders, thick thighs spread wide, arms that looked like they'd been forged for wrecking things. He wasn't just strong. He was comfortable in it.

And that was the biggest problem of all, wasn't it? He was unbothered. Loose-limbed, confident, completely at ease, as if he had all the time in the world to sit here and let her suffer.

She clenched her hands in her lap, glaring at the ceiling, focusing on the sounds of the night, anything but the heat licking along her skin.

Dawson stretched. A slow, lazy movement, the kind that made his muscles flex, the broad weight of his thigh shifting against hers. She felt it. Oh, she felt it. And damn him to hell, he knew it. He let out a deep, quiet sigh, low and rough-edged, like a man settling into something warm and slow.

Her breath hitched.

She hated him.

Hated the way he moved, the way he knew exactly what he

was doing, hated that she could still smell the faintest trace of him—woodsmoke and spice, something deeper, something masculine and unbearable.

"Something wrong, poppet?" Dawson tilted his head just slightly.

Daisy's teeth ground together. If she killed him, the estate finder's fee would be very much off the table. She relaxed her shoulders, exhaling slowly, forcing herself to be casual, unaffected, cool as a damn cucumber.

"Nothing at all," she muttered.

He hummed, clearly not believing her for a second. "Odd," he mused. "You seem... tense."

"Not at all," she said, far too quickly, pointedly not looking at him.

His grin deepened in the low lantern light of the carriage. Then he moved again. This time, he shifted toward her, just slightly, just enough that his shoulder brushed hers, his thigh pressing firmer against her own.

She inhaled sharply.

Voice barely a murmur now, low and devastatingly warm, Dawson leaned in. "You're breathing funny, poppet," he murmured, right at her ear. The deepest, slowest drawl, full of nothing but smug amusement.

She snapped. "I swear to every saint in the heavens," she hissed, whirling toward him, "if you do not remove yourself from my personal space, I will—" She stopped.

Because Dawson wasn't backing off. He was watching her now, really watching her, green eyes darkened, something hot and unreadable curling in his gaze. And God help her, she was looking back.

Looking at the cut of his jaw, the shadow of stubble, the way his throat moved when he swallowed, the soft, tired curve of his mouth, the one that always looked like it was a second away from saying something wicked.

She could kiss him.

Right now, she could kiss him.

It would be so easy. And damn it, she wanted to. Which was exactly why she needed to stop this. Immediately.

She did the only thing she could think of. The only thing that would break this unbearable, impossible heat. She blurted out, "I am an heir hunter."

Silence.

A long, heavy, charged silence.

"That so?" Dawson's brows lifted slowly, his smirk curling like a cat in the sun.

She inhaled sharply, regretting everything. "Yes," she muttered, scowling at her own idiocy.

"Hm," he said, rubbing his jaw. "And here I thought you were about to do something far more interesting." He tilted his head, gaze lazily dragging over her, studying her like a new, fascinating puzzle.

Daisy gasped. "Y-You—!"

He grinned.

She was going to kill him.

Or kiss him.

Or die trying.

Either way, this was going to be a very, very long night.

She should have known better. Should have been sharper, more on guard, less swayed by the thick, golden heat of the night, the lazy lull of the breeze, the steady hush of the summer fields. She should have kept her distance.

But Dawson Woodbridge was a man who took every inch of space and made it his. And right now, he was leaning toward her, his big, muscled body stretched out, the heat of him settling into the tight carriage like something tangible.

Daisy clenched her hands in her lap, refusing—*absolutely refusing*—to acknowledge the fact that she wanted to reach out and touch him. Not even because of the way his shirt hung open at the collar, revealing a ridiculous amount of golden skin. Or because of the way his thighs—his massive, ridiculous, tree-trunk thighs—brushed against hers whenever the carriage rocked. Or because of the gritty scrape of his voice, dragging over her like whiskey over a raw throat.

No.

None of that.

She was ignoring all of it. Because she had a job to do. And *he*—he was not helping.

"You must be very good at what you do," he murmured, low and slow, his voice just barely grazing her skin, curling warm in the hush between them.

Her breath hitched before she could stop it. And—oh. *Oh.* He'd heard it. His lips tipped up, just the barest bit, a lazy, knowing little smirk that said gotcha.

She fought the urge to scowl, lifting her chin instead, pretending she wasn't one wrong word away from climbing him like a bloody oak tree.

"I am, actually," she replied, voice steady, clipped, ignoring the way her heart had started beating a little too fast.

"Finder's fee, then?" Dawson mused, stretching his arms behind his head, like this was all just casual conversation, like he wasn't unraveling her with every shift of his ridiculous body.

She exhaled sharply. "Yes," she said, too briskly. "Twenty-five thousand pounds."

Letting out a low whistle, his green eyes flashed in the dim light. "That's quite the bounty, poppet."

Her stomach tightened. She shouldn't like that nickname. She didn't like it. And she definitely didn't like the way he said it, all warm and teasing and smooth as sin.

But it was late, and the air was thick, and he smelled like smoke and spice and everything she had no business wanting, and . . . she was losing this game.

She cleared her throat, trying to regain control. "It's not a bounty, you great oaf. It's an estate claim. An heir recovery. A completely legitimate and respectable profession."

He made a soft humming sound, tilting his head just slightly, watching her closely. Too closely. And that's when she felt it. The shift. The subtle, creeping realization that this entire conversation had never been hers to control. She thought she had been leading him toward the truth. But Dawson Wood-bridge was leading her.

And she had just walked right into his hands.

"You must be very sure about this," he murmured, voice lower now, his eyes dark and unreadable.

"Of course, I am." Daisy swallowed, forcing herself to hold his gaze.

He leaned in just slightly, just enough for her to feel the whisper of his breath. "Funny," he murmured, watching her too carefully, "because you don't look sure."

Her mouth went dry.

Damn him. Damn his thick arms and wicked voice and slow, knowing eyes that saw too much. She lifted her chin. "I never doubt my cases."

"Hmm," Dawson said, his lips curling, shifting just barely closer.

This was fine. This was completely under control. Except for the fact that she could feel every inch of him, that the air between them had gone heavy, thick with something entirely too warm, and that she was starting to realize—

He was letting her get comfortable.

He was letting her believe she had him. And God help her, she had just told him damn near everything.

Suddenly too warm, too tired, too everything, Daisy dragged her fingers through her dark hair, letting her head thump against the carriage wall.

He chuckled, the sound low and easy, like he'd already won.

And that's when it hit her. She was done for. She had no idea what he was going to do with this information. And worse? She was too bloody tired to care.

She shook her head, pressing her fingers to her temples, willing the exhaustion to stop clawing at her. It had been such a long day, and the night was so thick and warm, and the slight rocking of the carriage was so steady, so soothing, so...

Her eyes fluttered. Just for a second. Just long enough for her body to sink deeper, for her head to tip slightly, for the tension to finally slip from her shoulders. She felt herself drifting, slipping, the weight of exhaustion pulling her down, down, down.

Just before sleep claimed her, she thought she saw it. The barest twitch of Dawon's lips. The slow, deliberate curve of a grin.

Like he'd already won. Like he'd been waiting for this exact moment. Like she'd just made a terrible mistake.

But Daisy was too tired to care. She'd deal with him in the morning.

For now...

Her body gave in. Her eyes closed.

And the world faded.

Chapter Seven

She woke up slowly, the kind of slow that meant she had fallen too deep, too fast, dragged under by exhaustion she hadn't realized had been weighing on her bones.

The world was quiet, except for the soft snuffling of the horses, the occasional chirp of a bird in the hedgerow.

She stretched. Or rather, she *tried* to stretch and found that she could not. Her wrists wouldn't move. Her ankles wouldn't move.

Daisy's eyes snapped open.

Her first thought was: *Did I drink too much?*

Her second thought was: *Why can't I move my arms?*

Her third thought was: *Oh. Oh, that absolute, no-good, filthy, thieving, conniving, infuriating, smug as hell—*

She jerked forward, but her body barely shifted, her entire upper half pinned to the carriage seat, her arms looped together in front of her.

Her own bloody corset strings.

Her own. Bloody. Corset strings.

Dawson had unlaced the back of her corset while she was sleeping, pulled the stays and strings free, and used them to tie

65

her up like a package. For a brief, horrifying moment, her brain malfunctioned entirely, because that meant his hands, *his hands,* had been . . .

No. Absolutely not. Daisy jerked again, furiously, gritting her teeth, kicking at the empty space where Dawson had been last night. Oh, that smug little smirk she'd glimpsed—

"I AM GOING TO KILL HIM."

The horses snorted, shifting their hooves, utterly unbothered by her rage-filled shriek.

Dawson was long gone.

She wrenched herself upright as much as she could, heart pounding, scanning the quiet, sun-dappled countryside around her, looking for any sign of the infuriating devil who had done this to her.

Nothing. Not a damned thing. Just rolling fields, a few scattered trees, a distant farmstead.

No Dawson. No six-foot-something wall of crime-boss-raised muscle lurking nearby. He had vanished. And he had tied her up in her sleep before he did it.

She sucked in a furious breath, shoulders burning with frustration, hands twisting, trying to free herself. "*Ohhh,* you absolute bastard," she hissed, jerking at the knot. It was secure.

He had tied it well, which only made her angrier.

And he took her bloody corset stays with him, she realized. Not only had he trapped her here, but he had also ensured that whenever she did manage to get free, she'd be running after him half-dressed, with a bodice loose enough to make a dockhand blush.

Checkmate with a side of embarrassment.

She closed her eyes, inhaled slowly through her nose, and let the red-hot rage settle deep in her bones.

Alright, Dawson Woodbridge. You want to play dirty?
Fine.

Daisy Bramble could play dirtier.

* * *

Free of her bindings, she paced. Well, more like stomped.

Her corset stays were gone, her bodice was loose, her hair was half undone, and she was standing in the middle of the bloody Yorkshire countryside currently talking to two perfectly innocent horses because she had no sisters nearby to yell at. At least the brute had been in enough of a hurry to leave them behind. (side-note: *odd*) Who else could she have talked to about this mess?

"Alright," she announced, pointing furiously at the Irish Draught mare, who blinked at her in mild confusion. "For the sake of my sanity, you are now Violet."

The horse flicked its tail.

Daisy nodded sharply. "Good. That makes you Blossom," she said, turning to the Clydesdale gelding, who looked as if he wanted no part in this.

"Now," she continued, hands on her hips, barefoot because she had yanked her boots off in frustration five minutes ago, "we must use logic. And since my actual sisters are not here to talk sense into me, I shall use the two of you as proxy."

Violet, the horse, chewed her bridle, deeply unimpressed.

Blossom, the horse, let out a deep sigh, as if regretting all of his life choices.

"I know, Blossom," Daisy muttered. "This is not ideal."

She began pacing again, her feet kicking up dust, her mind racing as she tried to untangle just how thoroughly she had been played. Because Dawson Woodbridge—that big, arrogant, muscle-bound criminal with the audacity to be handsome while ruining her life—hadn't just escaped. He had done so with full knowledge of what she wanted, full advantage of her mistakes, and her bloody corset stays.

Oh, she could just picture him now, running through the countryside like some handsome rover who had never even heard of the word duke, grinning to himself, probably whistling, thinking he had won.

She stopped pacing, bristling with renewed fury. "Well," she announced to the horses, "what do we do?"

Violet stared at her.

Blossom flicked an ear.

"I agree," she muttered, folding her arms tightly, cheeks hot with frustration. "We hunt the big, fat jerk down."

Blossom let out a long, knowing sigh.

"Don't patronize me," Daisy snapped, scowling. "I had him, alright? He was right there, and then—" She threw her hands up. "Now he's gallivanting off into the countryside thinking he's won!" She exhaled sharply. "Alright. First, we track him."

Violet looked skeptical.

"Second," she continued, ignoring the doubt of her new equine sisters, "we subdue him."

Blossom snorted.

"Yes, I know, he's bigger than me," Daisy muttered. "But so were those two henchmen, and we all know how that turned out."

Violet gave a single, unimpressed blink.

"Don't judge me." Daisy huffed. "I can take him."

Could she? Well, that remained to be seen. But she could certainly outthink him. Dawson Woodbridge might have muscle, street smarts, and a smile that could melt bones—but Daisy Bramble had been tracking men like him for years.

He thought he was free. He thought he had won.

That was his first mistake.

"Alright, let's talk about the real issue here," she announced, gesturing wildly at her audience of two long-suffering horses. "Because I don't know about you, Violet and Blossom, but I was expecting something very different when I went looking for my missing duke."

Violet blinked slowly.

Blossom snorted in what she could only assume was agreement.

"*Right?!*" She threw her hands up. "Where, in any of my careful, meticulous research, was the part that said he was a crime boss's foster son?"

Blossom chewed thoughtfully, clearly pondering the depths of her suffering.

"He was supposed to be some lost, bumbling aristocrat! A sheep disguised as a man! A soft, stunned, grateful heir with no idea how to take care of himself." Daisy pressed her palms to her forehead, inhaling sharply.

She stopped. That was the real problem, wasn't it? Dawson Woodbridge was not helpless. He was not soft. No, Dawson Woodbridge was an absolute wolf of a man who knew exactly how to lie with a smile and had arms that looked like they could lift a bloody horse. A gorgeous, frustrating, utterly impossible man. And somehow, she was supposed to drag him back to London?

For twenty-five thousand pounds, yes, she absolutely was.

But how, exactly?

Daisy shoved her hands through her hair, pacing again. "I am a professional," she muttered, "I track people down for a living. I get the job done. And yet—" She stopped, gesturing furiously at the empty space where Dawson had been mere hours ago. "He is gone. And I am here. Tied up with my own corset strings, talking to two horses, and wondering how in the name of all things holy I am supposed to outmaneuver a man raised by London's most ruthless crime boss!"

The horses stared at her.

Daisy huffed. "Don't look at me like that, Blossom."

Blossom blinked, deeply unimpressed.

"I had a plan!"

Silence.

Daisy scowled. "I did!"

Violet let out a heavy sigh.

Daisy pointed at her. "I do not need your judgment either."

She resumed pacing, hands clenched, mind racing. Here was the truth: She had grossly miscalculated. And she had no idea what to do next.

Tracking men down was easy. But dragging a man like Dawson Woodbridge back to London against his will?

Oh.

Oh, hell.

She stopped pacing, inhaled sharply, and straightened her shoulders. "Alright," she said at last, voice steady, determined, despite the mess of problems ahead of her. "I am Daisy Bramble, and I do not lose. So here's what we're going to do."

The horses watched her, waiting.

"Back to my plan,," she said, "Like I said before I was so rudely interrupted. Looking at you, Violet. First, we track the impossible man."

Blossom nodded.

"Second," she continued, "we figure out a way to outsmart him."

Violet blinked dubiously.

"Third . . ." she hesitated. Third should be we haul him to London kicking and screaming and collect our well-earned reward. But was she ready for that?

She exhaled slowly, then muttered, "We figure that part out when we catch him."

Blossom let out another long-suffering sigh.

"Oh, shut up," Daisy muttered. "You're not the one who has to wrestle a six-foot-something crime boss's rogue foster son into a carriage. Again. And most likely this time without his consent." She paused. "Oh God."

Her stomach dropped.

She just realized something horrifying. If Dawson was raised by Mad Duggie Black, then that meant he had all the tricks. The grift, the muscle, the cunning, the street sense, the ability to slip away unnoticed.

She'd made a terrible mistake.

She never lost. But for the first time in her career, she was not entirely certain she was going to win.

Blossom (the human sister one) had warned her. *You're not prepared.*

She had laughed. Had brushed it off, had waved a hand in the air like a bloody fool and gone off on her merry way to collect her easy payday.

But this wasn't easy. Not even a little. Dawson Woodbridge wasn't some misplaced nobleman who had lost track of his birthright. He was not some helpless lamb, waiting to be brought back to the fold.

He had been raised by a criminal kingpin. He had vanished into the night like a ghost.

And she was standing barefoot in the middle of the countryside, half-dressed, recently tied up with her own bloody corset strings, talking to horses like a madwoman.

She groaned loudly, rubbing her hands down her face. "Damn it, Blossom," she muttered. "I hate when you're right."

If her sister had been right about this, then what else had she been right about? The warnings, the gut feelings, the uneasy weight of something not quite adding up?

Daisy exhaled sharply, tipping her head back, staring at the sky like it held the answers.

What the hell had she walked into?

She wasn't just hunting a man down. Oh no, she was hunting a man down who was actively hunting his own escape. A man who was smarter, faster, stronger, and far more capable of outplaying her than she had ever expected.

And she was starting to suspect that when she caught him— if she caught him—it wouldn't be the victory she'd thought.

"This," Daisy announced, gesturing wildly at the empty space where Dawson had been, "is why I do not like men."

Violet flicked her tail dismissively, utterly unmoved by her plight.

"Oh, don't start with me," she snapped at the mare, shoving her tangled hair out of her face, only for it to fall right back into her eyes. "I know what you're thinking. 'Daisy, how could you let him escape?' But in my defense, I had no reason to think the enormous pain-in-the-arse would be this much trouble!" She threw her hands up. "He was supposed to be some pampered, lost nobleman. Not a brute with thighs thick enough to crush a man's skull and the ability to tie knots better than the Royal Navy!"

Violet blinked impassively.

"You're right," Daisy muttered, twisting her hair up again, only for a chunk of it to slide free over her shoulder. "I shouldn't be talking about his thighs." She paused, then added begrudgingly, "But really, have you seen them?"

Blossom stomped a hoof.

Fine, she groaned. "I'll stop."

She fumbled with her wild mess of hair, grumbling as she tried to tuck the thick, tangled strands into some semblance of order. *Ugh.* She needed a ribbon, a pin, anything to tie it back before it drove her completely mad. Scowling, she stalked toward the carriage, yanking open the door to rummage through her things.

And that's when she saw it.

Something Dawson had left behind. Daisy stilled as the burn of fury reignited immediately, roaring hot and fast through her veins.

"Oh, you green-eyed bastard," she hissed, "You left that on purpose, didn't you?"

A single, well-pressed footprint in the damp earth, just beside the carriage.

And just next to it? A matchbook.

A challenge. *Chase him*, it urged. Was that why he'd also snagged her corset stays?

The chase?

Her pulse kicked up as she bent down, plucking it from the dirt, turning it over in her palm. The name of the establishment was stamped in gold across the cover, bold and unmistakable: The Fox & Fiddle.

She knew that place. A well-traveled tavern in a smaller village not far from here, a stopover for those coming and going between York and the outlying countryside. She knew it well enough to know that Dawson Woodbridge was probably headed there.

Daisy clenched her teeth. "Oh, you are going to regret this, you insufferable jerk." She stood, tucking the matchbook into her skirt pocket, and then spotted her stays under the carriage, bending back down to retrieve them. Huh, so he hadn't taken them. It helped, knowing he hadn't run off with them like some deviant.

Still, she didn't know why he was going to that pub. Didn't know if he meant to meet someone, if he was looking for something, or if he was just stopping to catch his breath while he waited for her in this little cat-and-mouse game he clearly wanted to play. But she did know this: He was *not* getting away.

She turned to the horses. Blossom let out another long, slow sigh, as if already regretting what was about to happen.

Violet flicked her ears back, shifting slightly, ready. Strong, sturdy, fast when she needed to be. She was the obvious choice.

But before she swung onto the mare's back, she took a moment to unhitch Blossom, giving the big Clydesdale a firm pat on his broad neck. "You're free to go, love," she murmured, watching as he gave a lazy flick of his tail and ambled off into the distance. No sense in leaving him tied up and at the mercy of whoever came sniffing around. Horses had better sense than men, anyway.

Done, she strode toward Violet, gathering her skirts, and slipping a foot into the wheel spoke of the carriage for a boost. She swung up bareback, legs settling tight around the mare's broad sides.

"Alright, girl." She leaned forward, stroking Violet's strong neck, heart pounding with a sharp, heated purpose. "Let's go find the biggest mistake of my career."

Chapter Eight

Dawson hung in the shadows, breath slow, steady, heart beating like a war drum. The alley stank of stale ale, damp brick, and the kind of bad decisions that festered after midnight. He shifted against the rough wall, pressing deeper into the shadows, the chill of the stone biting through his shirt.

He had always hated this smell. It clung to places like this. Places where men schemed and whispered, where oaths were made over broken bottles, and where the line between loyalty and survival blurred.

And now, here he was again. Back in the thick of it. Watching the past catch up to him in the form of three men he'd grown up around.

Jacko, Merritt, and Briggs.

They stood beneath a crooked wooden sign, huddled close, their words slipping through the humid air. Jacko was doing most of the talking, of course. He always did.

"... 'e's got to come back. Ain't no way around it."

Dawson stilled. His fingers curled against the brick, the

rough edge grating against his knuckles. They were talking about him.

Merritt, ever the practical one, shrugged. "Don't see why we have to be the ones to fetch him."

"Because, you idiot, we're the only ones 'e won't bolt from on sight." Jacko let out a bark of laughter.

Dawson's lip curled. *Oh, you'd be surprised.*

A gust of wind drifted through the alley, carrying the scent of soot and river water. A reminder of another time, another place. A reminder of Duggie's world.

Briggs, the youngest of the three, shifted uncomfortably. "Duggie was real mad," he muttered. "Never seen 'im like that before."

Jacko spat onto the cobblestones. "Because Dawson's a bloody ungrateful bastard, that's why. Duggie gave 'im everything, trained 'im, protected 'im, kept 'im outta the thick of it when any other street rat would've been drowned in the Thames years ago. And how's 'e repay 'im? By turnin' his back and runnin' like a coward."

Dawson's jaw tightened. The words landed heavier than he wanted them to. Jacko wasn't wrong.

Duggie *had* given him everything. Shelter. Food. Protection. A place to belong. And he had never forced him into the filth of his trade. Never made him spill blood, never sent him out to do the dirtiest work. He'd taken him in, raised him almost like a son.

But none of it had been free.

Which was precisely why he had taken his refusal to take over the gang as a personal betrayal.

Shifting his stance, Dawson rolled his shoulders to release some of the tension coiling tight in his muscles.

Jacko turned, his boot scuffing against the cobbles, and

reached down for a battered bag resting against the wall. Wait, was that his bag?

The sight of it sent a sharp, cold surge of fury through his veins. But no. It wasn't. Not upon closer inspection.

Dawson shifted, easing onto the balls of his feet.

"We move at first light. Duggie wants 'im found, and I don't intend to be the one givin' 'im bad news." Jacko slung the bag over his shoulder.

Dawson's heartbeat picked up. First light. That meant he had a window. A small one. But enough. He just needed a distraction, a split second to case their camp and grab the bag. He'd vanish before they knew what hit them.

He was just shifting to leave when a new sound cut through the night. Distant, but growing.

Hoofbeats. Fast. Steady. Furious.

Dawson's smirk faltered. Oh, hell. He knew that rider. Only one hellion could make her horse's stride sound spitting angry.

And he knew, without a single doubt in his mind, that he had about sixty seconds before Daisy Bramble came storming into his very delicate, very careful plan and ruined it.

He cursed under his breath, tipping his head back against the wall, letting his eyes slip closed for the briefest of moments.

And then he grinned. Couldn't help it. If there was one thing he loved more than a well-executed plan...It was a beautiful, furious woman charging into his life with no regard for the consequences.

He should leave. Right bloody now.

He knew that.

He had a plan. Track the thugs, get his bag, get his mother's hairpin, and disappear before this mess could drag him back under.

And yet . . . Dawson stood frozen, half-hidden in the shadows of an old stone building, his breath suspended in his chest, watching the most tempting mistake of his life ride straight toward him.

Daisy Bramble.

Her name had been torment the moment he heard it.

Now, seeing her like this?

Damn.

The sight of her was enough to make a man rethink his priorities.

The afternoon sun bathed her in gold, spilling over the wild waves of her dark brown hair, catching on the soft sheen of sweat at her collarbone, gleaming off the bare skin of her shoulders where the fabric of her tavern dress had slipped just slightly.

She rode like she belonged on horseback, back straight, thighs firm against the broad sides of her horse, her body moving effortlessly with each stride.

Violet was a good horse. He should be watching her. Instead, his gaze was locked on the woman riding her like she was the damn queen of the hunt, determined, fierce—the very embodiment of trouble wrapped in curves and sheer willpower.

Dawson swallowed hard, jaw clenching.

He needed to leave.

Needed to move.

Needed to stop watching the way the afternoon light made the warm bronze of her skin glow like she'd been kissed by every goddamn sunbeam in England.

She was coming closer now, slowing Violet to a steady walk, scanning the narrow street, eyes sharp and knowing.

Dawson stilled further into the shadows, heart hammering. She didn't see him. Not yet.

But oh, how he saw *her.*

And God help him, he wanted. Wanted to stay. Wanted to see what she'd do when she found him. Wanted to hear that sharp tongue, that wicked wit, that biting frustration that she wielded like a weapon.

He was no stranger to temptation. He'd spent his life dancing on the edge of it. But this?

This was something else entirely.

This was an ache. A hunger that twisted deep in his gut and had no business being there. Not for a woman like Daisy Bramble. Not when he had bigger problems to handle. When he had to disappear.

And still he lingered.

Watched her swing down from her horse, frown at the empty street, and mutter something under her breath as she pushed an errant strand of hair from her face.

Dawson's fingers itched to brush that lock of hair away himself. To feel the warmth of her skin beneath his fingertips. To do something monumentally stupid.

His throat went dry.

He had to go. Now. Before she saw him. Before she spotted him standing there, wanting things he had no right to want.

He forced himself to step back, deeper into the alley. Back to the plan. Back to getting his bag, his hairpin, and getting the hell out.

Ah, hell. Just one last glance. A single, lingering moment as he took in the sight of her, the fire in her eyes, the way she looked ready to burn the world down to find him.

Then he was gone.

* * *

The embers of the dying fire smoldered low in the campsite, casting faint orange flickers over the scattered mess of bedrolls, empty bottles, and discarded playing cards.

The place stank of sweat, ale, and cheap tobacco, but it was empty.

Dawson had made sure of that.

He set the bottle he'd pulled from his pocket down, smirking briefly at it. Had she already noticed it gone? Then he moved, silent as a shadow, rifling through the mess with quick, practiced hands. His gut twisted, half with determination, half with dread.

He needed to find his mother's hairpin. Needed to see it, feel it, know it was still there.

After a few minutes of searching, he discovered his bag shoved beneath a heap of discarded coats, as if tossed aside without a thought. His pulse kicked hard against his ribs as he crouched down and hauled it out, fingers already working the worn buckles. He reached inside. And there. just at the bottom, where his fingers knew to find it, the cool press of metal against his fingertips.

Dawson sucked in a sharp breath, throat going tight, lungs suddenly feeling too small. Carefully, almost reverently, he drew the pin out.

It was small, delicate. Old, but not fragile. The shape was intricate and uncommon here in England. A design he didn't recognize, but one that had been left with him when he was given up, according to Duggie, and tucked inside the wrappings of a child too young to remember the arms that had held him last.

It was the only piece of his mother he had. The only thing that belonged to him alone. Dawson sat back on his heels, staring at it. Everything inside him ached. He curled his fingers around it, breathing deep, trying to force himself to move past the moment, to not let it break him.

But God help him, the relief was staggering.

Standing as his chest went tight, his body coiled with the

weight of something too raw, too deep, too dangerous. Placing the pin back inside his bag, he gripped the leather handle tight. He was alone. No one could see him like this. It was okay.

"You absolute, stubborn bastard."

The voice was a whisper. Soft. Heated. Fuming.

And it was right behind him.

A shudder rolled through Dawson's body before he could stop it, and he dropped his bag. The warmth of her breath skimmed the side of his neck, sending a sharp, tight ripple of sensation straight through his veins.

Daisy.

She was right there. Close enough to touch. Close enough that if he turned his head, just slightly, his lips would be a breath away from her throat.

He didn't move. Didn't dare.

Because she was still talking.

"Do you have any idea how long I've been tracking you?" she whispered, voice like dark honey and sheer exasperation. "How absolutely *livid* I am?"

He swallowed hard. Oh, he could feel it. The heat rolling off her and the way her frustration crackled in the air like a coming storm. God help him, he wanted to let it break over him.

"You tied me up with my own corset strings, Dawson." Her voice dropped lower. Darker. "You made me chase you."

A muscle ticked in his jaw. She was still so close. So damn close. His fingernails curled into his palm, as if that tiny bit of pain could anchor him to something sane.

"And now I find you here, rifling through a pile of filth in the middle of the woods." Her breath brushed his ear. "I could just throttle you."

Heat shot through his body so fast it nearly knocked him sideways.

Jesus.

He couldn't breathe, couldn't move. If he did—if he so much as turned an inch—he would grab her. Press her back against the nearest tree and kiss her senseless. Breathless. Until she was wet and begging for him.

Exhaling slowly, deliberately, carefully, he kept his voice low and rough, fighting for control. "Poppet," he murmured, because he couldn't help himself. He felt, rather than saw, the way she stiffened. He smirked, just slightly, knowing that it infuriated her. "You're angry."

"Oh, *furious*," she whispered back.

"Good."

Before he could do something truly stupid, he should move. If he stayed a second longer? He was going to ruin himself over her.

And he wasn't sure he'd mind.

Daisy's breath hit his skin. Silken. Warm. Frustrated. "You took my stays and practically left me topless, you devil." Her voice was a whisper. A curse. A challenge.

And that was it. The final, breaking point of his control. He didn't think. Didn't plan. Didn't stop to remind himself that this woman was hunting him down like a hound on his trail. All he knew was that he wanted.

So he took.

With a low, rough growl, Dawson twisted, snatching her against him, one hand fisting in her hair, the other gripping the soft, full curve of her arse. She let out a strangled gasp, one of shock, of fury. Of something else entirely. And then his mouth was on hers.

Oh, bloody hell.

The first brush was a collision, a clash of heat and want and sheer, reckless temptation.

She was fighting him, and then she wasn't. Her hands, which had shoved at his chest, curled into his shirt instead. Her body, rigid with protest, softened, melting into him as though she had never been kissed like this before.

He made a sound in the back of his throat, a low, hungry thing. Because she was kissing him back. And he was ravenous for it.

His grip on her tightened, fingers flexing over the perfect curve of her arse, dragging her flush against him. He tilted his head, slanting his mouth over hers, deepening the kiss, pulling a sharp, startled sound from her throat that went straight to his blood.

She tasted like whiskey and absolute destruction.

He wanted to drown in it.

Her fingers clawed at his shoulders, her breath shattered between kisses, and *oh, hell,* she was ravaging him back. But he couldn't stay and play longer. He had to go. Had to leave her. Had to—

He tore himself away, breathless, burning, *leveled.*

Daisy staggered back, her hands flailing like a windmill in front of her, grabbing desperately for the breath he'd so unexpectedly stolen from her. Her huge brown eyes locked on him, dazed and disbelieving.

"You can't just *kiss* a person!"

Dawson's breath shuddered out of him, and he smiled. Slow. Wicked. His gaze dragged down her body, and he saw her breath stop altogether.

"I just did, poppet."

And then, like the scoundrel he was, he vanished.

"*Damn you, Dawson Woodbridge!*" Her shout echoed through the trees.

Now she had another reason to catch this heir.

Payback.

Chapter Nine

Rooted to the spot, Daisy clenched her fingers, her breath coming in short, sharp bursts.

The night was too quiet. The forest too dark. The only sound was the rapid pounding of her own heart.

She reached up, pressing a hand against her chest. It was still there. Still beating. Which was truly remarkable, considering Dawson had just tried to murder her via scandalous, knee-weakening, ruinous kiss.

Her lips still tingled, her body still hummed, and if she didn't move, if she didn't do *something*, she might actually catch fire. She sucked in a breath, stomped her foot, and then spun toward the trees where that absolute devil of a man had disappeared, hoofbeats trailing into the distance.

"Damn you and your delicious kisses!" The words ripped out of her, echoing through the darkened forest.

A few startled birds took flight. Somewhere in the distance, a fox let out a sharp bark.

Oh, he had done it now.

Her fingers curled into tight fists, her whole body thrumming with something dangerously close to rage. Or want. Or both, which was the absolute worst possible combination.

She took three steadying breaths.

And then she stormed toward Violet. The mare flicked an ear, blinking at her as if to say, *Oh? We're doing this again?*

Daisy pointed a finger at her. "Stop judging me."

Violet's tail swished, unimpressed.

"I'm sorry, am I being dramatic?" she snapped and threw up her hands. "Am I the one who just kissed someone senseless and then disappeared into the night like a criminal mastermind? No? No, I did not think so!"

She paced, her boots crunching against the grass, heat still coiling low in her stomach.

Why had he done that? Why had he kissed her like that? And more importantly, why had she kissed him back?

This was not part of the plan. It had been straightforward. Find the lost heir. Drag him back to London. Collect the bounty. Use the money to rebuild Bramble Hill Orphanage.

Because that—*that*—was what truly mattered.

Not him.

Not his stupid, smug mouth. Or the way his hands had gripped her like he couldn't help himself. Or even the way her entire world had tilted the moment his lips crashed against hers.

She needed a new plan.

Planting her hands on her hips, she glared at the mare. "Alright, lady, I have made a grave error."

Violet nodded her massive horse head.

"No need to be rude," Daisy huffed and began pacing again, gesturing wildly as she spoke. "This was supposed to be simple. Find the missing heir, convince him to come back, collect the finder's fee, and rebuild our home. That was it. A straightforward mission. But then . . ." She threw up her hands. "Then he had to go and be... Dawson."

She could still feel his hands on her. Could still hear his voice in her ear. *"I just did, poppet."*

A shiver chased down her spine, and she sighed, dragging her fingers through her hair. "I know, I know." She exhaled hard. "This isn't about him. It's about Bramble Hill." And that man's finder's fee was enough to make that dream real.

She clenched her jaw. He was not getting away. Not because of a kiss. Not because of the way he made her burn, or the way he had smiled at her like he knew exactly what he'd done to her.

No.

She was Daisy Bramble, Hunter of Men, and she was going to find him.

She strode to Violet, swung herself up onto the mare's back, and tossed back her hair. "Alright, girl." She adjusted her grip on the reins, eyes dark with renewed determination. "Let's go track down my heir."

And maybe, *just maybe*, make him pay for that kiss.

* * *

The Fox & Fiddle was exactly the kind of place a person went when they wanted to drink, gamble, and make some very questionable choices. It was also the perfect place for Daisy to do some thinking. Because what else was she supposed to do, really? Dawson had kissed her senseless, stolen every last ounce of her composure, and then disappeared into the bloody night.

"I just did, poppet."

She growled under her breath and threw open the tavern door with a bit more force than was strictly necessary. The rush of noise and warmth hit her all at once. The pub was alive with energy, and no one cared what time of night it was because the ale never stopped flowing. Laughter rang out from a crowded table near the hearth, where a group of men banged their tankards together, sloshing beer onto the floor.

A pair of women leaned against the bar, trading lazy smiles with the harried-looking barman she knew from her trips through was named Cecil. Someone was playing a fiddle in the corner, but half the notes were lost beneath the general din of shouting, betting, and the occasional drunken cheer.

Daisy blew out a breath. Now this was a proper place to seethe.

She strode up to the bar, plopped herself onto a stool, and slammed down a coin with more force than necessary. "Ale. Big one. Fast."

"Rough night?" The barman, broad and grizzled with a scar down one cheek and a missing tooth, raised a brow.

"I don't want to talk about it, Cecil."

"Fine by me. I'll get you that ale."

"Great. Thanks."

Cecil shrugged and slid a tankard toward her.

Daisy snatched it up, took a long pull, and groaned. It wasn't great ale, but it would do.

Now.

Time to think.

She needed a plan. A real plan. Not just *"track down Dawson and demand answers,"* but something smarter. She was dealing with a man who had been raised by a crime boss, had the instincts of a wolf, the body of a gladiator, and the ability to kiss a woman senseless and then vanish like smoke.

Which was unfair.

And rude.

She needed to work with what she knew. She tapped her fingers against the tankard, frowning.

What did she know?

1. Dawson Woodbridge had been raised by Mad Duggie Black, one of the most notorious crime bosses in London.

2. Despite that, Dawson had never actually been part of the East End Gang. Not in the thick of it, anyway, from what she'd gathered.

3. Duggie had tried to force Dawson into taking over the gang last year, and when Dawson refused, things had gotten ugly.

4. Dawson had run.

5. And now, the gang wanted him dead, or back. She wasn't sure which.

Her gut twisted. That meant he wasn't just avoiding her. He was avoiding *them*. Duggie's men had been sent to track him down, drag him back, and likely beat some sense into him.

And now, here Daisy was, doing the exact same thing. Except she wasn't planning to beat him. Just... tie him up, haul him back to London, and collect her twenty-five-thousand-pound finder's fee.

Because that was what this was about. Dawson wasn't just a job. He was a future for the girls who needed it. She had to remember that—no matter how tree-trunky and climbable his thighs were.

She took another long, steadying gulp of ale, trying to settle her thoughts. She could do this. Nice and rational and—

"—I'm telling you, Jacko, he was here."

The words snapped her back to attention. She froze, tankard still in hand. Her head tilted slightly, just enough to catch the conversation happening a few stools down.

Jacko. That was a name she recognized. She glanced discreetly up, scanning the tavern crowd. And now she was looking . . . oh. *Oh, bollocks.*

Sitting at the far end of the bar were two men she would

recognize anywhere. Jacko—thick-necked, broad, the kind of man who looked like he could punch through a wall. And Merritt—leaner, smarter, meaner. And a third one she didn't know at all.

Mad Duggie Black's men.

Dawson's thugs.

They were nursing ales, muttering low between them, but the moment she heard Dawson's name, she knew she was exactly where she needed to be. So long as they didn't recognize her.

Relaxing her posture, she took a slow, unbothered sip of ale, and turned just slightly on her stool. She was going to listen. Dawson Woodbridge had already escaped her once tonight. No way was she letting him do it again.

She kept her back to the thugs, her ears wide open, her tankard half-raised in an excellent display of casual disinterest.

"...Duggie don't care how we bring him back," Jacko was saying, voice low and rough, the kind of voice that sounded like it had spent years shouting through cigar smoke. "Long as he's alive."

Merritt snorted. "Alive and mostly intact. He don' want the bastard too roughed up, but..." He shrugged. "A little's fine."

Daisy's fingers tightened around the tankard. Bastards.

She should be thrilled. If Dawson's life was this complicated, it meant he was that much easier to persuade back to London. Surely, being a duke was better than being hunted.

But...her gaze flicked toward the froth in her ale, and a frown pulled at her lips. What kind of man was Dawson Woodbridge, really?

She had assumed he was a scoundrel, a rogue—dangerous in the way of men who thrived on chaos and charm. And he was. But he was also... more. She had felt it.

That kiss, God, *that kiss,* hadn't been careless. It had been hungry. Like a man reaching for something he thought he had no right to touch. Or like someone who had been running for too long.

And damn her, she was curious. Who was he, underneath all that clever mischief? What had his life really been like, growing up under the shadow of Mad Duggie Black? Did he see Duggie as a father? Had he ever wanted that life, or had he always been trying to escape it?

The thoughts made something tighten in her chest. Her grip on the tankard went white-knuckled. No. It didn't matter. He was a job. A paycheck. A very annoying, stupidly handsome, infuriatingly good-kissing job. Nothing more.

Daisy lifted the tankard and took a long, angry swig. "Focus, Bramble."

Jacko's voice cut through her thoughts. "Duggie said it's gotta be done before the week's out."

"Why the rush?" Merritt exhaled sharply.

Jacko shrugged. "Didn't ask. Don't care. Just know we've got 'til week's end to drag 'im back to London. Or we're the ones gettin' dragged."

Daisy stilled. That was new. A time limit. That meant Duggie was running out of patience.

And that meant Dawson was running out of time.

She took another slow, steady sip of ale, her mind sharpening, her pulse kicking up. This changed things, because if Duggie's men were on a deadline... she needed to find Dawson first, before they did. Before things got ugly.

Before she started thinking about him in ways that had absolutely nothing to do with money. Because that would be a problem. And Daisy Bramble *did not* make problems for herself. She solved them.

One heir at a time.

She needed another drink. *Badly.* Turned out that listening to two of Mad Duggie's thugs casually discuss how rough they could make Dawson's return trip to London—as if he were nothing more than a bit of wayward cargo—didn't sit well with her.

It made something in her twist. And twisting was dangerous. She needed to refocus. To remember why she was here, what she was doing, and that this was about business, nothing else.

Which meant an extra special drink.

Daisy reached toward her pocket where her bottle of Mrs. Buddersham's homemade honeyed whiskey should have been waiting. Her fingers met empty fabric. She stilled. *What?*

She patted herself down. Checked the other pocket. Looked inside her hidden liner pockets, then checked again, because surely, surely—

Nothing.

Her breath hissed through her teeth. She sat up straighter. Mentally backtracked.

Where was the last place she . . ?"

Oh. *Oh, no.*

Realization slammed into her. *The carriage.* When she had slept. When she had been too exhausted, too warm from the leftover buzz of whiskey mead, too utterly devastated from the absolute audacity of Dawson Woodbridge.

That was when that blasted man must have taken it.

Daisy's entire body went still. Her hands curled into fists. That low, steady burn of frustration that had been simmering in her gut roared into a full inferno. Dawson had stolen her whiskey. Her homemade, impossible-to-find-anywhere-else, beautiful bottle of Mrs. Buddersham's honeyed whiskey.

And she was going to kill him. Or kiss him again. Or kiss him and then kill him. She hadn't decided.

What she had decided, however, was that she needed

91

another drink. Immediately. She slammed her palm down on the bar so hard that Cecil, who had undoubtedly seen things he wished he hadn't, nearly dropped the glass he was polishing. "Another ale. Now."

"Already?" Cecil raised a bushy brow.

"Yes, already."

He gave her a look. "You realize you just ordered one three minutes ago."

"And?"

He sighed and poured another.

She snatched it up, muttering murderously under her breath.

The drink just wasn't the same. It wasn't the beautiful, rich, perfectly balanced whiskey mead that Mrs. Buddersham brewed in those big, old oak casks behind The Stag and Lantern, the kind that warmed a person all the way through. The kind that Mary had given her as a parting gift before she set off on this ridiculous hunt.

Now it was in the thieving hands of a man who did not deserve it.

Dawson Woodbridge could burn in the depths of hell, clutching that bottle, and she still wouldn't forgive him.

She took a long, angry swig of mediocre ale. Her thoughts churned. *That's it. That's the final straw. It's war now.*

The man had tied her up, stolen her sanity, and now her whiskey?

There was no redemption. She was going to catch him. And when she did?

"—Feck's sake, Jacko, I said he was right here an hour ago!"'

The words cut through the haze of her fury. Daisy froze mid-sip. Her focus sharpened like a blade.

Jacko and Merritt were still at the end of the bar. Still talking.

She steadied her expression, took another slow, measured drink, and leaned back against the bar. Because two things were now certain:

1. She was going to find Dawson before they did.
2. And when she did?

She was getting her honeyed whiskey back.

Chapter Ten

The next day was too hot.

The kind of heavy, humid heat that made Daisy's hair cling to the back of her neck, made her dress stick to her skin, made her entire body feel sluggish and overheated and absolutely in need of a bath.

Or a drink.

Or maybe revenge.

Yes. Revenge. Dawson was out there somewhere, drinking her whiskey, wearing that stupid, smug smirk, and not suffering nearly enough for his crimes.

She wiped the sweat from her brow, shifting slightly in her seat as Violet plodded steadily beneath her. She'd been riding for hours, straight through to daylight and beyond, tracking him across the winding countryside, following the trail of vague clues and gut instinct that had never failed her before.

The sound of rushing water cut through the thick summer air.

Her whole body perked up. A river. Finally. Violet deserved a drink, and so did she. And if she just so happened to dunk herself in up to her neck afterward, well, no one would be around to see it, now would they?

She guided Violet toward the tree line, the sound of rippling water growing louder, the shade beneath the branches a blessed relief from the relentless sun. Then she saw it. A break in the trees. The river, glimmering silver-blue beneath the golden light of afternoon.

Her stomach dropped straight to her boots. Someone was in the water. A very large, very broad, very wet someone.

Her brain short-circuited.

Dawson.

Bloody Dawson Woodbridge bathing in broad daylight with no clothes on.

Daisy froze, gripping the mare's mane like she'd just been struck by lightning. Her mouth went dry. Her pulse forgot how to function.

And oh, shite, he was . . . *oh, hell.*

Dawson was facing away from her, standing waist-deep in the water, his back a glorious expanse of sun-kissed, muscle-carved sin. She had never seen so much of a man before in her life. God help her, she was staring.

The broad sweep of his shoulders, the powerful lines of his arms, the way his muscles shifted with every small movement, it was indecent. And it wasn't even the worst part. No. The worst part was that he wasn't in a hurry.

He stretched, rolling his shoulders, letting his head tip back, shaking his wet hair out like some wild creature made of pure temptation. He ran his hands down his face, over his throat, down his chest . . .

Daisy nearly swallowed her tongue. *Good God, there's more of him.*

She quickly climbed off and anchored the mare, her eyes never leaving him. They *couldn't.*

She was going to die. Right here. Right now.

Violet let out a snort from the stand of trees where she'd just been tied.

Daisy jolted violently.

Dawson froze. Then he slowly turned.

She made a horrified choking sound and immediately snapped her gaze skyward, staring at the tree canopy as if her life depended on it. "Don't look down, don't look down, don't look—"

"Well, well," he drawled, voice thick with amusement and something darker.

She squeezed her eyes shut. She could feel his gaze on her. Feel the heat of it, even from across the river.

"This is unexpected," he continued, unhurried, unbothered, because of course he wasn't bothered.

The water shifted, the gentle waves lapping as he moved, and she risked a glance. Just a small one. To make sure he was actually covered.

He was.

Just barely.

The water licked at his waist, darkening the golden hue of his skin, his body still gleaming from the afternoon light, muscles flexing as he dragged his hands through his wet hair.

Her brain shorted out completely.

"Are you going to gawk all day, poppet?"

Her gaze snapped back up to his face so fast it nearly gave her whiplash. "I am not gawking," she hissed.

"Liar." Dawson's lips curled into a slow, wicked grin.

She scowled. "Why are you bathing in the middle of the day? In public?"

He tilted his head, clearly entertained. "Didn't realize I had an audience," he murmured. "Or that you'd be so scandalized, Miss Bramble."

She was not scandalized. She was furious. And hot. And sweaty.

And aware. *Very, very aware.* Her dress clung to her skin, the damp fabric heavy, uncomfortable, sticking to the curves of her body.

She *hated* him.

Dawson's eyes flicked over her, slow and knowing. Oh, he noticed. The sweat. The flush. The way her dress hugged her curves in ways it shouldn't.

His gaze darkened slightly. And then he slowly, deliberately leaned back in the water, sinking deeper, stretching out like he had all the time in the world. He was enjoying this.

He was torturing her on purpose.

Oh, he was going to pay for this.

But not yet. Not while he was still waist-deep in the water, looking like sin itself. Because right now she was the one suffering. And Dawson Woodbridge knew it.

She was burning from the heat and from the hours of riding in the sun. From the absolute indecency of the man lounging in the river like some ancient deity sculpted out of arrogance and temptation.

And worst of all? He knew exactly what he was doing. He was watching her struggle and enjoying it.

Daisy's jaw clenched so hard her teeth ached.

"Are you going to stay in there all day?" she snapped, voice higher than she would have liked.

He stretched again, muscles flexing, the glow of afternoon light turning the droplets on his skin into something downright naughty.

She looked anywhere but at him.

"Considering it, actually." He hummed, low and lazy.

"You can't just lounge there," she huffed, shifting uncomfortably in her boots.

"Oh, but I can," he murmured, grinning like the devil himself. "You seem to be the only one with a problem, poppet."

She flushed hotter. And *oh, hell*, he was smirking now, like he could see her discomfort. Could feel how much she was suffering. As if was memorizing every single second of her torment so he could tease her about it later.

Daisy inhaled sharply, stood tall, and forced her expression into something vaguely resembling dignity. "You are insufferable," she informed him.

"Am I?" Dawson tilted his head, pretending to consider it.

"Yes."

"Funny," he murmured, eyes gleaming with something entirely too wicked. "You weren't saying that last night."

"*Excuse me?!*" Her entire body jerked. Her face went scorching hot.

Dawson's grin spread. "Oh, you know. That little moment in the woods? Where you—"

"Don't."

"—were absolutely shook—"

"I will drown you."

"—from one little kiss—"

"*I will drown you and then steal my whiskey back from your lifeless hands.*"

He chuckled, slow and deep. "Now, now, no need for threats." He leaned back again, the water shifting around him as he moved.

She gritted her teeth. This was torture. He wasn't moving. He wasn't in any rush at all. And worse—*worse*—she could still feel the way his mouth had branded her, the way his hands had held her like he wanted to consume her whole.

And now he was acting like nothing had happened.

Like he hadn't stolen her whiskey mead.

Like he wasn't currently bathing in broad daylight without a damn care in the world.

Her fingers itched to throw something at him. "Just—get out of the bloody water, Dawson."

"Say please." His grin widened.

Her eye twitched. She was going to murder him. She was going to skin him alive. She was going to—

Dawson moved. Slowly. Unnecessarily leisurely like he had all the time in the world. Like he enjoyed this—watching her squirm, watching her suffer, watching her absolutely fail to pretend she wasn't looking.

He brushed his hands over the water, watching her with sharp, knowing amusement. "Problem, poppet?"

"You are the problem," she hissed.

He laughed. Actually laughed.

Then the bastard dunked himself under the water.

Daisy blinked. Frowned. Waited.

Nothing.

Dawson did not reappear. The ripples smoothed over. The river went still.

"...Dawson?" Daisy's stomach flipped.

Nothing. Her chest tightened. "Dawson, this isn't funny!"

Still nothing.

Her pulse picked up.

"Dawson, I swear to God." She was already moving toward the river's edge.

Just then a massive, wet, grinning brute exploded out of the water.

Daisy shrieked.

Dawson laughed.

"Why you—" She lunged.

He dove back, water splashing as he evaded her grasp.

She seethed.

He was smirking again, smug, insufferable, drenched, and still naked.

And Daisy was going to kill him.

But first? She needed to get ahold of herself. God help her—he looked good. And she was one step away from losing the last of her dignity. Which meant it was time to change tactics. So she exhaled slowly, straightened, and lifted her chin.

Oh, he wasn't the only one who could play this game.

She was about to scandalize him right back because he was too smug. Too pleased with himself, standing waist-deep in the river, looking like the kind of man who destroyed lives for fun.

He thought he was winning. That was adorable.

Daisy smiled. Sweet. Dangerous.

His smirk faltered—just barely. But, she knew he felt it. The shift in the air. The turning of the tide.

She tilted her head, trailing her gaze over him in a slow, deliberate perusal—one that she knew would get under his skin.

And oh, it did.

Dawson's shoulders went tense, his jaw ticking, his fingers flexing just slightly where they hovered near the water.

"Well now," she murmured, voice rich with exaggerated curiosity. Her smile widened. "Aren't you a fine sight, Mr. Woodbridge."

Dawson's eyes darkened. She pretended not to notice. Instead, she stepped forward, slow and unhurried, the sun casting a luminous glow over her damp skin.

He watched her like a man watching a storm roll in.

Good. Let him sweat.

"You know," she said, innocent as sin, "if I didn't know any better, I'd say you were trying to make me blush earlier."

His lips parted slightly.

She took another step. "But now that I think on it," she mused, voice dripping with mock-thoughtfulness, "it's rather unfair, isn't it? You standing there all confident, all comfortable, while I am simply suffering in this wretched heat."

Dawson swallowed hard, and her smile turned wicked. She reached for the laces at her wrist, pulled.

He went absolutely still.

She hummed, casually tugging at the loosened fabric, letting the neckline of her dress slip just slightly—just enough to make him look. And oh, he *looked*.

His throat worked around a swallow, his gaze dropping, dragging, lingering.

Daisy's heart was pounding, *but oh,* she was enjoying this. "You know," she purred, tugging just a little more, letting the damp fabric cling in all the right ways, "I could just cool off right here."

Dawson made a strangled sound.

She pretended not to hear it. "Right in this nice, cool, refreshing river."

He blinked. Once. Twice.

She leaned in slightly, tipping her chin up, letting the air between them thicken. She took a step back.

Dawson's brows furrowed.

She smirked.

"Well," she sighed dramatically, rolling her shoulders back, her dress clinging even more, "I suppose I'll just go find another place to cool off."

She turned on her heel.

Took a slow, measured step away.

And counted.

One... Two...

"You wouldn't."

Daisy grinned to herself. But when she turned back, she feigned utter innocence. "Wouldn't what?"

He narrowed his eyes.

"Are you... worried, Mr. Woodbridge?" Daisy tilted her head, all mock-confusion.

Dawson's jaw clenched.

Oh, she had him now.

Daisy lifted a single brow.

And then—

She turned and walked away.

Oh, she was nearly skipping as she walked away, feeling gloriously victorious. She had made him suffer. And that was enough.

Or at least, it should have been.

She had made it exactly four paces before—

"Come on, then, boy."

She froze.

No.

No, no, no.

That was not—

She turned just in time to see him smirk. A deep, wicked, unbothered smirk. A smirk that said he thought he had just flipped the game right back in his favor.

The bastard actually thought he was winning.

Dawson folded his arms, the absolute picture of smug satisfaction, waiting for something to approach from behind her.

"Well now, poppet," he drawled, green eyes sparkling, "I do hope you weren't planning to leave me stranded."

Daisy turned, knowing that he was expecting a horse trotting toward him—but nothing came. The air was silent. No hooves. No approaching horse.

Nothing.

Dawson's smirk faltered. His brows furrowed. He looked toward the tree where he'd left his horse only to find it empty.

A slow, terrible realization spread across his face.

And Daisy beamed. "Oh," she said sweetly, tilting her head, "were you expecting a horse to be there?"

Dawson's jaw tightened. "Poppet."

"Because—oh, wait!" she gasped, mock surprise dancing in her eyes. "Do you mean that bay gelding? The one tied to that tree back there? The one you likely commandeered from some poor unsuspecting soul after you kissed me stupid and took off last night?"

A pause.

A dangerous pause.

"What did you do?"

"Well," she sighed, shrugging dramatically, "he looked so terribly bored just standing there, so I may have... oh, I don't know... untied him and sent him off?"

Silence.

Dawson stared at her.

She smiled. The satisfaction was glorious.

"You didn't."

"I did."

"Daisy."

"Yes, darling?"

He exhaled slowly, nostrils flaring. Like a man trying very, very hard not to lose his temper. "And where, pray tell, did you send my horse?"

"Oh, I imagine he's well on his way back to the village stables by now," she said lightly. "I do hope you weren't relying on him."

Dawson cursed.

And *ohhh,* how she basked in it.

Because for once, finally, fully, the upper hand was hers. Oh, had she won.

She could still taste the victory—could still see the exact moment he realized his horse was gone.

It had been glorious. Absolutely glorious.

But then he smiled. Not the slow, smug smirk she had been expecting. No—this was different. This was lazily wicked, dangerous, and entirely too self-satisfied for a man currently stranded and very much naked.

Daisy's stomach dropped.

He moved straight out of the river. Casual. Unhurried. Like a man with nowhere to be and all the time in the world to ruin her life.

Her breath hitched. She barely caught a full second's glimpse before she threw her hands over her eyes, spinning on her heel.

"You can't just—" she spluttered, her voice a full octave higher than usual.

"You're the one who sent my horse off, poppet." His voice was closer now, deep and unbothered.

She squeezed her eyes tightly shut. "That doesn't mean you—"

"Doesn't mean I what?"

Oh, she hated him. Absolutely, furiously hated him.

Her palms burned against her face, and she debated whether it was safe to drop them, only to realize it absolutely was not. Because she could hear him dressing. The soft rustle of fabric. The lazy movements. The kind of deliberate, unhurried efficiency that meant he knew she was suffering.

And he was enjoying every second of it.

Bastard.

She focused on breathing normally.

She was fine.

This was *fine*.

"You know," he murmured—closer now. Much closer.

She felt him before she saw him. The brush of warmth just

behind her, the shift of air against her neck. Her spine locked tight.

"I'm afraid it's becoming an addiction," he continued, his voice slow and honeyed, "I've got no choice but to keep calling you poppet."

A shiver raced down her spine. Oh, hell no. *No, no, no.*

She would not be affected.

She would not react.

She was—

Dawson's hand brushed her waist. Just lightly. Just barely. The kind of touch that wasn't an accident.

The kind of touch that made her toes curl.

She sucked in a sharp breath.

Dawson laughed. Low. Amused. Thoroughly entertained.

She was going to kill him. Drown him in the river. Strangle him with his own damn cravat—if he had one.

But first she had to get her traitorous, burning body under control.

Somehow.

Chapter Eleven

D awson did not mean to stare.
Truly.
But *hell*.

The fire burned low, its glow casting flickering golden light over Daisy's skin, catching in the mess of her hair, dancing in the warm brown of her eyes.

She looked—

No.

He was not finishing that thought. Because Daisy Bramble was a menace. An infuriating, reckless, stubborn little hellcat.

And yet—hell. That firelight made her look soft. Like something warm. Something dangerous. Something a man could get used to looking at.

He shifted against the log, rolling his shoulders, trying not to feel the heat creeping up his neck. He was just tired. That was all.

He was tired, and the fire was playing tricks on him, and the last thing he needed was to—

A soft sound cut through the night. A low, quiet rumble.

Dawson tensed. For half a second, he thought something was coming out of the woods.

But then Daisy went still. Too still. And he realized that it wasn't something lurking in the trees.

It was her stomach.

She had gone rigid, arms crossing over her middle too quickly, as if she could somehow erase the evidence of her own hunger. And then a sharp, defiant glare across the fire.

Like it was his fault.

Like he had personally cursed her with the need to eat.

Dawson arched a brow. She did not look amused. She looked uncomfortable.

And that... did something to him.

Something he did not like.

Because Daisy Bramble was not supposed to look like that. She was supposed to be maddening and sharp, always quick with a quip or a glare.

But right now, she looked...hesitant.

And damn it, Dawson did not hesitate. He did not let himself think too hard about the feeling brewing in his chest.

He just moved.

"There's food in here somewhere," he muttered, rifling through the saddlebag he'd taken from Merritt's horse.

She didn't answer. Didn't say a single word. But he could feel her eyes on him as he dug through the bag, could feel her watching.

He found a bundle of bread and cheese, plus something that might have been salted meat in a past life, and tossed it onto the cloth between them.

"Eat."

Her brows lifted. "Are you feeding me, Dawson?"

"I'm feeding both of us, poppet."

A lie. He wasn't hungry, but she was. And he'd rather carve out his own ribs than watch her sit there pretending she wasn't.

She hesitated. And that hesitation damn near ended him.

"You'd rather starve than take food from me?"

"I didn't say that."

"You didn't have to."

Daisy exhaled hard and finally grabbed a hunk of bread. "Fine. But if it's poisoned, you should know I'll haunt you."

"Wouldn't expect anything less."

She took a bite, eyes closing briefly, and he had to look away. Had to focus on something else. Because there was no reason, no reason at all, for that sight to hit him like a punch to the chest. And yet . . . it did.

Which was why he rummaged deeper in the saddlebag, searching for something to distract himself. And his fingers brushed something cold. Dawson frowned, pulling it free. Handcuffs.

His brows lifted. Now, why the hell were these in here? Had they belonged to Merritt?

Didn't matter.

He turned them over in his palm, considering. And then, without hesitation, he slid them into his pocket.

Just in case.

* * *

"So," Dawson drawled, tipping his head lazily against the log, watching Daisy over the glow of the fire. "What exactly makes a person wake up one morning and think—'You know what sounds like a grand idea? Hunting down stray aristocrats for a living.'"

Daisy, settled cross-legged by the fire, tore off a piece of bread with her teeth like she was personally offended by it.

"It's not like I just decided it one day," she said, voice muffled through the bite. "It's a skill set. Takes effort, talent. Which I have in abundance, obviously."

"Obviously," Dawson murmured, stretching out his legs, watching the firelight lick along her cheekbones, glint off the tangled waves of her hair.

"And it's important work," she went on, pointing the torn hunk of bread at him. "Just imagine all those empty estates, all that wealth, just sitting there. Rotting. Forgotten. Some of these people don't even know what's owed to them. And I? Well, I make sure they do."

"How terribly noble of you, poppet."

"It is noble," she sniffed. "And quite lucrative, as you might imagine."

Dawson hummed, watching her a little too closely.

"So, it's about the money, then?"

A flicker.

Just a flicker of something in her expression.

A hesitation. A pause, so small it was almost nothing. "*Ohhh,*" he murmured, lips curling, leaning forward just slightly. "It's not just about the money, is it?"

Her chin lifted, brown eyes sparking. "Don't be ridiculous. Everyone needs money."

"True." He stretched, watching her now, letting his voice turn easy, smooth, as if this conversation meant nothing at all. "But not everyone spends their days chasing down long-lost dukes. Seems like a very... specific trade."

"It is," she said. "And I happen to be very good at it."

"Oh, I have no doubt. You're relentless."

"Thank you."

"That wasn't a compliment."

"I took it as one."

Dawson smirked.

109

Daisy narrowed her eyes at him, like she knew she was being baited but couldn't quite resist biting.

He leaned back again, watching the fire, watching her. "So where'd you learn all this heir-hunting business, then?"

She hesitated. Again, it was small. A brief shift of weight, a glance toward the fire.

"Bramble Hill," she said after a moment.

"Bramble Hill?"

"The orphanage where I grew up."

He stilled. "You grew up in an orphanage?"

Daisy flicked a glance at him, chewing the inside of her cheek, like she was debating something. Then she shrugged. "Yes, and?"

"Nothing, just..." He tipped his head, watching her more closely now. "Doesn't seem the kind of place to teach a girl how to hunt down missing nobles for a living."

"Oh, it wasn't," she admitted breezily, shifting to tear off another bite of bread. "That part came later. After it burned down."

He frowned. "Burned down?"

"Mmm." She waved a hand. "Tragic accident, really. Place went up like a matchstick. But we got out. My sisters and I."

"Sisters?"

"Not by blood, but by choice."

Dawson exhaled slowly, studying her. "And what? You all just decided heir hunting was your calling in life?"

"We had to eat," she said simply. "Turns out, when you're clever and resourceful and have nothing to lose, you can make a fine living doing what the nobility can't be bothered to do themselves—tracing their own bloodlines."

He didn't say anything to that. Because it made too much damn sense.

Daisy was proud of it—he could see that. Of what they'd built. Of what they'd made out of nothing.

Still, there it was again. That flicker. That thing beneath it all. The tiniest sliver of something else. Not regret. Not quite.

Just a whisper of something unsaid.

And Dawson, for reasons he did not care to examine, did not like the way it made his chest feel.

"What?" Daisy asked suddenly, catching him looking too long.

He blinked, his face slipping back into a smirk. "What, what?"

"You're staring at me all broody-like."

"Am I?" He made a show of tilting his head. "Broody-like, you say? I don't think that's a real word, poppet."

"It is now."

He chuckled.

"Well, if you must know, I was just thinking about how fascinating it is."

"What's fascinating?"

"That a woman who spent her childhood in an orphanage and then built a career chasing down lost aristocrats doesn't seem particularly fond of the ones she finds."

"Where on earth did you get that idea?" Her brows shot up.

He let his smirk deepen. "Just an observation." A true one. She could call it just a job all she wanted. But Daisy Bramble had opinions. And the way she spoke about the nobility? It wasn't hate. It wasn't even bitterness.

It was disdain.

She didn't just hunt heirs. She didn't just find them. She dragged them back to a life they never knew they had with absolutely no patience for their feelings about it. Like she didn't think they deserved the choice.

Dawson was watching her too closely again, and he knew it.

He forced himself to lean back, lazily stretching his arms above his head, as if this conversation was nothing at all. "So tell me, poppet—" he purred, voice low, smooth, teasing. "What happens if your stray aristocrat doesn't want to be found?"

Daisy scoffed. "Oh, they never do. But that's never stopped me before."

"No?"

"No."

"Sounds like a bloody hassle."

"It is. But a lucrative one, I remind you."

"And you just—what? Chase them across the countryside, wearing them down with your sparkling personality?"

"Precisely."

"And if they still refuse to return?"

Daisy smirked, her chin lifting. "Then I convince them."

Dawson arched a brow. "Convince them, huh?"

"That's right."

"And how exactly do you do that?"

Her lips curled. "Wouldn't you like to know."

"Oh, poppet. You have no idea."

He wasn't sure when exactly it happened. When the teasing shifted. When the hunt became something else. He'd started this conversation as a game. A bit of fun. A way to poke at her, tease her, make her bristle just because he liked the way she did it.

But somewhere along the way he forgot to stop watching.

Daisy was too easy to rile, too quick-witted, too sharp, too bloody fascinating.

And now, she was too close to the fire, her skin catching in the glow, the warmth of the flames licking along the deep, rich brown of her hair, casting golden glints that he should not be staring at.

But he was.

And he did not like the way it made him feel.

"You keep watching me like that, Dawson," Daisy murmured, tearing off another bite of bread, "I might start thinking you're interested in something more than just my profession."

He huffed a low laugh, watching as her eyes flicked—just for a second—down the length of his body before snapping back up.

Oh.

Oh, she was watching him, too.

"Can't a man be curious, poppet?"

"Curious about what?"

"You."

The word came out too easily.

And Daisy, who had been settling, relaxing, lowering her guard just slightly, suddenly went still. Just for a second. Just enough that he noticed.

Dawson took that second and pressed. "Your profession, sure," he said, voice too smooth, too lazy, like this conversation meant nothing at all. "But more than that."

Her chin lifted. "What more than that?"

Dawson tilted his head, considering her. "You're good at what you do."

"I know."

"You enjoy it."

"I do."

"And yet..." He trailed off, watching her too closely.

The fire crackled between them, the night thick with the scents of earth and woodsmoke, distant water and something faintly floral.

And Daisy was watching him like she was realizing something. Like she was piecing something together too late.

"And yet?" she prompted, voice just slightly wary now.

Dawson smiled. "You hunt down lost nobles. You reunite them with their birthrights. You make them whole again."

She stiffened.

It was small.

A flicker. A half-second hesitation.

But he saw it.

"Seems to me," he murmured, stretching his arms up behind his head, making sure she noticed, "you've spent an awful lot of time putting people back where they belong."

She said nothing.

He pressed. "But what about you, poppet?" His voice was quiet now, edged with something she would not like. "Where do you belong?"

Daisy inhaled too sharply. And just like that—

He had her.

Her fingers clenched around the torn bit of bread. Her body stayed still, too still. And Dawson knew. Whatever wound lay beneath all that fire, all that sharp wit, all that relentless chasing —he'd just found it.

And for some reason—

For some bloody, inexplicable reason—

He hated that it was there.

Daisy set the bread down too carefully. "Well," she said, too brightly, too suddenly, too bloody obviously, "it's getting late, and it's getting cold, and I, for one, would like to locate a blanket before I freeze to death."

He smirked. "Mm."

She stood, brushing off her skirt, turning away too fast. She bustled about their tiny camp. And he watched her movements, mesmerized by the shape of her.

That's how she caught him off guard.

One moment, she was huffing about a blanket, pacing

around like a little storm in brown skirts. The next, she turned on him. And oh, he had not been prepared.

"You know, Dawson," she murmured, stepping close, close enough that he felt the warmth of her skin through the firelit air, "I've been thinking about something all evening."

Dawson, who had been leaning back against the log, lazy and full of himself, barely had time to smirk before she brought him to his bloody knees.

"That so, poppet?" he mused, because teasing was all he had left. "What's been occupying that pretty head of yours?"

"The river."

He stilled. "The river?"

"Mmm." She lifted a hand, trailing a slow, featherlight touch over his chest, dragging her fingers down, down, stopping just short of dangerous.

His entire world tilted.

"That moment," she murmured, voice like silk and smoke, "when I walked up and saw you—" she tipped her head, her lips curving in something wholly unholy, "—in all your glory."

"Poppet—" His brain short-circuited.

"I only saw you for a second," she continued, like he hadn't just died right there, "but oh, it was enough."

That did it. That bloody did it. He breathed in sharp and stared down at his lap, like maybe, just maybe, he could will away the immediate, undeniable problem she had just created.

"Something wrong?" Daisy bloody well grinned.

Dawson growled.

Then she bent down and kissed him and everything else burned away. She kissed him slow. Deep. Unbearable. Her hands everywhere. His fingers spreading over her waist, her back, her hips, gripping tight.

A wolf, starving for something he shouldn't take.

Her lips moved against his with something dangerous, something deliberate, something lethal.

And he let her. Let her kiss him within an inch of his life because it was the kind of kiss that made a man forget his own fucking name. That made him forget everything but her.

It was dizzying, unraveling, devastating.

It was . . .

It was . . .

Wait.

Something—

Something wasn't right. A flicker of a thought. A whisper of a warning bell ringing in the back of his mind. Something about his pocket.

That was when she pulled back and stepped away.

And that was when he realized. *"Ohhh, bloody hell."*

She beamed, holding up the handcuffs she had just stolen right off him.

Dawson had never hated and adored a woman so much in his entire fucking life.

* * *

He was not a fool.

Yet here he was, a complete fool.

Dawson should have noticed the moment the game turned. Should have seen it in the way she glanced back at him, her dark, devastating eyes too steady, her expression touched with something he should have recognized as pure, calculated intent.

But he hadn't.

Because his brain had stopped working the second she looked at him like that. Like he was already hers.

Dropping before he could stop it, his gaze slid down the

length of her, down to the swell of her incredible breasts, the low, damp neckline of her off-shoulder blouse where sweat from the ride had left her distractingly clingy.

And just like that his mind fried beyond all recognition.

He stood. Didn't think. Didn't question. Just rose to his feet like a bloody puppet on a string.

She smiled. Oh. Oh, that should have warned him.

"There you are, Dawson," she murmured, her voice a purr, "I was starting to think you weren't interested."

He was interested.

He was so interested it was becoming a problem.

His tongue swiped over his lips. His fingers twitched. His chest rose too sharply, as if breathing had become a task rather than an instinct. "Daisy."

"Mmm, I like that." She tipped her head, eyes drenched in firelight and wicked amusement. "You saying my name like that."

She took a step closer. Dawson stood his ground. Barely.

"You've been looking at me all evening," she whispered, circling him like a huntress scenting blood, "but I don't think you've really seen me."

Oh, he had seen her. And he could not stop seeing her.

"Maybe I should help you out." Her fingers skimmed his chest. Light. Barely there. A whisper of heat over his linen shirt.

He sucked in a breath, harsh and ragged.

"You see me now, don't you, Dawson?" Her hand pressed, just a little. Just enough. And then she rose on her toes. And kissed him again. A dragging, open-mouthed, sensual thing that unraveled him down to his very bones.

Her hands—oh, her hands. Sliding up his chest, gripping into the hard muscle there, pressing closer, wrapping around his neck, tilting him deeper into her. Making him growl.

Christ, he was gone. Gone to the feel of her body against his. To the scent of her, wild and sweet, warm and dangerous. Gone to the way she kissed. Hungry, hot, perfect.

His arms wrapped tight around her, his hands gripping too firm, too desperate, like he could hold onto something he already knew would undo him.

Her tongue . . . bloody hell. His entire body tightened like a wolf starving for something he should not take. Should not claim.

Dawson kissed her back like a man drowning. Like she was air and fire and sin all at once. Her nails scraped into his scalp, sending a full-body shockwave down his spine. Damn, he liked that.

His fingers dug into her waist and pulled her flush. Made sure she felt what she was doing to him. And, oh, the little hellcat smiled against his lips.

That should have been his second warning.

But he was too far gone. Too distracted. Too entirely, utterly lost in her.

That was when she stepped back from him.

"Thank you for those cuffs," she purred, wiping at her kiss-swollen lips like she had just finished a damn meal.

He exhaled long and slow.

"Oh, poppet." And then, he laughed.

"I'd say this has been an enlightening evening." She twirled the cuffs between her fingers.

"You are going to destroy me." Dawson let out a deep groan of defeat.

"Mmm." She winked. "I already did."

That was when he heard the click. Felt the cool, solid, unmistakable weight of metal snapping shut around his wrist.

He froze. Slowly—so bloody slowly—he looked down.

There, shackled snugly around his wrist, was one half of the cuffs. And on the other end?

Daisy's wrist.

Attached.

To.

His.

Dawson blinked, clearly struggling to compute he'd been bested.

"There now," she chirped, far too delighted with herself, "this is much better."

"You didn't." He inhaled deeply, carefully, trying to reel back the raging desire to either kiss her again or throttle her.

"Oh, I did."

He yanked.

She yanked right back.

"You've shackled me."

"Brilliant deduction," she praised. "And here I thought I'd caught myself a criminal mastermind."

Dawson narrowed his eyes. "This is madness."

"This is preventative strategy."

"Preventative strategy."

"Mmm."

He breathed deep and slow, reining in every. last. curse. "You truly think I'd just run off while you were sleeping?"

"Um, Dawson?" she sighed, patting his chest like she was sorry for him, "You *did*."

Bloody. Hell. He let his head tip back toward the night sky, exhaling as if he were calling for patience from the gods themselves.

She patted his chest again. "Get some rest. We've got a long day ahead of us."

And with that, she yanked him forward, dragging him

toward their sleeping arrangements like he wasn't a fully grown man who outweighed her by at least four stone.

Dawson, utterly undone, shackled, and thoroughly bested, let himself be led.

Because he had no fucking choice.

Chapter Twelve

At first, Daisy was warm. Perfectly, wonderfully, deliciously warm. The kind of warmth that came from being wrapped up in a thick, muscled, devastatingly male body. The kind of warmth that felt entirely too good. The kind of warmth that made her want to stretch, sigh, and burrow deeper into it.

Which she did until her fingers twitched and touched something very large, and very firm. Something... very much not her own.

Her eyes snapped open. Her hand was on Dawson's—

Her breath caught and her stomach plummeted. And that's when she realized that his hand was on her breast.

Oh, holy mother of scandal.

Daisy froze, her entire body locked in sheer, unholy mortification. Her fingers were curled around something thick, hot, and—oh God.

And his fingers? Oh, they were rough, calloused, and perfectly covering her bare skin, because apparently her top had shifted in the middle of the night. And his big, warm, sinful hand was directly on her breast.

The worst part?

It felt *good*. Like, really good. Like, her breath hitched, her thighs clenched, and heat unfurled low in her belly kind of good.

Dawson's chest was rising and falling beneath her cheek. Slow and steady and controlled.

And, *oh no*, she could feel him wake up. Feel him breathing. Feel the solid, hard-packed muscle beneath her cheek shift as he tensed.

Her fingers twitched.

Dawson groaned.

She squeaked.

His grip on her breast flexed, just slightly.

Oh.

Oh no.

She had to . . . she had to move. Had to fix this.

Had to—

Dawson's voice, thick with sleep and something else entirely, rumbled low. "Poppet... I know you're awake."

She stopped breathing.

He released a long, slow breath.

His voice was low, rough, and altogether unfair when he asked, "Care to tell me what you're holding, sweetheart?"

Daisy's entire body combusted on the spot. Heat rushed to her face. Mortification flared in her chest, and for one brief, fleeting second, her brain went utterly blank.

Then the panic set in. Oh, hell. Oh, no.

She had two choices.

1. Admit she woke up clinging to Dawson Woodbridge's thoroughly impressive, absolutely massive, still-very-hard package like a woman starved.

2. PRETEND SHE MEANT TO DO IT.

Oh, it wasn't even a choice. She squared her shoulders,

steadied her breath, and said, with all the false confidence she could muster, "Just checking."

A beat. Silence.

Then Dawson's chest rumbled beneath her cheek. A deep, amused, thoroughly entertained sound. "Checking, were you?" He cupped her breast, flicking her nipple with the barest hint of a touch of his palm as he shifted it away.

She lifted her chin, refusing to back down, and refusing to admit she wanted his hand back on her posthaste. "That's right." She tilted her head, as if considering. "You've been lying to me all night. I figured it was time to see if you had anything else you were being dishonest about."

He went completely still. Daisy tapped her fingers lightly against him and his entire body tensed. She felt the ripple of muscle beneath her.

And oh, that was interesting.

She was pretty sure that Dawson was never caught off guard. But now? Now, she had him. And it was *fun.*

"What's the matter? You seem... tense." She tilted her head just so, feigning innocence and trying (mostly failing) to ignore his hard, strong . . .

A long, shuddering breath.

"Poppet," he said, voice thick, deep, gravelly. "You keep your hand where it is for one more second, and you're going to find out exactly how honest I can be."

Her breath caught and heat shot straight to her belly. Her fingers twitched again, involuntarily.

He groaned again. A low, utterly devastating sound.

And Daisy officially panicked. She yanked her hand back, shoving it under the blanket like it had never happened. Groping his privates, what?

"Well!" she said, voice far too high-pitched. "Now that we've established the truth, I think I'll go make some tea."

He watched her like a man who had far too much information now. "You do that, poppet."

She tossed off the blanket like it was on fire. Which, realistically, it was. Or rather, she was. Because oh, hell, she had just spent the entire night curled against his big, hard, very male body, and—and she wanted to do it again.

She was in so much trouble.

As she ripped her hand away from Dawson's very... solid predicament, she scrambled upright, breathless, wide-eyed, absolutely not thinking about how good he smelled. She fumbled at her wrist, cursing under her breath as she unlocked the damn cuffs.

He stretched out like a lazy cat, eyeing her with infuriating amusement. "If you wanted me gone so badly, poppet, you could've just said so."

Daisy threw the cuffs at his chest. "Don't tempt me, Woodbridge."

"Weren't you making tea?"

She nodded emphatically, turning on her heel. "Yes! Tea. A proper English morning calls for it. I'll just—" She took one confident step forward. Paused. Frowned. Another step. Stopped completely.

Her brain fully caught up with her mouth.

There was . . . there was no kitchen.

No stove.

No tea leaves.

No tea pot.

She was . . . *bum.* They were in the bloody countryside. There was no tea to make.

Dawson was still watching her. She felt the weight of his amusement, pressing thick and heavy against her back. And —*oh, nope.* She was not turning around to face that smirk.

"Actually," she said brightly, pivoting like it was all part of the plan, "I think I'll just check on Violet. See how she fared through the night."

"By all means," he drawled, propping his hands behind his head. Too relaxed.

Too entertained. Too damned smug.

She marched toward the horses, ready for any distraction. And then she stopped short.

Wait.

Wait, wait, wait.

There were two horses. Violet, her gorgeous, sleek, tolerant-of-her-chaos Irish Draught. And another. Bigger. Broader. Built like a damn warhorse.

"Blossom?" Daisy whispered.

The great gelding flicked an ear, huffed softly, and stomped a massive hoof.

"Blossom!" she shrieked, dashing toward him.

The Clydesdale gave her a long-suffering look before lowering his head, letting Daisy grab his enormous face and press her forehead against his soft nose. "Oh, you absolute beauty. You found your way back, you stubborn, wonderful boy!"

Blossom sighed. Because of course he did.

She turned toward camp and Dawson, positively glowing. "Look at him!" she beamed. "He's back! Violet must have called for him. Aren't horses incredible?"

Dawson just stared—a long, drawn-out, unreadable stare. And then, very, very slowly, his gaze lifted back to hers. "Poppet."

"Yes?" Daisy was too elated to notice the shift in his voice.

A slow, dangerous smile. "You do realize what this means, don't you?" He gestured lazily between them. "It means," he said, voice thick with wicked amusement, "you are officially out of excuses. Because now, poppet," he tipped his chin toward Blossom, "we can ride together."

"I-I'm not sure that—"

"I need your help."

What? Daisy blinked and turned slowly. One second, she'd been marveling at Blossom's triumphant return. The next, Dawson had gone and said something ridiculous.

"I'm sorry, I must've misheard." She tilted her head, expression perfectly innocent. "You need my what?"

"Help," he said, voice flat, clearly gritting his teeth.

She clasped a hand to her chest. "Why, Dawson." She let her eyes go wide and syrup-sweet. "That almost sounded like an admission of weakness."

"Don't start." He exhaled sharply.

"Oh, no, please. I'd like to savor this moment. It's not every day a man like you confesses to needing a woman's assistance. Shall I have it recorded? Perhaps chiseled into stone?" She arched a brow.

"Daisy."

"Yes?"

She saw his jaw tick. "The bag. The one I had when those bastards jumped me in the Shambles? It's still with them."

That sobered her amusement just a fraction because that bag and whatever was inside clearly mattered to him.

"And you want me to help you get it back?" She asked, crossing her arms.

"That's the general idea, poppet."

"What's in it?" Her eyes narrowed.

"Nothing of interest to you." Dawson gave a leisurely, deliberate shrug.

She snorted. "Oh, well, that's not suspicious at all."

He said nothing to that, so Daisy took the moment to study him. He was playing it casual, but there was something in the way he held himself, something in the too-loose posture, the steady weight of his gaze, the flex of his fingers at his sides. This wasn't just about a bag for him, but she wasn't about to let him win this game so easily.

"So let me get this straight. You need me, an utterly soft, delicate, incapable woman—"

"Christ." He pinched the bridge of his nose.

"—to help you retrieve your precious bag from men who would very much like to pummel you into the dirt. And you expect me to do this out of the goodness of my heart?"

He lowered his hand, his green eyes flashing. "That about covers it, yes."

"How unfortunate for you, then, that my heart is terribly selective about its generosity." Oh, she had him.

"What do you want?"

"Your cooperation." Daisy tilted her head and smiled at him.

He frowned. "I don't follow."

"If I help you, you don't make my life difficult. You don't try to run, you don't fight me on this heir business, and you don't make me chase you again. You come with me—and you stay with me. No more slipping off in the night, no more rogue antics. You are mine to track and mine to deliver. Agreed?"

He went very, very still. His jaw tightened. For a long moment, he didn't speak. So long, she thought he never might.

"Fine."

"Fine?" She narrowed her eyes.

"Fine, poppet. I'll be good." A slow smirk curled at the edges of his lips. "Would you like me to shake on it? Perhaps seal it with a kiss?"

Daisy huffed, stepping back. "I'd rather seal it with your continued existence. Don't make me regret this."

"I would never." He pressed a hand to his chest.

Lord help her.

She had a feeling this was going to be an absolute disaster. And she needed to be thinking about important things. Like her sisters. Like Blossom the Clydesdale's miraculous return.

Like the twenty-five thousand pounds that would rebuild Bramble Hill Orphanage.

And not, *not* about the fact that her entire body was hot and needy and restless from a single night of agonizing proximity to one very insufferable man.

Nope. Not thinking about it at all.

Except...

She was.

Oh, blast and damnation, she *was*.

Her skin still tingled where his rough, calloused palm had cupped her breast. Her fingers still remembered the heavy, solid heat of him in her palm. And her stomach—wicked, traitorous thing that it was—still clenched at the memory of waking up sprawled across him, pressed against all that impossible strength and warmth.

She squeezed her eyes shut. No. No, no, no. Absolutely not. She was a professional. She was here to collect her heir, not get all swoony over some lawless rogue with a wolfish grin and a body carved by the devil himself.

"You're quiet, poppet." Dawson's voice dragged over her like rough velvet.

She gritted her teeth.

"Am I?" she muttered. "How fortunate for you."

"Mm." His low, lazy hum was a wickedness all its own. "You weren't quiet last night."

"I—what—" Daisy whipped around, scandalized.

He leaned against a nearby tree with all the smug, loose-limbed satisfaction of a man who had not only won but was still relishing his victory.

"Tossing and turning. Sighing. Moaning my name in your sleep."

"I DID NOT."

"Didn't you?"

She marched toward him, jabbing a finger into his chest before she caught herself and yanked it away as if burned. Oh, why was he always so warm? Why did his skin feel like sun-drenched sin? Why did she want to climb him like a damn tree?

"I was not moaning your name."

"What were you moaning, then?" He arched a brow.

"I—" Daisy's entire face went up in flames.

Dawson grinned. "That's what I thought."

Oh, she was going to kill him.

Instead, she turned sharply on her heel, stomping back to Violet, using the horse as a barrier, as if that could somehow protect her from Dawson Woodbridge and his utterly infuriating effect on her body.

"You're avoiding me."

"No, I'm focusing on my very important bounty."

"Mm. Must be hard, with all those distractions."

Daisy bit the inside of her cheek. "Not at all."

"No?" Dawson strolled up behind her. Not touching. Just close enough that she could feel the heat of him against her back. "Pity."

"You're enjoying this."

"More than I should be," he admitted, voice low and rich and full of trouble.

She closed her eyes for half a second, fighting the violent urge to spin around and kiss the smirk off his face. But no, that would be giving him exactly what he wanted. And Daisy Bramble did not lose.

So she squared her shoulders, lifted her chin, and smiled sweetly over her shoulder. "Enjoy it while you can, Dawson

Woodbridge. Because when this bounty is done?" She leaned in, just enough to watch his eyes darken. "I'll be the one laughing."

The arrogant bastard just grinned. "We'll see, poppet."

Turning away, she straightened Violet's reins, pretending like she wasn't about to combust. All she had to do was get through the day without throttling, kissing, or otherwise compromising herself with him. Easy. Simple.

Absolutely, positively doomed.

Daisy squeezed Violet's reins, gripping them so tight her knuckles ached. This was fine. Everything was fine.

And then . . . Dawson chuckled. A deep, warm, rumbling sound. Low and lazy and laced with something she refused to name.

Her heart did a funny little flop. And then another. And another. She scowled down at her own chest, as if she could physically will the stupid, treacherous thing back into compliance.

Absolutely not.

She was not . . . she was never . . . this was not happening. Daisy breathed out, slow and shaky. Then she lifted her chin, set her sights on the road ahead, and absolutely did not look back.

But good hell, she wanted to.

Chapter Thirteen

Dawson had been fine. For all of three seconds. Then she swung onto her horse and that was the end of him

A gust of morning wind caught the edge of her skirts as she lifted her leg, revealing a flash of bare thigh. Not just any thigh —Daisy Bramble's thigh. And not just any part of her thigh. Oh, no. It was the soft, inner curve, disappearing up beneath her skirts like a damn invitation to wreck him permanently.

He saw his future in that moment. It consisted of wanting this woman in ways that would haunt him for the rest of his life.

And as if the raw, unbearable sight of her golden-bronzed skin wasn't bad enough, the blasted woman winced. Not much, just the slightest, tiniest hitch of her breath as she settled onto Violet's back. That was all. And yet, his blood absolutely roared.

Her thighs. Were sore. From bareback riding.

He almost fell off his own damn horse.

His brain shorted out. His hands clenched the reins so tightly it was a wonder they didn't snap. His body went hot, then hotter, then so catastrophically hard he actually groaned under his breath.

Because he knew exactly where she was sore. Exactly how soft and delicate her skin was.

Exactly how easy it would be to ease that ache—

Christ.

He was a goddamn disaster.

The woman wasn't even doing anything, and yet here he was, gritting his teeth against the throbbing, aching, unbearable proof of his downfall. And the worst part? The absolute cruelest part?

She had no idea.

She just sat there, riding ahead of him like trouble, adjusting the blanket she'd thrown over Violet's back to keep her thighs from chafing more, completely unaware that she'd just absolutely brought him to his knees.

Dawson scowled as if that might somehow help.

It didn't.

Instead, his gaze zeroed in on her again, to the mussed-up hair that she'd thrown into a loose knot, strands escaping wildly in the morning wind. To the curve of her waist and the way her hips rocked on horseback. To the fact that her clothes were now officially driving him insane.

It had been days. *Days.*

Why was she still in that damn dress?

Dawson had never cared about a woman's wardrobe in his entire life. But now? Now it was personal. The brown skirt had seen better days. It was rumpled, slightly dusty, and clinging to her far too much in places it had no business clinging to.

And that top.

That off-the-shoulder excuse for a shirt that kept slipping down and revealing more golden-bronze skin, more collarbone, more temptation, more destruction—

Right. That was it. She needed a new dress. He'd buy her one.

The thought hit so fast, so hard, so completely unbidden that he nearly reined his horse to a stop just to process what the hell had just happened inside his own head.

He did not buy women dresses. He did not care about things like this. He did not—

His gaze flicked back to her. Her skirts had shifted again.

He was buying her a new bloody dress.

Dawson cleared his throat, his grip on the reins tight enough to strangle. "So," he said abruptly, voice rough from the absolute war inside his body.

"Hmm?" Daisy glanced back at him over her shoulder.

Scowling at the view that greeted him—her mouth, the wind teasing at her hair, the curve of her hip that refused to quit being distracting, he gave up. Hell. He was never making it back to London alive.

In desperation, he went for the only thing that might not drive him straight into madness."This... dukedom," he muttered. "What's the deal with it?"

"The deal?"

"Yeah. The bloody deal." His jaw ticked as he stared ahead at the road. "Give me the details."

Daisy slowed her horse slightly, peering at him like he'd just asked her to recite Shakespeare backward. "You mean the duchies, lands, and investments of Ashby Hollow?" she said, still sounding a little suspicious.

"That's the one."

"So now you're curious." She let out a soft, amused noise.

Dawson shot her a look that could have set fire to stone. "No," he bit out. "I just need something to think about besides..." He clamped his mouth shut before he finished that sentence.

Still, she instantly perked up. Like a wolf scenting weakness. "Oooh," she cooed, grinning like a torment. "Besides what, Dawson?"

He glared at the road ahead and regretted not keeping his bloody mouth shut.

Taking a moment for his sanity, he looked around. Early morning. A golden, too-beautiful-for-how-much-he-was-suffering kind of morning. The sky was a crisp, washed-out blue. Rolling fields of Yorkshire glowed like honey beneath it. And the air smelled like dew, damp earth, and summer wildflowers.

"Tell me the deal about this dukedom, Daisy."

"Oh, with pleasure," she cooed.

He wanted to launch himself directly into the sun. Because across from him, riding like a smug little queen upon her horse, was Daisy about to destroy his whole damn morning with a story.

Christ, she looked too happy about it. Far, far too happy. Which meant he was going to hate this.

Suddenly she stretched—just to torment him, he was sure—before rolling her shoulders loose and giving him the kind of look that preceded truly unfortunate news.

"You mean to tell me," she said, sweet as honey and twice as smug, "that you—Dawson Woodbridge—have been running around all these years without realizing that you are spectacularly doomed by a family legend?"

"That's not what I asked." He glared at her.

"No, but it's what you should have asked." She flashed a smile, and he had precisely one second to prepare before she began her brutal tale. "The last duke? Oh, he died of ergotism. You know, that nasty little problem where fungus in grain makes you go mad as a hatter before you rot from the inside out? Hallucinations, gangrene—the whole shebang. They called him the Rabid Duke." She paused for effect. "And, well. He bit someone."

Dawson jerked the reins hard. "He what?"

"Oh, yes. Right on the arm. Poor woman nearly lost a chunk of flesh." She nodded, deadly serious.

"You're lying." He ran a hand down his face.

"I am not." Daisy continued. Relentless. "He was the seventh duke to die an untimely and grisly death. Every single one before him? Dead under mysterious or cursed circumstances. AND—" She held up a finger, smiling like she was having the best morning of her life. "They all died alone."

What in the actual hell?

"What kind of circumstances?" Dawson's stomach turned.

She ticked them off on her fingers, her smile only widening. "Poisoned. Drowned. Throat slit in his own bloody library. Trampled by his own horse. Set on fire. Struck by lightning."

He nearly choked. "Lightning?"

"And then the castle burned down."

"You're joking." He stared at her.

She held up a solemn hand. "I swear it."

This could not be real. But Daisy looked far too pleased with herself for it to be anything but the truth.

"Guess what else?" she asked, leaning a little toward him.

"Can't wait." He gave her a flat look.

"Their wives?" She widened her eyes for dramatic effect. "They all died young."

His stomach dropped. "That," he said slowly, his voice unnervingly steady, "sounds an awful lot like you're telling me the entire line of Ashby Hollow is cursed."

She beamed. "I am telling you that!"

"Bloody hell."

"Oh, and the estate is worth at least a hundred thousand pounds."

Dawson choked.

"And you, dear sir, are the rightful, legal heir to all of it."

Silence. The Yorkshire countryside stretched before them, golden and peaceful, a world untouched by curses, bad luck, and unwanted legacies.

Dawson stared straight ahead. He had no idea what to say to this. So he settled for, "Well, that's just fucking wonderful."

The hellion laughed. "Congrats! Your dear ol' dad was the Rabid Duke, a man who thought biting people was an appropriate farewell. I know I should be more sensitive, but this is . . I mean, come on!"

He squinted hard at the endless rolling hills ahead, trying to absorb what had just come out of Daisy's lovely, traitorous mouth.

"Say that again."

Daisy clasped her hands over her heart in mock sympathy. "Your father was the Rabid Duke, may he rest in peace."

"No." Dawson shook his head firmly. "Absolutely not."

"Oh, absolutely yes."

He scoffed. "My father was a nameless bastard from the rookery, not some unhinged blue blood with a fungal addiction and a tendency to maul people."

"Listen, I understand this is a lot to take in," she said, sounding far too delighted with the situation. "But you really should have expected something dramatic. Ashby Hollow doesn't exactly breed men who go quietly into the night."

"No," he agreed darkly, scrubbing a hand over his face. "Apparently, they go kicking, screaming, hallucinating, and biting." He glanced at her. "You're sure about this?"

"Beyond a doubt."

He swung in the saddle toward her. "What if you're wrong?"

She arched a defiant brow. "I'm never wrong."

"What if this is a mistake? A bureaucratic error? What if the real heir is some other poor bastard with a similar face and name?"

Daisy sighed and shook her head. "I traced your lineage."

"But what if you—"

"Birth records, lineage books, parish registries. Your name is on the document declaring the dukedom intestate."

Dawson groaned loudly and glared at the road ahead, as if he could outrun his own heritage.

"It's adorable how you think there's a way out of this." She patted his arm.

He inhaled deep, slow, steady. Then, "WHAT THE BLOODY, CURSED, GODFORSAKEN HELL?"

She nearly fell off her horse laughing.

"I mean it!" Dawson snapped. "There's no bloody way—what kind of nightmare inheritance—" He growled, raking a hand through his hair. "This is the worst goddamned news I've ever received."

"Oh, I don't know," Daisy mused. "I think the bit about being worth over a hundred thousand pounds is rather nice."

He whipped toward her, seething. "If I take the title, I'll be cursed! If I don't take it, the whole bloody estate goes to the Crown. England gets the whole lot. And what a tragedy that would be."

"They're rather good at keeping things. Bit of a hobby, really."

Dawson flung out a hand. "So now I've got the King of England as my bloody competition!"

She snorted. "Hardly. He's not exactly scouring the streets for wayward heirs, now is he?"

"So let's just take a moment to really appreciate my position here." He held up a finger. "Option one: I take the title, inherit the curse, and die horrifically in some absurdly avoidable way—"

Daisy hummed. "Oh, I do love a dramatic family curse."

He held up a second finger. "Option two: I don't take the title, in which case the entire estate gets swallowed up by the Crown, and I spend the rest of my life knowing I could have been rich, but instead I'm—"

"A wanted man?" she supplied, entirely too helpful.

"Exactly." He glared at her.

She grinned. "You're quite good at explaining your own doom."

"Oh, we're not finished." Dawson snapped, holding up a third finger. "Option three: I don't make it to London at all because Duggie's men finally catch up with me and gut me in an alley."

"Not ideal." Daisy winced.

"You think?" He ran a hand over his face again. "To summarize: I'm either dying from some ridiculous Ashby Hollow death-omen, getting taken out by Duggie's men, or I don't die and I have to spend the rest of my days knowing I could have been stinking rich, but instead I'll be in a ditch somewhere, regretting every decision I ever made."

She tapped a finger to her lips, considering. "You're missing an option."

"Do tell, Bramble." He looked skyward, as if begging the heavens for patience.

"You could just... take the title, stay alive, and be obscenely rich?"

"Oh, right, and I'm sure Mad Duggie would love to hear that his ex-protégé has gone off to become a duke."

"That would be awkward." She bit her lip.

Was she—was she about to laugh?

"This is all your fault." One hundred percent all hers.

"My fault?" Daisy's eyes widened, faux-offended.

"Yes! You found me! You could've left me alone in sweet ignorance!"

"I could have!" she agreed. "But then I wouldn't have been paid my twenty-five thousand pounds."

"Right. I just need to stay far away from London, outmaneuver Duggie's men, dodge my own inheritance, avoid all potential freak accidents, and hope that no stray lightning bolts decide to smite me before I sort it out." Swearing colorfully in at least three different languages, Dawson exhaled heavily and glared at the sky.

"Or," Daisy said cheerfully, "you could just embrace it all. Become a duke. Survive."

He stared at her like she'd just suggested he join a convent.

"Come on, Woodbridge," she encouraged with a grin. "Just imagine it: you, in a cravat. Owning land. Hosting balls."

"I'd rather be murdered." He physically recoiled.

"Duggie might just take care of that," she replied, cheerful and unhelpful as all hell.

Dawson groaned so hard his soul nearly left his body.

Chapter Fourteen

Daisy peeked through the tavern window, narrowing her eyes at the three ruffians occupying the table by the hearth. Jacko. Merritt. And a big, beefy one she'd dubbed Beefsteak, since she hadn't caught his real name and, frankly, didn't care.

What she did care about was the scuffed leather bag beneath Jacko's chair.

At first glance, it looked like any other travel-worn satchel. Nothing particularly remarkable. But the moment Dawson laid eyes on it, his entire body locked up. She'd felt the shift instantly. The tension rolling off him. The sharp inhale through his nose.

And then, in a voice so low and furious it practically vibrated, he muttered, "Fucking cockless, ball-bagging, rat-arsed sons of whores."

Well then.

She turned to him, one brow lifting. "Would you like to say that a little louder? I don't think the deaf man three villages over heard you."

Dawson ignored her, eyes still fixed on the bag, his fists clenched at his sides. His jaw worked, muscles flexing as if he were actively restraining himself from storming inside and tearing a man limb from limb.

Interesting.

"You all right there?" she asked, fighting the sudden, awful urge to comfort him. "You look like a man debating whether or not to bite through a table leg."

He exhaled hard through his nose. "That bag—" His voice was rough, clipped. "It's mine."

Right. That confirmed her suspicion. She turned back to the window, peering at the bag again. Then back at him.

"You're sure?" she asked, because of course she had to question him. It was fun.

"Yes, I'm fucking sure." He spun a glare at her, eyes flashing green fire.

"My, my, we are testy," she murmured, delighted. "And what exactly makes that bag of yours so special?"

"None of your damn business."

"Ah." She nodded sagely. "So it's something deeply important, then."

His nostrils flared. "I didn't say that."

"You didn't have to."

Dawson clenched his jaw, clearly realizing his mistake.

"Is it your secret collection of poetry?" she asked, watching the muscle in his jaw tick. "A bundle of love letters? Oh! An embroidered handkerchief with the initials M.D.B.?"

"Do you want me to strangle you?" His glare darkened.

"You say that like I should be frightened," she mused, eyes twinkling. "And yet, we both know you wouldn't dare."

He exhaled hard, rubbing his hand at the back of his neck. "Christ, poppet—"

"Not my actual name," she reminded him, grinning.

He dropped his hands, looking like he was debating how many more years off his life she was going to shave. "Are we getting my bag or not?"

She tapped a finger against her lips, considering. "That depends. Have you got a plan?"

Silence.

"Dawson?" She turned fully to him.

His mouth curved, slow and lazy. Wolfish. And then, he had the audacity to shrug.

"You do not have a plan." Her eyes narrowed dangerously.

"I do," he drawled. "It's just a... loose plan."

"Go on, then." Daisy folded her arms.

He gestured vaguely toward the window. "You go inside. Distract them. I grab the bag. We leave."

"That's it?" she deadpanned.

His grin turned infuriating. "You asked for a plan."

"That's not a plan," she scoffed. "That's wishful thinking."

Dawson let out a low, exasperated sigh, as if she were the problem here. "Fine. If you've got a better idea, I'd love to hear it."

"First of all, you fiend, we need a proper distraction." Daisy huffed, rubbing at her temples.

"Oh, I've got one."

She frowned at the glint in his eye. Suspicious. "Do I even want to know?"

He grinned. And shimmied. An unhurried, deliberate roll of his shoulders, a ripple of muscle through his shirt as he let his hips do a slow, scandalous grind that sent her reeling.

She made a strangled sound. He did not just . . .

"Oh, use your charms," he drawled, grinning like a rogue. "Bat your lashes, wiggle your hips—" He shimmied again, the absolute devil.

"Are you suggested that I flirt with them?!" Daisy nearly launched herself at him.

"I'm suggesting you use what you've got, poppet." Dawson replied, looking for all the world like he was about to burst out laughing.

The air crackled with her rage. "You—you—"

"Come now," he murmured, voice low and far too smug. "You can't tell me you've never used a bit of feminine wiles to get what you want."

"I hate you."

He barked out a laugh. And then, the bastard raised his hands, set them dramatically over his own chest—over his very broad, very infuriating chest—and cupped his imaginary bosom.

"Oh, sir," he cooed, mockingly breathy, rubbing his palms in slow, circular motions over where breasts would be. "Aren't you just sooo big and strong? Tell me, have you ever rescued a helpless little lady before?"

Her mouth dropped open.

But Dawson wasn't done. He slid his hands down his own torso, past his waist, tracing the curve of his hips like a woman smoothing down her skirts—and he swayed, the utter jerk, fluttering his lashes at her in pure wickedness.

Her entire brain malfunctioned.

"*Ohhh, Mr. Highwayman,*" he gasped, clutching his chest, swaying again, exaggerating every movement to obscene levels, "however will I repay you?"

Daisy choked.

Dawson just kept going.

"Perhaps with a kiss?" he purred, winking before sashaying an actual step closer to her, swishing his damn hips, his voice dropping into a low, sultry drawl. "Or maybe... you'd prefer something a little more, hmmm?"

Daisy whirled away, smacking her hands over her flaming

face. She was going to scream. Or laugh hysterically. Or tackle him to the ground and do things that would require a special church service to cleanse their souls.

Behind her, Dawson snickered, pleased with himself.

"You're ridiculous," she hissed, trying desperately to collect herself.

"And yet, you're still standing here, poppet."

Daisy's fingers itched to slap that smug, handsome face of his. Or kiss him. Or slap him while kissing him. Was that a thing? Could she do that?

No, no, focus, DAISY. "You are the worst human I have ever met."

"You wound me." He pressed a hand to his chest.

"That can be arranged." Happily, given her current mood.

His grin turned wolfish. "So violent."

"So deserving."

Dawson smirked, his green eyes glinting. "Come now, poppet. Admit it. You liked the show."

She huffed so hard her curls bounced. "I am ignoring you and coming up with a real plan."

"Suit yourself." He chuckled and leaned back against the building, satisfied, smug, gorgeous, and thoroughly infuriating.

Daisy was going to lose her damn mind. She sucked in a slow, measured breath, reining in the molten irritation bubbling in her chest before it could explode spectacularly all over the insufferable man in front of her. Because, damn it all to hell, he had a point.

A rare occasion, surely.

She cast a narrow glance through the grimy window of The Fox & Fiddle, eyeing the three thugs seated inside, their thick, low brows furrowed as they nursed their ales and muttered among themselves. Jacko, Merritt, and the other one. He looked like he smelled of onions and rotting cabbage.

They didn't know her. They knew Dawson. And as much as it pained her to acknowledge it, using herself as the distraction made sense.

Which was exactly why she wanted to murder him for suggesting it.

"You're thinking about it, aren't you?" Dawson murmured, far too smugly, his voice curling around the edges of her resolve like a match held too close to a fuse.

"No."

"Yes."

Daisy slowly turned her head toward him, her patience dangling by a frayed thread.

He lifted his brows and dragged his palms down his chest and waist in a slow, exaggerated motion, like some sort of mocking burlesque tease. "You know—" he mused, "you could give it a little... sway." He rolled his hips in a way that shouldn't have been attractive but somehow was. "Really sell it."

Her vision tinted red, and she clenched her jaw so hard her teeth nearly shattered.

He grinned wider, obviously sensing his impending doom and reveling in it.

"Oh," he added, lowering his voice to a low, sinful purr, "maybe if you bat your lashes real pretty-like, one of 'em might even offer you a nice warm lap to—"

Her fist connected with his stomach. Not hard enough to double him over, but enough to make him grunt.

He was still grinning. The bastard.

"Say that again," Daisy warned, "and you'll be singing soprano before we even get inside."

He coughed, then leaned down close, too close, his hot breath teasing over the curve of her ear. "You'd miss the bari-tone, poppet."

Oh, she loathed him.

145

And his voice.

And his ridiculous face.

And the way her entire traitorous body thrummed with awareness of him as he drew back, still wearing that damned smirk.

"I'll do it," she said. "But not for you."

"Oh, perish the thought."

She ignored him, turning her focus back to the thugs inside the tavern. Her heart began to pound—not from nerves, but from the thrill of the chase. She'd distracted bigger, meaner, and far more important men than these three in the course of her career.

And she was going to knock Dawson Woodbridge's smug arse to the floor while she was at it.

He thought she was just going to saunter in, toss her hair, and flash a smile? Oh, no. He was about to see how a professional did it.

"You owe me for this," she informed him.

"I do?" Dawson arched his scarred brow.

"Yes," she said. "And when this is over, you're going to do something for me in return."

"I can think of a few things." His smirk deepened as he lazily raked his gaze over her like he was already undressing her in his mind.

"Not that, you reprobate." Her fingers itched to smack him again.

He chuckled.

Daisy turned, flipping her hair over her shoulder, and marched toward the tavern door.

Dawson was about to eat his words. And by the end of the night, he'd owe her more than he ever expected.

She pushed open the door of The Fox & Fiddle, and a wall of noise and heat hit her square in the face.

The tavern was packed. Boisterous voices rang out over the clatter of tankards and boots stomping along to a lively fiddle tune being played by a questionably sober musician in the corner. The air smelled of spilled ale, roasted meat, and the distinct funk of unwashed men.

Perfect.

Chapter Fifteen

She didn't hesitate.

Daisy owned the space the moment she stepped inside, sashaying forward with purposeful ease. Not overdone, not exaggerated, but just enough to draw attention.

And oh, did she.

Heads turned. She wasn't the only woman in the tavern, but she was new. And men liked new.

Behind her, she felt Dawson linger near the entrance. Watching. Waiting. She could practically hear his smirk.

Smug bastard.

Fine. Let him think she was playing to his ridiculous "seduction" strategy. He had no idea what she was about to do.

She spotted Jacko, Merritt, and Onion-Breath at a table near the back by the hearth, hunched over their drinks, grumbling in low, serious voices. Dawson's bag sat at Jacko's feet, half-kicked beneath the table like a forgotten trinket.

Though hard, she resisted the urge to glance over her shoulder at Dawson and gloat.

Step one: Get their attention.

Daisy swept toward the bar with a swing of her hips and leaned in, letting her bare shoulders catch the dim candlelight.

"Evening, luv." The barkeep wasn't Cecil. This one, a balding man with a belly like a barrel, gave her a look that lingered a moment longer than necessary. "What's a pretty thing like you doin' in a place like this?"

"Oh, you know. Thirsty work." She let that hang in the air just long enough before tapping a coin on the wooden counter. "Give me something strong," she said, making sure her voice carried just enough. "Long day."

There was a moment of silence.

And then, just as expected—

"Well, well, well," a voice grated from across the room. "What do we have here?"

Hooked them.

Daisy turned slowly, as if she hadn't been expecting it. As if she didn't know exactly what she was doing.

Jacko was staring at her, his beady little eyes narrowing with interest. "Don't think I've seen you 'round 'ere before, sweets."

"No," she agreed, tilting her head and letting her hair tumble over one shoulder. "You haven't."

She took her drink from the barkeep and lifted it to her lips, making a show of taking a long, deep sip before licking a drop of ale from the corner of her mouth.

Jacko's thick throat bobbed. Merritt nudged him, grinning.

"You here alone?" Jacko asked.

Daisy laughed. And that's when she flipped the script.

She turned sharply, eyes locking onto Onion-Breath. "You." She pointed at him. "You look like a man who knows things."

The entire table blinked.

Jacko frowned. "Er—"

"You see," she went on, stepping closer and leaning in just enough, "I'm looking for a man."

"Aren't we all, sweetheart." Merritt grinned wider.

Daisy ignored him. She reached into her pocket, pulling out Dawson's matchbook. "This," she said, tapping it against her palm, "is from a certain someone you're after. And I have reason to believe he came through here recently, too." She let her eyes sweep the room, making a show of searching for her 'target.' "I'm after Dawson Woodbridge."

That got them. Jacko and Merritt stiffened. Dawson's bag, unfortunately, was still at Jacko's feet. And Onion-Breath shifted in his seat, glancing uneasily at his companions.

"What do you want with him?" Jacko asked carefully.

"I'd like to have a little... chat." Daisy smiled, letting just a hint of wickedness curl her lips.

"A chat, eh?" Jacko sat back in his chair, assessing her.

"Yes." She tapped the matchbook against her bottom lip, watching as their eyes followed the motion. "Now, if you fine gentlemen could point me in his direction, I'd be ever so grateful."

Merritt elbowed Jacko, muttering something low.

Daisy took one last sip of her drink, then casually flicked her gaze toward Dawson's bag. She let a fraction of a second pass before looking back up.

Jacko's jaw tightened. He knew. And now she knew that he knew.

The game was afoot.

Jacko's eyes were slits of suspicion now. Daisy could almost hear the rusty wheels turning in his thick skull.

"You're lookin' for Dawson Woodbridge," he repeated slowly, as if tasting the words. "A woman like you."

"What sort of woman am I?" She raised a brow, genuinely curious what he'd say.

Merritt leaned forward on his elbows, smirking. "Oh, I

dunno. A little too pretty. A little too polished. A little too...
smart."

She beamed. "Why, thank you."

Jacko wasn't smiling. He looked her up and down, then
grunted and took a long pull from his ale.

Daisy kept her expression light, playful, as if she didn't give
a single damn that she was playing a game with men who could
snap her like a twig if they wanted to. Because what they didn't
know . . . was that she played to win.

"So," she pressed, setting her drink down on the table and
leaning forward just a fraction, "where might I find our mutual
friend?"

Jacko exchanged a glance with Merritt. Daisy caught it. Oh,
they definitely knew something.

"And what do you want with him?" Jacko scratched his
stubbled jaw, eyes assessing.

She sighed dramatically, running a finger around the rim of
her tankard. "Well, you see, gentlemen," she said, keeping her
tone light, casual, "I happen to have something Dawson Woodbridge needs."

Merritt leaned in. "That so?"

"Oh, quite," she purred.

Jacko was still watching her, still calculating.

But Merritt? Oh, he was hooked.

Daisy turned her eyes deliberately back to Jacko. "I'll make
it worth your while."

Jacko grunted. "Yeah?"

"Absolutely."

"I'll buy you another round." She tilted her head, eyes
gleaming.

Silence. And then Merritt barked a laugh. "Cheeky little
thing, ain't she?" he said, nudging Jacko.

"Cheeky, perhaps. But also very determined." She slid a coin onto the table. "So, what do you say?"

Jacko studied her. His beady little eyes flicked to Dawson's bag, then back to her.

Daisy watched, waiting.

And then...

His posture shifted. Subtle. Barely noticeable. But there. A sliver of understanding passed between them. He knew that she knew Dawson's bag was his leverage.

And Daisy wanted it.

Jacko leaned back, slowly. "Dawson's got a lot of enemies," he mused.

"Does he?" She sipped her ale.

"Aye." Jacko rubbed his chin. "Mad Duggie's got us on him."

"Is that so?" Daisy's fingers tightened around her tankard. She kept her face neutral.

Jacko nodded. "We can't make 'im too roughed up, mind. But... a little is okay."

Her stomach clenched. She let out a hum, as if pondering. "Well," she said after a long pause, "I suppose I should find him sooner rather than later."

"If he don't want to be found, you won't find him." Jacko stated.

Daisy grinned. Oh, Jacko. He had no idea.

She took another slow sip of ale, then set it on the table and straightened. "Well, gentlemen, you've been most helpful," she said sweetly, dusting off her hands. "But I should be going."

She turned, only to suddenly stumble forward, bumping right into a wall of muscle.

"Easy there, poppet."

The voice was low, rough, and entirely too familiar.

Her breath caught. She looked up—straight into the green eyes of Dawson Woodbridge.

Everything went to hell in the time it took for Daisy to blink.

One second, she was staring into Dawson's wicked, infuriatingly gorgeous eyes, and the next—

"Oi! That's 'im!"

Jacko and Merritt lunged.

Dawson swore—a real proper one this time—grabbed Daisy by the waist, and twisted them both out of reach.

"Would you look at that?" he said over the sudden chaos, all smug and maddening. "Seems I don't need your help finding me after all."

"Oh, you great, arrogant—" Her curse was lost as a fist swung past her ear.

Dawson ducked, dragged her halfway behind him, and clocked the bloke in the jaw. The man staggered back, crashing into a table of rowdy gamblers.

A half-drunk tankard went flying.

A chair splintered against the bar.

And then all hell truly broke loose.

"WELL, NOW YOU'VE DONE IT!" Daisy shouted as a barmaid shrieked and a bearded patron jumped onto another man's back.

"ME?" Dawson argued, dodging another swing. "You're the one who started asking bloody questions!"

"You told me to be sexy and distract them!" Daisy ducked a flying pewter plate.

"And you didn't!"

"Because your idea was stupid and offensive. Oh, I am not taking the blame for this!" She elbowed a man in the ribs, grabbed a fallen broom, and whacked another in the knees.

The bastard choked on a laugh. "Well, that's one way to do it."

"This is all your fault!" She whirled and swung the broom at Jacko's head.

Jacko caught it, grinning ominously. "Bad luck, sweetheart."

Daisy just smirked. Then she yanked it forward toward her, making him stumble . . . and drove her knee into his bollocks.

Jacko made a sound like a dying cat and dropped like a sack of grain.

Dawson whistled. "Now that was impressive."

"I know." She quipped.

Merritt came at her next. Dawson cursed and stepped in, but she was faster. She spun, ducked, and landed a wicked right hook right across Merritt's unshaven jaw. He went down like a felled tree.

Dawson blinked. "Well, well," he drawled. "Boudica, is that you?"

"Who?" Daisy shook out her fist.

"Never mind."

The brawl raged on around them—fists flying, chairs breaking, ale spilling. Someone crashed into the bar, sending bottles shattering onto the floor. At one point she was pretty sure she even clocked Dawson during the chaos, but couldn't be sure.

"Time to go, poppet." Dawson grabbed her by the wrist and hauled her toward the back door.

"But your bag!"

He swore again. "Fine. You get the bag, I'll get us an escape."

"Deal." Daisy sprinted toward the table where she'd last seen it only to find some broad-shouldered brute picking it up. She skidded to a stop. The brute looked at her. She looked at the brute. "Oh, bloody hell."

The brute grinned, all yellowed teeth and unfortunate decisions.

Daisy barely had time to brace before he swung. Pain

exploded across her temple. The room lurched, everything tilting sideways.

A roar, low, furious, and utterly feral split through the chaos. Her vision blurred. Was that... Dawson? Yes. Dawson.

That roar. Raw and unhinged, terrifying. For her.

Because of her.

Her knees buckled. Her body swayed, weightless. The floor rushed up to meet her. Strong arms—his arms—caught her just before she hit the ground.

Her lips parted, but she couldn't speak.

The last thing she felt was his warmth and strength, the hard press of him. And the last thing she heard was his voice, savage and shaking.

Then—

Blackness.

Chapter Sixteen

She crumpled.

One moment, Daisy was fighting like a hellcat. The next—gone. The sound of her body hitting the floor might as well have been a gunshot.

Dawson saw red. Saw nothing else. Everything in him—everything base, raw, primal—SNAPPED.

The bastard who hit her barely had time to breathe before Dawson was on him. His fist collided with flesh. Bone crunched. The man yowled, stumbling back into a table that splintered beneath him.

Somewhere in the distance, someone cheered.

Another lunged at him. He turned, caught the motion, but he was too slow. A fist slammed into his ribs. He barely felt it. Not when Daisy was still on the floor. Not when she wasn't moving.

"DAISY!" he roared.

A chair swung. He ducked, grabbed it midair, and drove it straight into the bastard's gut who'd punched him.

Gasps. Laughter. Cheers. The Fox & Fiddle had turned into a damned venue of high entertainment. Somewhere, mugs were still being lifted, coin exchanged over bets. The brawl had taken on a life of its own. A chaotic, drunken spectacle.

But Dawson didn't give a bloody damn about any of it. Not when Daisy—his infuriating, impossible, too-clever-for-her-own-good Daisy—was knocked out cold.

His heart was a hammer and his hands trembled. His bag—his mother's pin—was somewhere on the floor still. Probably by the bar.

Daisy was closer.

He hesitated. Just for a breath.

Fuck the bag.

Dawson dropped to his knees. His hands found her face, her pulse, her warmth. "Come on, poppet," he muttered hoarsely, his thumb brushing her cheek.

She didn't stir. The roaring in his blood didn't quiet. Didn't slow. Something ugly curled inside him. He'd fought. He'd stolen. He'd survived the darkest parts of London.

But he'd never felt this.

This wild, unrelenting thing in his chest. The sharp, unbearable need to protect her. To get her out of here. To not let go.

Dawson's jaw locked. His arms slid beneath her, lifting her effortlessly. She was smaller than she had any right to be for someone with such a lethal right hook.

He held her close. Closer than necessary.

His bag.

Dawson gritted his teeth. He was not leaving without it. He adjusted Daisy in his arms, the warmth of her tucked against his chest making his gut clench in ways he didn't want to examine.

He forced himself to look away from her face—the ridiculous curl of her lashes against her cheek, the way her lips parted just so—and scanned the chaos.

There. Right in front of Jacko's stupid, meaty boot. Fucking brilliant.

Jacko, battered but upright, was busy throwing a punch at a stranger who'd clearly joined the fight for sport.

Merritt? Unconscious. The third one? Nowhere in sight. A small mercy.

He gritted his teeth. He had one shot. Shifting Daisy higher in his arms, he bent low and snatched the bag up in one smooth motion.

A grunt came from behind him. Jacko had seen.

Dawson's fingers curled tight around the strap.

"That what you been after, Woodbridge?" He stepped closer, rolling his shoulders. "Shoulda known."

His grip tightened on Daisy.

"I'd love to stay and chat," he said smoothly, "but as you can see, I'm a bit occupied."

He turned, pivoting for the door. Jacko blocked his path. The bastard was smart enough not to take a swing while Daisy was in his arms. But that didn't mean he wouldn't.

Jacko lifted his beefy hand, palm out. A demand. "Leave the bag."

Dawson's pulse hammered. His mother's pin was in there. His only connection to her.

Like hell.

"Now, Jacko," he said slowly, adjusting his stance. "You and I both know that's not gonna happen."

Jacko narrowed his eyes.

The tension stretched.

Suddenly, a crash. A table collapsed to their left, sending drunken men sprawling.

Jacko's head whipped toward the noise.

That was all Dawson needed. He moved fast. A sharp shift of his weight. A sudden, explosive kick to Jacko's gut.

The man stumbled, cursing.

He was already gone. He barreled through the door, Daisy still limp in his arms.

The cool air slammed into him, a sharp contrast to the heat seething inside him.

The horses were where they'd left them. Violet stomped impatiently, sensing the urgency. Blossom, massive and steady, stood just beyond, where Dawson had tied them both safely away before heading inside.

He barely felt the sting of his split knuckles. His focus was singular: Daisy. She was out cold against him, her long lashes brushing her cheeks, her breathing soft and steady.

She was his responsibility now.

He had no business thinking that way, he knew. No right to feel this twist in his gut. But he did.

He had to get her out of here.

Duggie's men inside wouldn't stay down long. The whole tavern was still in fighting mode, fists flying, tables splintering under the weight of brawling bodies. If Jacko and Merritt weren't already awake, they soon would be.

He shifted Daisy more securely in his arms and moved fast, leading both horses down the narrow alley behind the tavern, keeping to the shadows.

"Dawson!"

He stiffened.

The call came from inside the tavern. A rough, familiar voice, echoing just over the din of the fight. "Duggie wants you back in London, mate! Stop feckin' running!"

His entire body went cold, but he kept going.

"Dawson, you stubborn feck! I mean it, Duggie wants you back in London! Tanuki ain't been right without you!"

The words slammed into him harder than any punch Jacko had landed.

Duggie wants you back.

His stomach twisted. That didn't make sense. Mad Duggie had made it clear as day that if he ever set foot in London again, he was dead.

So, if not to kill him, why the hell would his old gang be chasing him down now?

Dawson's jaw locked. No time to think. No time to react. He had to leave.

He threw himself into the saddle he'd put on Violet halfway through the trip here, concerned for Daisy's tender inner thighs. One arm kept Daisy secure, the other gripped the reins.

He whistled low and sharp. Blossom pricked his ears, and followed. Then, with a flick of his wrist, Dawson spurred Violet into a gallop.

They shot out of town like a phantom in the early pre-dawn light, hooves thundering against the dirt road.

She shifted against him. A little sigh. A small frown.

Her hand brushed his chest, and Dawson went rigid. That soft touch. That barest hint of warmth.

It sent fire through his blood.

He clenched his jaw, forcing himself to focus.

She wasn't awake. Not yet. Which meant he had a few minutes to decide what the hell he was going to do. Because he wasn't just holding a woman. He was holding the most infuriating, intoxicating, utterly impossible creature he'd ever met.

And for reasons he didn't want to examine, he couldn't let her go.

* * *

Dawson had never been a man prone to regret. But as he rode through the Yorkshire countryside, Daisy's warm, soft weight tucked against him, the steady drip of guilt and something worse made his grip tighten on the reins.

Her head rested against his chest, light glinting off the deep brown waves of her hair. He could feel the warmth of her breath against his neck, the occasional soft sigh escaping her lips as Violet carried them forward in a steady, rocking rhythm.

Daisy was asleep. He didn't know how long she'd been out. Didn't know what exactly had knocked her under so hard—the brawl? The blow? Exhaustion? He only knew that he didn't like it.

Didn't like how small she felt curled against him. Didn't like how still she was, how much trust it took to sleep against a man she should be furious with.

If there was one thing he did know, it was that Daisy Bramble should be raging at him. Instead, she was breathing with him. And fuck, but he liked the weight of her against him too much.

It wasn't the first time he'd had a woman pressed against him in broad daylight. Wasn't the first time he'd felt the soft curves of a body leaning into his. But this wasn't about sex. It wasn't about winning.

This was different.

His hand flexed against her waist, fingers instinctively curling into the fabric of her dress, as if holding her closer would fix something. But nothing about this was fixable. She was warm and soft and smelled faintly of temptation and whiskey, and he wanted to keep her there.

Which was not the plan.

He had no business feeling like this.

Not over a woman he barely knew. Not over some loud-mouthed, sanity-thieving, heir-hunting menace who had spent the last two days making his life increasingly difficult.

Yet here he was, riding under the full blaze of the Yorkshire midday sun, holding her like something precious.

And it fucked him right up.

Blossom's hooves clopped steadily behind them, the rhythmic gait of the big Clydesdale a steady presence, but all Dawson could focus on was the weight of her in his arms.

Daisy hadn't stirred much since they'd left the village, but now, as Violet picked her way along the country road, he felt her shift just a little, her body pressing in closer, her nose brushing his collarbone.

A muscle in his jaw jumped. Goddamn her. She was soft where he was hard, warm where he was tense, and Christ, she smelled good. Like sun-warmed skin, wild honey, and something else—something that curled in his gut and made him grip the reins tighter.

Her dress was a mess of wrinkles, smudged with dust, but somehow, the more worn it got, the more it clung to her. And when she moved just a little, just enough to press herself into his chest with a sleepy sigh . . . Dawson lost the last of his patience.

His fingers flexed against her waist, curling into the fabric of her too-thin skirts, and before he could stop himself, before he could think better of it, he dipped his head and kissed her forehead.

Gentle.

Lingering.

Her skin was warm beneath his lips, smooth, *and fuck,* he was an idiot. Because it felt good. Too good.

And then she sighed. "Mm... knew you'd catch me..." The words came out sleep-soft, barely a whisper against his throat, and it was over for him.

His chest went tight. Dawson didn't want to be that man. Didn't want to be the one who caught her.

But he had.

And now he didn't know if he could let go.

He wasn't a religious man, but he was fairly certain that if he'd ever wronged a saint or spat at a priest in his lifetime, this— this—was divine retribution.

He felt it all. Every. Single. Inch.

The weight of her, slumped against his front. The ridiculous softness of her body, all supple curves and warm, yielding lines. The faintest tickle of her wild, tangled brown hair at his throat. The press of her cheek against his bare collarbone where her gown had slipped slightly aside—oh, for the love of all things unholy.

His jaw locked. His fingers curled tighter around the reins, trying to ground himself in the rhythmic motion of the horse's steady gait, but the problem with holding onto the reins was that he couldn't hold onto her. Not properly. Not how he wanted to.

So instead, he stewed.

And muttered.

God help him, he muttered aloud like a damned fool because the woman in his arms had reduced him to this—a half-feral, utterly besotted wreck of a man, so entirely undone that he was talking to himself. "God save me, you are actually trying to kill me, aren't you, poppet?"

Daisy made a little noise against him, somewhere between a sigh and a murmur of contentment. And then she nuzzled deeper.

His spine went rigid. His heartbeat tripped over itself, tumbling into something uneven and raw.

Her nose brushed the bare skin at his collarbone, her lips parting just slightly against him, her breath hot and feather-light where it touched.

"Christ almighty." Dawson actually groaned. Out loud.

She didn't wake. Didn't even stir, except for the sleepy shift of her body as she burrowed closer.

Oh, this woman.

She'd laid out two of Mad Duggie's hardest bastards with nothing but a bottle and sheer audacity, had tricked him into letting her cuff him to her, had damn near killed him with that kiss back at the campfire—

And yet, here she was, tucked so trustingly against him, her body instinctively drawn to his warmth, his presence, his touch.

Dawson swallowed hard. *She shouldn't trust me.* The thought came unbidden, cold and sharp against the molten heat of his torment. *She doesn't know me, not really. Not what I've done. Who I've been. Who I was raised to be.*

She thought he was an heir—some errant, misplaced duke waiting to be shoved into his rightful place. She didn't know that he had never belonged anywhere. Not to London's society, not to Duggie's world of crime, not to any single thing except his own two hands and what he could take for himself.

And yet. She trusted him. The realization shook him. And it ruined him.

"Mmm... Dawson..."

He stopped breathing. Everything stopped. His grip on the reins tightened to a vice. His entire body went still, taut, strung so tight he might snap.

And then she did it again. She turned her face further into his throat, nuzzling there like she belonged there, and whispered his name like it meant something.

Like it meant everything.

Dawson clenched his teeth so hard he nearly cracked a molar. "You absolute torment," he muttered, his voice rough, hoarse.

But he didn't pull away. Didn't shift her. Didn't even try to loosen his grip. Instead, he rode on, the weight of her warm and inescapable, the scent of her clinging to his skin, his heartbeat a wild, furious thing against his ribs.

Stewing.

Seething.

Burning.

Because this wasn't supposed to happen. Daisy Bramble wasn't supposed to feel like this.

Like his.

Without a doubt, he was absolutely not going to survive this.

Daisy was warm and pliant in his arms, tucked up against him on horseback like she belonged there—which she absolutely did not. And now, as the golden, wretched, traitorous Yorkshire sun bathed her in the kind of light that made her look like a goddess, she stretched in his lap like a spoiled, drowsy kitten.

His brain ceased to function.

Her back arched. Her arms reached up, making a sleepy little noise that sent hot agony flooding straight to his groin. The motion pressed her full, soft, perfect body flush against his, the gentle bounce of the horse making it worse—so much worse—and he actually felt lightheaded from the sheer force of his own suffering.

And then—because the universe had decided he hadn't suffered enough—she sighed, nuzzled her cheek against his chest, and murmured sleepily, "Mmm, you're so warm, Dawson."

Dawson Woodbridge, who had survived fistfights, brawls, thugs, and all manner of street dealings, nearly fell clean off the damn horse.

Warm?! Was she—?! Did she have any idea what she was saying?!

His body was a furnace of torment, every muscle tense, every nerve on fire, and all she could say was that he was *warm*?

His hands flexed violently around the reins. His jaw locked so tight it could snap. He had to get her off of him. Had to get off this damn horse. Had to get away from her and the heat of her, and the smell of her, and the softness of her, and the fact that his body was rock-hard and his breeches were actively trying to murder him.

And the worst part? She was completely, blissfully unaware.

Her fingers curled lazily in his shirt. She shifted slightly, her thigh brushing up against—

NOPE.

Dawson was about two seconds away from losing all semblance of control.

"Daisy," he ground out, voice rough as hell.

"Mmm?" she hummed. Sweetly.

His eyelid twitched.

The stone manor inn he was taking them to was mercifully close, its ivy-clad walls and inviting candlelit windows promising salvation—or hell, depending on how you looked at it.

He muttered something vicious under his breath, a half-strangled curse, just needing something to say, something to focus on that wasn't the warm, curvy woman in his lap trying to end him.

And of course, because life hated him, she perked up slightly, blinking blearily up at him. "What was that?"

Oh, he was going to commit atrocities.

He glowered at her, grumpy and desperate, trying not to notice how her lips were still slightly puffy from sleep, how her skin had warmed against him, how—

NOPE AGAIN.

"Nothing," he snapped, finally replying.

Daisy frowned at him, clearly sensing something was wrong, but blissfully ignorant of the fact that he was barely holding himself together. And then she had the absolute audacity to smile. And not just any smile—a slow, sleepy, utterly devastating smile.

That's it.

He yanked the reins, halting the horse just outside the inn's stable, and with way too much force, swung down from the saddle. He did not trust himself to help her down.

But of course, Daisy expected him to. She looked at him in confusion as he backed up like a man who had just realized he was standing in a field of explosives.

"Dawson?" she called, her voice soft and a little hoarse from sleep.

He did not look at her. He could not look at her. Instead, he muttered one last curse, turned sharply on his heel, and stalked off toward the inn like a man fleeing a crime scene.

Because if he didn't take care of this problem right now, he was going to end up doing something incredibly, dangerously stupid. Like hauling her into the nearest dark corner, pressing her up against the stone wall, and—

He was going to find a very, very cold basin of water and throw himself into it.

Or take himself in hand and deal with it before he lost his damn mind.

But first—

Whiskey.

Strong whiskey.

And maybe a prayer for mercy.

Chapter Seventeen

"**D**awson?"

The early evening air had cooled since they'd arrived, a whisper of a breeze curling through the trees, rustling the golden summer leaves. The heat of the day still clung to her skin, but not nearly as much as the heat left behind by his body.

And now...now he was walking away from her.

Daisy scowled, blinking the last remnants of sleep from her. Excuse her? After holding her for miles, keeping her pressed against his impossible warmth, kissing her forehead in a way that had utterly melted her bones—he was just going to leave her in the saddle like a sack of grain and stalk off without a word?

Absolutely not.

"Oi! Dawson!" she called, sharper this time.

The man in question stopped. His shoulders bunched, hands flexing at his sides, tension coiled into every hard, unforgiving muscle beneath his coat. He stayed that way for a long moment, like a predator on the verge of flight or fight—or something much, much worse.

Daisy hated how much she liked the sight of him. And how much she liked that it was her that had done this to him.

Slowly, he turned.

Oh.

Oh no.

Her breath hitched.

Because that was not the expression of a man who was thinking reasonable, logical, rational thoughts. That was a man teetering on the knife's edge of control. His pupils were blown, his jaw tight, his chest rising and falling just a bit too fast.

Even the newly lit lantern light from the inn flickered strangely against his eyes, making them glow wolf-bright, like something prowling just beneath the surface. Something hungry.

Oops.

She swallowed. And, very carefully, held out her arms. "Are you going to help me down or do I have to make a very undignified attempt at it myself?" Not that she couldn't get down on her own. She just . . . she just wanted his hands on her again.

Dawson exhaled, a sharp, ragged thing, and then strode back to her with the kind of lethal determination a man had when he was about to make a very bad decision.

She was prepared for many things.

She was prepared for the long ride back to London. For the fact that she still hadn't managed a proper bath. For Dawson to remain a grumpy, growly rogue who could charm and infuriate in equal measure.

She was not prepared for what happened when he helped her off the horse.

His hands closed around her waist—strong, firm, big. A perfect fit, as if they were made to hold her. And hold her, he did. Not hurriedly. Not practically. Not in any way that made sense. He should have just lifted her down, quick and efficient. Instead... instead, he pulled her close.

Her feet left the stirrups, and for a moment, she hovered in the air, heart knocking against her ribs, fingers curling against the front of his unbuttoned coat. Then—the descent.

Her body slid flush against his.

Every. Last. Inch.

The heat of him—God, he was all heat and hard muscle and impossible strength—burned through her clothes, branding her. She felt the ripple of his stomach, the tautness of his thighs, the broad expanse of his chest as she skimmed down it. The rough graze of his shirt against her bare arms sent shivers up her spine.

And oh, she felt something else, too.

Low. Pressed right against her.

Daisy sucked in a sharp breath. Her boots hit the ground, her body flushed, reeling, shaken.

Dawson didn't step back. His hands still gripped her waist. His breathing was off, rougher, shallower. She could feel it ghosting across her cheek.

He felt it too.

She knew it in the way his fingers flexed against her, in the tautness of his frame, in the way his green eyes—damn those eyes!—lowered, tracking over her lips.

A shiver swept through her. She cursed it. He felt that, too. His lips curled in a smirk.

The bastard.

His smirk deepened, his grip tightening just a fraction. Just enough to make her breath catch. Just enough to remind her, as if she could ever forget, that he was big, strong, and entirely too male.

And worse—entirely too aware of her.

The knowing gleam in his eyes? Infuriating.

The amused quirk of his lips? Infuriating.

The hard, undeniable proof of his arousal still pressed against her belly? Infuriating. (And maybe, just maybe, a little thrilling. Not that she'd admit it.)

Daisy lifted her chin, ignoring the delicious, devastating heat curling deep in her stomach. "Well," she said, arching a brow, keeping her voice as unimpressed as humanly possible when faced with a very impressive situation. "That was quite the thorough dismount, Woodbridge."

He leaned in, right at her ear. His breath was warm. Rough. Full of things that made her stomach drop and her pulse riot. "Did you enjoy yourself, poppet?"

The absolute audacity.

She shoved at his chest. Not because she particularly needed him to move, but because if she stayed pressed against him a moment longer, she might do something spectacularly stupid.

Like kiss him.

Again.

She already knew what that was like. Hot. Ruinous. Wicked. She couldn't afford another taste.

Dawson let her push him back, just barely. Just enough to let her breathe.

He was still close. Still towering over her, watching her with that damnable smirk, looking so infuriatingly smug over the way he'd just melted her brain into a puddle of hot uselessness.

"Feeling warm, are we?" he teased.

"No warmer than usual. Unlike you, I don't overheat at the first sign of contact."

A bold-faced lie.

They both knew it.

"Is that so?" His eyes gleamed. Oh, he was enjoying this. Too much.

"We're in public, you menace." She threw out her arms,

gesturing to the people moving toward the inn, carriages rolling in, the bustle of an evening's arrival. She made a noise of irritation, stepping back, reclaiming her space, her sanity.

And just like that, the moment shattered. Reality came rushing back in. Daisy swallowed hard, forcing the awareness of him down, down, down to the farthest corner of her mind.

There was an inn to enter, a room to secure. She turned on her heel, needing distance before she combusted entirely, but she'd only made it three steps before a hard hand wrapped around her wrist.

He caught her. Not just by the wrist, not just with words—but with his hands, his heat, his entire maddening presence.

One second, she was marching away, flustered, fuming, and very much trying not to think about how his big, rough hands had slid her down the length of his very hard, very warm, very unfair body. The next she was against him again.

A single, sharp tug, and she stumbled right back into his arms, right into the solid wall of his chest.

"Dawson—" she started, breathless, indignant, utterly unprepared—

And then his mouth was on hers. His lips were hot and demanding, rough from the sun and wind, moving over hers like he'd been waiting for this, aching for this, absolutely bloody starving for her.

And worse?

She let him.

Worse than that?

She wanted it.

His kiss was not a question. It was a claim, a challenge, a bloody undeniable fact as his hands curled around her waist, dragged her closer, pulled her in deep.

Daisy made a high, strangled sound, part gasp, part protest, *part oh, this is exactly what I've been dying for.*

And Dawson groaned. A deep, low, utterly shattered sound that lit her up from the inside out.

His lips slanted over hers, his tongue licking deep, coaxing, teasing, demanding, and she shuddered, hands fisting in the fabric of his shirt as she clung to him like he was the only solid thing left in the world.

And then his hands slid lower. Over her back. Over her hips.

Lower.

Her knees nearly buckled. What in the devil was he doing to her? Heat coiled low, her entire body thrumming, desperate, starved.

His fingers flexed, possessive, relentless. She gasped, and he swallowed it down, kissed her deeper, hotter, rougher.

Daisy had kissed men before.

She had never been kissed like this.

Never been devoured, undone, unmade by lips and tongue and heat and need. Dawson Woodbridge was kissing her like a starving man who had just been given his first taste of heaven. And she was bloody well drowning in it.

A reckless, wild whimper left her lips, a sound she barely recognized as her own.

He growled, and tore his mouth from hers, breathing ragged, harsh, his forehead pressing against hers, his voice raw. "You drive me mad, poppet."

Daisy had no reply. Because she couldn't think. Couldn't breathe. Her lips were swollen, tingling, aching for more. Her entire body burned. She wanted to shove him away. She wanted to pull him back in.

And that—that was the problem.

She wanted.

She wanted him.

Dangerously.

Which meant this had to stop.

Now.

With every last ounce of willpower she possessed, she shoved at his chest—not too hard, but enough to make it clear.

His lips quirked, lazy and smug, his green eyes so damn wicked. And then, just to torture her further, he leaned in again, let his lips just barely graze her jaw, her throat.

Her entire body shuddered.

"Still thinking about the river, poppet?" he murmured against her skin.

Daisy made a sound of pure frustration. This was not supposed to happen. She was supposed to be tracking her mark. She was supposed to be focusing on twenty-five thousand bloody pounds and the noble, respectable cause of rebuilding Bramble Hill Orphanage. Not melting against the very man she was meant to deliver to the Crown's bloody paperwork vultures.

Not gripping his shirt like he was the only solid thing in the world.

Not letting her heart do whatever foolish, reckless thing it was doing inside her chest—fluttering, flipping, practically singing over a man who was entirely, utterly, unattainable.

Oh, this was bad.

Very, very bad.

She did not shove him this time. No, she escaped. Whirled, stormed toward the inn, her entire body flushed, aching, ruined.

Damn him.

Damn her.

Damn her traitorous, stupid, utterly besotted heart.

As she stormed through the entrance of the inn, chest heaving, lips tingling, knees still weak from that bloody kiss, she had to admit that things had gotten away from her rather spectacularly.

The air inside was thick and warm, scented with beeswax,

old wood, and a dozen different kinds of smoke. Pipes, candles, the crackling hearth. It all mixed with something richer—the heady musk of rain-damp wool, aged whiskey, and the unmistakable smell of excitement.

The place hummed with noise. Murmurs, conversations, the scrape of chairs and the clatter of tankards. But there was something else, too. A... buzz. A low, thrumming energy beneath the usual tavern din.

It wasn't until she finally looked around that she realized why.

What in the devil...?

The inn was packed. Absolutely filled to the bloody rafters. Not just with the usual travelers and merchants but—oh.

What. The. Hell.

A woman in full Tudor-style mourning garb swept past, black lace trailing, a black veil drawn over her face. And a man in an absolutely enormous, ridiculous velvet cloak was flipping through an old leather tome, muttering about ectoplasmic manifestations.

Nearby a group of earnest scholars and wide-eyed spiritualists huddled by the hearth, animatedly discussing The Science of Spectral Energy and Astral Residue. A table of serious-looking ghost hunters compared instruments—odd contraptions full of brass and wires, clicking dials, and even a set of dowsing rods.

What the actual f—

Daisy blinked. Did she step into another world?

A woman beside her suddenly turned and stared at her—eyes wide, dramatic, and a little unnerving. "You have a most haunted aura, my dear."

Daisy almost choked. "I beg your pardon?"

The woman's veiled face tilted. "Tragic. Deeply tragic. And bound to him."

"Bound to—" Daisy started, but then—

Of course.

Dawson strode in behind her. And everything in the room shifted. The hum of voices dimmed. A few heads turned.

And Daisy, traitorous, foolish Daisy, knew exactly where he was without even looking. Her body knew. A prickle at the base of her spine. A heat creeping up her neck. A wicked, awful, thrilling awareness of the man who had just kissed her senseless in the courtyard.

The same man who now stepped up beside her, looming, his massive body heat pressing into the space between them like he had every bloody right to stand so close. "You're letting ghosts get in your head, poppet." His voice was low, rough silk against her ear. Still raw from their kiss.

Daisy's stomach did a violent, swooping turn. She scowled at him with all the righteous fury of a woman desperately trying to ignore how bloody delicious he smelled.

"I do not have a haunted aura."

Dawson made a thoughtful noise. "I don't know. You have been following me around the countryside like a woman possessed."

She gasped at his audacity, whirling toward him before she even realized that was a mistake. Oh hellfire. He was right there. Close enough that her breath hitched against his chest. Close enough that she had to tilt her chin up way too far to glare at him properly. Close enough that she was far too aware of his lips.

Lips that had been on hers not five minutes ago.

Lips that had been devouring her.

Daisy braced herself, gritted her teeth, and refused to take a single step back. She was not letting him win. "Don't flatter yourself, Woodbridge."

His lips tipped. Slow. Knowing. Wicked. "Too late."

Damn him.

Daisy's spine went rigid. She turned away before she did something stupid—like punch him, or gods help her, kiss him again.

She did not get rattled.

She did not get undone by broad-shouldered, green-eyed, infuriating men who kissed too bloody well for their own good.

Focus. There was one thing she needed right now.

"Excuse me," she called to the closest innkeeper, ignoring Dawson entirely. "I need a room."

The innkeeper, a short, harried-looking man in an apron, looked up from his ledger. "One room left, miss."

Daisy exhaled, nodding. Good. Finally, something was going right.

"And it's got a nice view, too. Top floor. Lovely little attic room. Single bed."

Daisy blinked.

Wait.

One bed?

Just one?

Chapter Eighteen

D aisy's heart stalled.

Oh. No.

Behind her, she could feel Dawson's slow, curling grin. "Well, well, poppet," he murmured. "Looks like you really are haunted."

She was staring at the harried little innkeeper, waiting for him to tell her he had another room somewhere, anywhere—and instead, he flung a hand toward the madness around them.

"You're lucky there's any room left at all, miss! It's the Greymoor Widow anniversary, after all."

Daisy's stomach dropped.

"The what?"

"The Greymoor Widow!" he repeated, as if that explained everything. "Happens once a year, like clockwork. Ghost lovers, hunters, scholars—they all come to witness the hauntings. Booked solid every season. Most everyone else booked ahead for the event.".

Daisy finally took a good look at the crowd. She had been so focused on trying not to think about Dawson's mouth, she hadn't actually noticed that much beyond that initial weirdness.

There were all sorts. Tall men in dark frock coats, holding books of folklore. Women in unnecessarily flowy gowns, their hair trailing loose, whispering of energy and spirits.

A red-faced man was gesticulating wildly to another group, shouting, "I TELL YOU, IT WAS THE MIST! THE MIST MOVED ON ITS OWN! I SAW IT WITH MY OWN EYES!"

And over by the hearth, two elderly women were hunched over a glass orb, murmuring something about 'lingering sorrow.'

She opened her mouth—closed it.

And then, beside her, a deep, smug voice drawled, "Told you curses were real, poppet."

Oh, for the love of—

Daisy did not turn to look at him. She did not acknowledge the barely restrained amusement in his voice. She just took one deep, slow breath and forced a tight smile.

"And... this last room?" she asked the innkeeper, praying for salvation.

The innkeeper gave her a big, apologetic grin. "Like I said, sweet little attic space. Top floor. Cozy."

"Oh, that's wonderful," Dawson murmured behind her, voice pure wicked delight.

Daisy ignored him. "Fine," she snapped, shoving a coin onto the counter. "We'll take it."

The innkeeper happily pocketed it.

Just as Daisy reached for the room key, a pale, slender hand shot out, snatching her wrist.

Daisy startled.

It was her. The woman from earlier. The one with the big eyes and the dramatic stare and the whole nonsense about her 'haunted aura.' And now, she was staring even harder.

Gulp.

"My dear," the woman whispered, voice low, urgent, eerie. "Love will lift it."

"I—what?" Daisy's nose crinkled.

"The curse," the woman murmured. "The curse that clings to him."

Daisy froze. She could feel Dawson stiffen beside her.

The woman's pale fingers tightened ever so slightly on Daisy's wrist. "You are part of it now," she whispered. "Part of its end."

"I—" Daisy's blood ran cold.

"You carry the key," the woman continued. "You always have."

Daisy's pulse stuttered. Her throat went dry. For one, terrible moment, she swore the inn felt too still. Too warm. Like something had shifted in the air. Like something—or someone— was listening.

Dawson's voice was low, flat, dangerous. "What the hell is that supposed to mean?"

The woman's gaze flicked to him. To his rigid stance, his clenched fists, his jaw tight with fury. She did not answer. She simply smiled.

And then, softly, "The bloodline always calls for home."

Daisy's stomach dropped.

Dawson's teeth clenched so hard she heard it.

No. No, no, no, absolutely not.

Daisy's pulse hammered in her ears. This woman—this utterly unhinged, ghost-obsessed, dramatic creature—she couldn't know. She couldn't possibly know.

And yet.

And yet.

Daisy's heart was slamming in her ribs. Dawson had gone still as death. For a long, terrible moment, neither of them spoke.

Finally, Daisy snapped out of it. Nope. Not doing this. Not entertaining crazy. "Right. Well."

Daisy yanked her wrist free, grabbed the key, and spun on her heel. She was halfway toward the staircase before she felt Dawson fall into step beside her.

Still quiet. Still watching her. Still a problem.

Don't ask, don't ask, don't ask—

"So," Dawson said.

Daisy braced.

"Are we going to talk about what she just said," he continued, far too casually, "or are you just going to pretend it didn't happen?"

She marched faster. "Pretend it didn't happen," she replied confidently.

He chuckled. Of course the bastard chuckled. Then, before she could storm ahead, his fingers curled around her wrist. Like the old woman had downstairs. Only his touch was warm. Solid. Steady.

Her pulse jumped. She turned, ready to tell him off, but . . . he wasn't smirking. He wasn't teasing. His green eyes weren't even on her face.

They were on her temple.

On the slight, sore bump from where she had hit the floor back at the tavern.

His jaw went tight. "He got a good hit in, didn't he?" he murmured.

Daisy blinked. "What?"

"The one who knocked you out."

His voice was low, gravelly. A sound of barely restrained fury.

She had thought she was over it. It had been just a hit. Nothing she hadn't taken before. But the way Dawson was looking at her now—like he was barely stopping himself from marching back to the tavern and putting that bastard through the floor—it sent a strange, warm jolt through her chest.

Not good.

Not safe.

"Dawson," she said, trying for exasperation, though it came out way too breathy. "I'm fine."

"You're not."

"It's nothing."

"It's not nothing." His eyes flashed.

Daisy sighed. "Are you about to storm back down to The Fox and Fiddle and avenge my honor?"

Dawson's jaw ticked. "...Yes."

A completely inappropriate laugh bubbled up in her throat and she barely swallowed it down.

And that was when she noticed the faint purple bruise blooming along his jaw.

The humor fizzled from her lips.

She reached out before she could stop herself. Her fingers skimmed gently over the bruised skin, brushing along the sharp cut of his jawline. Warm. Firm. A little rough beneath her fingertips.

Dawson stilled. His eyes—so damn green, so damn watchful —flicked to hers.

She swallowed. "You got hit," she murmured.

The barest twitch of his mouth. "By you."

"What?" Daisy's brows shot up.

"In the brawl."

His fingers were still wrapped around her wrist. His body was close. Too close.

Her breath caught. She vaguely remembered swinging at someone. Vaguely remembered connecting.

"Oh," she said, horrified.

Dawson's mouth quirked because she was still touching him. Her fingers were still curled along his jaw.

And he was still watching her, his eyes just slightly hooded, something low and dangerous brewing in their depths.

Daisy's heart skipped. And then she did something very, very stupid.

She leaned in and kissed him. Not on the mouth. Not in a way that was meant to destroy them both.

Just a soft, slow brush of her lips to his bruised jaw.

Warm.

Lingering.

An apology. A confession.

A terrible mistake.

Because Dawson—because she felt him shudder.

Felt the way his fingers flexed around her wrist, like he wanted to grab her, pull her in, hold her there.

And then just as suddenly he let go. Like she burned him. Like he burned himself.

Daisy blinked, breath coming too fast, too sharp. Mortified. Panicked. Laid bare.

She stepped back and turned. She stormed straight to their room and didn't look back.

Didn't dare. Didn't see the way Dawson stood there, jaw tight, hands flexing open and closed at his sides, looking like a man seconds from doing something very, very stupid.

But she felt it. Oh, she felt it. And that—that was the problem.

Because she wanted.

She wanted *him*.

And it had just cost her whatever peace she had left.

Chapter Nineteen

Dawson stepped into the attic room—and immediately wanted to turn around and walk straight into the damn sea.

Of course. Of course this would be their room.

He didn't know what he'd been expecting. Some drafty little hole, perhaps. A stiff, lumpy cot in the corner. Bare walls, a crooked chair, a damp-smelling rug.

What he had not been expecting?

This.

This soft-lit, cozy as hell, too-small-for-his-sanity attic room, with its sloped ceiling, wooden beams, and one singular, horrifically inviting bed tucked against the window, all plush quilts and overstuffed pillows. The kind of bed meant for long, lazy mornings and tangled limbs.

The kind of bed where a man could lose himself in a woman for hours.

He hated everything about this.

The room smelled too nice. Like beeswax candles, fresh linens, and the faintest hint of lavender. The little window seat was draped in a hand-knitted throw, the oak floorboards gleamed warm in the glow of the lantern, and the fireplace in the corner flickered with a soft, amber glow that only amplified the absurdly intimate atmosphere.

Dawson barely resisted the urge to slam the door shut behind him and swear until he passed out.

Instead, he just stood there, his jaw tight, fists clenched, silently raging at the universe for once again putting him in the worst possible position.

Behind him, Daisy stepped in and made a small noise. A soft, surprised exhale.

Dawson shut his eyes. He already knew exactly what she was about to say.

"Oh." Her voice was far too delighted for his well-being. "This is quite... lovely."

He dragged a slow, deep breath through his nose. "Don't."

"Don't what?" she asked innocently.

He opened his eyes and looked at her. She was peering around the room with wide, shining eyes, her fingers brushing lightly over the quilt, her lips parted just slightly. She loved it. She bloody loved it.

He gritted his teeth so hard his jaw might crack.

"I see the innkeeper wasn't joking," Daisy mused, her voice all warm amusement and secret laughter.

"Joking about what?"

"He said it was romantic." Her eyes danced as she turned to him.

He made a horrible strangled sound.

She smirked. Oh, she was enjoying this far too much.

He glowered at her, hands still fisted at his sides. "You did this."

"Did what?" She blinked innocently.

He gestured vaguely to the romantic death trap of a room.

"Are you accusing me of personally curating this experience?" Daisy placed a hand to her chest, mock-offended.

"Yes," he said flatly.

She grinned. "Well, I didn't. But I do rather like it."

Dawson turned away and pinched the bridge of his nose. He was so close to losing it.

"This is quite possibly the nicest place I've ever stayed." She sighed happily, twirling once in place.

Dawson did not respond. He was too busy praying for strength.

She beamed up at him. "You don't think it's lovely?"

"I think it's a goddamn trap."

"You are ridiculous." She laughed.

"And you are—" He stopped himself. "You are entirely too delighted by this situation."

"I'm simply making the best of it."

He pointed to the bed. "You're taking that. I'm sleeping on the floor."

Daisy shrugged. "Suit yourself."

Of course she didn't argue. Of course she had no issue taking the nice, soft, warm bed while he suffered on the hard, cold floorboards. That was exactly the kind of woman she was.

This was going to be the worst night of his life.

* * *

Dawson lay on the floor, flat on his back, arms crossed over his chest like a corpse in a crypt. The floor was not that bad. Truly. Hard, sure. Unforgiving, absolutely. Cold, without a doubt.

But it was a hell of a lot safer than the alternative.

That alternative being the entirely too soft, entirely too inviting bed just above him. The bed where Daisy had just

186

curled up, all warm and content and entirely unconcerned about the absolute agony she had inflicted upon him.

He breathed slowly, purposefully, while staring at the dark beams of the ceiling.

A long, heavy silence stretched between them. For a moment, it seemed like they might actually just go to sleep. It seemed like Dawson might actually be granted peace. A reprieve from all of her and the way she blew through a man.

"So," she said cheerfully. "What's your favorite part of the ghost-hunting convention so far?"

Grunt.

"Oh, come on," she pressed. "Surely you have a highlight."

"Yes," he muttered. "The part where I did not get roped into an attic lovers' suite with a woman who has made it her life's mission to battle me."

A beat of silence. Then, a soft laugh. Low. Warm.

Damn dangerous.

"That's your highlight?" she teased.

"It's a very low bar, poppet." Dawson scrubbed a hand over his face.

A pause.

A shift of movement above him.

"I liked the part where the woman with the haunted aura told me I was part of the curse," Daisy mused.

He stared up at the ceiling. "That was your favorite part?"

"It was interesting."

"It was nonsense."

"You don't know that," she defended.

He turned his head, squinting up at the edge of the bed where her dark waves spilled over the pillow. "Oh, do enlighten me."

She hummed, clearly enjoying herself. "Maybe it was nonsense," she allowed. "Or maybe I am part of the story."

Sigh. "Do you ever just... stop talking?"

Daisy made a thoughtful noise. "Mmm... no."

Of course not.

Dawson stared at the ceiling again, wishing for death. Or sleep. Or some form of divine intervention that would make his cock stop aching like he had been denied salvation itself.

"I did rather like the haunted widow tale though," Daisy continued idly. "And the inn itself is lovely, don't you think?"

He didn't answer. Just glared at the ceiling.

She went on anyway. "It's very charming. I like all the stone and wood. And the candlelight." A pause. "And this tiny, romantic attic room."

His chest squeezed too tight. "You are enjoying this far too much."

"Oh, immeasurably."

* * *

Silence fell again and Dawson almost relaxed.

Then the bedsheets rustled above him. A soft shift of weight. Christ, his entire body went tense. Because she was moving. Because she was right above him. And he was very, very aware of the way the mattress dipped with her weight, the way the floorboards creaked slightly beneath her shifting body.

And oh—oh, he hated himself for noticing. For picturing her there, curled up, drowsy, warm, wearing whatever soft, sleep-rumpled thing she had on under that damned dress.

Dawson clenched his jaw, willing himself not to think about it. Not to think about her. Not to think about anything.

A long, heavy silence stretched between them.

"Dawson?"

His eyes snapped shut. "What."

"Goodnight."

He sighed and rolled his shoulders. Shifted, trying to get comfortable. "Goodnight, poppet."

A soft exhale. A rustle of sheets. And then, at last, silence. Blessed, peaceful silence.

He took a long, slow breath.

Fuck.

He was still painfully, unbearably hard. And now she was asleep. He was alone. Now he could finally, finally do something about it . . . maybe.

Above him, the bed creaked as Daisy shifted beneath the covers, sighing sweetly. He clenched his jaw. His fingers curled into the folded blanket he'd been using as a sorry excuse for a pillow.

She was right there. Close enough that if he reached up, he could trail his fingers along the wooden slats of the bed frame. Close enough that he could hear her breathing. Unaware of the absolute hell she was putting him through.

Dawson rolled onto his side, trying to find a position that didn't feel like slow, torturous agony.

This was fine.

He could do this.

He was a grown man.

A man who had survived plenty of hardship. He had run jobs for Mad Duggie Black at the age of twelve. He had stolen from some of the most dangerous men in London. And yet—this was somehow worse. This aching, impossible, maddening feeling of knowing she was just inches away, warm and soft in that bed, sleeping peacefully while he lay here, every muscle in his body tied into knots.

It was humiliating.

He'd made it twenty-eight years without letting a woman undo him like this. And now? Daisy Bramble—his favorite vice, his tormentor, his utterly maddening obsession—was unmaking him.

Slowly.

Ruthlessly.

Without even trying.

A miserable sound rumbled in his throat, and Daisy shifted again, mumbling something in her sleep. He stilled. Listened.

Her voice was soft, barely a whisper. "...whiskey, Mason..."

He snorted. Of course. She was dreaming about bloody whiskey.

That should not have made his chest feel warm. That should not have made him grin into the dark. And yet, here he was. A full-grown man, sleeping on a cold wooden floor, smiling at the fact that the woman he was completely losing his mind over dreamed about whiskey.

Dawson scrubbed a hand over his face.

This was bad. This was really, really bad. He needed to get a grip before this woman destroyed him completely. Before she—

Above him, the bed creaked again, followed by the smallest, sleep-slurred sigh.

He went still. Too still. Because that sound. That little sigh that left her lips—sleepy, content, warm—shot straight through him like a bolt of lightning.

His blood turned molten. His body—already painfully tense—hardened instantly. He squeezed his eyes shut. No.

No, no, no.

This was not happening. Not here. Not now. Not with her. He took a long, steady breath, gritted his teeth, and willed his body to calm the hell down.

It did not.

Obviously.

So he rolled onto his back. And then, in a moment of absolute, desperate weakness . . . he slid his hand beneath the blanket. Just one quick stroke. Just enough to ease the unbearable edge. Just enough to make his body settle.

Dawson bit back a groan. He could be quiet. So quiet.

But then . . . somewhere above them . . . the inn creaked.

His entire body locked up and he froze. His hand stopped moving. His pulse slammed into his throat.

Another creak. Steady. Deliberate. Like someone, or something, was walking above them.

A shadow passed over the small sliver of moonlight seeping through the window.

"Dawson?" Daisy blinked down at him, drowsy and confused, hair tumbling in soft waves around her shoulders, lips slightly parted.

Perfect.

Just perfect.

She had no idea. No idea that she had just caught him at the absolute worst moment of his life. That his entire body was locked tight, frozen in a state of unspeakable, agonizing, hand-halfway-to-salvation disaster.

She stretched, spine arching, her hands lifting above her head, and the blanket slid down, exposing the smooth, satin skin of her collarbone.

Dawson nearly died.

His pulse slammed in his throat.

His cock throbbed painfully.

She made a sleepy, contented sound.

Dawson made a dying, strangled sound.

"Did you hear that?"

He nearly choked. Shite! Had she heard him?

No—no, she meant the noise. The creak. The one that had startled her awake. Not the noise he had just been silently, shamefully making.

Relief and mortification tangled in his gut, because this was somehow worse. Because now, he had to talk. And move. And pretend he had not been about to wank off while she slept six bloody inches away.

Dawson swallowed thickly, tried to sound normal. "What?"

Daisy's brows pinched, still hazy with sleep. She frowned, tilting her head. "I thought I heard..." she trailed off, shaking her head. "Footsteps."

He was not in a place to process that. Not when he still had one hand under the blanket and a cock harder than a damn iron bar.

Another creak.

His body went rigid.

Daisy stilled. "That," she whispered.

Dawson's stomach dropped. That hadn't been the inn settling. That hadn't been the wind.

That had been footsteps right above them on the widow's walk. The small, open-air balcony that wrapped around the uppermost part of the old manor inn. A place that—according to the inn guests he'd overheard—was where the Greymoor Widow had last been seen before she vanished into the night over a century ago.

He was not a superstitious man. But he was also not a man who enjoyed watching Daisy go pale in the dark.

Her hand gripped the blanket. "Someone's up there," she whispered.

Dawson hesitated, pulse still trying to catch up with the absolute catastrophe that had just been his life. And then, a soft knock at the window.

His entire body snapped to attention. (Which was deeply unfair because he had just barely gotten his arousal under control.)

Daisy let out a quiet, panicked sound.

He sat up fast, hand yanking free from under the blanket like he hadn't just been doing unholy things beneath it, and he reached for the nearest weapon, which, unfortunately, was just a bloody candlestick. Still, he gripped it like he meant to commit murder.

Daisy was sitting up fully now too, clutching the covers, eyes wide.

They both stared at the window. Nothing. The wind howled softly through the trees outside.

Another creak.

Another slow, careful sound right above them.

Bloody fantastic. This night just kept getting better.

"Dawson?" Her voice was small.

Another knock at the window. Measured. Like someone—or something—was waiting.

Dawson's grip on the candlestick tightened. His heart pounded against his ribs, but he kept his face carefully neutral. If Daisy saw even a flicker of uncertainty in him, she'd panic. And he didn't panic. Not over ghosts. Not over anything.

He took a step toward the window.

She sucked in a breath. "Dawson, don't."

He ignored her. Another step. The candlelight flickered, casting strange shadows against the low ceiling. He reached out, fingers brushing the dew-kissed glass.

Silence.

Then, a whisper. Low. Faint. Just barely audible over the wind. "...*Come outside.*"

Dawson went still.

He saw Daisy's fingers curl tighter around the blanket, her breath shuddering out. "Tell me you heard that."

"Yeah, poppet." He swallowed hard, his throat tight.

Another whisper, this time just a little clearer. "*Come find me.*"

The floor above them creaked again, like someone was pacing the length of the widow's walk.

He reached for the latch on the window.

Daisy shot forward, grabbing his arm. "Are you mad?" she hissed. "You don't open the window for ghosts!"

He looked down at her, brows raised. "Is that a rule?"

"Yes!"

"Well," he murmured, smiling faintly, "good thing I don't believe in ghosts." Before she could stop him, he flicked the latch and shoved the window open.

The cold night air rushed in, sweeping through the room in a whispering gust.

The candle flickered wildly.

Daisy sucked in a sharp breath.

And outside, just beyond the window . . . everything was empty.

Chapter Twenty

The weight of the night pressed against Daisy's skin, thick with unanswered questions and the kind of tension that had nothing to do with ghosts.

Dawson was still standing by the window, his broad shoulders taut, hands flexing at his sides like he wasn't sure if he was about to fight a specter or run his hands through his hair in frustration.

She should have let him stay there. Should have turned over, pulled the blankets high, and ignored the way her pulse had been thrumming ever since he stepped toward that window.

Instead, she whispered, "Come to bed."

He turned, slowly, green eyes unreadable. "What?"

"I don't want to sleep alone."

A long, slow pause. Then, "Poppet, that's a bad idea."

She knew it was. She didn't care. "It's just sleep," she lied.

Dawson exhaled roughly, gaze flicking to the too-small bed, to her, back again. "This bed barely fits one of us."

She lifted a brow. "Are you afraid of a bit of closeness?"

His jaw ticked. "No."

Liar.

She patted the empty space beside her. "Then get in."

For a long, excruciating moment, he didn't move.

Then he very slowly walked toward her, the air in the room shifting with each step. When he sank onto the mattress, his weight made it dip, shifting her closer.

Daisy swallowed.

Too close.

Not close enough.

His voice was low, rough. "You sure you know what you're asking for?"

She wasn't sure of anything anymore. But still, she whispered, "Yes."

Dawson exhaled sharply, rolling onto his back. One arm tucked behind his head. The other resting perilously close to hers.

They lay there. Silent. Staring at the ceiling. Daisy, fighting the urge to reach for him.

When he finally spoke, rough and lazy, voice like molasses over gravel—it was the beginning of her undoing. "Can't say you weren't warned, love."

She had thought she could handle this. It was just sleep. Just company in the dark. But she hadn't accounted for how solid he'd feel next to her. How the heat of his body would seep into hers, warming every inch of space between them.

She swallowed.

Bad. This was bad.

She had spent years keeping her head level, her priorities straight. Her sisters, the finder's fees, the orphanage—that was what mattered.

Not this. Not him.

But her body? Her body was a traitor.

The mattress dipped with his weight, his shoulder brushing hers—just barely—but enough. Enough to make her inhale sharply, enough to make her wonder how easy it would be to just . . . no. Daisy fisted the blanket in her hands, gripping tight like it was the only thing keeping her tethered to sanity.

"You're quiet, poppet." His voice was rough-edged, dangerously lazy.

Daisy's pulse skipped. "And you're talkative."

A deep, quiet chuckle.

"You asked me into your bed," he murmured, shifting slightly, just enough that the mattress moved beneath them, just enough to remind her how close they were. "And now you don't want to talk to me?"

Daisy desperately willed her body not to react. "Some of us would like to sleep," she muttered.

"That right?" A slow, knowing hum.

Her jaw clenched. That tone. That low, teasing drawl that always meant trouble.

He was too relaxed. Too at ease. And she, well, she was losing her mind.

"I think you're regretting this already," he mused.

Daisy's fingers curled tighter around the blanket. She would not rise to his bait.

A beat of silence.

"You keep clutching at that blanket, sweetheart," he murmured, voice barely above a whisper. "Anyone would think you were nervous."

She stilled. Oh, he was enjoying this. Her eyes flicked to him, meeting dark amusement in those wicked green depths.

Damn him.

She lifted her chin, keeping her expression neutral. "I've shared a bed before, you know."

He grinned, all slow danger. "Have you?" he mused. "And did they make you this tense?"

Daisy's breath caught. She hadn't realized, not until now, how stiff her body had become, how tightly wound she was.

Damn him. *Damn him.*

"I am not tense," she snapped, rolling to face him fully, determined to glare him into silence. And that was a mistake because now she was close. Too close.

The low lantern light flickered over his face, casting deep shadows across the sharp cut of his jaw, the curve of his mouth. And his eyes—green, naughty, knowing.

A challenge.

Her throat went dry.

Dawson's voice dropped lower, even rougher. "I could help with that, you know."

Her stomach flipped. He was playing with her. Toying with her. It was awful.

And worst of all—*she liked it.*

Her voice was not steady when she said, "Help with what?"

"Your tension, poppet." The corners of his wicked mouth tipped up.

Daisy felt it before she saw it. The break. One second, Dawson was just a man beside her in bed, warm, contained, tightly leashed.

The next—

The wolf took over.

He moved before she could catch her breath, before she could think better of this, before she could remind herself of all the reasons why this was a mistake. His body rolled into hers, the weight of him pressing her down into the mattress, solid and demanding and unignorable.

A sharp inhale caught in her throat. Oh. Oh, this was not the same man who had smirked at her in the candlelight. Not the same rogue who played at being a scoundrel just for fun. This was something else entirely.

His eyes—dark, unrelenting, focused solely on her.

His breathing—shallow, uneven, a man at the absolute edge of restraint.

His body—heat and power caging her in, his muscles flexing like he was barely holding himself back.

He wasn't teasing anymore.

She should have felt uneasy. She should have been terrified at the sheer intensity of him, at the way he looked at her like he was about to consume her whole. But she wasn't.

She was burning for it.

"You don't know what you've done." His voice was nothing but gravel and darkness.

Her breath hitched.

Dawson didn't give her time to respond.

His mouth crashed onto hers, heat and hunger and pure devastation wrapped up in the way he kissed her. Not soft. Not tentative. Not careful. She gasped, but he didn't let her escape.

His hand slid into her hair, gripping just enough to keep her exactly where he wanted her. His tongue traced the seam of her lips, demanding entrance, and she . . . she gave in so easily that it sent a sharp thrill through her chest.

A sound rumbled in his throat, something almost like a growl. And then, his hands. Broad, rough, possessive. Sliding down, tracing the curve of her waist, gripping her like he was learning her. Mapping every inch, memorizing how she fit beneath him.

Daisy arched instinctively, her body betraying her, craving more even as her mind struggled to catch up.

She should stop this. She should—

His hands found her breasts, and she forgot how to think. She forgot how to breathe. Because Dawson—this man, this rogue, this wolf in human skin—was not holding back anymore.

His hands molded to her breasts, firm and knowing, a man

who had clearly touched before, had taken before, but never, never, like this. Never like she was something he wanted to worship and wreck all at once.

A strangled gasp caught in her throat as his thumbs dragged over her peaked nipples, teasing, testing, feeling her shudder beneath him.

Dawson's mouth tore from hers, breath hot and ragged against her lips. "That's it, poppet," he murmured, voice deep, seductive. "You like this, don't you?"

She should have denied it. But his fingers pinched lightly, rolling, coaxing, and—oh, *oh*. Her body arched before she could stop it, chasing the feeling, chasing *him*.

"Bloody hell, look at you." His lips brushed her jaw, her throat, hot and wet and teasing, before he dipped lower, mouthing along her collarbone, nipping just enough to make her gasp. "You should see yourself, sweetheart." His voice was ragged, like he was barely holding on. "Squirming under me, all needy and wet. Bet you've never looked like this for another man, have you?"

Daisy's stomach flipped violently. She should have told him to shut up. Should have reminded him that he was an utter scoundrel. But his thumb flicked over the tight, aching peak of her nipple and she gasped instead.

Dawson laughed darkly, his mouth moving lower. "Oh, love." His voice was honey-thick and amused, deep with something darker. "You're not even pretending to fight it anymore, are you?"

She couldn't even answer because his mouth was on her now.

Heat. Wet heat. His lips closing around her nipple, his tongue swirling, flicking, teasing. She cried out, her fingers flying to his hair, twisting, pulling. "Dawson!"

He groaned, his hips shifting between her thighs, solid and

hot and so, so hard. "Fucking hell, Daisy," he rasped against her skin, voice shaking. "You're gonna kill me." He sucked harder, dragging her deeper, undoing her completely.

She had never felt anything like this. His mouth, his hands, the weight of him pressing her down. Her clothing, raking against her skin—then gone. The way he was devouring her, completely unashamed. Like he'd been starving for this. For her. Her nails bit into his scalp, her back arching again, chasing more, needing more.

And Dawson—oh, Dawson noticed.

"So damn greedy," he murmured against her breast, his breath hot and wicked. "Want more, do you?" His teeth grazed over her nipple, just enough to send a sharp jolt through her. She whimpered, and he groaned like a man in pain, his fingers digging into her hips. "You sound like a dream, sweetheart." His mouth trailed lower, lower, lower . . .

She was lost. Utterly, completely, deliciously lost. Dawson's mouth was a brand on her skin, trailing heat and need and a hunger that matched her own. He moved lower, his breath hot against her belly, his hands firm on her hips, holding her steady as he worshipped her with lips and tongue and teeth.

She couldn't think, couldn't breathe, could only feel—the scrape of his stubble, the press of his fingers, the wet heat of his mouth as he tasted her everywhere. "Dawson," she gasped, her fingers tangling in his hair, pulling him closer, needing more. He growled against her skin, the vibration sending a shiver down her spine.

"You taste like the reason I won't make it to heaven, poppet." His voice was dirty and dark and filled with a desire that made her burn.

She arched into him, lost in the sensation, in the way he made her feel. Like she was the only thing that mattered, the only thing he wanted. "Please," she whispered, not even sure what she was asking for, only knowing that she needed him, needed this.

He lifted his head, his eyes dark and filled with a promise that made her heart race. "Tell me what you want," he said, his voice a low growl that sent heat pooling in her belly.

She met his gaze, her breath coming in short, desperate gasps. "You," she said, the word a plea, a demand, a surrender.

He smiled then, a slow, wicked curve of his lips that made her pulse quicken. "Then you shall have me," he said, his voice filled with a filth that sent a shiver of anticipation through her.

And then he was on her, over her, surrounding her with his heat and his strength and the overwhelming intensity of his desire. His mouth claimed hers in a kiss that was all-consuming, his hands roaming over her body, leaving a trail of fire in their wake.

She was gone. Lost in the heat, the weight, the sheer power of him pressing her into the mattress.

Dawson was everywhere. His mouth on her throat, sucking, teasing. His hands trailing lower, fingers skimming over bare, too-sensitive skin. His breath against her belly, warm, wicked, and so devastatingly knowing.

She couldn't think. Couldn't breathe. Just feel.

And oh, she felt.

His lips ghosting lower.

His tongue, hot and slow, tracing the soft dip of her hip.

His teeth—a sharp, hungry graze—dragging over skin so sensitive she nearly arched off the bed. "Dawson."

His grip tightened. Firm. Possessive. A silent warning.

She barely had time to gasp before . . . his mouth.

Low. Lower.

His tongue, sliding like he had all the time in the world over her throbbing wet womanhood.

Oh, God. Her breath hitched, pleasure coiling so sharp it stole her thoughts.

"Bloody hell, sweetheart," he growled against her. "You don't even know how good you taste." He licked the length of her, dipped his tongue between her swollen folds. "Fucking beautiful pussy."

Daisy clutched at the sheets, mind spiraling, body thrumming like a live wire.

She shouldn't—

She couldn't—

But she did.

She let go. Let him devour her, unravel her, destroy her piece by piece. She was unraveling. Writhing. Gasping. Coming apart beneath him.

Dawson's mouth was relentless, his tongue working her with slow, devastating precision, his lips teasing, sucking, destroying her.

She was gone. Gone. Fisting the sheets. Arching into him. Her body straining toward the pleasure he was building inside her, coiling tighter, sharper, hotter.

"Look at you, poppet." His voice was dark and drugged and so unbearably smug. "So fucking perfect like this. Falling apart just for me."

Daisy whimpered. Her hips bucked, desperate, instinctive, and he groaned like a man wrecked.

"That's it." He tightened his grip on her thighs, holding her open, holding her still. "Let me have you. Let me taste you." His tongue flicked, slow and deadly, and Daisy sobbed. "Come for me."

She was too close. Too far gone. Pleasure clawed up her spine, white-hot and unbearable.

Dawson sucked hard on her, his mouth closing around her, tongue pressing just right—

And Daisy shattered. A sharp, helpless cry tore from her throat as her body bowed off the mattress, pleasure ripping through her in waves so strong she thought she might break. And he swore hard, refusing to let up, drawing it out until she was shaking beneath him, overwhelmed, unraveled, lost.

When she finally collapsed against the bed, breathless, trembling, completely ruined . . . Dawson kissed the inside of her thigh, slow and reverent. And smirked against her skin.

Daisy was laid bare. Shaking. Gasping. Barely clinging to reality.

But he wasn't done. Oh, no. She felt the lazy drag of his tongue, the hot press of his mouth, and her entire body jolted. A desperate sound escaped her lips. "Dawson!"

"Hmm?" The bastard was teasing her. His voice full of wicked amusement as he kissed the inside of her thigh, leisurely and knowing. "You think I'm stopping, sweetheart?"

She whimpered. Because he wasn't stopping. Because he wasn't done with her. Because his mouth was already back on her, his tongue licking deep, slow, thorough—making her arch, making her clutch the sheets in a helpless, broken grip.

"Oh, fuck!" The curse left her lips before she could stop it, before she could even think.

Dawson growled like a man possessed. "That's it." His voice was ragged, edged with something dangerously close to obsession. "Let me hear you, poppet. Let me feel you fall apart on my tongue again."

And she did.

Hard.

Fast.

Heat, pleasure, a white-hot burst that sent her spiraling into the abyss, her body shaking, her breath breaking apart. Her fingers tangled in his hair, clutching, pulling, desperate for something solid, something to hold onto as he pulled another orgasm from her like he owned her. Like he'd never stop.

And he didn't.

He stayed right there, devouring her, tasting her, until she shuddered beneath him one more time, pleasure crashing through her in a violent, helpless, completely devastating wave.

Dawson finally pulled back, breathing hard, his lips wet, his expression dark and satisfied. And then he moved, crawling up her body, his weight pressing her into the mattress, his mouth trailing open-mouthed, hungry kisses over her skin.

Daisy couldn't move. Could barely breathe.

And then—oh, God—

He pressed his lips against her ear, his breath hot and thick with want, and whispered, "Sweetest fucking thing I've ever tasted."

Chapter Twenty-One

Daisy stretched luxuriously in her chair, her limbs all loose and languid, like a cat who'd spent the night curled up in a patch of sun. Because, well... she felt fantastic.

Relaxed. Satisfied. Glowing, even.

She speared a bite of warm, buttered toast with her fork, humming softly at the golden crunch, the lingering sweetness of honey. Breakfast was perfect. Life was perfect. And across from her?

Dawson was not having a good morning.

Oh, he looked devastating. Scruffy-jawed, rumpled, all dark circles and tense muscles, broad arms crossed over his chest, fingers tapping against his biceps like he was barely holding himself together.

His hair? A disaster. A thoroughly ravaged mess, like a man who had spent half the night lying awake, staring at the ceiling, too furious to sleep. (Which, to be fair, was exactly what had happened.)

She was . . . kind of eating it up.

She let her eyes drift over him, taking her time, letting her lips curl just slightly around the edge of her mug. Because oh, she knew exactly what that frustration was about. Knew he hadn't found any relief last night. Knew his self-restraint had been an ironclad, painful thing.

And, worse for him?

She knew that he knew that she knew.

She took another slow, indulgent sip of tea, her body still thrumming with aftershocks of pure, glorious pleasure. But he hadn't touched his food. Not a single bite.

He just sat there, brooding, glaring at his untouched plate like it had personally offended him. She could see it, in the stiff set of his shoulders, in the way his grip tightened around his fork, in the flicker of his gaze that kept drifting—just for a second—before snapping back up.

Oh, she knew exactly what was happening in that gorgeous, tormented head of his. What had happened had been, well —*whew*. She stretched lazily again, letting her arms rise just enough to arch her back, let her body lengthen, let the fabric of her dress pull snug.

Dawson's jaw ticked and glared at her dress.

Well, it wasn't the dress itself, exactly, that he was glaring about. She was pretty sure that it was the fact that he had been under it last night. That he had pushed it up with his hands, with his mouth, with his shoulders. That he had dragged his fingers over her bare thighs, spread her open, made her fall apart again and again until she had been nothing but pleasure in his hands.

"Not hungry, Woodbridge?" She licked a drop of honey from her lip, eyes dancing.

His eyes snapped up to hers, dark and unreadable. "Oh, I'm fucking starving."

Daisy choked on her tea.

Oh.

Oh, this was fun.

Her pulse skipped, but she fought to keep her expression as innocent as possible. "Well, you should eat, then."

"I'm finding it a bit difficult." Dawson's jaw flexed.

"Why?" she mused, eyes full of faux concern. "Sleep poorly?"

His nostrils flared.

Ah. Yes. This was truly the best morning of her life.

"Oh, young man!"

Dawson flinched.

Daisy turned toward the next table where three ghost hunters they'd met yesterday, Dr. Whittaker, Mrs. Pruitt, and the overenthusiastic Arthur Timmons, were watching Dawson like he was the newly discovered spirit of the Greymoor Widow himself.

"We were discussing last night's disturbances. Did you hear the knocking? The footsteps? The whispering?" Dr. Whittaker leaned in eagerly.

"There was something out there, I tell you!" Mrs. Pruitt clutched her necklace.

Arthur sighed dreamily. "A lost soul, calling out for peace..."

Dawson, a man who was absolutely clearly not in the mood for this conversation, closed his eyes slowly.

Daisy bit her lip to keep from laughing. Oh, this was just cruel and beautiful.

"Tell us," Mrs. Pruitt pressed, eyes sharp behind her spectacles. "What do you think it was?"

Daisy sipped her tea, eyes locked on Dawson, waiting for his suffering.

He did not disappoint. He exhaled, slow and controlled. "I think it was the wind."

A scandalized gasp from Mrs. Pruitt.

Arthur's entire face crumpled. "No! No, it was much more than that!"

"We think it may have been her." Dr. Whittaker nodded gravely.

Dawson's jaw ticked. "Could have just been the innkeeper making sure his guests got their money's worth."

Daisy smiled into her toast.

"Heavens! Our esteemed host would never!"

"Of course not," he grunted. "My mistake."

"Hmph."

"You were awake when it happened, weren't you?" Mrs. Pruitt narrowed her eyes.

Daisy nearly snorted into her tea.

Dawson's broad shoulders went rigid. Oh, he'd been awake, all right. Wide. Awake. They'd both been.

She could not handle this. She covered her mouth with her fingers, barely keeping the laugh in.

"I was awake," Dawson said, voice gritted, strained. "But I heard nothing unusual."

Mrs. Pruitt huffed. "How disappointing."

Dawson's eyes snapped back to her, wicked and full of pure debauchery

Oh, oh my. The man was a positive wolf.

Daisy just smiled all sweet and satisfied at him.

Best. Morning. Ever.

Or so she thought, until it happened. Dawson shifted, reaching for his coffee.

His coat shifted too and something glinted. Something small. Something gold. It was tucked into the fold of his inner pocket, half-hidden by the fabric, but she saw it.

A hairpin.

An unusual, elegant hairpin. Gold, worn with age, but unmistakable.

209

Her heart dropped. She had seen this shape before. In books. In documents. In books and documents about legends.

Daisy set her tea down slowly, her hands suddenly unsteady. Because—oh, shite. This had to be the key. The key to the legend of Ashby Hollow. It was exactly how Violet had described it the morning before she'd left, when she'd filled Daisy in on all things Ashby Hollow related.

The key to the legend. The key to Dawson's past. Irrefutable proof that he was the Rapid Duke's son, the rightful heir to the dukedom. That was, if that hairpin in his pocket fit into the lock designed to take it. A lock that reportedly resided somewhere on the estate grounds.

She felt the world tilt.

Dawson, still glaring at her, still grumpy and flustered and starved, had no idea. No idea that in this moment, everything had just changed.

No idea that Daisy—who had spent the last several days chasing him, teasing him, pushing him—was now the one breathless. The one spiraling.

Her fingers curled against her lap, and she forced her breath to remain steady. Her heart did a slow squeeze in her chest. Not because of Ashby Hollow. Not because of the legend. Not because of the finder's fee that would change her sisters' lives.

But because this was Dawson's history. A piece of a past he didn't even know he held. And for a moment—just a moment—something in her ached. Something small and quiet and deep. Something she couldn't afford to feel.

Daisy blinked. Breathed. Forced herself to let it go. Reminded herself that this wasn't about him. It couldn't be.

This was about the job.

About her sisters.

About the life they had built and the future they were fighting for.

So she lifted her tea again. Took a slow, even sip. And when Dawson met her eyes across the table—still scowling, still simmering, still utterly undone by her—she smiled.

Because whatever she was feeling?

She could control it.

She had to.

Chapter Twenty-Two

Dawson followed her up the stairs like a man walking toward his own damnation.

Her hips swayed. Not intentionally. Not because she was trying to torment him. But because that's just how she moved.

And he, a man who had spent the entire night with his hands on her, his mouth on her, his body between her thighs, knew exactly how she felt in his hands. Knew the lush weight of her arse when he'd palmed it, kneaded it, dragged her closer while his tongue had been buried deep inside her. Knew the exact way she rocked when she was grinding against his face, the way her thighs had clenched, the way her body had trembled apart for him.

Now she was walking ahead of him, oblivious, confident, relaxed. Like she hadn't completely flattened him. Like she wasn't the reason he'd spent the last hour gritting his teeth through breakfast, pretending he didn't want to haul her into his lap and bite every inch of exposed skin. Like she wasn't the reason he was hard, aching, and completely fucking feral.

Dawson barely remembered walking up the stairs. Barely

registered the inn's creaky floorboards, the low murmur of voices from the hall below. Because all he could see was her. All he could think about was how good she'd felt under him. How fucking perfect she had been when she had . . .

She reached their room, fingers brushing the doorknob. Turned it. Pushed the door open. Walked inside.

He followed, the door clicking shut behind them.

Daisy turned—only to find herself suddenly backed against the wall, trapped between the solid heat of him and the rough wooden panels at her spine.

"Dawson," she gasped.

"What," he growled.

Her lips parted, eyes flicking up to his, wide and startled. "What are you so grumpy about?" she challenged, brows rising in smug amusement.

That was it. Something inside him snapped. A last, frayed thread of control shattered.

Grabbing her wrists, he pinned them to the wall, and crashed his mouth to hers.

It wasn't gentle.

It wasn't careful.

It was a claiming.

A deep, hot, desperate kiss, all teeth and tongue and hunger.

Daisy made a small, shocked sound. Then she melted, Right into his body, his grip, his mouth.

Dawson growled, shoving his knee between her thighs, pressing up against the heat of her, feeling how warm she already was for him.

"Fuck, poppet," he rasped against her mouth. "You get wet just from me looking at you?"

She shuddered, and he felt it. Felt the way her body responded, the way her pulse fluttered at her throat, the way her hips arched into him.

"You're fucking ruined for me," he murmured, dragging his mouth down her jaw, nipping, kissing, sucking.

Her breath hitched. "You think highly of yourself."

He laughed darkly. Then he reached under her skirt and slid his fingers between her thighs. Pressed against her. Felt the soaked heat of her through her underthings.

Head falling back against the wall, Daisy moaned. He rocked his hips against her, let her feel how hard he was, how much he needed her.

"You *are* ruined," he muttered, voice filthy, rough. His fingers moved, teased, stroked over the damp fabric.

Daisy whimpered.

He grinned. "Say it."

"Say what?" She bit her lip.

His fingers pushed harder, dragged slow and purposeful over the place he knew was aching for him. "You know what," he whispered.

She whimpered again, body arching into him.

"Christ," he groaned. "I should make you beg for it."

She let out a shaky breath. Dawson felt her heartbeat hammering under his lips, under his fingers, everywhere. But then she tipped her chin up, met his eyes. And smirked. A small, wicked thing.

And suddenly he was the one in danger. Because Daisy wasn't just responding. She was enjoying herself.

"Poppet," he said against her mouth, his fingers pressing into that soaked, aching place between her thighs. "You feel how ready you are for me?"

Daisy shuddered.

He grinned wickedly.

He was winning.

She was soaked. Swollen. Slick and eager and absolutely his for the taking.

He should have known better.

Just as he was about to push further, just as he was about to make her beg—she moved.

Fast.

Deliberate.

Her hands slid down, down, down. And then—she cupped him. Right through his breeches.

Dawson's entire body seized.

His breath ripped out of him in a strangled growl. His forehead dropped to hers, his entire body bracing against the sensation. "Bloody hell, Daisy," he ground out.

"Oh," she murmured, squeezing just a little. "You're—" She paused. Grinned. "You're so hard."

He let out a dark, strained laugh. "You just figuring that out now, poppet?"

Her hand moved, exploring. Dragging over the thick, aching length of him through the fabric.

He gritted his teeth. Oh, he was in danger. She was playing with him. Testing. Teasing. And he was about three seconds from falling to his knees.

She tilted her head, voice all honeyed curiosity. "You were hard at breakfast, weren't you?"

Fuck, fuck, fuck.

"Thinking about how you had me," she continued, her hand stroking unhurriedly, cruel, his favorite hell. "Thinking about how you made me come on your tongue. Thinking about how you—"

"Jesus fucking Christ." Dawson's hand shot out, gripping her wrist, stopping her movements before she sent him over the edge like a fucking virgin.

Daisy laughed.

He was done. Done thinking. Done fighting. Done pretending there was a single goddamn ounce of control left in his body.

Daisy had taken it. Had wrapped her fingers around his cock, stroked him slow, teased him soft, gutted him completely.

Now he was about to take her. No more waiting. No more teasing. No more games.

His mouth crashed back over hers, hard and claiming. His hands shoved her skirts higher, higher—"Fucking need you," he muttered against her lips, dragging his fingers over the soaked heat of her pussy, ready to push them inside—

BANG. BANG. BANG.

A sharp knock at the door.

Dawson froze.

Daisy froze.

For a second, neither of them moved.

"Young man!"

His entire body went tight. Oh, hell no.

That was Mrs. Pruitt, one of the ghost hunters at their door. While he was seconds away from being buried inside Daisy.

He clenched his eyes shut.

"Young man!" Mrs. Pruitt banged again. "We must come in immediately!"

Daisy let out a strangled sound that was half-laugh, half-mortified groan.

He was about to commit a crime. "Absolutely goddamn not," he muttered under his breath.

"We must!" Mrs. Pruitt insisted. "There have been sounds!"

Daisy, still pinned against the wall, still flushed and breathless, bit her lip, eyes glinting with mischief. "Oh, there have been sounds, all right."

"Don't," Dawson growled.

She grinned. He was in so much trouble.

Another knock. Another aggressive knock.

Dawson braced both hands against the wall, breathing like he had just been physically removed from heaven.

"The Widow is communicating!" Dr. Whittaker declared from behind the door.

Now there were two of them outside the door? What the fuck? Dawson's eye twitched.

"Her moans!" Arthur added. "We heard them so clearly!"

Daisy gasped. And then she broke. A full, uncontrolled burst of laughter.

Still achingly hard, still pressed against her, still ready to throw his entire future away for one more second between her thighs, Dawson was losing his goddamn mind.

Mrs. Pruitt banged again. "Come now, let us in!"

Daisy couldn't stop laughing.

He couldn't breathe. His cock was throbbing, his blood was on fire, and now there were elderly ghost hunters shouting about moaning outside their door. He tilted his head back, let out a long, slow exhale, and muttered, "I am going to murder every single one of them."

She was dying. And not because she was being ravished by him against the wall. No—because she was laughing. Laughing. While Dawson stood there, hard enough to break stone, breathing like a beast, moments from fucking her into the wall.

"I am going to commit a crime, Daisy."

She giggled.

He gripped the wall to keep himself from grabbing her again.

Mrs. Pruitt banged once more. "Young man!" she snapped. "We demand entry at once!"

Dawson's eye twitched so hard it might never recover. He forced himself to take a breath. Then another. Then one more, for the love of God, before he did something that got them thrown out of this bloody inn.

Daisy, still laughing, finally—mercifully—pushed him back. "Go," she whispered, grinning like the hellion she was. "Answer the door before they break it down."

"Give me a fucking second." How worked up he felt right now, that's about all he'd need.

"We know you're in there!"

Dawson yanked his shirt down in an utterly pathetic attempt to cover his still very large, very present problem, and stomped toward the door.

Completely unhelpful, Daisy whispered, "Might want to walk slower, love. Wouldn't want to—"

"Daisy," he ground through his teeth. "Shut up."

He yanked open the door, and there they were. Mrs. Pruitt, prim and furious, holding her dowsing rods like she was about to beat him with them. Dr. Whittaker, positively vibrating with excitement, peering into the room as if expecting a ghost to be standing right behind Dawson. And Arthur, looking like a man who had witnessed something truly profound.

"Sir," Arthur said gravely. "Are you aware that your room has been experiencing heightened paranormal activity?"

For several beats Dawson just stared at him. Then, very slowly, he turned his head. Daisy was still against the wall, lips red, hair mussed, dress wrinkled, looking entirely too pleased with herself.

He turned back to Arthur. "Yeah, mate," he said flatly. "I am painfully aware."

Mrs. Pruitt huffed.

"We heard the noises," Dr. Whittaker said breathlessly. "The moaning. The Widow! She was speaking!"

He closed his eyes. Saw his life flash before them.

"Sir," Arthur pressed, "did you feel a presence?"

"Yeah," he said, dragging a hand down his face. "I felt something."

Mrs. Pruitt lit up. Arthur nodded gravely. Dr. Whittaker looked like he might faint.

"And?" Mrs. Pruitt demanded. "What did you feel?"

Dawson looked them dead in the eyes. "Aroused."

Daisy snorted so hard she nearly choked.

Mrs. Pruitt gasped, clapping a hand over her mouth.

Dr. Whittaker actually did faint.

And Arthur? He stared at him like he had just been given a message from the beyond. "I see," he whispered.

"No," Dawson muttered, "you absolutely fucking don't."

Chapter Twenty-Three

Daisy still wasn't sure how Dr. Whittaker had fainted more dramatically than a swooning debutante, but at least he was breathing again.

Mrs. Pruitt had fussed over him, Arthur had taken out his notebook like this was the greatest discovery of his life, and Dawson had stood there like a man contemplating his own violent demise. He'd been scowling since the moment she'd revived Whittaker by gently slapping his cheeks. He'd been grumbling under his breath when she helped get the ghost hunters back downstairs.

And he'd been watching her like a wolf since the moment she led them back to their room.

Which was... a problem because she needed to tell him something important. And it wasn't about how incredibly unfair it was that he still looked like an orgasm-drenched dream, all mussed hair and seething frustration.

No.

She needed to tell him what she'd seen in the dining room. Needed to tell him what she thought she knew.

The door clicked shut behind them, sealing them in the

quiet, cozy attic room once again.

Dawson sighed heavily. "Poppet," he grumbled, voice low and still entirely too rough from what they had almost done. "If you're about to make another joke at my expense, I swear to—"

"I saw your hairpin."

He froze, his hand stilled mid-motion.

Daisy took a breath. Steadied herself. "I saw it this morning," she continued. "In your pocket."

His expression didn't change, but she could feel the shift. Something tensing. Locking up.

She pressed on. "I only caught a glimpse," she admitted, choosing her words carefully. "But something about it—it looked different."

He still didn't speak. Didn't deny it. Didn't confirm it. Just watched her.

But she knew what she saw. The shape. The edges. The strange, delicate ridges worked into the design.

Not just an heirloom.

Not just a pin.

She licked her lips. Pushed forward. "I think it's a key," she whispered. "An actual, physical key."

Dawson's jaw ticked. His fingers curled into fists at his sides.

She maybe should have heeded those warnings, but she didn't stop. "And not just any key." A breath. A heartbeat. "The actual, real life key to the legend of Ashby Hollow."

The air in the room changed. Tightened. Hummed with something unspoken. And for the first time since she had met him, Dawson looked shaken.

The silence stretched. Thick. Charged.

Then the man laughed. Low and rough and not amused.

Daisy's stomach tightened.

"That's a hell of a reach, poppet."

"Is it?" She lifted her chin.

Dawson sort of mirked, a lazy, unimpressed thing. False. "Yeah," he drawled. "You see a bit of metal in my pocket and suddenly you think I'm truly the heir to some haunted dukedom?"

Wrong choice of words. Daisy narrowed her eyes. "It wasn't just a bit of metal, and I wouldn't be here if you weren't the actual ducal heir."

"No?" He arched a brow.

"It looked like a key. One that I've seen sketches of before in some odd reference books that Violet uncovered."

"Did it now?" Another laugh. This time, sharper.

Daisy folded her arms. "And you know what else?"

He sighed dramatically. "No, but I reckon you'll tell me."

She stepped closer. "You've had that pin for as long as you can remember, haven't you?"

The smug half-grin twitched. Just slightly. Like something beneath his skin pulled too tight.

She pressed in. "You fidget with it. You keep it close. And you won't get rid of it, even though I'm sure it's just some useless little trinket, right?"

His jaw ticked, and the room felt smaller. The candlelight cast deep shadows across his face, catching on the sharp angles of his cheekbones. God, he was masculine in every right way.

"You're reaching," he muttered. "Plenty of men carry things from their mothers."

"Plenty of men's mothers weren't married to the last Duke of Ashby Hollow."

That did it.

That struck.

His smirk faded, and the scoff died on his lips. "No," he said flatly.

"No?" she repeated, certain she'd misheard him.

Dawson's fingers flexed. His voice came low, measured, like

a man forcing himself to keep his footing on crumbling ground. "It's a hairpin, Daisy, that once belonged to my mother," he murmured. "Nothing more."

"And if you're wrong?" she asked softly.

Dawson's throat worked. His fingers flexed at his sides. He was losing ground, and they both knew it.

"Let's say you're right," she murmured. "Let's say it's just a hairpin. Then it won't open anything, will it?" she said. "It won't fit into a lock, won't turn, won't reveal some long-buried secret."

Silence.

His green eyes burned into hers.

"But if I'm right?" she whispered. Another step toward him. "And if your mother left you more than just a scrap of metal?"

His breath hitched.

Daisy saw it. Felt it. And something tightened in her chest.

Dawson didn't do roots. Didn't do history. Didn't do past.

But this was his, and where he came from. Whether he wanted to admit it or not, it mattered. Otherwise he wouldn't have kept it all these years.

"Don't you want to know, Dawson?"

A muscle jumped in his jaw. Still, he said nothing. But Daisy could feel it. The fight. The way he wanted to deny it. Scoff. Shrug it off. The way he wanted to run. And the way, deep down, he couldn't.

Not from this.

Not from her.

"And if I don't?" he finally spoke.

Daisy didn't hesitate. "Then I'll find out for myself."

The words hit their mark.

Dawson's eyes flashed. Something wild and furious. Because he knew her. Knew she wasn't bluffing. She'd track down Ashby Hollow on her own and chase the legend to the ends of the earth. She'd dig up every secret, every scrap of truth, with or without him.

She had him and they both knew it.

He ran a hand through his hair, the motion frustrated as hell. His eyes burned into hers. "Let me get this straight, poppet." His voice was soft and dangerous. "You think I've been carrying around a bloody hairpin all my life—"

"A key," she corrected.

His nostrils flared. "A key," he bit out, "to a legend about a haunted estate that I have zero interest in claiming."

"That about sums it up." Daisy shrugged.

Dawson huffed a bitter laugh, and shook his head. "Christ," he muttered. "You really don't let things go, do you?"

"Not when I'm right." Daisy smiled sweetly.

"You're impossible."

"And yet," She tilted her head. "I have your attention."

A muscle jumped in his cheek. He was still fighting it. Still trying to push back.

"Just look at it, Dawson." She went for the kill, whispering, "Unless you're afraid."

He snapped. Not loudly. Or obviously. But she saw it. The way his fingers curled. The way his shoulders went tight. The way his breath came just a little sharper.

And then . . . he reached into his pocket. Pulled the pin free. Held it up between them.

"Fine," he muttered. "Have a look."

She reached for the pin, steady, measured. Not because she wasn't buzzing with triumph. Not because her heart wasn't pounding from the sheer, impossible reality of this. But because Dawson was watching her, and he wasn't laughing anymore.

His smirk had faded. His teasing gone. He stood still. Too still. Like a man standing on the edge of something—and not entirely sure if he wanted to jump.

Daisy ignored the sudden tightness in her chest. Ignored the strange, unsteady thrill of his warmth so close.

Her fingers closed around the pin. Cool metal. Delicate. And yet... strong. She turned it over between her fingertips, inspecting every curve, every groove.

She saw it, and her breath hitched.

Dawson must have caught it because his jaw tightened. "What?" he muttered.

She swallowed, running her thumb over the subtle notch near the base. Over the faint, precise ridge along the tip. It was so small. So cleverly designed. But she'd seen enough locks. Enough hidden compartments. Enough secrets.

"It's definitely a key," she murmured, forcing herself to focus on the truth in her hands. "This isn't just a pin," she said quietly, turning it over again. "It was made to fit something. A small lock, by the size of it."

Daisy finally looked up. And saw it.

The war.

The storm brewing behind his eyes. His shoulders tense, rigid. His pulse hammering just beneath the skin of his throat.

She licked her lips. Held his gaze. "You know what this means," she whispered.

"Yeah," he grunted. "I do."

"Then we have to go to Ashby Hollow."

A muscle jumped in Dawson's cheek. His hands flexed. His whole body bristled, like she had just asked him to walk through fire. And maybe, in his mind, she had.

If this was real, (It was.) and if this key really belonged to his past (It did.) then everything he thought he knew about himself was about to change.

She softened, just slightly. While she waited for his response, she ran her thumb over the smooth metal. Over the delicate grooves, the subtle notches—the undeniable mechanics of a key.

A flicker of something on the underside.

She tilted the pin, angling it just right in the lantern's glow, and there, so small, so easily missed—D.A.H. Etched into the metal.

D.A.H.

Her pulse thrummed. Her breath came faster, sharper. She traced the letters, as if her touch could confirm what she already knew. Daisy swallowed hard. And then, almost without thinking—she whispered it aloud. "D.A.H."

"What?" Dawson's eyes snapped to hers.

Daisy wet her lips and turned the pin toward him. Showed him. "Engraved initials," she murmured. "Right here. D.A.H."

She looked up at him—and the storm in his eyes was a hurricane. His chest rose and fell, too controlled. Too forced. Because he knew. God, he knew.

D.A.H.

Duchess of Ashby Hollow. His mother.

The proof was right there in his hands.

"You don't have to want it," she whispered again. "But don't you think you should at least see?"

A long, weighted pause. Dawson's fingers curled into fists. His throat worked.

And then finally, hoarse, and resigned, "Fine. We go."

* * *

The closer they rode, the heavier it got.

Not the air. Not the sky. Not even Daisy's expectant, smug little glances that were driving him up the bloody wall.

No. The weight pressing down on Dawson's chest was entirely his own.

Because there it was.

Ashby Hollow.

And it was ridiculous. Massive. Brooding. Unnecessarily dramatic. Like a haunted castle and a stately manor had a love child and let it be raised by too much money and bad decisions.

The medieval stone towers jutted into the sky like the ribs of a dead thing, while the newer Georgian wing sprawled beneath it, all ivy-draped balconies, gleaming leaded windows, and sweeping terraces that overlooked acres of untamed green.

It was... breathtaking. Not crumbling. Not forgotten. Just untouched. A place waiting. Holding its breath. Waiting for the lost heir. Waiting for him.

Dawson's fingers tightened on the reins.

No.

He wasn't waiting for it. He never had been.

"This is it." Daisy's voice was too damn full of triumph.

He did not look at her. If he looked at her, he might actually have to acknowledge that she was right. And he was not about to do that. Instead, he exhaled slowly, eyes locked on the estate as they drew closer, and muttered, "Well. It's a proper mess."

She hummed. *Hummed.* Which was the most infuriating thing she could have possibly done.

Dawson shot her a glare.

"It's gorgeous, actually."

"If you like things that are entirely too much."

She turned fully toward him now, brows lifted in faux surprise. "Oh, I do."

He had to look away. If he let himself stare at her any longer, his thoughts would go somewhere he absolutely did not need them to go.

Not now.

Not here.

Not when he was about to walk into the past he had never asked for.

He didn't want the bloody estate. Didn't want the title. The inheritance. The past. And yet—he didn't *not* want it, either. And that was the part that was scrambling his entire existence.

Because he should have been indifferent. Should have been able to scoff at the grandeur of it, at the ancient ivy-covered stone and the ridiculously sprawling estate that had been sitting empty for fifteen years, waiting for an heir who wasn't supposed to exist. Instead, his chest felt too tight.

And then there was Daisy. Sitting astride Violet, like a vision straight out of some maddeningly beautiful dream. That tattered dress still clinging to her in ways he couldn't ignore, and still wrapped around her because he hadn't gotten her proper clothes, because he hadn't provided for her, and that simple fact itched under his skin like something unbearable.

And there was her hair. All those wild strands in the summer breeze, catching the afternoon light.

Dawson swallowed hard. Something inside his chest pinched. Tight. Unrelenting.

And he hated it.

He shoved a hand through his hair, his scowl deepening. "You're still in that bloody dress."

Daisy tore her eyes away from the estate, looking at him instead.

She smiled. *Smiled.* Like she knew exactly what he was doing. Like she knew that he was fighting this unfamiliar, burning need to take care of her.

And she was eating it up.

Dawson clenched his jaw. Scowled harder. His hands tightened on the reins.

"You don't like my dress, Dawson?" Daisy arched a brow.

No, he didn't like her dress.

228

Because it had been under his hands last night. Because it had been bunched up around her hips while he was on his knees for her. Because he wanted her in something new. Something soft. Something that he had gotten for her.

Because he was losing his fucking mind.

He exhaled sharply, shaking his head, as if that would clear the tangled mess of thoughts in his brain.

It did not.

Daisy was still looking at him like that. And this place—this beautiful, infuriating, impossible place—it felt like it had been waiting for her. Like she belonged here.

And Dawson was absolutely not prepared for that realization.

His pulse kicked hard. His hands flexed. And before he could stop himself, before he could think, he reached for her. Fingers curling around the back of her neck. Pulling her in before he even knew what he was about to do.

She gasped, but didn't pull away. Didn't fight him. Just watched him. Eyes dark, lips parting.

He thought he was going to kiss her hard. Thought he was going to take and take and take until this unbearable need stopped clawing through him. Until he'd shed himself of this delirium.

He kissed her soft.

Tenderly.

Deep and lingering.

Like something inside him had finally stopped fighting. Like something had finally given in.

It wasn't just hunger. It wasn't just lust. It was something more. Something he wasn't ready to name.

Something he would never be able to take back.

Chapter Twenty-Four

His hand was warm, strong, the fingers curling firm at the back of Daisy's neck, his thumb brushing just below her ear.

Dawson kissed her.

Not how she expected. Not the way he had before—hot, consuming, desperate, like he was trying to brand her from the inside out.

No.

This one... lingered.

It pressed. It curled. It held. It sank into her like a unhurried, deep breath of something lethal. Something seductive.

His lips weren't demanding, but *entreating*. A slow, soul-melding, breathtaking kiss that had no right to be coming from the mouth of Dawson bloody Woodbridge.

Daisy's stomach flipped. Her heart turned over in her chest. This wasn't just lust. Not this.

This was something far worse.

A shiver traced down her spine. Not from the chill, but from the way he kissed her. From the way he moved, so reverently, as if she were something rare.

As if she was something worth holding onto.

Her fingers curled against his chest, instinctively gripping onto the fabric of his coat—a mistake—because she felt the heat of him through the layers, the steady thrum of his heartbeat, the solid, broad strength of the man who had somehow become the most infuriating, dangerous, intoxicating part of her life.

Daisy swayed.

Just a little.

Just enough to—

A sound cut through the air, high-pitched and strange.

A wailing, whining call—not human, not wind, but something... else.

"What was that?" Daisy jerked back, pulse slamming.

Dawson's hand flexed at the back of her neck before he let her go. She immediately felt colder. More unsteady.

He didn't answer, his own brows drawn tight, his breathing too uneven for a man who had only just kissed her like—like he felt something. Like he didn't know what to do with it.

Like he was as punched in the gut as she was.

Her fingers twitched. She should say something. She should demand something. But the way he was looking at her like his entire world had just shifted under his feet and he didn't know whether to chase her or run from her . . . she couldn't handle it.

So she ran first. Before he could say a word, before she could lose herself in his damn green eyes any further, Daisy yanked on Violet's reins and took off.

"Daisy!" Dawson snapped behind her.

She ignored him. She was not ready for that kiss. Not ready for what it meant.

Not ready for what she had felt.

So she did what she did best. She grabbed her horse and ran, straight into the wild, breathtaking ruins of Ashby Hollow estate. She rode hard and fast, her heart pounding louder than

Violet's hooves as they thundered over the untamed, overgrown paths leading toward the abandoned grandeur of the great manor.

She didn't have a destination. Didn't have a plan. She only knew she had to move. Had to escape whatever had just passed between them in that kiss.

The heat of Dawson's mouth still lingered on hers, the press of his hand at the back of her neck still branding her skin. But it was the way he had kissed her that truly unraveled her. Raw. Soul-stealing. A kiss that had whispered of possession, of knowing.

She could not let that happen.

The sound of thundering hooves behind her sent a shiver through her bones. Daisy knew it was Dawson. Of course it was him.

There was no one else.

No one who would follow her into the crumbling ruins of a forgotten dukedom. No one who would always, always give chase. She grinned, wild, reckless, and unchained.

The manor loomed ahead, rising from the hills in all its rugged, neglected splendor. The oldest parts of it, a castle keep and a tower, still stood, their ancient stone veined with ivy and time. The newer manor wings stretched outward, their massive windows staring like vacant eyes, their columns cracked but proud.

It was magnificent.

It was a kingdom long abandoned.

It was his.

She exhaled sharply, pushing down the twisting feeling in her chest, and leaned low into the gallop, speeding toward the main courtyard.

Behind her, Dawson growled. Not a word. Not a curse. Just

a low, frustrated, absolutely feral sound that sent a bolt of heat straight through her stomach.

Oh, he was furious.

She smiled wider. He deserved it. If she had to suffer this storm in her chest, then so did he.

She burst into the courtyard and reined Violet hard, the mare sliding to a halt in the overgrown grass. A beat later, Dawson's horse galloped in behind her. Blossom stopped with a heavy stomp, snorting clouds of breath into the air.

Dawson was already out of the saddle before his horse had fully stopped.

Her pulse spiked.

Oh, hell.

She had pushed him too far.

Daisy swung off Violet, backing toward the massive wooden doors of the estate, laughing breathlessly. "Easy, Woodbridge."

His jaw ticked. His hands flexed at his sides. His eyes, dark with something dangerous, locked onto her like a predator closing in. "This is funny to you?" His voice was a low rasp.

"You seemed like you needed a little air." She shrugged, stepping further back onto the marble steps.

Dawson's lips curled. Not in humor.

In promise.

"Oh, poppet," he murmured, stepping forward all casual, watching like a wolf closing in.

Daisy's breath caught.

He was too close. Too big, too broad, too ruinous.

She turned on her heel, racing inside the grand abandoned foyer, her boots echoing on the stone floor. She didn't have to look back—she knew he was following.

She felt it.

The weight of him, the heat of him—the damn gravity of him.

Her heart pounded and her breath came fast as she dashed through the shadows, into the vast, empty ballroom, light filtering through dust-covered windows.

"Daisy," Dawson's voice was closer.

She bit her lip, pressing a hand to her chest as if that would slow the frantic beat of her heart. She ducked into a hallway, weaving through the grand old corridors. Marble busts stared at her with their solemn, hollow eyes. Old chandeliers dangled from towering ceilings, still waiting to be lit. The ghosts of ballroom whispers and forgotten scandals clung to the walls.

And then, the main tower staircase.

She took the steps two at a time, her skirts flying behind her, her boots light on the worn stone. Up, up, up. Her laugh echoed in the stairwell. "Come on, Woodbridge! I thought you were fast."

A rough curse from below.

A thunder of boots.

Oops.

Daisy gasped as he caught her halfway up, a firm hand closing around her waist, spinning her into the stone wall. She collided with warmth, with strength, with Dawson. She barely had time to breathe before his hands were on her hips, his body caging her in, his breath hot at her ear.

"You like being chased, don't you, poppet?" His voice was dark and dangerous.

She twisted out of his grip at the last second, breath catching in her throat as she darted into the afternoon light. His fingers grazed her waist, just shy of catching her. She was breathless from running, from teasing, from the sheer wildness of this place.

The tower chamber was a dream.

Light spilled through vaulted windows, stretching high into

the gorgeous old stonework. Everything felt ancient and vast, and yet undeniably alive.

She spun, arms wide, drinking it all in. "All of this could be yours!"

The second the words left her mouth, she knew she'd said something wrong. Gone too far. She'd meant it as a joke. A bit of fun.

But Dawson wasn't laughing. No, he was looking at her like she'd just sunk a blade between his ribs. And worse, like she was the only thing left in the world that could pull it back out.

Her chest tightened. She should have stopped there. Should have let it go. But because she was an absolute terror and never knew when to quit, she took it one step further. Pushed farther.

Daisy spread her arms, turning in a slow, dramatic circle. "A shame, really. It's all quite spectacular. Pity you're too much of a rogue to want it."

That did it.

The shift in him was immediate. Dangerous. The air changed.

Dawson's jaw ticked, his shoulders rolling back as he straightened to his full height. A wolf scenting blood. And then he took a slow, measured step toward her.

Daisy's heart skipped.

Another step.

Her pulse raced.

Another.

"Dawson." She swallowed.

He cut her off, voice gravel rough. "You think I don't know what it means to want something, poppet?"

She went stock still. Because that voice. It wasn't the usual, lazy drawl he used when teasing her. It wasn't cocky, or smug, or playful.

It was dark.

And it wasn't a question.

Daisy's throat went dry. Oh no. She'd thought she was teasing him. But she wasn't. This wasn't a game to him. This was real.

Her mouth opened, but nothing came out.

Dawson exhaled sharply through his nose, shaking his head like he couldn't bloody stand himself. Then, suddenly, he was right there, so close she could feel his body heat, his breath against her cheek. And oh hell, was he looking at her.

His gaze dropped to her mouth. Lingering. Burning. And then it dropped to her throat, to the bare stretch of skin at her collarbone, where his mark had faded too much since last night. His hands flexed at his sides.

And for a breathless, endless moment, Daisy thought he was going to devour her whole.

Instead, he shocked them both again. Because Dawson, world-class rogue, didn't kiss her like a scoundrel. He kissed her like a man coming apart.

And Daisy—against all reason, all sense, all self-preservation —let herself fall into it. Just a little. Just enough to feel the truth of it.

And oh, what a mistake that was.

He groaned. Her heart clenched. And suddenly, there was no more air left in the world. No more distance. No more battle.

Just this.

Just them.

She felt it happen. Felt the moment she should have pulled away, but didn't.

The truth sent her reeling and she yanked away. "Dawson, I—"

I can't believe I'm falling in love with you.

She needed space. Air. Anything.

Daisy ran. Again.

Chapter Twenty-Five

Dawson followed her. A predator who knew his prey had nowhere to run. She could pretend all she wanted, could tell herself she was focused on her damn keyhole hunt or simply exploring, but Dawson saw the way her pulse leapt at her throat. Saw the way she refused to meet his eyes.

Saw right through her.

And he planned to make damn sure she knew it.

Daisy darted ahead, stepping through another arched doorway into a long, dimly lit corridor, lined with tall, narrow windows and tapestries so old the colors had faded into dusky shades of time. She was moving fast, determined, her fingers trailing along the stone like she was actually looking for something.

Liar.

Dawson smiled. His steps were heavier than hers, the rhythmic, methodical echo of his boots letting her know exactly where he was, how close he was.

She turned a corner sharply, her skirts swishing, and disappeared through a door into what looked like another tower stairwell.

His smile deepened. Oh, she was running all right. Running from the heat between them. Running from what she wanted. And she was leading him right where he wanted *her*.

He followed her into the narrow stairwell, steps purposeful, his chest tight with something he couldn't name. The air was different here, warmer. And at the top of the stairs, he pushed open an old wooden door and stepped into another tower room.

Smaller than the last one. Cozier. More intimate.

On the far wall was a deep arched window seat, cushions still plump despite years of dust. Dark wooden beams were overhead, a massive fireplace along one wall, and shelves full of forgotten books, softened by time, lined the old stone.

And there, just beyond the window and down below, lived a garden. Wild, overgrown. Heavy with fruit trees, their branches thick with figs and plums, the scent of them ripe and heady even through the open panes.

Dawson stepped further into the tower room, the door creaking as it shut behind him.

Daisy stood in the center of the room, still pretending, still looking for something to keep her hands busy.

"Lovely place you've led me to, poppet," he murmured, voice a slow drag of heat.

"I didn't lead you anywhere." Daisy lifted her chin.

"Didn't you?" he hummed.

Her hand tightened on the edge of a bookshelf.

He stepped closer. "You can't help it, can you?" he mused, voice dropping lower, smoother.

"Help what?"

Moving another step closer, Dawson watched the way her breath caught. "Running."

"I'm not—"

"You are."

Another step.

She backed up instinctively. Right against the bookshelf.

Dawson braced one arm on the shelf beside her head, caging her in. "You could've led me anywhere in this estate," he murmured, voice like velvet and woodsmoke, his lips just inches from her ear. "But you brought me here. To this little, hidden, perfect place."

His fingers lifted—just barely—trailing along the ribbon at her waist.

Daisy swallowed hard.

"Now, why do you think that is?" He tilted his head, watching her.

"I was looking for a keyhole. You know that. It's the whole reason we're here."

"Were you?" Dawson chuckled, low and knowing. His fingers traced the edge of her corset ribbon. "Or were you hoping I'd keep following you?"

Daisy sucked in a sharp breath.

He pressed closer. His breath was warm against her temple, his scent all heat and spice and Dawson. His voice dropped to a whisper. "Were you hoping I'd catch you?"

She thought she could run. She thought she could escape. But Daisy Bramble had never truly been hunted before. Not like this.

Not by him.

Desire slammed into his gut. She wet her lips, but that fire in her eyes still burned.

"I wasn't running," she said lightly, ducking under his arms and slipping away. "I was searching for the lock to your mother's hairpin key like I said."

"That's funny," Dawson snorted.

"You think I'm lying?"

"I think," he said, moving slowly toward her, "you don't give a single damn about finding a lock right now."

"I—"

"I think you're running because you know exactly what's coming."

She was backed up against the cushioned window seat now, that glorious, golden Yorkshire light pouring over her. His stomach tightened at the sight. She belonged here. In his home. In his life. Under him.

Her throat moved as she swallowed. "Dawson..."

"Mmm," he mused, tilting his head. "Now, that's interesting."

Her eyes narrowed. "What?"

"You're breathless." His voice was wicked. Dark. "I've barely touched you, poppet, and you're already coming unraveled."

She stiffened. "I am not."

"Liar." Another step toward her. "Shall I prove it?"

"You seem very sure of yourself."

He smiled. Sharp. Wolfish.

And then he reached for her. Not rough. Not rushed. Just... inevitable.

His fingers curled around the delicate, fine column of her throat, just enough for her to feel the weight of him there. His thumb brushed the frantic beat of her pulse. And Daisy, proud, stubborn Daisy, swayed. Just slightly. Just enough for him to see it.

He leaned in, voice dropping to a rasp. "You keep running, poppet." His lips ghosted over her cheekbone. Not kissing. Not yet. "And I keep catching you."

Her fingers flexed against his chest. No doubt torn between pushing him away and pulling him closer.

He nipped at her jaw, unhurried. "You know what I think?"

Her breath shuddered out of her.

"I think," he continued, "you're desperate for me to do something about it."

Her hands fisted in his shirt.

His lips brushed the corner of her mouth. "You want me to catch you in the worst fucking way, don't you, Daisy?"

A whimper. Soft.

Scorching.

And that was it. Dawson was done pretending. He took her mouth like a man past the point of salvation.

Daisy met him head-on.

Her taste—God help him, her taste—hit his tongue like a slow-burning brand, searing through every last ounce of restraint he'd been clinging to.

Too long.

He'd been good for too bloody long.

She'd let him have this—let him chase, let him catch, let him have his bloody mouth on hers like she wanted it just as badly as he did. She wasn't pulling away. She was leaning in.

And fuck if that didn't set him ablaze.

Dawson groaned, deep and rough, hands greedy as they gripped her waist, tugging her closer, pressing her tight against him. Soft curves against hard, unrelenting need.

She moaned and he swallowed the sound, taking everything she gave, sliding one hand up the curve of her spine, tangling his fingers in the riot of dark waves that had driven him to madness since the moment she stormed into his life.

"You like being hunted, don't you?" he murmured against her lips, voice thick with wicked pleasure. "You like when the roles get reversed, Daisy Bramble, Hunter of Men."

She shuddered. Tried to shake her head. Failed so miserably it was beautiful.

Dawson chuckled darkly, triumphant. "No use denying it now, sweetheart."

She trembled in his hold.

So damn strong. So damn fierce. And yet utterly undone in his hands. And fuck, if that didn't slay him.

"Say it," he growled, his mouth tracing the delicate line of her jaw, the soft, scandalously tempting skin just beneath her ear.

She let out the smallest, sweetest, most damning sound.

He tightened his grip. "Say it, Daisy."

She panted against his cheek, shaking, hands clutching the fabric of his shirt like he was the only thing keeping her standing. "I like it," she whispered, clearing hating that she admitted it. Hating even more how true it was.

Dawson groaned, dropping his forehead against hers, utterly destroyed. "God, poppet..." His lips crashed against hers again, wilder, deeper, rawer.

She gave as good as she got. Her fingers dug into his chest, dragging him closer, her teeth nipping at his bottom lip like she wanted to test just how much restraint he had left.

Spoiler: none.

He growled against her mouth, took her breath, took her body, took everything. And when she gasped at the hard, unmistakable length of him pressing against her belly—when her fingers fumbled at the buttons of his shirt, tugging—Dawson lost his goddamn mind.

He lifted her, his hands firm and possessive, gripping the perfect, tempting fullness of her arse.

She moaned as his teeth grazed the sensitive skin of her neck, and he felt the sound straight in his cock.

"You want me to stop?" he asked, voice rough, dangerous.

A challenge.

A warning.

Because if she asked now—if she asked now, he'd stop. But if she didn't, if she begged him to keep going . . . there would be no stopping.

Not this time.

Daisy's breath came fast and shallow, her fingers clawed at his shoulders. And then she breathed one word, "No."

Heaven. Hell. And every wicked thing in between. That's what she tasted like on his tongue. Daisy Bramble—his torment, his temptation, his fucking undoing. And now?

Now, she was *his*.

Dawson dragged his hands down her body, his fingers rough and hungry as he found the hem of her dress, curling his fists around the fabric, bunching it higher, higher, until the last goddamn barrier between him and her perfect skin was gone.

The moment the dress slipped off her shoulders, sliding down her curves, his breath caught. "Fuck me, poppet..."

She was breathtaking. The fading sunlight slanted through the arched windows, painting her in molten gold, her skin flushed from his kisses, her breasts heaving, bare and perfect and utterly unfair.

He swallowed hard. Tried for a single, fleeting moment to be a better man. And failed spectacularly.

His hands smoothed up her shapely thighs, tracing every scandalous inch, the way he'd imagined a hundred times—but this time was real. This time, he wasn't dreaming. His fingers brushed the soft, sensitive skin just beneath her belly, and Daisy sucked in a sharp, helpless breath.

"Dawson," she whispered.

He groaned. Hard. Because she wasn't stopping him. She was arching into him.

He caught her under the thighs and shifted her, pinning her against the window seat, spreading her legs just enough to make her breath catch.

"Oh, you're going to be so fucking sweet for me, aren't you?" he rasped, voice utterly starved.

Her lashes fluttered, her mouth parting, her breath a soft, needy pant.

"Poppet." He dragged his rough palms up her thighs. "I can feel how warm you are. How ready you are for me."

She trembled beneath his touch. "Am not."

"Oh, you so are, love." And he was hungry.

His mouth found her breast, and he sucked her nipple between his lips, agonizingly slow and deliberate, savoring the way she moaned, the way her fingers dug into his shoulders, fisting his shirt like she needed something to anchor her. "Dawson."

"You like that, sweetheart?" A dark chuckle rumbled from deep in his chest.

Her sharp, shuddering inhale was answer enough.

His teeth grazed the tight bud of her nipple before he licked over it, hot and lingering, driving her mad on purpose. Because if she thought he was going to rush this? She had no bloody idea what was coming.

He moved to the other breast, lavishing it, sucking and licking like he had all the time in the goddamn world.

Daisy—fucking hell, Daisy—she arched and moaned like she was already gone. And he wasn't even close to finished with her.

Dawson lifted his head, his lips wet, his eyes dark with pure, primal hunger. "You taste like honey and fucking temptation," he murmured against her skin, pressing hot, open-mouthed kisses down the center of her belly.

She shivered. And she was watching him now, her eyes wide, her lips kiss-swollen and parted, her breath coming fast and uneven. Like she knew. Like she knew exactly where he was going next.

Dawson smiled against her skin and kept going. Because he was going to learn every single inch of her.

She was about to learn exactly how thorough he could be.

Christ, he was gone for her. Utterly. Completely. Ruined beyond salvation.

And he didn't give a single fuck.

Bare beneath him, Daisy sprawled across the plush window seat, her golden-bronze skin glowing in the late afternoon light, her breath a desperate, needy thing.

Dawson was a man starved.

He let out a low, feral sound, hot palms sliding down her back, slow and possessive, feeling every sinful curve, every soft, beautiful line of her body. "So fucking perfect," he growled, voice rough and utterly depraved.

She barely had time to breathe before he flipped her over, pressing her gently but firmly onto her stomach, sprawling her across the window seat. She gasped, hands fisting the cushions, her hips rising instinctively.

"Oh, you like this, don't you, poppet?" His hand slid up, cupping the back of her neck, his fingers tight, controlling, owning her in a way that had her thighs pressing together in aching desperation.

"So responsive," he murmured, smiling darkly, his mouth finding the nape of her neck, and biting down just enough to make her whimper.

Fuck, that sound. That sound nearly ended him right then and there.

His tongue flicked out, soothing the sting of his teeth, his other hand dragging down her spine, nails grazing her skin, making her shudder, arch, beg.

"And you wanted to run from me, didn't you, sweetheart?" Dawson taunted, his mouth dragging lower, hot, wet kisses pressing down the delicate curve of her back.

Daisy let out a breathless moan, her hips shifting, seeking. "Deserved it."

He laughed low and wicked, palming her waist, spreading her wider beneath him.

And then, he kissed her ass. A deep, slow, filthy kiss. Right on that perfect, gorgeous curve.

"Oh!" She jerked, a startled, helpless moan escaping her throat.

"*Ohhh,* poppet." His hands kneaded, squeezing and gripping her like she was his to take, his to devour. "Look at you," he murmured, pressing another slow, debauched kiss to the other cheek, his teeth nipping just enough to make her gasp. "Fucking beautiful."

She was panting now, her body trembling under his hands, her thighs clenching, her back arching just the way he wanted. "Damn it, Dawson," she gasped.

He was absolutely losing his goddamn mind. His mouth traced lower, tongue flicking, teasing at the delicious, sensitive place between her thighs. Her pussy was heaven's gate. Hell's paradise. Fuck if he wasn't going to worship.

Daisy let out a ragged, breathless sound, her fingers digging into the cushion, her whole body shuddering.

"That's it," Dawson groaned, voice dark, desperate, reverent.

He licked her again. Right between her gorgeous cheeks.

"Fuck—Dawson—" She nearly sobbed.

"Mmm" he murmured, lazily stroking his tongue against her again, making her tremble so violently he had to hold her down. He pressed a kiss to the inside of her thigh, his hands gripping her hips, steadying her. "I could eat you for hours," he muttered against her skin, his breath hot and teasing, making her arch, writhe, beg for more. "You should let me," he purred, dragging his tongue devastatingly slow against the most gorgeous part of her.

Daisy let out a helpless cry, her whole body quivering beneath his hands. She was not surviving this, because he wasn't stopping until she screamed his fucking name.

He barely gave her time to breathe before he kissed her beautiful quim again, a deep, lazy, torturous press of lips, his tongue flicking just enough to make her cry out, helpless and shaking.

"D-Dawson!"

"Mmm, that's my girl," he purred, his grip tightening on her hips, holding her steady as he devoured her from behind, so thoroughly, like she was the finest meal he'd ever had.

She let out a desperate, ravished moan, her fingers clawing at the cushion, her mind unraveling by the second. "Oh, hell—Dawson, I—"

"What? Too much?" His tongue flicked a teasing, wicked, agonizing stroke that had her back arching like a bowstring.

"Y-you know it's not," she panted, shuddering beneath him.

"Fuck, poppet." His hands flexed against her hips, his breath hot and heavy against her skin. "You've been driving me mad for days."

Daisy bit back a moan, hips shifting, restless, wanting. "Yeah?" she managed, breathless, teasing, even as she shook beneath him. "And whose fault is that?"

"Yours. You and your bloody dress," he growled, sliding his hands up her waist, over her ribs. "You and your smart mouth, and your gorgeous body, and your—" He bit her thigh, sharp, punishing, delicious.

She jerked. "You absolute bastard," she panted, breath shaking, fingers twisting into the cushion.

Dawson laughed darkly, his hands sliding up, cupping her breasts, thumbs flicking over her already sensitive peaks. "Say that again," he demanded, his voice low, debauched, utterly unrepentant.

"You bastard," she gasped, pushing back against him, feeling the shudder that went through his body.

"Oh, poppet." Dawson let out a low, dangerous growl. "I like it when you talk dirty to me."

And then he was flipping her over, dragging her into his lap on the window seat, his mouth crashing into hers in a desperate, filthy kiss.

Chapter Twenty-Six

D aisy was shattered.

Absolutely, utterly, deliciously destroyed. And she wanted more. She wanted to watch Dawson fall apart.

She slid onto his lap, straddling him, the heat of his cock searing between her legs, even through his breeches. He was achingly hard beneath her.

His hands clenched on her hips, fingers digging in, like he was holding on for dear life. His jaw was tight, his breath unsteady. His eyes—oh, his eyes.

Daisy watched them shift, that sharp, wicked green going darker, turning pure, devastating green-black as she slid her hand between them, cupping him through his breeches.

"Christ, Daisy." He swore under his breath, hard and dirty.

She grinned, stroking up and down at a meandering, teasing pace, and feeling the way he shuddered beneath her, how his hips jerked like he couldn't help himself. His head tipped back against the window seat, throat taut, his hands flexing, gripping her, as if he were one second away from snapping.

"That's better," she murmured, watching the way his eyes

went heavy-lidded, how his breath caught when she squeezed, just a little.

Dawson let out a low groan, his hips lifting into her hand, helpless and wild. "You're playing a dangerous game, poppet," he gritted out, his voice thick with barely-leashed hunger.

"Am I?" Daisy tilted her head, utterly unrepentant.

He let out a shaky breath, his eyes flashing like molten emeralds. "Oh, you are." His hands tightened on her hips, urging her closer, pressing her down against him until she felt every inch of him, thick and hard, right against her.

She let out a sharp moan, heat flooding her, need curling hot and deep in the pit of her belly.

"Feel what you do to me?" he asked, his voice a rasp of heat against her lips.

Daisy swallowed hard, stroking him again, watching the way his hips twitched, the way his lashes fluttered low with pleasure. "I like watching you like this," she whispered.

Dawson let out a harsh sound, his eyes locking onto hers, glinting hotly, savagely.

"You want to watch, poppet?" he ground out. "Then watch." He grabbed her wrist and gently pushed it away, freeing his length for her view.

She thought she might die from the way he looked at her, all wicked, dirty sin. But then she climbed off and stepped back to see him—and nearly did.

Oh my.

He leaned back against the cushioned window seat, one arm draped over the back, looking like a king on his throne. Except somehow he'd lost his shirt during all this and he was naked from the waist up. And his other hand was still wrapped around his thick, aching cock.

And she was watching. Wide-eyed. Breathless. Because he wasn't just holding himself. *Oh, no.*

He was stroking.

Long and lazy. Like he had all the time in the world to make her fall apart for him. Like he was enjoying this far too much.

And, God help her, she was too. Watching him. Watching the way his fingers tightened, slid lower, teased, spread the wetness already slicking the head.

Her thighs clenched, and she felt a rush of heat, of hunger, of pure, wicked want. Dawson saw it. Knew it. And the bastard smirked.

"You looked curious before, poppet." His voice was a provocative, husky tease. "Still curious?"

Daisy hated him.

No, she didn't. Not at all. God, he was intoxicating. Stronger than the most potent whiskey.

The only thing she could do was nod.

Dawson's gaze darkened.

His pace slowed.

"Come closer."

Her breath stopped. "Dawson, I—"

"Closer, poppet." His voice dripped with pure sex, and he stroked himself again, making sure she saw every inch of it.

Before she even realized she'd moved, she was right in front of him.

Dawson exhaled roughly, his free hand sliding up her bare thigh.

"You want to touch me now?" he murmured, pressing his mouth to the inside of her knee.

Daisy swallowed hard.

Yes.

God, yes.

"Say it." His lips brushed higher. "Ask for it."

"I want to touch you." She confessed on a whisper, hands fisting at her sides.

He let out a dark, approving sound. He let go of himself and sat back. Spread his legs wider.

An invitation. A dare.

When Daisy finally reached for him, wrapped her fingers around the thick, hard heat of him . . . he let out a filthy, guttural groan that shot straight through her.

His cock was hot. Heavy. Velvet steel against her palm.

And when she stroked—

He shuddered. His head tipped back against the window seat. His breathing turned ragged.

"That's it, poppet. Just like that."

Oh, hell.

Daisy felt herself pulse. Wet. Desperate. So utterly needy. She wanted—no, needed—his mouth on her again, right where she throbbed the most.

When Dawson lifted his head again, found her eyes, and grinned . . . her stomach flipped.

"Would you like to see all of me, love?"

Oh, God yes. Yes.

And all she could do was nod.

He chuckled hotly. And then, Dawson stood. Slowly, torturously, gloriously, he began to undress. She couldn't breathe. Couldn't think at all when he was finally before her utterly, completely bare.

Good Lord above, he was a revelation.

Daisy's eyes trailed over him, unable to stop, unable to look away. His shoulders were broad, powerful, with sun-kissed skin stretched over lean muscle. His chest—toned and dusted with just the right amount of hair—tapered down to the sharp ridges of his abdomen.

The trail of hair dipped lower . . . lower . . . and then . . .

Oh.

Oh.

Her mouth went dry.

Her knees actually wobbled.

Dawson's cock in plain sight, with no hand wrapped around it, was... enormous.

Her pulse roared in her ears, her entire body turning hot and restless and so incredibly needy. She had felt him before. But seeing him like *this*?

Dawson's arms flexed, his stance shifting like he was fighting the urge to close the space between them. He was watching her as he sat back down. Watching the way she stared at him. And when she finally, finally dragged her eyes back up to his . . . oh, she was done for. Because those green eyes had gone dark with possession. With heat. With need. With the kind of raw, burning desire that made her legs press together in a desperate, useless attempt at relief.

Her heart pounded, her lips parted. And before she could stop herself, before she could even think, out came, "You're enormous."

"You flatter me, poppet." Dawson barked out a laugh. Rough. Filthy. His hand ran through his messy hair, his cock jerking slightly at her words.

Daisy could barely speak, barely move. Because he was still sitting there. Still letting her look. Still giving her the space to drink him in like a greedy thing.

And God help her, she *was* greedy. Her fingers twitched. Her breath shuddered. And then, shakily, she reached out. Because she needed to touch. Because she needed to know what he felt like everywhere, needed to feel all that power beneath her fingertips.

He stilled. A low rumble sounded in his chest. And the fire in his eyes nearly set her ablaze. Her nipples puckered at the intensity, craving more.

Lost in the heat of it all, Daisy dropped to her knees

between his legs. A hand braced against his thigh, the other wrapping around him.

Lord help him, Dawson was an aroused, groaning, muscle-clenching disaster. His head fell back against the cushion of the window seat, his chest rising and falling in heavy, ragged breaths. And his cock—his thick, heavy, gorgeous cock—was right in front of her.

Waiting.

Needy.

God, he was so hard. So hot and velvety soft over iron. And she could see everything. The way he throbbed in her grasp. The way he leaked for her, proof of just how much he wanted this. The way his fingers were flexing against the window seat like he was barely holding himself together.

Daisy moistened her lips.

She bent forward.

And licked him.

"Bloody fucking hell." Dawson's entire body jerked. His hand shot out, gripping her hair at the base of her skull, a ragged, almost pained sound tearing from his throat. "Jesus Christ, Daisy."

She swirled her tongue over him, humming softly, her eyes flicking up to his face. "Mm, tastes good."

He choke-groaned, his hips jerking toward her. "Fuck. *Fuck,* you dirty little beauty."

And oh, he looked ravaged. His jaw clenched so tight a muscle ticked in his cheek. His tree-trunk thighs trembled beneath her hands. And his eyes—God, his eyes—were dark and feverish, locked on her with an intensity that made her stomach tighten.

"Just like that, love—" he rasped, his grip in her hair tightening, just a little. "Take me all the way in that sweet mouth of yours."

She did.

She wrapped her lips around him, sliding down, taking him deep, feeling the silky hot weight of him against her tongue. Dawson cursed, loud and filthy, his hips jerking involuntarily.

And then he was talking.

Dear God, the man could talk.

"You're so good at that, aren't you, poppet?" he purred, his voice all smoke and ruin. "So bloody perfect. So fucking greedy. You love this, don't you?"

Daisy whimpered around him, her body clenching at the sound of his voice, at the taste of him.

"That's right, love," he groaned, his other hand tangling in her hair too, guiding her, slow and deep. "God, I love watching you. Look at you, on your knees for me. So pretty, so perfect, so fucking eager."

His words were wrecking her. His voice was wrecking her. She could feel it—his body tensing, his abs flexing, his breath turning ragged and desperate.

He was close.

Too close.

With one last lazy, delicious drag of her tongue, she pulled away.

Dawson nearly shouted. "*What the—?*"

But she was already moving, already crawling up his body, already sliding over him. She didn't think. Didn't hesitate. Didn't give him time to catch his breath.

She needed him.

Now.

She took him inside her in one slick, glorious slide.

"Fuck, Daisy!" He lost his goddamned mind. His hands snapped to her hips, his head thudding back against the window seat, his muscles flexing as he fought for control.

There was none.

Because she was already moving. Already riding him. And God, it was good. The stretch. The heat. The full, thick, perfect fit of him.

"Oh, Dawson," she moaned, loving how big he was.

"That's it, poppet," He gripped her tighter, guiding her, his own hips rising to meet hers. "Take what you need. Take everything."

She did.

She rode him like she meant to ruin him. Fast. Hard. Deep. And he met her thrust for thrust, driving up into her, hitting her just right, making her moan—louder, wilder, completely untethered.

"Christ, look at you," Dawson praised, his eyes locked on her, drinking in the way she moved, the way she arched, the way she trembled every time he hit that perfect spot inside her. "You were made for this. Made for me."

Daisy shattered. The pleasure ripped through her like lightning, raw and annihilating, her entire body clenching tight as she came, crying out his name.

He snapped.

In one motion he flipped her, slamming her back against the cushions, pinning her beneath him, his weight pressing her down, anchoring her as he drove into her, hard and relentless. "You think you can ride me like that and get away with it?" he growled, his breath hot against her ear.

She whimpered. "Dawson . . ."

"No, love." He dripped seduction, catching her wrists, pinning them above her head. "Now I ride you."

And he did.

So deep. So hard. So perfect. She was clawing at him, her body arching, her moans turning wild.

"You feel that?" He demanded to know, his lips trailing fire along her throat. "You take me so bloody well. You feel so fucking perfect around my cock. Tight, hot, mine."

"Oh God, Dawson," she sobbed, clawing at his back in blind, consuming desire.

The pleasure built again. Higher. Stronger. Until it was too much. Until she was breaking.

Until he was right there coming with her, groaning her name, spilling deep inside her, shuddering with every pulse.

They collapsed together.

She was breathless. Shattered. Completely, utterly blown.

And as Dawson pressed his forehead to hers, still inside her, still breathing her in like she was the only thing anchoring him to this world . . . Daisy knew.

She was his.

And, God help her.

He was hers.

Chapter Twenty-Seven

Morning light slanted through the high, arched window, spilling golden warmth across the stone floor.

The tower room smelled like her. Like Daisy. Like warm skin and spent pleasure. Like something irrevocable.

Dawson was a goner.

His arm was heavy over her waist, his body pressed against the glorious curve of her back. He was sated, wrecked, ruined... and yet somehow not nearly finished.

Because she was soft and warm and breathing so peacefully against him, like she belonged there. Like they hadn't just ravaged each other the night before. Like he hadn't spent the entire night alternating between devouring her and trying to remember how to breathe.

His fingers traced the bare skin of her hip, light, lazy. He shouldn't touch her like this, shouldn't feel so easy in the aftermath. But he couldn't seem to stop himself.

She shifted slightly, a sleepy hum leaving her lips, and his already half-hard cock gave a warning throb against the curve of her arse.

Jesus Christ.

Hadn't he just spent half the night inside her? Hadn't he just fallen apart for her again and again?

And yet—here he was. Starved.

His hand slipped lower, skimming over the bare curve of her thigh, and she made that breathless little noise that had undone him every damn time. "Mm, Dawson..."

His eyes nearly rolled back into his head. Christ, his name had never sounded better than it did on her lips, all sleepy, sweet, edged with heat.

He pressed a slow kiss to the nape of her neck.

She shivered. And Dawson fucking felt that shiver in his soul. Dangerous.

She shifted again, stretching like a satisfied cat, her hips pressing back just enough for his cock to slide against her slick, warm skin.

He gritted his teeth. He should be content. They had done everything. And yet... it wasn't enough. It would never be enough.

His fingers flexed against her hip, gripping her just a little tighter.

Daisy let out a soft, knowing little laugh. Still facing away from him, still relaxed against the mattress, but utterly aware of what she was doing to him.

"Oh, you think this is funny, do you?" He kissed her shoulder, nipped gently.

Her voice was pure, wicked morning-rasp. "A little."

Dawson exhaled roughly, half in frustration, half in pure, fucking worship.

She had no idea what she was doing to him. Or worse—she did. And Christ, did he love that about her.

She shifted again, grinding back against him just enough to make his vision go white-hot for a second.

His hand snapped to her hip, gripping her hard enough to still her. "Daisy." His voice was hoarse with warning.

"Yes?" She hummed, utterly unaffected.

"You trying to get fucked this morning?"

Her laugh was pure gorgeous temptation.

He swore under his breath. Then his patience snapped. In one swift motion, he rolled her onto her back, covering her, caging her in.

Daisy blinked up at him, breathless, so damn pretty it hurt to look at her. That golden-brown gaze gleaming with mischief and heat. That wicked little smirk on her swollen lips.

He shook his head, voice raw. "You're dangerous, poppet."

Her fingers dragged slowly over his chest, over the still-racing thump of his pulse. Soft as a sigh, she breathed, "So are you."

Dawson was lost.

Again.

Always.

She was warm beneath him. Still sleepy, still loose-limbed from last night, still so fucking perfect it made something inside him twist and snap all at once. She stretched, slow and utterly unbothered by the way he had her pinned beneath him, and Dawson nearly lost the last scrap of his control.

The golden light streaming through the tower window kissed her skin the way he had all night, turning her into something otherworldly. His mouth went dry. God help him, but he wanted her again. Like this. Soft and drowsy and tangled up in him.

His cock twitched, already so hard he ached, pressing against the heat of her inner thigh.

"Something on your mind?" Daisy's wicked, knowing little smile nearly killed him.

"Yeah. You."

Her fingers dragged through his hair, nails scraping just right against his scalp, and he swore softly under his breath. This woman was going to destroy him.

"Mmm. That so?"

Dawson gritted his teeth, grinding against her just enough to feel the slick heat waiting for him between her thighs.

Her breath went thready.

His grin was deadly. "Yeah. That so."

Daisy's eyes flashed wide when he caught her wrists and pinned them above her head like he did last night, sinking deep and deliciously heavy against her.

He murmured against her lips, low and rough and barely human anymore, "You want me to say it, don't you?"

She bit her lip, hips lifting, chasing the friction he was barely giving her.

He smirked. Wicked. Starved.

"You want me to tell you how fucking perfect you felt last night?" His voice was pure filth. "How your pussy fit me like you were made for me?"

Her breath came faster.

"Want me to tell you how many times I nearly lost my damn mind with you riding me?"

A soft, mewling little sound left her throat.

Dawson groaned and took her mouth in a deep, drugging kiss, tasting every breathless gasp she made.

Then, lazily, deliberately, he trailed lower. Across the curve of her jaw. Down the column of her throat. Over the swell of her breast.

Daisy arched, moaning, as his mouth closed over one of those gorgeous, sensitive nipples.

Fucking ruined. That's what he was. A man slayed.

She whimpered. Clutched at him.

"Still think it's funny?" He grinned against her skin.

She gave a strangled little laugh. "Not... quite as funny anymore."

Growling his approval, he flicked his tongue over her nipple before sucking it deep into his mouth.

She cried out, writhing beneath him.

That was it. That passionate, desperate sound of hers. It drove him mad.

He rolled his hips, grinding his aching cock against her heat. She was so slick, so ready for him, and he swore he felt his vision black out for a second.

Dawson dragged his teeth gently over her nipple, earning another desperate sound. "That's my girl," he breathed roughly.

His.

Fucking *his*.

He lifted his head, green eyes dark and wicked as they locked onto hers. "Gonna ride me again this morning, sweetheart?" His voice was gravel, his grin, oh, so naughty.

Daisy went molten beneath him. "Not this time."

And just like that he knew he was about to die happy.

She wrapped her legs around his waist and pulled him close, took him in. So warm.

Dawson shuddered, pressing his forehead to hers, trying to breathe through it, but she was so tight, so perfect, so damn *his* that he nearly lost it before he even started moving.

She groaned luxuriously, hips lifting, chasing more.

His control snapped. Dawson swore and thrust deep. Daisy cried out, back arching as she clutched at him, fingers tangling in his hair, nails digging into his shoulders.

Gone.

He was *gone*.

Dawson buried himself to the hilt, so fucking deep, grinding into her until she felt him everywhere.

"Fucking hell, Daisy." His voice was raw, ragged. "You feel—"

She cut him off with her mouth, kissing him hot, needy, demanding. He growled against her lips, rolling his hips and thrusting, he dragged a gasping, breathless moan from her throat.

Her nails dug in deeper. "Dawson," she panted. "Dawson, you—"

He caught her wrists, pinned them to the mattress, and fucked her like a man who had lost all reason.

Daisy gasped, moaned, clung to him like she never wanted to let go.

And God, that did something to him.

Something dangerous.

Something that felt like forever.

Her breath shattered, her thighs tightening around him, her hips meeting him perfectly as he drove her higher and higher. He felt her tighten around him, felt her body shudder beneath him, heard the way she moaned his name like he was the only man who had ever existed.

And then she broke apart. Came hard, screaming his name.

Dawson's vision went white. His body seized up as his climax hit him like a bloody runaway carriage. A strangled groan tore from his throat as he thrust deep one last time, grinding against her as he spilled inside her, body shaking, completely at her mercy.

Panting beneath him, Daisy was blissed-out, golden and gorgeous, her lazy, satisfied little smile nearly sending him over again.

He collapsed onto his forearms, pressing a slow, lingering kiss to her temple.

She sighed, content, utterly melted into the cushions. Then she grinned up at him. "Okay," she whispered. "Maybe you were right. I did want you to have me again this morning."

Dawson huffed a laugh, his heart still hammering in his chest.

"Damn right, poppet."

Chapter Twenty-Eight

Daisy smoothed out her wrinkled dress, ignoring the ache deep in her thighs, and the way her skin still hummed from where his hands had gripped, had claimed, had worshiped.

She didn't dare look at him yet. Because she knew what she'd find. And she didn't need to see Dawson lounging there, all bare and satisfied, watching her like she was the best damn thing he'd ever tasted, to feel the heat of it.

But she heard him shift. That lazy, sinful stretch, the creak of the cushions beneath his weight.

She squared her shoulders, tugged her bodice into place . . . and said it. "So, tell me, Dawson, do you mean to laze about all day, or do you plan to find the lock to your family legend like we came here for?"

A long, thick pause.

Then his voice, low, rough, and laced with amusement. "Poppet, I'll tell you exactly what I plan to do today."

She knew that tone. A low, simmering heat unfurled in her belly before he even finished.

"First, I'm going to have you again." His gaze burned into

her, wicked and knowing, and it didn't matter that she had turned away, because she could feel him, lounging there, bare and sprawled and addicting.

"Then," he drawled, "we'll look for your precious lock."

She swallowed. Smoothed her hands down the front of her skirt. Ignored the sharp throb between her thighs that said *yes, please, now.*

Daisy tossed her hair over her shoulder and finally, finally, turned to face him. Big mistake.

There he was. Stretched out on his side, propped up on one arm, all smooth, tanned skin and hard muscle, completely unbothered by his own nakedness.

And worse?

His gaze.

The way it flicked down her body, lingering and knowing, like he was remembering every place he had touched, kissed, tasted.

Her pulse stuttered.

Dawson's green eyes darkened when he landed on her dress. This time, the look he gave it was different. Not just hungry. Not just hot. There was something else, something new. A tension in his jaw. A flicker of something unreadable in his gaze.

His brows pulled together just slightly, his lips pressing into a thin line. "I'm buying you a new dress."

The words were gruff. Decisive. Almost offhand. But Daisy heard it. The weight.

"Oh?" She tilted her head, watching him.

"Yes." Dawson's gaze flicked to the wrinkled bodice, the fabric his hands had pulled down and pushed up and fisted between his fingers. His voice was lower now, rougher. "I'll buy you a hundred of them."

And just like that something in her chest squeezed. Tight

and sudden. And she had no idea why. It was just a dress. Just words. Just Dawson being Dawson.

Right?

* * *

Exhaling, Daisy tossed Dawson a side-eyed glance as she bit into a slice of dried apple from his bag. The grounds of Ashby Hollow stretched before them, morning light slanting through the thick summer trees, dappling the long, overgrown pathway as they walked the property.

It was breathtaking. The kind of place that felt like stories were spun from its very bones. The towering ruins of the old castle loomed in the distance, their weathered stone walls wrapped in ivy and legend, while the newer manor sprawled beside it, grand and magnificent, but unmistakably empty. It had been abandoned for years, and yet, it felt like it was waiting.

Waiting for something . . . or someone.

Waiting for him.

She stole another look at Dawson as he tore off a chunk of bread with his teeth. He was barely paying attention to the landscape, all broad shoulders and restless energy, his brows drawn low, his expression unreadable.

She knew that look. He was thinking too hard. Which, frankly, was her job.

"So," she said lightly, tearing off another piece of dried apple, and deciding that sharing something from her childhood would help lower his protective barriers, and let her in, where—surprise!—she discovered was a place she really wanted to be. "When I was eight years old, my sister Blossom and I snuck into the orphanage kitchen, stole three entire loaves of bread, and buried them in the garden."

Dawson stopped chewing his bread. Slowly turned his head

toward her. "...Poppet." He swallowed, blinking. "Do I want to know why?"

She grinned, tossing the rest of the apple slice into her mouth and chewing. "We wanted to make our own treasure hunt. Thought it'd be a grand adventure." She shrugged. "Ended up forgetting where we buried them, and the loaves were never seen again."

He snorted. "You buried perfectly good food?"

"Oh, we tried to find them!" She sighed dramatically. "Spent weeks digging up every inch of that poor garden, but the loaves had vanished. Completely gone. We decided a ghost must've taken them."

He huffed a quiet laugh, shaking his head as he tore off another piece of bread.

"Mrs. Granbury, the old headmistress, was furious, of course," Daisy continued, grinning at the memory. "We had to peel potatoes in the kitchen for a month as punishment. But we never found those loaves." She chewed her lip. "I still think about them sometimes. Where they might've gone."

Dawson gave her a skeptical look. "You're haunted by missing bread?"

"Well, when you put it like that . . ."

His grin was lazy, teasing. Warm.

And just like that, her heart did something it absolutely should not be doing.

Daisy cleared her throat. Straightened her shoulders. "Point is, I was a brilliant little investigator even then. I knew how to track things, how to uncover lost things, even if I never found my damn bread."

Dawson chewed thoughtfully, watching her in that too-intense way of his. "And what is it you think you're tracking now, exactly?"

She tilted her chin, pushing past the warmth blooming in her chest. "You."

His chewing slowed.

The words had just... slipped out.

"I mean—the lock." Daisy glanced away, her mouth suddenly dry.

Too late.

His green eyes flickered with something dark, something sharp, something that saw right through her.

"That so?" He swallowed, licked a crumb from his lip.

Daisy absolutely refused to be affected by the low, knowing way he said it. She turned ahead, stepping over a fallen branch, ignoring the way her pulse had started hammering. "Yes. We're going to find the lock your key it fits into."

A beat of silence.

"You sure you don't just want me to unlock something else for you, poppet?" His voice was low and lazy and wicked as midnight.

She choked on absolutely nothing.

Her foot caught on a rock, and before she could pitch forward onto her face, Dawson's hand snaked out and grabbed her wrist, steadying her with an effortless pull of strength.

Heat sizzled between them.

Daisy stared at him, breathing hard.

His grip was firm. Sure. His green eyes gleamed, full of that cocky, carnal knowledge.

She exhaled sharply. "You are insufferable."

"And yet, you still want me."

Oh, he was lucky she didn't push him into the nearest fountain.

She shoved his chest and stormed ahead, because she absolutely could not look at him right now. Not when her pulse was a mess. Not when her thighs still ached from his touch.

Not when he was completely right.

Behind her, Dawson chuckled—knowing and unbearably smug.

And damn it all...

She was smiling too.

* * *

The morning grew warm, the kind of June warmth that sank gently into the skin without smothering, kissed by sunlight and the scent of wild roses blooming thick along the crumbling stone walls.

The castle ruins and manor stretched before them, ancient and golden, half-wrapped in ivy and mystery. But it was the darker place beneath the crawling ivy that caught Daisy's eye. A stone archway, barely visible beyond a tangle of overgrown greenery.

She veered toward it without thinking, brushing past Dawson as she did. He didn't stop her, just fell into step beside her, watching her with that slow, knowing gaze that made her heart do something highly inconvenient in her chest.

The moment they stepped through, the temperature dropped a few degrees, the shade wrapping around them like a secret. It was a cool, tucked-away place, a reprieve from the warming morning.

And for a second, Daisy forgot the legend, the lock, the key. Forgot everything but Dawson and what they were seeing.

It was beautiful.

A hidden courtyard, enclosed by weathered stone walls, dappled with gilded light where the vines had given way. A moss-covered fountain sat at the center, long gone dry but still elegant, carved with strange, twisting creatures. And there, just beyond the fountain, a low stone ledge, warmed by the sun, practically begging her to sit.

She turned in a slow circle, taking in the sun-dappled, secret world of the courtyard. It had the feeling of a place left untouched, meant only for those who wandered into it by accident—or fate.

She loved it immediately.

Dawson, however, was silently watching her.

She felt his eyes tracking her movements, hot and possessive, like he already knew exactly what he'd done to her body last night and how much she still felt it this morning. Like he'd happily do it all over again against the sun-warmed stones if she let him.

He hadn't stopped looking at her like that since she'd climbed out of his lap, breathless and boneless, an hour ago.

She absolutely refused to acknowledge how much she liked it. Instead, she plopped herself onto the low stone ledge of the fountain and stretched out in the warmth of the morning, pressing her palms flat against the smooth rock. "Oh, this is far too romantic," she said airily, tilting her face to the sun. "Should I be worried?"

Dawson's chuckle was low and wholly indecent. "Terrified."

She refused to look at him, knowing if she did, she'd see that wicked smirk, the one that had left her breathless and begging the night before.

So she focused instead on the stone creatures carved into the fountain, trailing a finger along one's moss-softened head. "Violet would love this," she mused. "It's so... overgrown and wild and untouched."

"Violet?" His brows flicked up. "The horse?"

"My sister," Daisy said absently, still admiring the fountain. "Well, one of them. The youngest, the sweetest, the most annoyingly impulsive." She grinned. "Looks like a fresh and whole-some milkmaid but fights like a bloody prizefighter."

"Sounds familiar." Dawson let out a low laugh.

She threw him an arch look but didn't argue. Instead, she let her hand slide down the fountain's edge, her fingers tapping idly.

She didn't mean to say it.

Didn't mean to let him in like this.

But the place was too lovely, the morning too warm, and he was looking at her too damn closely. So the words tumbled out. "When I was sixteen, I nearly got locked inside the Guildhall Library overnight."

"Oh?" Dawson's head tipped slightly, amused curiosity flickering in his sharp green gaze.

She sighed dramatically. "Blame Lark, Juniper, and Ivy. We were all the same age and got into a shameless amount of trouble together."

"Of course you did."

Oh, the way he drawled.

"It wasn't my idea," she defended, which was only a half-lie. She'd certainly encouraged it.

He gave her a look.

She huffed. "Fine. It was slightly my idea."

A low chuckle. "Go on, then."

Daisy leaned back on her elbows, stretching her legs out. "We snuck in," she said, "because we'd heard there was a restricted book that detailed how to seduce a man with just a glance."

Dawson actually barked out a laugh.

"What? It seemed important at the time." She mock defended.

He was grinning now, full and wicked and absolutely devil charmed.

God help her.

"What happened?" he prompted.

"Well," she replied, "we did not get the book, but we did get caught."

"Of course you did."

"Luckily," she continued, "we had plausible deniability. I mean, who wouldn't believe four eager young ladies simply wished to further their education?"

Dawson was watching her like a man thoroughly enchanted. "Utter scoundrels, the lot of you."

She laughed. "And proud of it."

His eyes dipped down her body, languid and heated, and something in his gaze changed—not just desire, but something deeper. Something unfamiliar.

Daisy's chest seized.

That awful, knowing, wicked smile spread across his face.

And she actually forgot how to breathe. She needed to look away. Needed to rein herself in.

But all she could think about was how much she liked him looking at her like that.

Her pulse thumped wildly in her throat.

He leaned in slightly, his voice whiskey-rough and deliciously smug. "So tell me, poppet... have you mastered the art of seduction with just a glance?"

She narrowed her eyes.

Suddenly—a shriek. A wild call from beyond the stone walls that sent her skin crawling. "What the hell was that?" she said, glancing over her shoulder.

She looked back and saw Dawson go utterly still. His frown deepened, the muscle in his jaw flexing hard enough to crush stone. His whole body went rigid, shoulders coiled like a predator catching an unfamiliar scent on the wind.

Well, now. That was interesting.

Daisy cocked her head, fingers settling on her hips. "You look like you've just seen a ghost—oh, wait. That was nights ago at the inn."

No smirk. No cutting retort. He didn't even look at her. Instead, his head tilted slightly, the way a hound might when tracking prey.

The fine hairs at the back of her neck prickled. "Alright, you clearly know something. Spill it, Dawson."

He exhaled roughly, dragging a hand through his hair, making the already-mussed strands even more unfairly rakish. "Not sure," he muttered, his gaze distant. "Just... it sounds familiar. But not quite right."

A high, eerie keening echoed through the trees again.

"Not quite right how?"

Dawson shifted his weight, exhaling sharply through his nose. "I don't know. Can't quite place it."

Another call, this time closer.

She nudged his arm, forcing a bit of lightness into her tone. "Maybe it's just a really ugly fox."

His nostrils flared. "That's not a fox."

"Okay," she said, believing him.

She tore her gaze away from Dawson, which was unfairly difficult to do. Cruel, even.

Like a reward for her bravery, something caught her eye. Near the base of the stone bench against the wall, half-covered in overgrown grass and clover, was an etching, And not just some careless graffiti left by a bored gardener. A careful, deliberate carving too symmetrical to be random.

She stood and walked toward it, brushing dirt away with the side of her boot. Once she did, she saw clear as day a delicate engraving of a woman's profile.

It had to be the Duchess of Ashby Hollow.

Daisy's stomach jumped.

It was unmistakable—the sharp yet elegant curve of the nose, the regal tilt of the chin. It was not some idealized version, like a portrait. But a personal, intimate carving. Someone had done this with care.

Her heart thudded hard against her ribs.

A high, eerie cry from the trees made her glance back at Dawson.

He still hadn't moved. But something about him was... off. Not only the tension in his shoulders, or the set of his jaw, or the way his hand twitched at his side like he wanted to reach for something. It was deeper than that. Something in his bones.

Daisy exhaled, forcing her focus back to the bench.

This was something. And she had a feeling—one of those deep, instinctual gut-feelings that had never once led her wrong —that whatever she was looking was about to change everything.

She crouched down and ran her fingers over the grooves of the carving, heart thudding. It wasn't just a carving. It was a seam.

The faintest hairline split in the stone, so precise it nearly disappeared unless you looked for it.

She glanced up at Dawson, but he was still distracted, his whole body tight with tension. Fine. She'd just have to snap him out of it. "Oi, Lord Long-Legs—are you planning to keep staring into the void all day, or do you want to see something interesting?"

He shook his head, the haze in his dark green eyes clearing just slightly. Then stalked over, rubbing the back of his neck like she was the source of all his problems. "What could possibly be so—"

His words cut off because he saw it. The engraving. The faint seam—a small, near-invisible slot just beneath the duchess's carved throat.

"What is that?"

"Pretty sure it's a hidden compartment."

"You're sure?"

Daisy shot him a look. "No, I just enjoy sticking my fingers into questionable crevices for sport."

Dawson's mouth quirked—just slightly. Then he crouched down beside her.

Her pulse ticked up. Up close, Dawson smelled like warmth and worn leather and that impossible mix of wild and refined that made her stomach do stupid things.

Which was hardly the point right now.

She forced her focus back. Brushed away more dirt and pressed against the groove. It gave and a small section of stone shifted outward.

Not a drawer. Not a door. A box. A solid, rectangular stone box.

Hidden inside the bench.

Her heart slammed against her ribs. Suddenly this wasn't just a curious engraving of a duchess anymore.

This was intentional. It was planned. A message.

And she was fairly certain she knew exactly who had left it here. She swallowed hard and turned to Dawson. "Pull out the key."

His brows drew together. "What?"

She nodded toward his pocket. "The hairpin."

His fingers flexed at his side, instinctively going to his pocket before he even knew why. And that's when Daisy knew. Knew that this was real.

Really real.

Chapter Twenty-Nine

Dawson stared down at the stone box. Silent. Still.

It shouldn't have meant anything. Just another bit of trickery left behind by some long-dead aristocrat with too much time and money and not enough sense.

But it did mean something and he hated that he knew it.

His hand flexed near his hip. The key, his mother's hairpin, felt like a weight in his pocket. A thing he'd carried for so long it had become part of him.

A stupid, sentimental bit of metal. The only thing that ever been his.

His jaw ticked.

Daisy wasn't saying anything. She wasn't rushing him. Just watching. Waiting.

And he couldn't move.

Because he already knew what this was. Not the what—not the details. But the feeling. A deep, clawing certainty that whatever sat inside that box would change his life.

His pulse throbbed in his throat. His fingers twitched.

He reached into his pocket.

The hairpin was warm. Not just from his body heat, but from years of being kept close.

He turned it over in his fingers. Felt the tiny engraved letters with his thumb. Felt the shape of it, the shape he'd traced so many times in his life he could have carved it from memory.

A slow, sharp breath raked through his chest. Then—finally —he held it out.

Daisy's eyes flicked to his. Then to the key. Then back to him.

Dawson clenched his jaw and pressed it firmly into her palm. "Go on then, poppet." His voice came out rougher than he meant.

She turned to the box.

For once in his life, he didn't have a quip. Didn't have some dry remark. His throat was too damn tight.

Daisy, sensing his rare silence, was careful. She took the key with both hands, as if the small, battered thing deserved some kind of reverence.

And as she turned toward the hidden compartment, fitting the key into the tiny, near-invisible keyhole inside the carved-out space, he had to fight the sudden, gut-deep urge to snatch it back. Because if they opened this . . . if they saw what was inside . . .

It was real.

It wasn't some half-formed, unspoken dream. It wasn't a legend. It was his life. And that, more than anything, scared him senseless.

The lock gave a quiet click.

Daisy inhaled sharply.

His stomach dropped.

She reached in.

Dawson fisted his hands against his thighs, watching as she carefully lifted out a small wooden box. It was modest. Dark-stained wood, a bit of gold detailing worn at the edges. Just large enough to fit in both her hands. She looked at him, waiting.

He nodded once.

Daisy lifted the lid.

A folded letter lay inside. Yellowed. Unmistakably old. Beneath it, something smaller.

Her fingers trembled as she picked up the letter, the paper fragile with age.

Dawson couldn't move. His breath was lodged somewhere between his ribs. He could already see what lay beneath it. He knew what it was.

A locket.

Oval. Delicate. The kind of thing a lady would keep close to her heart.

Daisy lifted the letter, holding it with careful fingers.

He couldn't look away.

The paper shook slightly in Daisy's hands. Her eyes scanned the first few words. And then she went completely still. "Oh," she breathed. "Oh, Dawson."

He staggered back like he'd been gut-punched. Like the air had been ripped straight out of his lungs.

His chest locked.

His heart slammed hard once, twice.

Daisy lifted her head, her expression soft with something he couldn't face. "Dawson..." she whispered.

But he couldn't hear her. Not over the way his own blood roared in his ears. Or the feeling that his entire world had just flipped beneath him.

His hands shook, and he did not shake. Not when a blade was held to his throat. Not when he'd spent half his life surviving London's underbelly. Not even when Daisy had kissed him so thoroughly he'd forgotten how to breathe.

But this—this letter. His fingers trembled as he took and

unfolded it, the parchment delicate with age, the ink faded but legible.

A mother's hand.

He swallowed, something thick and painful in his throat as his gaze locked on the first words:

To my dearest son,

If you are reading this, then I am gone. And I am sorry, my darling. More sorry than words could ever say.

I never meant to leave you.

I never meant for any of this.

If there is anything I need you to know, it is this: I loved you. I loved you so wholly, so desperately, that I would have done anything—anything—to save you. And I tried. God help me, I tried.

Your father was not a kind man. You must have heard the whispers, the things people said about the Dukes of Ashby Hollow. Their cursed lineage, their doomed wives. But the truth is simpler, colder than that.

There is no curse. Only cruel men who never learned to love. Your father was one of them. And I—I was his prisoner. From the moment I took his name, my life was not my own. And when I fell pregnant with you, I knew—I knew—he would do to you what he had done to me.

Break you.

Beat you into something ruthless, something unrecognizable.

And I could not—would not—let that happen.

So I made a plan. I told him you had died in the days after your birth. And when he raged, when he locked himself away in his suites to nurse his broken ego, I took the chance. I gave you away, my love. To a man feared in the darkest corners of London.

A man whose hands were stained in blood, but whose word, I was told, was ironclad.

Mad Duggie Black.

It was supposed to be temporary. A few weeks, no more, until I came for you.

I had everything arranged. I would fake my own death, slip away in the night, and return for you. We would have a life. A better life.

But something went wrong. I didn't immediately make it back. And if you are reading this, then that means I never did.

I need you to know, my darling boy, that if there was any way I could have crawled from my grave to find you, I would have. I would have burned the world to hold you again.

But I was only a woman and I was not strong enough. So I leave you this—the truth. And my locket, because it was all I had left of my heart when I lost you.

You are not your father. You do not have to be the man he was. You are better. You are loved.

And you have always, always, been worth saving.

With all my love,

Your Mother

The paper blurred.

Dawson's breath came in short, sharp bursts. His chest was tight, too tight. He stared at the words, at the truth.

It shattered him.

This was everything. Everything he never let himself hope for. And everything he had spent his life pretending he didn't need.

Daisy was watching him. Gentle. Careful. Too careful. Like he might break. Like she knew, really knew, what this meant.

He reached into the wooden box, his fingers clenched

around the locket, the small weight of it pressing into his palm like a brand.

Proof.

That he had been loved.

That his mother had tried.

That he had never been unwanted.

Something inside Dawson cracked. A wound he hadn't even known he'd been carrying split wide open. And suddenly he couldn't breathe.

He stared at the letter, the words burning into his mind, branding him.

His mother had loved him. She had fought for him. She had died trying to save him.

And he had never known.

His whole bloody life, he had thought he was nothing. A throwaway. A mistake.

But he had mattered.

He had been worth saving.

His throat burned. His hands curled into fists around the parchment, like holding it tighter would keep it from slipping through his fingers, like everything else in his life. A sharp breath—too sharp.

Daisy moved closer. "Dawson," she murmured, so damn gentle, reaching for him like she thought he might crumble if she touched him.

He recoiled. Fast. Too fast. The letter crinkled in his grip as he paced away, heart pounding, head spinning, breath coming in ragged, uneven gasps.

It wasn't real.

It couldn't be real.

Because if it was—if every word of that letter was true—then everything he had ever known about himself was a lie. He wasn't just some nobody off the streets. Wasn't just Mad Duggie Black's bastard stray.

He was the lost son of a duchess—a woman who had fought with everything she had to save him. And she had died for it.

His heart slammed so hard he thought it might crack his ribs.

Daisy moved again. Just a fraction, but he felt it—felt her. Always too damn perceptive. Always knowing when he was on the edge of something unbearable. "Dawson," she whispered. "Talk to me."

His jaw locked so tight it hurt. Talk to her? About what? How his entire existence had been built on lies and loss and agony? How everything he thought he was—every piece of armor he had built, every survival instinct, every fight, every damn thing—had been for nothing?

Because he wasn't nobody.

He was somebody.

He was the fucking Duke of Ashby Hollow.

And his mother—his real mother—had loved him. Had tried to save him. Had undoubtedly been beaten to death for it.

His stomach lurched. A sick, twisting feeling clawed up his throat. He bent at the waist, bracing his hands on his knees, sucking in ragged gulps of air. It was too much.

Too much.

Too much.

A warm hand brushed his shoulder. Daisy. Always Daisy. Her touch was light, tentative, as if she were afraid he might shatter beneath it.

He shoved away. Hard. Like her touch burned.

Because it did.

If he let her touch him, if he let her in right now—he would break.

He straightened, forcing his breathing to steady, but his

chest still heaved, his vision still swam, his hands still trembled with too much, too fast, too real.

Daisy's eyes—God, her eyes. Big, searching, full of something raw.

He had to get out.

Now.

Before she saw the truth. Before she saw just how close he was to losing it. "I need to go," he rasped.

Daisy stiffened. "Go where?"

He didn't know. Didn't care. Just away. He turned, already moving, his boots crunching over the overgrown path.

"Dawson—wait." She grabbed his arm.

And *fuck, fuck, fuck.*

He shouldn't have stopped. Shouldn't have let her touch him. Because the second her fingers curled around his wrist, something snapped.

He wrenched free, turning on her too fast, too hard, too furious. "You don't get it, Daisy." His voice was low, rough, shaking with something ugly. "You don't know what it's like to wake up one day and realize you've been living in a lie your whole damn life."

Daisy's mouth parted.

He didn't let her speak. Didn't give her the chance to say something kind, or soft, or fucking understanding.

Because he couldn't take that right now. Couldn't take her. Couldn't take the way she was looking at him.

Like she saw him.

Like she felt every bit of his breaking apart.

He exhaled sharply, shaking his head. "This was a mistake."

Daisy flinched.

But he couldn't stop, not with the storm raging inside him, ripping him apart, piece by piece. "I never should've come here," he growled. "And I sure as hell never should've let myself—"

He cut himself off.

Too close.

Too much.

Daisy's throat worked on a swallow. "Let yourself what?" she whispered.

Feel. Want. *Love.*

He ripped his gaze away. Didn't answer. Couldn't. Not when it felt like his whole chest was being torn open, bleeding out everything he'd tried so hard to keep locked away.

Daisy's voice wavered. "Dawson, don't do this."

But he already had. Because if he didn't leave now, he never would. And she deserved better than a man like him. A man who was too angry, too broken, too much of a damn coward to face what was in front of him.

He turned, walked away.

Daisy's voice chased after him, shaking, hurting. "Dawson."

He didn't stop.

Didn't look back.

Didn't let himself feel the way his name sounded on her lips —like she wanted to chase him, like she wanted to fight for him, like she cared too damn much.

Dawson walked away.

Leaving Daisy, and everything he'd ever wanted, behind.

Chapter Thirty

The tavern was loud. Too loud.

Men shouting over their drinks, chairs scraping against sticky floors, the sharp clatter of dice rolling on wood. A woman with a voice like broken glass was belting out some tragic ballad about a lover lost at sea.

Dawson barely heard any of it.

He just sat there, slouched in the corner, his chair tipped back against the wall, an untouched tankard of ale in front of him. Whiskey was the only thing that burned enough to make him feel something. And even that wasn't working.

His bones ached. His chest felt like it had been caved in with a sledgehammer. With her sharp tongue and wicked grin, Daisy had broken him. Daisy with her warm, steady hands, her relentless determination, her impossible, inconvenient ability to see right through him.

Daisy, who had never needed him, only chased him.

And he had let himself believe, just for a moment, that maybe... maybe she was chasing him for more than the bloody title. God, what a fool. He should have known better. He did know better. And still, he'd wanted. Still, he'd hoped.

Fucking stupid.

She really was an heir hunter. And she really had been hunting him.

For his title.

Half-drunk already and working on the rest, Dawson held the whiskey glass loose in his fingers. The bottle sat heavy beside it, half-gone. Not enough. Would never be enough.

He took another slow sip, the burn sliding down his throat, pooling warm and deep. Whiskey. Sweetened with honey.

Just like that night. That damned night.

The first night he met her, when she had smelled of smoke and wildflowers and that sweet liquor she'd been hoarding in her pocket. When she had knocked him clean on his arse. Not just from the force of her body hitting his—but from her. From that sharp tongue and those dark, laughing eyes and the way she had tossed him in a carriage and run off with him.

He had known, right then. Not what she was to him. Not what she would become. But that she was trouble. The kind of trouble that got under a man's skin. The kind that tangled in his veins and refused to let go. The kind that could make him believe in things he had no business believing in.

Like home.

Like hope.

Like *love*.

Dawson let out a slow, bitter breath, tilting the glass in his hand, watching the golden liquid swirl. He could still see her. Standing in the sunlight, arms thrown wide, spinning in that wrinkled dress, laughing like she belonged there, like she belonged to him.

All of this could be yours.

She had meant the estate. But fuck him—he had wanted her. More than anything he had ever wanted in his life. And that was exactly why he had left.

Jennifer Seasons

Because Daisy Bramble wasn't for keeping. Not for the likes of him. Even if she had been, he couldn't give her what she needed. She wanted a duke. She wanted that finder's fee, wanted to rebuild her orphanage, wanted to take care of all the girls like her who had nothing and no one. Dawson could never take that from her, even if it destroyed him.

He drained the glass in one long swallow and reached for the bottle.

"Well, well." A voice, low and rough behind him.

Dawson went still. The hairs on the back of his neck rose. Jacko. And company.

"Here we were, tracking you all the way up to this miserable little nowhere, and you just walk right into our laps. Isn't that convenient?"

Dawson closed his eyes briefly. Let the glass clink back to the table. Then, slow as syrup he turned his head.

Jacko grinned, teeth flashing, Merritt at his side. Two more men hovered just behind them.

Perfect.

He should have known the bastards wouldn't give up. But for the first time in his life, he didn't give a damn about them. Because all he could think about was Daisy.

Jacko leaned his arms on the back of a chair, all easy-like, grinning that stupid, cocky grin. "Didn't think we'd find you, did you, mate?"

"Duggie ain't happy. You know 'ow he gets when 'e ain't happy." Merritt cracked his knuckles, looking less amused."

Dawson gave a slow, sharp exhale, rolling his glass between his fingers. "Oh, I don't know. I'd wager he's a right ray of bloody sunshine."

Jacko chuckled. "Oh, yeah. A feckin' delight, 'e is. Real chuffed about his foster son running off an' pretending 'e don't exist. Not even a bloody note, mate. Duggie's sentimental, you know that."

Dawson snorted. "Sentimental? You mean possessive. Man doesn't give a damn about me—just his pride."

Merritt frowned, eyes dark. "You're talking about the man who raised you."

Dawson's jaw ticked. "Aye. I am."

Silence.

Jacko whistled low. "Feck me, you really are different. Used to be, you'd've taken that as a compliment."

Dawson took another sip of whiskey. "Used to be, I didn't know any better."

That got him a look.

Merritt tilted his head. "So that's it, then? You're just done wi' us?"

Dawson didn't answer right away. Didn't know how to. Because was he? Was he done with the only family he'd ever known? Because they were his family. Duggie had been a bastard, but he'd kept him alive. Jacko, Merritt, the lot of them—they'd watched his back since before he could throw a punch.

And now he was about to stand here and tell them that some woman had unraveled all of that in a matter of weeks?

That one stubborn, infuriating, clever, beautiful woman had undone everything? That he'd rather rot than go back to the life he'd lived before her?

Jacko's grin had gone sharp. "Ahh. I see it now." He flicked his gaze toward the empty glass in Dawson's hand. "This ain' just any old misery drinkin', is it?"

His teeth clenched.

Merritt leaned in. "A woman, then?"

He didn't answer.

Jacko let out a bark of laughter. "Holy hell. It is." He

clapped a hand to his heart. "Dawson 'I don' need anyone' Woodbridge go' 'imself proper fecked by some bird."

His nostrils flared. His grip on the glass went tight.

Jacko wasn't done. "Who is she then, mate? A duchess? No —wait. Tha's the job, innit? You're playin' some game, runnin' from your real life ta play tickle wi' some cunt in a dress?"

Dawson stood.

Slow.

Deadly.

Jacko's grin didn't falter. "Oh, hit a nerve, did I? Must be some prize quim."

He rolled his shoulders, tilting his head side to side with a crack. "You've always had a way with words, Jacko."

"Some things never change, aye?"

Dawson's smile was sharp as a knife. "Oh, some things change." And then he punched him.

Hard.

Jacko's head snapped back, blood spraying from his nose as he staggered, eyes wide with pure, shocked delight.

Merritt swore. "For feck's sake—"

Dawson turned just as Merritt swung. He dodged. Just barely. The bastard was quick. They were all quick. Because they'd grown up in the same fucking gutters.

A second later, the entire tavern exploded into chaos.

Fists flying.

Chairs toppling.

Mugs shattering against walls.

Dawson was in the thick of it, gritting his teeth, fighting with everything he had. And for the first time in his life, he wanted out. He didn't want this. Didn't want these men, didn't want this life, didn't want the bloody cycle of it all.

He wanted her.

Daisy.

Fuck.

Another punch landed. Dawson barely felt it because something in his chest had cracked wide open. And it wasn't the impact of the fist. It was her.

Her smile.

Her eyes.

Her voice, sharp and teasing, calling him out, calling him forward. Calling him *home*.

He needed to go back to her. He needed to fix this. He needed to do the one thing he had never done for anyone in his entire life.

He needed to choose someone else over himself.

Daisy was so fucking worth it.

He shoved Merritt off him. Wiped his mouth. Stepped back.

Merritt was panting, wiping blood from his lip. "You done?"

Dawson nodded once. "Yeah."

Jacko groaned from the floor, grinning through bloodied teeth. "Feck me, mate. You're worse than ever."

"Tell Duggie I'll see him soon."

"Not before you see her first, aye?" Jacko chuckled, wiping his nose.

Dawson turned for the door and didn't even try to deny it.

His ribs ached. His knuckles throbbed. His lip was split, whiskey-stung, and fuck if he didn't deserve every bit of it.

But none of it—none of it—compared to the wreckage inside his chest.

It wasn't just his body that hurt.

It was her.

It was the loss of her.

And the stupid fucking truth of it? He'd done it to himself.

Dawson rolled his shoulders as he stepped over the splintered remains of a chair and made for the door.

"Oi, Dawson," Jacko called from the floor, grinning through bloody teeth. "You actually love this bird, don' you?"

Dawson didn't stop. Didn't turn. Didn't want to admit it.

But he wasn't a liar.

Not about this.

"Yeah," he said, voice rough, jaw tight. "I do."

And fuck if saying it out loud didn't make his chest squeeze so hard he could barely breathe.

He'd never done this before. Never wanted someone enough to say it. Never needed someone enough to fight for it.

Daisy deserved that fight.

Duggie could fucking wait.

Dawson had a woman to get back. A woman to beg forgiveness from. A woman to give his whole damn self to—if she'd have him.

He grabbed his horse from the stables. Tightening his grip on Blossom's reins, he swung into the saddle, and kicked off down the road.

Toward Ashby Hollow.

Toward Daisy.

Toward *everything*.

Chapter Thirty-One

Daisy crossed her arms as she stood in the garden and eyed the two tiny, masked hooligans who had just trotted straight out of a bush like they owned the place. They stopped a few feet away, fluffy tails curling over their round little bodies, black eyes locked onto her with an entirely too much awareness for a pair of small, woodland creatures.

"Well," she muttered, still seething from everything she absolutely was not thinking about—which meant she was definitely thinking about it. "I don't suppose either of you happen to be knowledgeable in the field of heartbreak, male idiocy, or general betrayal?"

Silence. The little beasts blinked.

Daisy huffed. "Didn't think so."

The morning was too beautiful for how utterly foul her mood was.

Sunlight slanted through the trees, warm and gilded. A gentle breeze rustled through the overgrown garden, sending sweet, earthy scents drifting through the air. Flowers bloomed riotously in untamed patches—roses, honeysuckle, wild lavender—and if she hadn't been actively suffering the most infuriating morning of her life, she might have actually enjoyed it.

As it was?

She was pissed off.

So, naturally, she directed all of that anger at the only living creatures in sight. "Let's get one thing straight," she told the two little masked interlopers. "I am not heartbroken. I am simply peeved. Livid. Aggrieved, if you will."

More blinking.

She scowled. "I was not stupid enough to fall for a man I was hunting for a bounty, that would be preposterous. What kind of reckless, softhearted fool does that?"

One of them tilted its head.

Daisy pointed at it. "Don't give me that look."

It gave her that look harder.

"Oh, this is absurd," she muttered, dragging a hand through her unbound hair.

They were watching her like they understood her. Not like regular animals. Not even like the smart ones, the ones that could be trained.

No.

These creatures—whatever the hell they were—were fully focused, fully aware, fully judging her. And honestly, she was too tired to deal with being critiqued by wildlife this morning. So, she dropped onto a flat, sun-warmed stone bench, ignoring the way the folds of her dress pooled around her legs.

She hadn't exactly planned on going full woodland sprite, but here she was.

And the little beasts? Oh, they were sitting down now, too. Like they were settling in to hear the full extent of her grievances. Which was deeply concerning. But also? Fine. If they wanted to listen? They were going to listen.

She leaned forward, leveling them with a hard stare. "Would you like to know what my first mistake was?"

More blinking.

Daisy huffed a humorless laugh. "I trusted him."

The words felt foreign on her tongue. Uncomfortable. Because she didn't do that. She didn't trust people. Not fully. Not easily. Not after everything she and her sisters had been through.

And yet, she had trusted Dawson. Trusted him enough to let him in. To let herself fall.

And he had left. He had ridden away into the night without looking back.

Without her.

Her stomach twisted, but she ignored it. She'd been foolish. That was all. She'd fix it. She always did. "Falling for him was not part of the plan," she muttered, mostly to herself.

One of the little creatures twitched its tail. The other yawned, clearly unimpressed with her crisis.

"Oh, well I apologize for not being more entertaining for you." Daisy scowled.

More blinking.

Unbelievable.

She exhaled slowly, rolling her shoulders, trying to ease the tension in them. "Anyway," she said, her tone lighter now, almost playful, "what exactly are you two supposed to be, then? I've never seen creatures like you before."

They blinked again. One of them tilted its head in the opposite direction, like it was waiting for her to figure it out.

Daisy squinted her eyes. "You're not... raccoons, are you?"

No reaction.

"...But you look a bit like them."

Silence.

She sighed, eyeing their plump, round bodies, their masked faces, their little black noses. They were... similar to raccoons, but not quite right. Their legs were shorter. Their bodies were more compact.

And their eyes were sharp.

Too sharp.

Almost... knowing.

Her stomach turned. Because if she didn't know any better, she'd say they were truly listening.

A sound cut through the morning stillness. Low. Eerie. Rising into a shrill, bone-chilling wail.

Daisy's heart leapt into her throat.

The little creatures perked up immediately. They turned toward the sound. Toward the trees beyond the garden, toward something unseen, something waiting.

She went very, very still. Because that sound was the sound from yesterday. And that was the sound people whispered about.

That was the sound that spawned the legend of the Banshee of Ashby Hollow.

Another wail. Closer.

All the little creatures stood up. They looked toward the trees. The eerie wail still hung in the air, shivering through her bones.

She did not move.

Did not breathe.

She was about to be banshee-murdered in a garden full of flowers and judgmental little beasts, and honestly? It was exactly the kind of poetic injustice the universe would serve her right now.

But then . . . footsteps. Slow. Steady. Solid. And not from the trees.

From behind her.

She whipped around, her heart in her throat, fists clenched, ready to punch a ghost if necessary.

Dawson.

Standing at the edge of the garden. Ruffled, road-worn, shadow-jawed. So bloody beautiful she could have screamed.

And she very nearly did scream. Not from fear. Not from shock. But from the absolute, searing onslaught of emotion that seeing him again brought crashing over her. Because he left. And now he was back. And she had no idea what the hell to do with that.

Her breath shook. Her heart clenched. And then her fury kicked in.

He opened his mouth, but Daisy beat him to it.

"Are you actually kidding me right now?" she demanded, voice sharp.

Dawson stopped dead.

She advanced. "You left, you bastard."

He flinched.

"You left," she repeated, voice thick with something dangerously close to hurt, but she barreled past it, charging straight into anger instead. "And now you just stride in here like . . . like," she gestured wildly, "like you didn't just rip my heart out and stomp all over it?"

He raked a hand through his hair. "Daisy."

"No." She held up a hand. "You do not get to 'Daisy' me right now."

"Poppet." A muscle jumped in his jaw.

Her eyes blazed. "Oh, you can shove that right up your—"

"I'm sorry."

She stumbled to a halt. Her mouth snapped shut. "Wha—?"

297

"I'm sorry."

He said it.

And he meant it.

Dawson 'Cocky, Smug, I-Don't-Apologize' Woodbridge just apologized. And he looked wrecked over it.

Daisy swallowed hard, heart still racing, still screaming, still not sure whether to forgive him or punch him straight in his stupid, beautiful face.

He took another step closer. "I mean it," he murmured, voice gravelly, quiet, low.

She hated how much she felt it. Hated how much she wanted to just throw herself at him and bury herself in him and pretend none of it had ever happened. But it had happened.

And she deserved more than pretty words.

"What exactly are you sorry for?" She lifted her chin, eyes still blazing.

He exhaled sharply. His gaze dropped. For the first time, he looked like a man stripped bare. "I was a coward," he admitted.

Daisy's heart stopped.

He lifted his gaze back to hers, green eyes raw. "I let the past swallow me whole. I let it dictate my future. I let fear make my choices." He shook his head, voice gutted, gravel rough. "And worst of all, I left the best thing that's ever happened to me standing in a garden all alone."

Her heart squeezed so hard she actually felt a little faint. Because . . . because he meant it. Every single word. She could see the truth in his eyes.

She stared at him, pulse stuttering, trying to breathe past the tidal wave of emotion crushing her chest. She should say something. Should make him grovel harder. Should tell him she wasn't just going to roll over and forgive him because he looked at her like she was his whole world.

A tiny, high-pitched chittering noise broke the silence.

Daisy nearly died.

The two little raccoon-dog things were still watching. Watching her. Watching him. Watching the sheer bloody emotional carnage of the moment like it was a riveting bit of street theater.

And when she looked back at Dawson, he was staring at them like they had just slapped him across the face.

She frowned. "What?"

He took a step back, his face draining of color. He shook his head once. Swallowed hard.

Very quietly, very hoarsely, very much like a man having the single worst revelation of his entire life, he swore, "Bloody hell."

Daisy narrowed her eyes. He was staring at the tiny, strange little creatures, their masked faces and bushy, not-quite-raccoon-not-quite-dog tails twitching as they peered back at him with an uncanny sort of knowing. He looked as though someone had just walloped him upside the head with a frying pan.

"What," she said, hands on her hips, "exactly are you staring at?"

Nothing.

No response.

Dawson just kept looking at the little furballs like they were ghosts from his past come to haunt him personally.

Daisy huffed. "Oh, come on. You've got to be joking. You disappear, you storm off in a fit of male self-destruction, you leave me to fester in my own fury and heartbreak, and now you show up again and you're just going to ignore me in favor of those . . . those . . . those beasts?" She threw out an arm toward the furry little creatures, who were watching all of this unfold with great interest.

Still, Dawson said nothing.

Daisy made an exasperated sound and planted herself right in front of him, blocking his view. "You left."

His gaze snapped to hers.

Oh. *Oh.*

That was guilt in his eyes. That was something raw and regretful and so full of unspoken things it nearly stole her breath. And still, he had the audacity to stay silent.

Her chin lifted. "I'm going to let you try that one more time, Dawson Woodbridge, because I am nothing if not a gracious woman. You. Left."

His throat worked. His hands flexed. His glorious, unfairly perfect chest rose and fell on a deep, unsteady breath. "Yeah," he said roughly. "I did."

Daisy's fingers curled into the skirts of her dress, digging in, because hearing him say it out loud hurt in ways she hadn't expected. But she wouldn't let him see that. Not yet.

Instead, she forced herself to glance down at the furballs. "And now you're back. Because of why?"

Dawson's gaze flickered. He hesitated. Then, he did something she absolutely was not prepared for. He reached out, curled his big, calloused fingers around her waist, and pulled her flush against him.

She sucked in a sharp breath, but before she could say a single thing, before she could remind him she was supposed to be mad at him, Dawson crushed his mouth to hers in a kiss that stole her breath. That made her heart slam into her ribs, made her fingers curl against his chest, made every ounce of her resistance flicker and falter and finally, finally crumble.

When he broke away, his forehead pressed to hers, his breath uneven and full of everything they weren't saying, he finally whispered, "I came back for you."

Daisy's heart thumped painfully in her chest. No. No. She was not going to just let herself melt like some ridiculous, besotted fool.

Except... she was already melting.

Dripping, more like.

His forehead was still pressed to hers, his breath warm against her lips, and he smelled like whiskey and regret and the damn woods, and she was fighting a losing battle.

But she could at least make him sweat for it.

She swallowed, tilted her chin just enough to meet his gaze, and—because she had not spent her entire life being independent and stubborn just to fall apart over one very well-placed kiss—she said, very primly, "Well, I suppose that's a decent start."

Dawson huffed a soft laugh, but he didn't let her go. His hands stayed firm at her waist, his fingers flexing, like he wasn't quite ready to lose contact.

And... she wasn't, either.

Damn him.

Damn him and his rough hands and low voice and the way he made her feel like she was the only thing in the world worth looking at.

She was not finished making him work for this.

So, she exhaled sharply, pulled back just enough to glance toward the little masked creatures still watching them, and arched a brow. "And what about them? Did you come back for them too? Whatever they are."

Dawson's fingers tightened at her waist. A muscle in his jaw ticked. And then—a slow realization seemed to dawn in his expression.

She saw it happen in real time. The flicker of memory, the narrowing of his gaze, the way his fingers twitched like something had just slotted into place.

"Oh, bloody hell," she murmured. "You do know what they are."

Dawson inhaled deeply. Then, finally—reluctantly—he nodded.

She crossed her arms, ignoring the way she still felt his touch like a ghost at her waist. "Alright then. What are they?"

He glanced back at the little creatures, his expression unreadable. With all the weight of something he'd only just begun to understand himself, he said, "Raccoon dogs."

Daisy blinked. "Raccoon what?"

His mouth twitched, but it wasn't quite a smile. "Raccoon dogs," he said again, voice rough and a little stunned. "That's what they're called, I think. At least, that's what Duggie always called his."

His.

Her stomach flipped. She looked at the little creatures, really looked at them, and something clicked in her mind. "Duggie had one?"

Dawson exhaled roughly. "Not just one." He dragged a hand through his hair, still staring at the damn things like they'd personally rearranged his entire life. "He's got the last descendent of a breeding pair. Had them since I was a boy."

"And you think..." She trailed off, a slow, creeping realization forming in her chest.

Dawson nodded once, grimly. "Yeah, poppet. I do."

Daisy blinked rapidly, processing. Somehow, they were connected. All of it was. She tilted her head, eyes flicking between Dawson, who looked like he'd been hit by a runaway carriage, and the strange little creatures still watching them with bright, knowing eyes.

"Alright," she said, breaking the silence. "You're going to have to explain. And preferably in words I don't have to decode."

Dawson inhaled sharply, dragging a hand through his hair, eyes locked on the beasts like they might sprout wings and fly off at any second. "Duggie had a pair," he said, voice flat. "When I was a kid. Grew up with the damn things."

She lifted a brow. "And you never asked what they were?"

He shook his head, eyes distant. "Didn't need to. They were Duggie's."

Her lips twitched, though it wasn't funny. "So, what? He just collected odd little creatures the way the gentry collect paintings?"

"No. Just them." Dawson let out a short, humorless breath, and his jaw tightened. "He was proud of them. Real proud."

"Why?"

He finally looked at her, something unreadable in his eyes. "Because they were rare," he said quietly. "A bloody status symbol. Duggie made sure everyone knew it. He paraded them through the East End. First the pair he had when I was a kid. Then—" He exhaled sharply. "Then Tanuki."

Daisy blinked. "Ta-what?"

"Tanuki. That's what he called the last one. His favorite. The only one left now." His lips pressed into a thin line. "He put a collar on him. A fucking jeweled necklace."

Daisy's stomach twisted.

"Oh," she said slowly.

Dawson glanced at her, brows pulling tight. "What?"

Daisy's mind worked quickly—pieces slotting into place, clicking together so seamlessly she couldn't believe she hadn't seen it sooner.

The duchess.

Duggie.

The bloody necklace.

The status symbol.

Her breath hitched.

"Dawson," she said, voice low, steady. "That collar . . ." She licked her lips. "Where did it come from?"

He stilled.

And Daisy saw it, the exact moment he realized. The way

303

his throat worked, the way his eyes darkened, the way his fists curled . . . Dawson knew. All the pieces fit. His mother had given Duggie the creatures. And his mother had given him the necklace that he used as a collar.

Further proof that his mother had made a deal with the devil to save her son's life.

Daisy watched every flicker of realization as it rippled through him, waiting for the explosion—the snarled curse, the fury, the gritted-teeth reckoning she was sure was coming.

Instead, Dawson grinned. That slow, wolfish, utterly rogue, too-damn-charming-for-his-own-good grin that should not be allowed under the laws of nature, physics, or general fairness.

"Oh, no," she said flatly. "What is that look?"

He tilted his head, all lazy-wicked amusement, green eyes glittering. "That," he drawled, "is the look of a man with a bloody brilliant plan."

"And am I going to like this plan?" Daisy crossed her arms, eyed him hard.

He tapped a thoughtful finger to his chin. "Not sure."

"Dawson."

He exhaled, dropping to a garden bench and draping an arm over the back, looking for all the world like a man without a single problem. Like he hadn't just unraveled his entire past and put it back together again with the kind of revelation that could send lesser men spiraling into the abyss.

He pulled her in. God, he smelled good. Too good.

"We're going to steal Mad Duggie's pet, Tanuki."

Daisy stared. "I'm sorry, we're going to what?"

Dawson's grin deepened, and she could feel herself toppling further into whatever this was between them.

"We," he said slowly, deliberately, maddeningly, "are going to steal Tanuki."

"We?" she repeated, half-sputtering, half-panicking,

because dear God, her heart was fluttering. "What do you mean 'WE'?"

He just kept smiling, kept looking at her like she was the most fascinating thing he'd ever laid eyes on.

And Daisy felt it happen.

That last, final, irreversible slip of her stupid, reckless heart.

Chapter Thirty-Two

"You're enjoying this way too much."

Dawson didn't even have the good sense to look guilty. If anything, his expression turned positively wicked. "Course I am. Can't recall a better way to spend an afternoon."

Daisy scowled, crossing her arms tight over her chest, only for him to reach out and uncross them, sliding his hands over her shoulders with an infuriating gentleness.

"None of that now, poppet." His voice dipped into something low and knowing, the kind of teasing purr that always set her teeth on edge. "You need to look inviting."

"I don't need to look anything." Her scoff was immediate.

"Oh, but you do." He smoothed his thumbs along the curve of her shoulders, his hands featherlight as he adjusted her. Like she was some damn shop display.

And then . . . he gripped her sleeves and tore them clean off.

Daisy gasped. "Dawson Woodbridge, I will murder you!"

"Will you?" He flicked the scraps of fabric away without a second thought, his green eyes full of laughter, but also something else—something darker, heavier, brimming with a satisfaction she absolutely should not be enjoying.

He was looking at her. Not just at her arms. Not just at her dress. At *her*.

Like he'd had her beneath him in that tower room and he would very much like to have her there again.

She swallowed hard, suddenly very aware of how close they were standing in this tucked-away little park on the edge of the East End of London.

Dawson made a thoughtful sound, then reached for the already battered neckline of her dress.

She smacked his hand away. "Absolutely not."

His grin only widened. "Can't have you looking too proper," he said, that roguish smirk deepening as he skimmed his fingers under her chin. "Not when you're supposed to be luring them in, love."

"I hate you."

"You love me."

Daisy sputtered.

He laughed. And then he squeezed his own chest together with both hands, dramatically mimicking cleavage. "Show them all your bits, sweetheart."

"Oh my God."

Dawson was enjoying himself entirely too much. And for one wild moment, Daisy entertained the idea of just shoving him straight into the nearest horse trough.

But instead, she squared her shoulders, gathered her composure like armor, and gave him the sultriest, slowest, most deliberately wicked smirk she could manage.

His grin faltered.

She leaned in close, just enough to let her lips graze his ear. "You mean the bits you spent hours worshiping?"

His grin vanished.

His hands clenched into fists.

She felt the sharp inhale of his breath against her skin, the way his chest locked tight, how his entire body coiled like a trap just waiting to spring. Then she stepped back, smiling sweetly. "There. That should settle you."

Dawson stared at her. Scrubbed a hand down his face, muttering something under his breath. "Christ, poppet." He dragged his palm over his mouth before flicking his gaze back to her, a new kind of heat in his eyes. "You're going to kill me."

Daisy just beamed. "Good. Now, shall we?"

They moved out of the park, slipping into the side streets near Mad Duggie's compound.

Daisy's pulse was thrumming. She was too aware of Dawson's heat beside her, of the fact that this was absolutely the worst idea either of them had ever had.

But it was going to work. Because Dawson knew what he was doing. And because apparently Duggie was utterly obsessed with his pet, Tanuki.

If they pulled this off, they'd have the only leverage strong enough to force the most dangerous man in London into a deal.

She'd always liked impossible odds.

Daisy had walked the streets of London more times than she could count. She'd prowled the back alleys, slipped through the markets, ghosted through the worst parts of town with nothing but her wits and her sharp tongue to keep her safe. But never, not once, had she walked them like this. With Dawson bloody Woodbridge beside her. With his rolling, confident stride, his loose-limbed ease, his damnable swagger that belonged here, in the way only a man raised in the streets of London ever could.

It wasn't an act. He was East End born and bred, right down to the way he tilted his chin up ever so slightly at the men who eyed him, as if to say *Try me, mate. I dare you.*

They looked away. Because Dawson Woodbridge had a

reputation here. He wasn't just anyone. He was Mad Duggie Black's protege, whether he wanted to be or not. And that unsettled her.

Daisy kept her gaze moving, tracking the sights and sounds of the East End as they slipped deeper into the warren of streets leading to Mad Duggie's compound. Barkers called out in thick accents, pushing their wares. Fishmongers sloshed buckets of water over stone streets, gutting the day's catch. Children weaved through the crowds, hands quick and eager in unsuspecting pockets.

She knew these streets. Had walked them a hundred times over. Had lived among them once, long before Bramble Estate Investigations, long before her name carried any weight. She knew how to keep her coin tucked close, how to hold herself just dangerous enough that she wouldn't be picked as an easy mark.

But she also knew that none of that mattered with Dawson beside her. The moment they stepped into the real heart of the East End, the part ruled by Mad Duggie Black's men, all eyes had landed on him.

He didn't acknowledge it. Didn't turn his head. Didn't let his shoulders tense or his step falter. But Daisy felt it. The way the air tightened, the way the city seemed to bend around him, the way people moved aside without thinking.

Dawson hadn't belonged anywhere in this world for a long time.

But here? He wasn't forgotten. And that, more than anything, made her heart tighten.

She swallowed, pushing past it, keeping her gaze moving as they turned down a narrow, twisting lane lined with aging brick buildings. Somewhere ahead of them, just beyond the next turn, lay Mad Duggie's compound. They were close.

"What's the actual plan, then?" Daisy adjusted the already battered neckline of her dress, shooting Dawson a look.

He grinned. That slow, wicked, all-teeth grin that spelled trouble in the very best and worst ways. "Oh, you're going to love it, poppet."

She sighed.

She already hated it.

And she should have known. Should have known that the plan he cooked up would be the most ridiculous, infuriating, and impossibly reckless thing she'd ever been roped into. And she'd grown up with Violet.

She crossed her arms and stared at him. "Let me get this straight. You really weren't joking when you tore my dress back in the park? You weren't just being an arse with your . . ." she gestured a vague, sad attempt at a shimmy.

Dawson, standing beside her in the shadows of the narrow, grimy alleyway in the East End, grinned. That lazy, wicked, far-too-pleased-with-himself grin. "Nope."

Daisy resisted the urge to punch him.

"You want me," she said, voice flat, "to distract the guards—"

"Mm." He interrupted, nodding. "That's right."

"—by using my body."

"Your very lovely, divine body, yes."

Daisy shut her eyes. Breathed in. Breathed out. *Don't murder him in public.*

She snapped them back open. "So, let me guess. You'll be doing all the hard work while I just stand there being ogled?"

He placed a hand to his heart as if she'd wounded him. "Poppet, you wound me. This is hard work. Very vital work. You must be absolutely alluring. Mesmerizing, even."

"Oh, I'll mesmerize them, alright," she muttered, hands flexing like she was already picturing wrapping them around his thick, smug throat.

Dawson tsked, stepping closer into her space. "You're not getting into it. You need to sell it. Here—"

His hands shot straight for her dress.

"Dawson!" she yelped. "What in the devil—"

A tug at the bodice. A swift, shocking dip.

"You absolute cad!" Daisy swatted at him and stabbed a finger at his chest. "Do that again and I will kill you."

He just grinned harder.

God, she hated him. (Except, no. That was the problem, wasn't it? She didn't.)

She huffed. "Fine. If we're going to do this, I might as well look the part."

Dawson's brows lifted with deep, obvious appreciation as his gaze roamed her body.

The bastard.

"Stunning," he murmured. "Truly. I may have to fight the guards off myself."

Daisy rolled her eyes and turned away before he saw the heat rising in her cheeks. "Come on, then, Your Grace. Let's go steal a raccoon dog."

Chapter Thirty-Three

Dawson was having a grand old time. Truly. A riotous time. Daisy, for all her brilliance and sharp wit, was not a born femme fatale.

She was good at a lot of things. Incredible, even.

But seduction as a strategy?

No.

And watching her attempt it was possibly the greatest entertainment of his life. He smothered a grin as she huffed under her breath, yanking at the low neckline of her dress—which he had adjusted himself, thank you very much, much to her annoyance.

She tugged her skirts higher, flashing just enough ankle to make a nun faint and a rogue smile, before glaring at him. "If one of them touches me," she muttered, "I'm going to stab you first."

He folded his arms across his chest. "Now, poppet, if you're going to show them all your bits, you have to commit."

Daisy hissed his name in warning, smacking his arm. "Don't make me punch you! This is your ridiculous idea!"

He nudged her toward the compound. "Go on, then. Bat your lashes, swish those hips . . ."

She turned, rolling her eyes so hard she probably saw yesterday, and sauntered toward the gate.

At first, it was hilarious. Daisy, in all her fake coquetry, playing up the helpless-woman-lost act to the three thugs guarding Mad Duggie's entrance.

Dawson took that as his cue to slink into the shadows, scanning for his opening. He had one job: Slip in. Grab Tanuki. Get out. Simple.

Only, it wasn't.

Because her act stopped being funny.

He was about to slip away when she tilted her head just so, lips parting in an entirely too familiar way. One that made him ache.

One of the guards leaned in toward her, murmuring something with a smirk.

Dawson's jaw clenched so hard it nearly shattered.

Another of Duggie's guards swept his gaze down Daisy's body, too slow, too hungry.

Dawson's vision went hazy. He stopped moving. His breath came short. His fingers curled into fists at his sides.

What had been amusing to watch was now intolerable.

His breath ran hot through his nose. His muscles locked tight. He needed to go. Needed to get inside. He needed to not stride over there and snap the necks of three poor bastards who didn't know better than to ogle what belonged to him.

Because Daisy did belong to him. He knew it now, with a kind of savage, possessive certainty that should probably terrify him. But it didn't. What terrified him was the fact that he'd left her. That she could have left him. That he could have lost her.

Dawson swallowed hard, forcing himself to look away—to

keep his focus on the job. Tanuki. The bloody furred menace was the reason they were here.

Not his jealousy. Not his unholy need to stake a claim on Daisy so thorough that no man would ever dare look at her like that again.

Then one of the guards reached out to her. A fingertip, just the lightest touch, barely grazing the fabric of Daisy's sleeve.

It was nothing.

Dawson saw fury.

NO. The thought cracked through him like a whip. No one touched her. Because she was his.

And they were about to fucking learn it.

Dawson moved. Fast. Too fast. His fingers twitched for the blade at his belt, for the rage at the back of his throat.

But then . . .

The little hellion saved her own arse. She whipped her arm back, slapping the guard's hand away with a sharp gasp, her brown eyes going wide and scandalized. "Oh, sir!" she exclaimed, her voice so saccharine and sweetly offended, Dawson almost believed it.

The guard stammered, hands lifting in an *oh-shite-I-didn't-mean-to-get-slapped* panic.

Daisy turned her big doe eyes on the other two men. "Did you see that?" she gasped, pressing a hand to her chest, making damn sure they did, in fact, see that. "A lady wanders in, lost, and a gentleman takes such liberties—"

Dawson bit his tongue.

Because—by all the saints above and devils below—that little minx was actually loving this.

She wasn't just distracting them. She was punishing him. For making her do this. And hell if she wasn't enjoying it.

His cock ached. His fingers itched to punch. And if he

wasn't so close to ripping her off the street and kissing her sense-less, he might have been proud of her performance.

Instead, he forced himself forward. Slipping through the shadows. Moving fast. And when he reached the cottage-sized kennel, he found exactly what he was looking for: Tanuki.

Sitting. Staring. Waiting. A lazy, unimpressed little furred king on his pile of plush cushions.

Dawson sighed roughly, shaking his head. "Come on, then," he muttered. "Let's get this over with."

Tanuki, like the little traitor that he was, hopped up imme-diately—ready to be stolen. But then the damned pet realized it was him and all hell broke loose. A sharp, high-pitched trill of excitement, a blur of fur launching at him . . . and then he had an armful of wiggling, whining, delighted Tanuki.

"Fuck's sake," Dawson hissed, catching the overexcited crea-ture before he knocked them both over. "Shut it, you little menace."

Tanuki did not shut it. No, Tanuki sang the song of his people.

Loudly. Incessantly. And with great enthusiasm.

Dawson barely managed to stop the little beast from climbing straight up his chest and licking his face raw like an overzealous lover. He cursed under his breath, glancing over his shoulder. Still clear. For now. But this was a delicate operation. A crime so daring and dangerous, it required absolute stealth, total discretion.

Tanuki yipped happily and licked his jaw.

"This is a theft, you insufferable little bastard," he muttered under his breath, adjusting his grip. "You could at least try to act kidnapped." He scowled, holding him at arm's length.

Tanuki blinked at him, then wriggled like a delighted eel and licked Dawson's thumb.

Exhaling sharply, he fought a grin. Because he was being

mugged by a fluffy, smiling, overgrown raccoon-creature in a jewel-studded gold collar.

Of course this was his life.

Dawson bit back a laugh, tucking Tanuki securely under his arm, already slipping back into the shadows. "Right then. You're comin' with me, you ridiculous thing."

Tanuki squeaked cheerfully, his little paws gripping Dawson's shirt like a pirate monkey. Cursing, he moved faster, because this was not a normal dog. This was a very expensive-looking, very beloved, very heavily-guarded crime lord's pet.

And the thing was wearing a fucking fortune around its neck.

The thick, gleaming gold collar, adorned with fat-cut rubies, emeralds, and sapphires, was so obscene, it could probably fund a small country. Or at least buy Daisy as many bloody dresses as he could stand.

Dawson kept to the edges, heart hammering against his ribs as he took in every sight, scent, and sound of the East End compound. The sour tang of coal smoke curling in the muggy air. The shouting and laughter from men drinking and gambling near the main house. The metallic clang of a blacksmith's hammer in the distance, mixing with the chatter of merchants and street hawkers peddling their wares just beyond the walls.

He moved like a shadow, slipping between barrels, crates, and empty carts, inching his way toward the gate. He had to get gone, get his girl, and get the hell out of London before Duggie realized what he'd done.

A sharp whistle cut through the air.

Dawson's blood froze.

"Oi!" a voice bellowed. "Who's got the bloody dog?"

Dawson muttered a low, vicious curse under his breath. And then he ran like hell.

"OI! I SAID, WHO'S GOT THE BLOODY DOG?"

He was already moving before the last syllable finished echoing. Tanuki wiggled in his grip like this was the best fucking day of his life.

Dawson, on the other hand? Not having fun.

"Shut it, you furry little traitor," he muttered under his breath, shifting Tanuki closer against his chest. If the creature so much as made a sound . . .

Tanuki yipped happily.

Dawson cursed savagely.

Footsteps. Heavy ones. Moving fast.

Shite.

He ducked behind a stack of wooden barrels, chest heaving, ears straining for pursuit. Too loud. Too many of them. And too damn close. This was not ideal.

Dawson tightened his grip on Tanuki's ridiculous gold-jeweled collar, keeping a hand firm on the little beast's scruff. Tanuki squirmed like a fish, utterly thrilled, licking his fingers like they were made of roast duck.

"I am going to kill you," he whispered.

Tanuki beamed.

The footsteps grew louder as angry voices barked orders, the sound of men scattering to search the compound.

His stomach clenched.

Time to go. He adjusted Tanuki under one arm, tightened his stance, and bolted. He ran like hell, dodging past barrels, crates, and carts, vaulting over a stack of broken chairs, and sliding like a thief possessed behind a row of stacked grain sacks.

Yelling behind him. So much yelling. More boots hitting the ground. Someone had seen him.

"FIND THE BLOODY DOG!"

Dawson sprinted faster. A tight alleyway was up ahead. He took it only to run into a rickety wooden fence. He jumped it.

Tanuki shrieked with glee.

"Not helping!" Dawson hissed, landing hard and sprinting toward the nearest open passage to the streets.

A brick wall loomed ahead. shite. No time to stop. He kicked off a crate, caught the ledge, and hauled himself up while Tanuki clambered onto his shoulders like a goddamn hat.

He threw a leg over and dropped to the other side. Right into the cramped, noisy bustle of a London street. He landed in a crouch, his head snapping up.

And there she was.

Daisy. Standing just outside the alleyway, hands on her hips, watching him like a woman who had long since run out of patience.

He froze mid-breath.

Her brown eyes flicked to the raccoon-dog clinging to him and her brows shot up. She exhaled heavily. "That," she said, pointing at Tanuki, "is the thing that just nearly got you killed?"

"We," Dawson panted, "are calling it a success." He adjusted the excited fluffball on his shoulders and grinned wolfishly.

Daisy's mouth pressed into a thin line. She smacked him hard on the arm. "You absolute menace," she seethed.

He chuckled, catching her by the waist before she could whack him again. "Missed me, then?"

She made a frustrated sound, but she didn't pull away. Instead, she tilted her head, eyeing Tanuki. The creature blinked innocently at her, curling his fluffy tail around Dawson's neck like a feather boa.

"He's wearing an actual treasure around his neck, Dawson." She inhaled deeply.

"Ain't he just?"

Daisy huffed. And then, to his utter delight, she laughed. It was sharp, exasperated, and utterly gorgeous.

His grin widened.

And just like that, he knew.

She was it.

She was everything.

And if he wanted to keep her, he had to finish this. Properly.

"We're going to ransom the little bastard back," he told her, voice low. His grip tightened on her waist, his green eyes gleaming with something dangerously determined.

He leaned in, brushing his lips against her ear, his next words pure, wicked sin. "Then I'm coming home with you, poppet."

Daisy, the woman who could outwit the world, outfight fate, and outfox him, did not argue.

* * *

Dawson adjusted his grip on Tanuki, the creature's ridiculous jeweled collar catching the sunlight as they wove through the crowded London streets. Daisy, beside him, was walking fast, her skirts swishing, eyes sharp.

He, on the other hand—not as composed.

Because Tanuki, the little furry shite, would not sit still. He wriggled. He wobbled. He twisted his fluffy body every which way, licking Dawson's neck, his jaw, his damn ear.

And cooed.

Cooed.

He gritted his teeth. "For the love of—would you settle, you overgrown rat?"

Tanuki chirped happily.

Daisy, who had not spoken for the last two blocks (probably because she was still debating whether or not to throw him into the Thames) snorted.

"Not a word." Dawson shot her a glare.

She raised her hands. "I would never."

Tanuki licked his temple.

He exhaled murderously.

"Bloody thing loves you," Daisy observed, amusement creeping into her voice.

He muttered something about "traitors and their terrible taste."

They turned down a quieter street, the narrow road lined with rows of mismatched buildings, brick and timber, some clean and orderly, others sagging and full of secrets. Dawson's gut pulled tight. They were deep in the East End now.

"Where are we going, poppet?" he asked, keeping his tone casual.

Daisy glanced at him, eyes dark and unreadable. "I know just the place," she murmured.

Dawson lifted a brow. "That so?"

Daisy did not elaborate. And just as he was about to press her, Tanuki let out an absolutely ungodly yowl. Loud. Piercing. Echoing through the alleyway like a bloody war cry.

Dawson froze.

Daisy whipped her head toward him, panic flashing in her gaze. "Tell me," she hissed, "that Duggie's men don't recognize the way that thing sounds!"

Still holding the wiggling, delighted, screeching animal, he cleared his throat. "Ah. Well. The thing is . . ."

Daisy smacked a hand over Tanuki's mouth. Instant silence. Instant, complete, absolute silence.

Dawson blinked.

She smirked. "That's how you do it," she said smugly, removing her hand.

Tanuki stayed quiet.

"Now you listen?" He scowled.

Daisy patted his shoulder. "I've got a way with stubborn creatures."

Dawson, who was very much a stubborn creature himself, narrowed his eyes.

She grinned. "Come on, thief. Keep up." And she set off ahead, leading them toward whatever plan was cooking in that brilliant, devious mind of hers.

He, still carrying a now perfectly well-behaved Tanuki, sighed.

They ducked down side streets, weaved through carts, cut across a market square, and somehow, miraculously, made it out of the East End without getting their skulls cracked in.

Tanuki wiggled excitedly in Dawson's arms, his too-big paws scrabbling at his chest, licking wildly at his chin like a lovesick tart. "Would you calm down," he muttered, adjusting his grip as the creature made a ridiculous little chirping noise.

"He's just happy to be free of that godforsaken compound." Daisy glanced over.

He shot her a look. "Didn't see you running for freedom in the last few minutes, love."

"That's because I was too busy saving our arses with my—" she gestured grandly to her chest "—magnificent bosom, as per your orders."

He huffed a laugh, but he didn't like how right she was. Or how those sods had looked at her. His jaw ticked at the memory, but before he could say anything, Tanuki, the little traitor, squirmed right out of his arms and plopped down at Daisy's feet, looking up at her with total, utter devotion.

Daisy arched a brow. "Seems like he's chosen a favorite."

"Traitor."

"He's got good taste." Daisy squatted down, ruffling the ridiculous furball's ears. Tanuki made a low, delighted grumble, then promptly flopped over and showed her his belly. She grinned triumphantly. "See? He likes me better."

Dawson sighed, long and aggrieved. "Just tell me you know where we're going, woman."

"As a matter of fact, I do." She rose gracefully, dusted off her hands, and tossed him a slow, smug smile. Then she pivoted on her heel and strode confidently down the street, Tanuki trotting happily at her side.

He sighed again, then followed. Because of course she bloody well did.

Chapter Thirty-Four

The familiar street of Salisbury Court bustled with afternoon life, but Daisy still couldn't shake the feeling of being watched.

She checked over her shoulder . . .

No sign of Duggie's men. Yet. But that didn't mean they weren't coming.

She lifted a hand, signaling for Dawson to wait. He scowled but stayed put near the alley entrance, one hand tight on Tanuki's collar as the creature wriggled excitedly, his bejeweled necklace catching the bloody sunlight.

Saints above, could he shine any brighter?

Moving quickly, Daisy darted to the side entrance of Bramble Estate Investigations. Far less conspicuous than the main door. She pulled out a key, unlocked it, and slipped inside first. Then turned and yanked Dawson in after her, Tanuki wiggling between them like an overly enthusiastic accomplice.

She shut the door fast, bolted it, then exhaled.

Safe.

For now.

She turned to Dawson as he set Tanuki down. "See? That was easy."

Dawson snorted. "Poppet, you're still breathing hard."

Before she could smack him, a familiar voice cut through the office. "Daisy?"

A rustling from the back room.

"DAISY BRAMBLE, WHERE THE BLOODY HELL HAVE YOU BEEN?"

Violet.

A second voice joined in, sharp as ever. "And why is there a blasted raccoon in my office?"

Blossom.

Oh, bugger.

Daisy barely had time to brace before her sisters stormed in from the back rooms.

Violet got there first, her sharp blue eyes taking in her disheveled hair, the unfamiliar dress, the ridiculously over-dressed raccoon-fox hybrid thing prancing around their office . . . and then Dawson, looming behind her like a proper rogue with his arms crossed and an expression that screamed '*I have indeed ruined your sister, what of it?*'

Fantastic.

Blossom appeared right behind Violet, taller, steadier, and visibly unimpressed. "Where," Blossom said, voice deceptively calm, "have you been?"

Daisy opened her mouth.

Violet beat her to it. "And why," she demanded, pointing an accusing finger, "is that thing wearing a necklace worth more than our office?"

Tanuki chose that exact moment to stand on his hind legs and paw at Violet's skirts, his big fluffy tail wagging as if he were a common dog rather than a notorious crime lord's most prized possession.

Dawson snorted.

Daisy shot him a glare. Not. Helping.

Violet reeled back, eyeing the animal like he might explode.

"It's fine," Daisy rushed to say. "He's harmless. Sort of."

"Sort of?" Blossom echoed.

Daisy ignored that. "And he's called Tanuki."

Violet made a face. "That is not a real thing."

"It absolutely is."

Blossom crossed her arms. "It's a raccoon."

"Nope." Daisy shook her head.

Violet squinted. "A fox?"

"Not that either."

Violet narrowed her eyes. "A weird cat?"

Dawson huffed a quiet laugh behind her, and Daisy shot him another look that very clearly said *shut it.*

"Tanuki," she repeated. "A rare breed of animal from Japan. Apparently, the nobility used to collect them as status symbols. This one belonged to . . ." she glanced questioningly at Dawson.

He cleared his throat. "Belongs to Mad Duggie Black."

Silence.

And then, "WHAT?!"

Daisy winced as both her sisters yelled at the same time.

Violet grabbed her by the arm. "You stole something from Mad Duggie?"

Blossom, ever the practical one, turned to Dawson. "How dead are you?"

He lifted one shoulder in a lazy shrug. "Depends. How sentimental do you think Duggie is?"

Tanuki let out a happy little chirp and nuzzled against his leg.

"Very." Daisy sighed.

"You absolute lunatics." Violet clutched her head like she was getting a headache.

Blossom, however, was still staring at Dawson. Calculating. Studying.

And Daisy noticed the way he stared right back at them. Watching. Measuring. Taking in all of it. It made something in her belly go warm. Because—this was her family. Loud, nosy, sharp-tongued, and utterly, unshakably hers.

And Dawson, this man who had been so alone for so long, who had just lost the only truth he had ever known, he was watching them like they were something impossible. Something rare. Something he might want.

Her heart gave a stupid, aching squeeze. Which was ridiculous. So she rolled her eyes, ignored it entirely, and turned back to her sisters. "Are you two done gawking?" she asked. "Or do you want the full story?"

Blossom's gaze sharpened. "You mean the part where you ran off chasing a duke and somehow wound up committing grand larceny instead?"

"Exactly." Daisy grinned. She clapped her hands together. "So. Who wants to hear about our brilliant plan?"

Violet groaned. "There's a plan?"

Dawson finally spoke. "It's a good one."

"That remains to be seen." Blossom gave him a flat look.

Daisy elbowed him. "See? They're already intrigued."

Blossom sighed, pinching the bridge of her nose. "Fine. Tell us what absolute madness you're dragging us into this time."

* * *

She had just finished dramatically recounting how they had executed The Great Tanuki Heist (complete with hand gestures, perfectly timed pauses, and Dawson leaning against the desk, smirking like an absolute scandal) when Blossom took her by the elbow and steered her straight into the back room.

Not a word. Just grabbed her and walked.

"Uh," Daisy tried. "Blossom?"

The moment they were alone, Blossom turned and leveled her with that look.

Oh no. Daisy straightened. "Alright," she said breezily, hands on her hips. "What's this, then? About to scold me like a governess?"

Blossom just crossed her arms. "Daisy."

Oh. That tone. That was not the 'you reckless idiot' tone. That was worse. That was the older sister tone.

"What?" Daisy acted innocent.

Her sister sighed. "See, I told you it wouldn't work out like you thought."

"What's that supposed to mean?"

Blossom gave her a knowing look. "You went and got your heart involved."

"I did not," she scoffed immediately.

Blossom's lips twitched. "Oh, of course. You let a man who was supposed to be your bounty stick his tongue down your throat for what? Strategy?"

Daisy flushed violently. "Blossom."

"Then you had him in your bed."

"Oh my GOD, I never said that part out loud—"

"And then you stole a tanuki together—"

"That is entirely irrelevant."

Blossom arched a perfect brow. "You love him."

Daisy froze. Her pulse slammed into her throat.

"You do, don't you?" Her sister tilted her head, soft but firm.

She opened her mouth. Closed it. Opened it again.

Blossom just watched her. Waiting.

And Daisy felt it—the roaring, terrifying truth trying to claw its way free.

Her heart was in this. Had been for longer than she wanted to admit. And suddenly the weight of it nearly knocked her flat.

Her sister sighed, softer this time. "You can lie to yourself all you want," she said gently. "But you can't lie to me."

Daisy stared at her sister, throat tight. Because, bloody hell.

She was in love with Dawson Woodbridge.

And she was so, so screwed.

Daisy stormed back into the main office like a woman on a mission. That mission? Avoid her feelings at all costs.

Shoving past Blossom, she muttered something about fetching tea, despite the fact she didn't even like tea that much.

The moment she stepped into the main room, Dawson was there. Leaning against her desk, arms crossed. Looking at her. And not just looking. Watching. Like he'd been doing that whole damn time. His green eyes—sharp, knowing, too damn perceptive—tracked her movements as she marched toward the tea service like she wasn't completely unraveling inside.

Violet and Blossom bickered over whether Tanuki should be allowed on the furniture. He had, in fact, already made himself comfortable in Violet's chair and looked entirely unwilling to leave.

But Dawson wasn't paying attention to any of that. He was looking at her. Like he knew. Like he had always known. Like he was just waiting for her to figure it out.

She refused to engage. Instead, Daisy poured herself a cup of tea she absolutely did not want and stirred it with far more force than necessary. And pretended she wasn't completely coming apart at the seams.

"That bad, poppet?" He smirked at her. Knowing. Infuriating.

Her spine snapped straight. She turned to glare at him, cup in hand. And immediately regretted it.

Damn him.

That lazy, rogue's slouch. The open collar. The absolute bastard way his eyes dropped just slightly before flicking back up, like he knew exactly what he did to her. She wanted to launch her tea straight at his stupid, too-handsome face. Instead, she took the most scalding sip of her life and promptly burned the absolute hell out of her tongue.

Dawson's grin widened.

She hated him. So, so much.

And, worse, she wanted to kiss him again. Which exactly why she needed to get rid of him before she did something irreversibly stupid.

She slammed her cup down onto the desk, narrowed her eyes. "Are we planning a ransom or what?"

Dawson chuckled.

And, God help her, that sound sent a shiver right down her spine.

"That eager to be rid of me, love?"

Daisy opened her mouth. Closed it, and tried very, very hard not to panic. Because she was starting to think that no matter how this whole steal a gangster's pet for ransom situation ended, she was never getting rid of Dawson Woodbridge.

Chapter Thirty-Five

Dawson hung in the shadows of the old dockside warehouse, rolling his shoulders loose. The room smelled like brine, damp wood, and the sharp, lingering tang of spilled rum—Duggie's kind of place. Unremarkable. Forgettable. Perfect for dealing with problems.

And right now? Dawson was the problem.

He flexed his fingers. Took a slow, steady breath. And waited.

The door creaked open. A gust of cool, salt-laced air rushed in. Then Duggie stepped inside. He looked the same. Same dark coat, same steady, near-predatory gait, same unreadable expression.

It was Dawson that felt different. For the first time in his life, he wasn't looking at Duggie as his past. He was looking at him as his choice. That this was something he got to choose for himself.

Duggie's gaze flicked over him, quick and sharp, taking him in like he was counting all the ways Dawson had changed. Then his eyes slid past him to Daisy and they narrowed. The energy in the room shifted.

Dawson's pulse kicked up fast and hot.

Duggie's gaze returned to him. And his voice, low, even, and edged with something dangerous, cut through the silence. "You've got some fucking nerve, boy."

"Only just noticed?" He smirked, cocking his head.

Duggie exhaled slowly through his nose, and for a beat, neither of them moved. The air between them stretched tight before Duggie's voice dropped into something quieter, more lethal. "Where is he?"

"Safe." Dawson didn't blink. Didn't twitch.

"Dawson." Duggie's jaw went tight.

"Oh, he's happier than a pig in shite." Dawson smirked. "Little bastard's livin' the dream."

Duggie's shoulders tensed. "You stole my fucking dog."

Dawson shrugged. "I liberated your dog."

A muscle jumped in Duggie's jaw, and for a long, charged moment he just stared. Measuring. Calculating. And then something flickered behind his gaze—fleeting—but Dawson saw it.

Saw what he wasn't saying. What was really happening here. It suddenly hit him like a bull at full charge.

Duggie wasn't just furious that Dawson had outplayed him. He wasn't just furious that he had taken Tanuki.

He was furious because Dawson had left. Period. This wasn't really about the damn dog. This was about Dawson walking away from him.

Dawson's chest tightened. For all his life he thought Duggie only ever wanted to own him. To use him when convenient. To keep him as a name, as a weapon, as an extension of his empire. Fuck, even as a sort of pet, like Tanuki.

But that wasn't it. Not at all. Duggie had loved him in his own twisted, feral way.

Now, he was losing Dawson all over again.

331

Duggie's voice came low and edged with something raw. "You walk away from this life, you don't come back. Not ever."

Dawson swallowed hard. The air in the room thickened. This was it. The moment. The choice.

The ending.

But this time—it wasn't just about him.

It was about her.

Daisy.

The woman who set his blood on fire and made him want more. The woman who would not break beneath him, who would not settle for half of him, who would take every damn part of him or nothing at all.

He inhaled, lifted his chin, and spoke. "I love her."

Duggie went still.

His throat was tight, but he kept going. "I'm gonna be a proper fucking duke. I'm gonna give her that finder's fee she came after me for. I'm gonna give her that damn orphanage, and I'm gonna love her with everything I've got for the rest of my life." He exhaled sharply. "And you? You're gonna let me go."

A long, hollow silence.

Then, Duggie laughed. Low and rough and just a little bit broken.

But when he finally spoke, his voice was quiet. "You got bollocks the size of ham steaks, lad. I'll give you that. Fuck me, I knew this day was coming. Knew it when your mum handed you over that day. Christ, I've known since the beginning you'd one day leave for your title, and I knew I was gonna hate it. Which I do. Fuck me, I do." Something vulnerable and raw flickered across his face. "You gonna let me visit?"

Dawson's chest went tight. The final gut punch. Duggie's version of *I love you.*

"Well," Dawson's voice was gruff, but certain. "There's a

whole colony of raccoon dogs on the estate, so I expect so. Tanuki's got a lady friend waiting for him there."

"More tanuki?" Duggie's head snapped up. "You mean the duchess had more than the two she gave me?"

"A damn near infestation." Dawson confirmed. "They'll make fine pups."

Duggie stared at him a long while before slowly, finally nodding. "Tanuki ain't so young anymore. He deserves to be with his own kind. He likes you better anyways."

And just like that, it was done.

Dawson turned to Daisy. And she, well, she was watching. Already seeing. Already knowing.

And hell, that did it.

Whatever was left of his restraint, whatever thin, pitiful string of control he had left—snapped. He didn't give a damn about Duggie. Didn't give a damn about Duggie's men watching. Didn't give a damn about the whole bloody East End seeing him lose himself to this woman.

Because Daisy was it.

She was the only thing in this world that could unmake him and make him whole again in the same breath. And he needed to touch her. Now.

He was on her in two strides, grabbing her, yanking her right up against him so fast her breath punched out in a gasp. "You," he growled, voice rough and low, pure possession.

"Me?" she murmured, almost dazed. Her wide brown eyes flicked up to his, surprise and heat tangled together in her gaze.

Dawson exhaled sharply, a rough, shaky thing, because hell, she didn't even fight it. She didn't push him away. Didn't tell him to slow down. She didn't do a single damn thing except look at him like he was already hers.

And that—that wrecked him.

He bent low, his lips brushing her ear, his breath hot, his

voice pure sin. "I'm going to love you so hard and so deep, poppet, you'll feel me for days." His hands tightened on her waist, fingers digging in. "Every time you move, every time you breathe, you'll remember exactly where I've been. Exactly where I belong."

She shuddered. And he felt it. Felt it all the way to his bones.

Her breath caught, and her fingers curled into the front of his shirt like she needed something to hold onto, something to steady herself.

He wasn't done.

His lips ghosted down the line of her jaw, slow, teasing, meant to drive her mad.

"You love me." His voice was a wicked rasp, thick with everything that was between them. "Say it."

Her breath came fast, unsteady. "Dawson—"

"Say it, Daisy." His teeth scraped her skin, his tongue following after, soothing, tempting, ruining.

She whimpered. Then, so softly, so breathless, so real, she gave it to him. "I love you."

Fuck.

Dawson crushed his mouth to hers. Right there, in front of Duggie, Jacko, Merritt, and every last thug watching. In the middle of the East End, where he had been raised, where he had fought and clawed and survived. Where he had once been lost.

She opened to him like she was made for him, and hell, maybe she was.

He took his time ravishing her. Slow. Deep. Tongue teasing, claiming, owning. Until she was clinging to him, melting into him, whimpering into his mouth—and he knew. This was his future.

This woman.

This life.

And he was never letting her go.

He finally broke the kiss, breathing hard, forehead pressed against hers, his lips still damn near touching her swollen, kiss-bruised mouth. He grinned, slow and wicked. "Well, poppet," he murmured, voice rough with satisfaction, "looks like I'm getting a ducal estate, a fortune, and a pack of bloody raccoon dogs." His thumb swiped across her lower lip, gaze dark and gleaming. "Tell me, does that make me the wealthiest bastard in England, or just the most ridiculous?"

Daisy blinked up at him, cheeks flushed, eyes dazed, lips swollen from his kiss. Then she laughed. "A bit of both, I'd say."

Duggie grumbled something unintelligible behind them.

Dawson didn't care.

He just kissed his woman again.

Epilogue

S *ome months later . . .*

Daisy stood in the wild, overgrown gardens of Ashby Hollow, hands on her hips, staring at what had become her new, ridiculous reality.

God help her, but she loved it.

Sunlight poured through the tangled canopy of flowering vines, dappling the stone pathways in shifting golds and greens. The scent of roses, thick and heady, mixed with damp earth from the morning rain, and in the distance, the rolling Oxfordshire countryside stretched out, hazy with late summer warmth. It was stunning. Unapologetically grand.

And currently overrun with a bloody menace.

Three raccoon dog pups (because of course there were more of them now) were absolutely ruining what was left of a once-respectable estate garden. One was currently digging furiously in a patch of violets, another had climbed halfway up

336

a toppled stone sundial, and the third ... Daisy's gaze narrowed.

Because the third was gnawing on Dawson's very expensive ducal boot.

He stood beside her, arms crossed, watching the chaos unfold with a look of pure, amused arrogance. He had no right to look so pleased with himself.

"You knew this would happen," she accused.

Dawson exhaled, stretching luxuriously in the morning sun, utterly unbothered. "Define *knew*."

She shot him a look. "Oh, don't you bloody dare."

Blossom, who was seated gracefully on a stone bench, shook a mischievous tanuki pup off her skirts and gave Dawson a long, assessing look. "He definitely knew."

Violet, cross-legged in the grass, happily letting one of the pups tangle itself in her hem, only grinned. "And he's delighted about it."

Dawson didn't even bother to deny it.

"I *cannot* believe this is my life now." Daisy sighed, rubbing her temple.

His palm landed on the small of her back, sliding lower. "You share it with me, too, poppet." The deep, wicked promise in his voice sent a sharp, treacherous shiver through her. But she wasn't about to let him distract her.

Not when she had to know. Daisy poked his chest, eyes narrowed playfully. "One last question, Woodbridge."

He smirked, grabbing her finger and kissing the tip. "Anything, poppet."

"Mrs. Buddersham's honeyed whiskey. You know, the bottle you stole? The one I used to save your delightful backside?"

He chuckled, the sound deliciously wicked. "Left it behind at Jacko's camp, I'm afraid. Though it served a noble purpose, knocking those blighters senseless."

Daisy hummed thoughtfully. "Then it's only right we fund Mason's brewery expansion as repayment."

Grin widening, Dawson's eyes gleamed. "A drunken investment? Love, you truly are my perfect duchess."

Speaking of investments . . . they needed to discuss the future of Bramble Hill Orphanage now that she had that hefty finder's fee.

"This is the perfect place for it," Violet said like she'd just read Daisy's mind, pushing a stray curl from her face as she surveyed the sprawling estate. "For the new orphanage. Not the brewery. Plenty of space, privacy, land to expand—"

"It's *not* going here," Dawson cut in smoothly.

Daisy turned, hands on her hips. "Oh?"

He smiled. Slowly. Dangerously. The kind of smile that made her want to kiss him senseless and throttle him in equal measure.

"Perhaps," he drawled, "one of my *other* estates would do."

And *oh*, she knew exactly what that really meant. The man was not about to give up their tower room with its magical window seat.

Blossom gave him the look. The Blossom Look that could unravel lesser men.

He only arched a brow.

But before she could change the topic, something flickered at the edge of the ruined abbey. A whisper of movement. A shiver of fabric.

Daisy barely registered Dawson tensing beside her, his hand tightening at her waist.

"What is it?" she murmured.

He exhaled sharply, running a hand through his already mussed hair. His voice, when he spoke, was lower than usual. "Holy hell," he muttered. "I think I just saw the Widow."

"Good heavens!" Violet gasped, bright-eyed with absolute delight.

Blossom released the longest, most suffering sigh in existence. "Don't encourage him."

Daisy chuckled. She couldn't help it.

Dawson turned, scowling. "What's funny?"

"I *told* you this place was haunted."

The breeze shifted, carrying the scent of roses and summer earth. The ruins stood silent. The moment stretched.

"You," he muttered, "are insufferable."

Daisy winked. "That's Daisy Bramble-soon-to-be-Woodbridge to you, Your Grace."

He rolled his eyes. "Oh, for hell's sake—"

"Do you know what I do, Dawson?" she interrupted, voice honeyed and sharp with satisfaction.

He arched a brow. "You spend an ungodly amount of time making my life difficult?"

She tsk'd, stepping closer, pressing her fingers flat against his ridiculously well-formed chest, her dark eyes glittering. "I'm an heir hunter, love."

Dawson's smile flickered. "Oh, I know."

Her fingers curled into his shirt. "And tell me," she murmured, drawing him down, lips just a whisper from his own, "what does an heir hunter do once she's found her heir?"

His breath caught.

"She *keeps* him." She smiled against his mouth, her body flush to his, hands gripping the broad expanse of his shoulders as she dragged him down, down, down for the most scandalous, soul-stealing, toe-curling kiss in all of history.

But just before she ruined him completely—just before she utterly wrecked this man who thought he was the one who did the ruining—she whispered against his lips, all smug and sinful,

"Oh, by the way, the legendary Banshee of Ashby Hollow?" She paused. Let it simmer. Felt his breath catch. Then she delivered the final blow. "Just a lovesick raccoon dog in heat."

Dawson stilled. Properly, fully, absolutely stilled. Then he pulled back just enough to gape at her. Like he wasn't quite sure if she was telling the truth or just having him on. "You know," he drawled, squinting toward the tower, "when the female started howling for Tanuki that first night... it hit me. Took a while, but I remembered the sound. The old female when I was a lad used to wail just like that."

Daisy blinked. "Wait. You're telling me *you* figured it out?"

Dawson shrugged, the picture of smug male pride. "Eventually." And then . . . he laughed. A deep, guttural, body-shaking, utterly scandalous laugh. A laugh that sent heat roaring through her chest. One that nearly dropped her to her bloody knees.

And oh, how she loved that sound. Loved the way it rumbled through his broad, powerful body. Loved the way he looked at her in that moment, like he was well and truly done for.

"Bloody hell, poppet," he rasped, his fingers tightening against the small of her back. "You really do ruin all the fun."

"No," she murmured, gaze locked with his, the whole damn world narrowing down to this man, this moment, this impossible, unbelievable, heart-stealing thing between them. "I find things." Her lips brushed his, soft, slow, devastating. "It's what I do."

And then, she kissed him again. Thoroughly. Filthily. In front of God, the universe, her highly entertained sisters, and the absolute chaos of tanuki pups tumbling at their feet.

And Dawson—gruff, impossible, sin-drenched Dawson—let her. Let her take everything. Because somewhere, deep in that wicked, untamed heart of his, he knew.

Daisy Bramble had found him.
And he would never be lost again.

THE END

Did you fall for Daisy and Dawson just a little too hard?

Yeah... same. 🌚

If this story made you laugh, swoon, fan yourself dramatically, or stay up way too late, would you mind leaving a review?

Your words help this book find new readers, and they make this author happy dance like a scandalous barmaid on market day.

Stars are love.

Words are magic.

And you? You're the absolute best.

Thanks for reading. Truly. You're the reason I write.

Love and mayhem,

— *Jennifer*

📝 Leave a review here.

Up Next in The Heir Hunter Series:

One Bramble sister found her duke.
Now it's Violet's turn.
Only... her guy's not exactly noble.
He's a bruised-up prizefighter.
She kidnapped him.
They're "engaged." (It's complicated.)
And the Highlands will never be the same.

📚 Preorder now before someone ends up shirtless. Again.

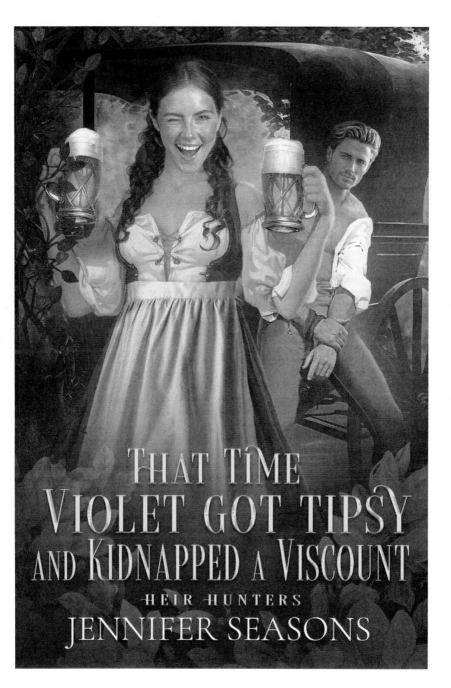

THAT TIME
VIOLET GOT TIPSY
AND KIDNAPPED A VISCOUNT
HEIR HUNTERS
JENNIFER SEASONS

About the Author

Jennifer Seasons has written 30 swoon-worthy romances, from Regency hijinks to contemporary charm, all with her signature blend of sizzling chemistry, sharp wit, and heart-melting moments. A California native now calling the mountains of Massachusetts home, she spends her days wrangling words, horses, and an unreasonable amount of cozy cardigans.

When she's not lost in writing (often by hand, coffee in reach, cat in lap), you can find her riding through the countryside, baking dangerously good chocolate chip cookies, or attempting to grow the perfect tomato.

Want to stay up to date on her latest books and behind-the-scenes mischief? Sign up for her newsletter here: Newsletter

Also by Jennifer Seasons

HISTORICAL ROMANCES:

HEIR HUNTERS
That Time Daisy Got Tipsy and Rescued a Duke
That Time Violet Got Tipsy and Kidnapped a Viscount (June 2025)
That Time Blossom Got Tipsy and Bet a Baron (September 2025)

THE CASTLEBURYS
Mayfair Misfit
Duke Undone
Dockside Duchess
London's Leading Lady
Bow Street Baron

FORGOTTEN BRIDES OF BELGRAVIA
Fake It Till You Rake It
Wallflower Most Wicked
Cold-Hearted Duke

MISTLETOE MIRACLES
The Duke's Christmas Wish
Miracle on Bond Street

FLIRTATION WITH A ROGUE

Romancing Colonel Northam

Sins of a Scoundrel

A Rogue by Night

Every Rake Has His Day

Highlander and the Bluestocking

Laura's Croft

CONTEMPORARY ROMANCES:

DIAMONDS AND DUGOUTS

Stealing Home

Playing the Field

Throwing Heat

Major League Crush (Confessions of a Secret Admirer Anthology)

The Big Play

Home Base

FORTUNE, COLORADO

Getting Lucky

Talking Dirty

Playing Rough

STAND ALONES

After Him

Romancing Livingstone

BOXSET COLLECTIONS:

Flirtation With A Rogue

Click here to go directly to Jennifer's Amazon page to check out her books: https://amzn.to/37ZI8OC

Made in United States
Cleveland, OH
09 April 2025

15956217R00210